The Other Side of Bad

By R. O. Barton

Cover design by Emmett Barton

ISBN: 1490423966
ISBN-13: 9781490423968
Library of Congress Control Number: 2013911220
Createspace Independent Publishing Platform
North Charleston, South Carolina

For Margie, I miss you everyday. I will always love you.

And

For Emmett, the best son a man could have. Without their very existence, I might not still be alive today.

Thank you both for saving me from myself.

Book One

"ELEVEN"

prologue: The full moon peered down like the jaundiced Cyclopean eye of God, coldly observing me as I struggled to inch up through the hot fetid fog to escape the red horror below. I was covered with blood. It dripped mournfully from my body, with pain and sorrow in every drop.

My arms and legs were laden with fatigue. My lungs unbearably steamed with each breath. My eyes were welded shut. The exertion of trying to open them was ripping my head apart. If I could free my hands, I could pry my eyes open. But my hands were getting me away from the crimson hell below. I was screaming; I could feel it in my throat. I was crying; I could feel it my heart. There was no sound. Just silence that shrieked with grief and pain. I had to get away. I had to wake up. I must wake up. My mouth was full of blood; I was drowning in it. Wake up! Please God, let me wake up. Let me wake up or let me die in this sea of blood. Now! Please . . please . . . please . . .

When I awoke, I was on the floor. I must've fallen off the bed.

She was sitting on the edge of the bed, looking down at me with concern. She was naked. My beautiful wife, my childhood sweetheart, my lover, my best friend.

"What's wrong sweetie, are you all right?" she asked sleepily.

I looked around, still not fully awake. The dream's mired gravity was physically pulling on me.

I was so happy to see her and the familiar surroundings. Our bedroom and all its furnishings were recognizable, but in some way chimerical. I was having difficulty climbing out of the nightmare.

"I must have fallen off the bed," I said, as I crawled on hands and knees towards her, struggling with the dream's quicksand sucking at me, trying to drag me back down.

On my knees, I anchored my arms around her hips and buried my face in her lap, her small feet between my legs. I could feel the tears coming and could do nothing to stop them.

"I had a horrible dream," I sobbed. "I dreamed you were dead. It was awful."

I couldn't stop shaking, so I hugged her hips harder and breathed in her sweet fragrance. The smell of her so reassuring, my heart wept with relief.

"There, there," she said. "I'm right here. It's okay honey, its okay. Sshhshh . . . I'm right here. I'm not dead. Feel me. Touch me." She was rubbing the back of my head.

With my face still buried in her lap, I completely inhaled her, just to make certain I was awake.

Squeezing her harder, I said, "It was terrible, you were dead and had been for a long time."

I was beginning to settle down. The calm that only she could bring was starting to course through me.

"It was so strange," I said. "I was this middle-aged guy and you had been gone for a long time, like twenty years. I'd had relationships with different women, it was so real, like memories. Shannon had found Patricia but you never got to see your grandchildren. I had a son who was from another woman. I loved him so much, but I missed you terribly. The pain was killing me. I longed for you."

I was starting to cry again. In a deep, cloudy carrel of my brain, was a fleeting query over my lachrymose behavior. I felt something was slightly askew, like a library book that's on the correct shelf but in the wrong space.

"Hey . . . hey, look at me," she said, as she put her hands under my chin, lifting my face from the security of her lap.

"I'm right here. I'm fine. I'm not going anywhere, you know that. You know you're never going to get rid of me," she consoled me, with that little throaty laugh I loved.

I looked up and through the long auburn hair framing her face, I could see her clear blue eyes, like two azure gemstones flecked with gold.

"It was so real, the memories. I had memories of killing."

"Everything's all right, you aren't in that business now. You don't even carry a gun anymore. Remember?"

Then, she said, "You're an artist now."

She pulled me up to her face and kissed me with her sweet mouth. It was so extraordinarily powerful, like coming home after being lost for decades.

I slipped from her lips and buried my face in her neck.

"What a trip. Must have been something I ate," I said with a teary eyed chuckle, trying my best to lighten up.

I felt her hands on the back of my head, soothing away the nightmare. I started to drift off. I tried to wake up, so I could lie down beside her and hold her, spoon with her. I became a weightless mist ascending on a soft confectionous cloud of euphoria.

I awakened, opened my eyes to the dark and patted the bed next to me, searching for her, the nightmare an unfading memory that required expunging by her touch. I had to reach further than usual, as she always slept close. She wasn't there: she must be in the bathroom.

As my eyes grew accustomed to the shadows, I became disoriented. Where was I? This was not our room. No! No! God, don't do this to me. . . please.

The red digital numbers on the clock to my left said it was 2:44 in the morning. I sat up on the edge of the bed and through the blue nightfall could see a door to my right. I stood, walked over to the door, entered and touched the light switch on the wall. I was in a bathroom, my bathroom.

I looked in the mirror and saw a middle-aged man, as tears from despondent eyes traversed his face to pool a deep crescent scar in his left cheek, that would forever mar his soul.

Chapter 1

It looked like three against one, to me. Me, being the one. Even though the one in the middle was the man who'd hired me this morning over the phone, Samuel Bench—real-estate tycoon.

I read in the Tennessean that he had an intuitive genius for finding cities that had let their downtown riverfront properties go to seed, buying it for next to nothing, then planting new ones. These new seeds were the ideas and plans for the revitalization of the properties, including a riverfront park complete with floating stage that would draw crowds of fat-walleted people. Not just tourists, but locals as well. He had breathed new life into many major cities throughout the United States and in the late eighties, Nashville was no exception. After the makeover, which for the most part he persuaded the city and small groups of investors to pay, the real-estate was worth ten times what he'd paid for it. These properties leased and sold like hot cakes at the I-Hop on seniors Sunday.

When the limo pulled into the designated pickup, the Kroger parking lot on Harding, and the door opened, the only available seat was the one that put my back to oncoming traffic and the driver, separated by tinted glass. It wasn't a stretch, but one of those sleek black Lincolns you saw politicians in, with just the two wide seats that faced each other. The interior smelled faintly of expensive cigar smoke and fine whiskey. For one I'd developed a taste, but wouldn't be indulging tonight. The only expression that looked more stressed than the soft gray Corinthian leather was Mr. Bench's.

Not one of the three faces looked happy to see me. Their expressions differed: The man to my left looked at me like I was an interesting pimple; Mr. Bench looked me up and down in mild shock; and the man to my right looked out-and-out hostile. The men to either side of Bench were his personal body guards, clearly discontented he employed me.

"Do you own a suit Mr. Tucker?" Samuel Bench asked between his tight thin lips.

I looked down at my cowboy boots and jeans with a black t-shirt tucked into them. I wore a very nice black on black herringbone silk sport coat and fairly new Diamond Gusset jeans. The sport coat was one of my favorites, it also made it easier and quicker to get to my .45.

They all wore dark suits with ties. Mr. Bench had gold cuff links.

"You said to dress casual," I said.

"I meant that it wasn't black tie," he said, with heavy condescension.

I really don't like it when people talk to me in that manner, and to compound it, I'd been having a bad feeling about this job since taking it. It was October 11th.

I once dated a woman who was heavily into psychics, astrology and numerology, phenomena of that nature. One day she dragged me to a numerologist and had my number calculated.

When all the pertinent information was in and the numerologist punched the last button, finishing her calculations, she said, "Uh-oh, you're an 11."

I asked, "What's that mean?"

She answered with, "It's a tough road. Eleven means constant spiritual awakenings."

At which point I said, "Yeah, tell me about it."

Things tended to happen to me on the 11th; not all of them good. One of them was being born. I sometimes wonder if that was a good thing or a bad thing. The verdict fluctuates.

I looked over at Mr. Bench and said, "Your tie is black."

He was a small man, maybe five-seven or eight, a hundred and thirty pounds, around 40, very trim and right now, a skosh irate.

"I don't believe I care for your tone, Mr. Tucker," he said, visibly swelling and stirring his two bodyguards.

It had been a long time since I felt the need to win a popularity contest. Furthermore, I was not well-known for my obsequious nature.

I reached over the seat with my left hand and knocked on the window behind the drivers head. The dark brown window slowly receded, and as soon as I could see the driver I said, "Would you please pull over? I'm getting out."

In the rearview mirror, the driver, a very large black man with a bald head that resembled a 15 pound bowling ball, glanced past me to Bench.

"Keep driving James," Bench said, with a minute speculative laugh. Then to me, "Captain Spain said you were somewhat of a hardass."

As the window was going up, I tapped on it again; it lowered and when I could see the driver's eyes in the mirror, I said, "Is your name really James?"

He laughed loudly, showing large white even teeth and with a wink that told me his Uncle Tom accent was assuredly exaggerated, said, "Yes sah, Meesta Tucker. It shorely is."

I nodded with crinkled eyes and as I turned to look at Bench, I heard the whirring of the window going up, partitioning me from my only ally.

We sat like that, studying each other, for a full minute.

He gestured to his right and said, "This is Mike Powell."

Powell looked to be about five-ten, mid-forties, a little portly and I'd bet was either retired or booted early FBI. Mike Powell didn't offer his hand, which was fine with me. It was a long way over there, and by the look on the other bodyguard's face, I didn't want anyone holding my right hand.

"You've got a reputation of never losing a fight," Powell said with the pride of a man who has done his research.

Yep, a feebee.

I looked out the window on my left, saw we were headed downtown, and said, "I don't."

"You don't what?" Powell asked.

"Fight."

"In our line of work it's hard to avoid physical confrontations," he said.

Bench's stare was intense.

"I'm very good at that," I said.

Powell laughed and said, "What's your secret?"

Prior to 1982 my coveted secret was fear. Fear of being hurt and not just physically. Paramount was the fear I would be seen as the coward I was. Whenever I felt violence was imminent, the fear induced chemicals coursing through my veins altered me. For the last twenty years my only fear was going to sleep and . . . waking up. But, old habits do die hard.

I wasn't looking at Bench, but could feel his eyes.

Still looking out the window, I said, "If I get even the faintest inkling that things may get physical I do an 'U-F-F-F' move."

Powell said, "What's that?"

I turned and caught his eyes as they darted from the scar on my face, and attempting to smile, said, "Unexpected, fast, first, and final. That way there's no real fight and whoever I am working for doesn't get hurt . . . nor do I. I've found action is always faster than reaction."

I could tell he considered himself a jovial chap, but he swallowed the laugh that was about to emerge.

I surmised my effort at smiling was futile; I hadn't done jovial for 20 years.

"Yeah? Where'd you learn that?" the other bodyguard sneered.

Nothing jovial about this one.

"This is Trent," Bench said, with an 'I'm sure you've heard of him' tone.

I looked at him. I could physically feel the air between us snap with current. There wasn't a pleasant molecule in it. He was at least six-two, also mid-forties, clean shaven, angular, sharp, with a squared away crew cut. He appeared very fit, an almost military bearing, but not quite.

"I asked you where you learned that so called move," he reiterated, his voice followed his gaze, coming from his nose with a mild West Virginia accent.

Flashing sorely behind my eyes were the years of surviving the humidity induced short tempered mean men of Louisiana, the arid racist vigilante border violence of Texas and the cold envious hatred of desperado Mexicans who suffered the flagrant and blatant injustice of their own country.

"No one particular place or time," I said, returning his stare, minus the dislike. At least I tried. I looked out the window on his side and said, "It was a slow learning curve."

"Yeah, well I checked you out after Mr. Bench told us you were coming in tonight. I don't think we need anyone coming in to help us in the 11th hour, but he's the boss."

Upon hearing the number 11, the skin on the backs of my arms started to crawl. I continued to look out the windows. I was apparently the only one in the vehicle doing so. I perceived the two bodyguards apathy as being on the job for too long without any action. I've felt it myself and used it as a barometer to leave the employ of whomever I was working for. Besides it scared the hell out of me. Not just for myself, but for the person who'd employed me.

Maybe I didn't have all the information.

Still looking out the window, I said, "Is this vehicle bulletproof?"

"No," they said in unison.

Bench looked as if it just occurred to him.

Powell smiled and started looking out his window.

But Trent was unfazed, as he continued, "As far as I can tell you're a very good gunsmith who's also good at shooting holes in paper targets."

Before I could thank him for the encomium, he added, "I also found out you travel around and actually teach tactics to police departments. What qualifies you to do that?" His tone held more disdain than Bench's had earlier.

I *really* don't like it when people talk to me that way.

"Something you evidently don't have," I said, looking at him, and the aversion just tiptoed out all by itself.

"Yeah, what's that?"

This man had perfected the act of sneering into an art form.

"Common sense," I said. I found the last two fingers of my right hand hooked around the edge of my coat. I wasn't conscious of it, it was a reflex. For some reason this man saw me as a threat, and he didn't seem the insecure type.

It became very quiet and thick inside the limousine. He looked down at my hand and placed both of his hands on his knees. His sneer faded as the data was computed.

Okay, so he has some common sense.

To show good faith, I placed my hands on my knees. We sat like reprimanded school children.

He clearly felt more at ease, because he just had to ask, "Have you ever had to shoot anyone? Ever been in a *real* fire fight?"

It's also been a long time since I've felt the need to answer every question I'm asked, especially rude ones.

It was Mr. Bench who broke the long silence that followed with, "What have you to say to that Mr. Tucker? I would like to hear it."

I held his gaze as I answered, "You're not paying me to talk."

"That may be true, but *I am* used to being answered by my employees when I ask them a question."

He was beginning to resemble something I'd wipe off my sleeve with a tissue.

"Mr. Bench, please have James pull over so I can get out. I won't charge you for the joy ride."

As if James heard me, the limo started to slow. Over a speaker James said, "We're here Mr. Bench."

Earlier that morning Samuel Bench had told me he was throwing a dinner party for ten of his top sales people at Pete's, one of Nashville's finer restaurants. He bought out the whole restaurant for the night, and Chef Pete was cooking just for them: men and women with their spouses or significant others . . . wow. He also said he'd had a bad feeling about tonight and talked me into helping out his two full-time bodyguards.

He actually had to talk me into it and pay me twice my normal fee. I mean, after all he said about having a bad feeling and the fact that it was the 11th, I wasn't chomping at the bit.

We both must have been thinking the same thing. He suddenly didn't seem too keen on me leaving his employ. He looked as small as he was.

"Please stay and work the night Mr. Tucker. I'll have James drop you off where we picked you up, after he takes me and the boys home." After a pause he added, "I'll give you a bonus."

The *boys* didn't look any happier at the mention of the bonus. He actually looked scared. What the hell, in for a penny in for a pound.

"Sure," I said.

By now the limo had come to a stop and James opened the door on my left. There was a sizable crowd around the entrance to Pete's. The walk under the maroon awning, from the door to the road, was lined with people. Many appeared to be those who'd come to Pete's to eat without reservations, and unable to get in, were milling around. The others seemed to be Bench's employees and their partners. They were actually clapping. It looked like a mini academy awards ceremony, without the red carpet.

Powell got out first, stood and looked around just like a body-guard should.

Before I could move I heard Trent say, "You get out last."

I knew he wasn't talking to Bench.

"Okay," I said, without looking at him. I was watching the crowd. I thought, this is where I would cut the dogs loose. I wondered who Mr. Bench had angered to the extent to need three body-guards. Not only who, but what he had done to anger them.

Powell bent down and looked at Samuel Bench and said, "Okay, Mr. Bench, it's clear."

Clear?

Bench got out, followed by Trent. For a moment, I thought Trent was going to close the door in my face.

People were standing in front of Bench, shaking his hand, patting him on the back. These were for sure, employees. Powell was on his left and Trent on his right. All three only one man deep. They were not letting anyone get to either side of him. I was three feet behind Bench, about 15 feet from the limo, and still 20 feet from the door to Pete's when I remembered an old swamp axiom: 'It's always the second man the water moccasin bites.'

That's when things started to move into slow motion. That's when I knew; for me, slow motion has been an effective harbinger for extreme violence and it has never lied.

The skin on my back felt like there were ants crawling under it. The cool October night felt too warm, and there was light where there should be darkness and darkness where there should be light. The crowd disappeared, and there was only Powell, Bench, and Trent in front of me. I felt a presence behind me.

I spun my head to the left, over my shoulder. There were two men in the street, ten feet from and just over the hood of the limo. I was vaguely aware of other people in the shadowed street to either side, but knew there was no one behind them. James was still standing by the back door, his wide white smile glistening and contradicting the impending doom.

Both the men in the street wore dark suits, coats unbuttoned, their faces ghostly white in the changing light. They were just starting to spread out when they saw me spot them. One was a big man; beefy in the shoulders and small in the hips. The other was as small as Bench.

"Behind us!" I yelled, as my body followed my head to the left, putting my back to Bench's back, my left hand reached behind me to make sure he was there, and stayed there.

There was a gun in the smaller man's hand, and it was aimed at me. The big man's gun was by his side, coming up fast. My .45 bucked twice in my hand. I didn't hear it, didn't even know I'd pulled it. I saw flame come from the little man's gun. To my left, someone was tugging at my coat. I'd felt it before. My .45 bucked two more times, now aimed at the big man's chest. I shifted back to the little guy, he was still up but somehow shorter.

He must have body armor.

In a two handed squared stance, I shot him once more. He went down hard, disappearing behind the hood of the limo. I moved forward, looked over the hood, then shifted to the big guy. He was sitting in the street, holding himself up with both hands, one at each side. I could see the gun under his right hand, I shot him once. The back of his head hit the street so hard, it bounced back up into a bright red mist that was hanging in the air. I still couldn't hear anything over the sound of rushing fluid in my head, like water straining through a pipe. I've heard it before.

I slowly and deliberately turned my head to look at Bench. He was just starting to lie down, being pushed by Trent. I couldn't believe how long it was taking him. He should have been down a long time ago. Powell and Trent both had their weapons out and were looking at me like I had feathers. Somewhere in a small pocket of my brain, I wondered what I had done wrong.

I knew I'd shot six times, so I reached into the left hand pocket of my coat, pulled out an extra magazine, pushed the magazine release with my right thumb dropping the partial magazine into my left hand. With the full one between thumb and forefinger I rammed it home, putting the partial into the empty pocket.

I walked around the limo and looked down at the little guy. He was on his back, his feet tucked under him, one under each butt cheek. He'd been on his knees when I shot him the last time. There was no body armor, just a lot of blood. I didn't need to look at the big guy.

My hearing was coming back. Both ears were ringing from the muzzle blasts I didn't hear. Life once again moved at a normal pace.

Trent was looking at me wide-eyed, shaking his head. Powell was pulling Bench to his feet.

I wondered why I didn't hear the sirens of approaching police cruisers. I could hear women screaming, and suddenly, everything was sharper, brighter; the colors more brilliant and the eyes of everyone staring at me were magnified, too close to me.

Holstering my Colt, I walked over to the limo, and James was still standing in the exact same spot, like he was holding the door open for me. He was no longer smiling.

I got in and sat in the middle, away from the crowd and the bodies in the street. I faced the front of the car and waited for the police to arrive. Staring straight ahead, I couldn't see anyone at all. More importantly, I felt no one could see me.

Suddenly, I felt the beautifully aged, cherry-stained, birds-eye maple trim inside the limo, gawking at me.

I was later told the whole thing took place in the space of 3 to 4 seconds, probably closer to 3. It wasn't the gravity of my actions that ground that data into insignificant unobserved electrons, but the eyes. I couldn't get the eyes of those people out of my head. They looked at me like *I* was one of the *bad* guys.

Chapter 2

What if? Have you ever played what if? Most people have, but it's usually, 'what if I won the eighty million dollar lottery'.

But, what if you knew beforehand, the exact moment, that pivotal moment in time and space, that moment you made the decision to turn right, to answer the phone, or to take that other route home? That crucial decision that would hurl you into a series of independent, seemingly logical actions, which would create in your world so much pain, so much violence, so much grief and guilt, that at times you didn't think you'd survive. At other times, you were afraid you would. If you knew this beforehand—would you make that turn? Would you answer that phone? Probably not. For in most cases it takes years, sometimes many years, to know that the decision you made at that moment—the moment that facilitated all that violence, pain and grief—that horrific decision making nano-second . . . could make you a better human being.

Nashville, Tennessee   Present Day

I was focused at my workbench, easing the slide onto a Smith & Wesson 9mm when the phone rang. Startled, I jerked it up, "Tucker's."

On the other side I hear in the slowest of southern drawls, "Hey, ya wanna punch holes in some paper?"

It was Brad Spain, a Captain with the Nashville Metro P.D., who heads up the elite Murder Squad. He's a little full-blooded Cherokee Indian, who talks sooo slow, in a deep brown monotone voice, that it is sometimes grueling. His words were cut short and exact, his voice strained, as if he were lifting something heavy, all with a drawl, but he was a competitive shootist. I've known him for twenty years, since 1 a.m., Dec. 11th, 1982. The night my wife was killed.

"Brad, it's always good to hear from you," I said.

Notice I didn't say, 'good to hear the sound of your voice.' But, Brad was a friend, a friend of a definite kind, the kind who has shared something horrific, tragic, and sacred with me. When I did hear from him, it usually meant some kind of work was coming my way. It would just take me a long time to hear about it. Spain was instrumental in the transformation of Tucker Arms to Tucker Security.

"What's up?" I asked.

"I've got the range at Gun World for six tonight. Feel like a friendly wager?"

There was a time we could do our shooting at the police range, but certain knowledge as to the identities of some of my clients had become privy to Metro PD, and I had fallen out of favor.

I looked down at the Citizen Aqualand watch on my left wrist. It was 4:30. It's a big watch and has nice big green numbers, so at night I could almost read by their luminescence, and if needed, it could be taken off and used as a blackjack.

I said, "Kind of short notice, isn't it? What've you been doing? Practicing for this and planning to slip up on me?"

"Naw, just a friendly little shoot-out," he replied.

I don't have time to do the gunsmithing I used to, but I looked at the two pistols remaining on my bench that I had yet to finish. One was my favorite to work on and to shoot, a 1911 Colt .45. Archy in Boulder, Co sent it to me. The attached note said, 'smooth it out, quicken it up and make it shoot straight.' Usually 1911's shoot where they're pointed, tells me a little about Archibald from Boulder. The other one was a third generation Smith and Wesson Model 5904 9mm that had a little too much on the trigger pull. I owned one myself. Nothing I couldn't do tomorrow.

"Spain, I'd love to take your money, but I'm swamped here."

Thought I'd play hard to get and raise the bet.

"Money," he says lazily. "Who said anything about money? I don't have any fuckin' money. If I can't pay for it with a credit card, forget it. How about the winner buys dinner at the Three Little Pigs."

Aha. It worked. It's a great Bar-B-Q place that serves excellent smoked turkey breast and has Haake Beck, a fine fake brew, and it's just around the corner from Gun World. But, I can tell he's holding something back.

"I don't think so . . . " I started, but before I can get it all out, he spilled his guts, in slow motion.

"Tucker, I need to see you. There's someone who is interested in meeting you. He wants to set up an interview. Tucker, this might be a big one, and there's something else going on I'd like to talk to you about."

I traced the scrimshaw etchings on the ivory handle of the Colt with my finger and said, "So I've got to embarrass you at the range. Then make you buy me dinner just so you'll tell me. Tell me now and save yourself."

I wonder where dead-eye Archy from Boulder got his ivory. It didn't look old enough to be legal.

He said, "I can't. I'm at my desk, it could get a little touchy . . . embarrass me! Just show up and I'll show you who gets embarrassed. Besides, if you beat me, I may not tell you."

Listening to Spain was like trying to wheedle a half inch of thick brown molasses out of a gallon jug. After it was all out, you realized it would've been faster to break the jug and scrape it out.

"Okay. What are your terms?" I asked. "You always have some."

"No fast draw. Semi-automatics on the bench. Five shot groupings. We go on a three count.

I felt like he was right behind me, fixing to take my scalp.

"All right, Spain, who's doing the counting, you?"

"Naaw, I'll give you a break. We'll let Spark do the counting."

Spark owned and operated Gun World on Murfreesboro Road. He looked like a slow-moving catfish with a Clark Gable mustache, black glasses and a black receding hairline, and his favorite expression to me was 'Well, I don't know, Tucker.' He would say this in a cavernous bass voice with no southern accent, since he originated in Connecticut. He usually said this right after I'd done something with a pistol he just couldn't wrap his mind around.

"I'll be there even though I smell an ambush," I said.

"Good, see you at six." His chuckle sounded like he was rubbing his hands together.

Chapter 3

My past has a way of slipping up behind me, with the subtlety of a freight train. I don't hear it coming. First, I feel it, like a wave of shimmering energy being pushed ahead of it. Then the train arrives and slams into my occipital ridge with a force that used to take me to my knees. Towed behind the locomotive is a row of boxcars that contains everything meaningful, and most times traumatic, that has happened to me. It's a long train.

For someone who battles with staying in the present moment, this can be difficult. But isn't that what life is?

Over the years I've learned through different modalities of study to watch this train from a higher point of view. Like an eagle soaring above the train. Observe the train. Don't be the train.

Each car being towed is full of actions and feelings. They're baggage cars and they are full. Who I am at this moment, is the sum total of the mistakes made and lessons learned inside each one of those cars.

But, I am not at this moment any one of those actions or feelings. I am not anger, I am not violence, I am not guilt, and I am not grief. I'm supposed to be love. Love for everything that has happened to me, no matter what it was. Because like Stuart Smalley said, 'I love myself.'

There are times when I feel more love than other times. I can be any one of many feelings. This time I'm numb. Numb is good.

From my eagle's eye view, everything happens at the same time. So my future has already happened. I just can't see it. The decisions I make now, in the present moment, determine that.

Ahh . . . there's the caboose.

I stared at the backs of my hands that were spread out over the Colt. They weren't big hands, as hands go, especially attached to my Alleyoop arms that were affixed to a 48-inch torso. They were strong hands. I believed the smallness of them was a major factor in the hand speed I've always had. The knuckles were different shades due to scar tissue. There was a perfect little round scar just to the left of my right index knuckle, exactly the size of a .25 caliber bullet. The exit scar on the other side was not as perfect.

Sporadically spaced about the backs of both hands were scars of varying sizes, shapes and shades. The little finger on my right hand was bent under at the last knuckle, due to my first fight out of the ring when I was 13 (I never got past Golden Gloves). I didn't close my hand tight to make a hard fist. Instead of hitting him with the first two knuckles, I caught him with the last two, and the force of the blow pushed the little finger into my hand and the bone decided to peek out and see the world.

I knew at that moment, hitting a man in the head with my bare fist, while summoning the speed and strength I was capable of, wasn't going to work for me. I was five- nine and weighed 160 pounds when I was 13. I wasn't fat.

The man I hit was 35 and about 185 pounds. The last punch of a five-punch combination was a straight right that caught him over his heart. He wet his pants on the way down. I got the knuckle sequence right that time.

My cell phone rang. I pick it up, "Tucker's."

"Hiii Paw Paw!"

I felt my heart smile.

I said, "Hey, Little Margie."

My mouth felt funny. I must have smiled. Smiling, according to some, was something I didn't do enough of. It's been said my smiling was often a precursor to violence. It may be hereditary. The Major use to smile before he smacked me.

I remember the day my daughter, Shannon, called and asked my permission to name her firstborn after her mother, my late wife.

I knew the inescapable red horned demons that stalked me in my slumber and crept up on me with the stealth of stagnant swamp water while I was awake, were not my daughter's problem.

I answered with, "Shannon, you don't have to ask my permission. You name your daughter anything you want."

"But Dad," she replied, "I'm worried that it'll be hard for you. I know how much you still miss Mom."

Bowing to my ambiguous sensibilities, all I could do was reiterate, "You name your daughter anything you want. I appreciate your concern. I'll be just fine with it, really."

I also remember I wasn't so sure of that at the time.

Now, I love to say her name. Her being named Margie was a healing for me. Now, she's *my* 'Little Margie'.

"What are you doing, Paw Paw?" Margie said, enunciating every syllable.

"Oh, you know, just foolin' around the office."

"Are you working on a gun? When are you going to take me shooting? I want to go hunting. I want you to take me fishing too," she said, without taking a breath. Her voice, so mature for a girl not yet a teenager.

"You're not quite old enough to hunt yet, Margie. Besides, do you think you could really kill an animal, like a duck? They're so pretty." I figured to shock this burgeoning young lady with some hard reality.

"Sure," she chirped. "I love your duck gumbo. I could kill a duck for sure."

So much for shocking reality. She was so sure of herself. I couldn't help but notice how much she was like her namesake.

I did something alien. I laughed out loud.

I said, "Maybe this summer we can start shooting a .22 rifle. You and Max (her little brother) can come out to the house, and we will make a day of it. Maybe you guys can spend the night."

"That would be cool," she said, delighted.

Cool, the word of generations. The fact that it still worked was cool in itself.

"Paaaw Paaaw! Take me fishing!" Max yelled into the phone.

I said, "Maxoman, can you hear me?"

When he was just starting to say my name and I came into the house, he would yell 'Paaww Paaww!' and I would yell back 'Maaaxxoooommmannnn'. I sounded like someone that just spotted Superman flying through the sky. He loved it.

"No, Paw Paw. He can't hear you, I've got the phone," Margie said, her voice dripping with 'how stupid can you be?'

"Margie, give the phone to your brother."

"Ohh. Okay," she said, exasperated. As she handed the phone to Max, she said, "Max, don't hang up before you give it back."

"Hi, Paw Paw. When are you going to take me fishing? I want to go too," Maxoman said.

Both children were being home schooled by their father, Roger. Roger is incredibly bright. He graduated Magna Cum Laude from Vanderbilt in computer science. He worked out of the house consulting, so was there to teach them. They both spoke succinctly beyond their years.

"Let's let the weather get a little warmer, and we'll go. Okay? It's too cold outside right now, Maxoman." It really wasn't too cold, but he didn't know that.

"Paw Paw, it's not that cold. I was just outside playing, and the Koi aren't frozen in the pond."

Maxoman's a lot like his dad.

"Not for the fish, Maxoman. It's too cold for Paw Paw," I said, then added, "Spring and summer are for fishing. Winter is for hunting."

"How old were you when Mom was born?" he asked.

"Give me the phone, Max!" Margie yelled, positively vexed.

I could hear the scuffling over the phone, then Little Margie said, "Paw Paw, how old were . . . Huh? Oh, okay . . . " I could hear Shannon's voice in the background, then more phone scuffling.

"Hey, Dad," she said, when she got the phone from Little Margie.

Shannon's laugh came from her throat, like her mothers.

"What's that all about?" I asked.

"Oh, we were looking at the pictures we took the other night with the digital camera. There's a really good one of you in that black sport coat. Margie said you were too handsome to be a Paw Paw."

"Well, I am," I said matter of factly. "You agreed with her, right?"

"Yeah right." She said sarcastically, with a smile in her voice. "Anyway, she asked me how old you were when I was born and I told her if she wanted to know that, she'd better ask you. I don't want her to hear from me how young you and Mom were. She's already looking at boys, and I would like her to wait awhile before she gets married."

"I see. So this way, if she gets married too young, you can blame it on me. It'll be my fault, and you can skate."

"Exactly," she said.

I wasn't sure if she was teasing.

After a long pause, she said, "She's really a handful, Daddy."

"Sounds like she takes after her mother," I said, which she ignored.

"Are you working tonight? You *know* what I mean."

After the rodeo that took place the night I was watching over Samuel Bench, Shannon and I agreed it would be best if she didn't know when I was doing that kind of work. She was having a hard time living up to her end of the bargain.

"No." I said.

"You wouldn't tell me if you were, would you?" she asked quietly.

"No."

"You know what I'd say to you if the kids weren't here, don't you?"

Among her closed circle of friends and family, Shannon was known and admired for the eloquent profanity that could roll off her tongue with the ease and grace only attractive southern women could get away with. Her beauty and timing would spin the connotations into colorful and amusing anecdotes.

"You're lucky the kids are in the room," she threatened.

"Yeah, I know. Let me talk to Margie."

"Okay. I love you. And Dad, you *are* too handsome to be a grandfather."

"Thanks. I love you too."

She's so much like her mother, and other than her mother, she's the only person I've ever been truly afraid of.

"Paw Paw?" Little Margie's voice was all business now.

"Yes, Baby, what is it?" I asked.

She loves it when I call her Baby. It makes her feel all grown up. It's what I sometimes call her mom. It's also what I called her grandmother.

"Mom said it would be all right if I asked how old you were when she was born."

I could hear Shannon in the background denying all culpability.

"Sure, no problem. Let's see, let me think . . . I was ten. Yeah . . . yeah. That's the ticket, ten years old."

"Nooo waay!" she yelled, giggling at same time.

"Okay, twelve, that's right, twelve."

"That's really gross Paw Paw," she said, but her tone implied she was intrigued.

"I tell you what. When you reach the age I was when your mom was born, I'll tell you then. How's that? That seems fair. Then you'll better understand just how young your grandmother and I were."

"Oh no, that's not fair. I want to know now," she said, pouting.

"Now be a big girl and let's compromise. Okay?" I asked.

I was starting to sweat.

Wait until she finds out how old we were when her aunt Mary was born. Mary is our oldest daughter, the one we had to give up for adoption, who we named Patricia Elain. Her new parents renamed her Mary. Shannon found her about seven years ago. That's another story altogether.

"What's the compromise?" Margie, the business manager, asked.

"Ah, that I'll tell you later. When you're older."

"That's not a compromise. Don't I get something for a compromise?" She asked.

Little Margie can be a lot like her dad, too.

"Okay, I'll take you duck hunting."

"When?" she demanded.

"Before I tell you how old I was," I said, thinking 'I've got her now.'

"When was that?" she asked, with an '*I've got him now*' tone.

I must escape.

"Little Margie, I've got to go now. I have to close up the office and lock up the apartment."

"I love your apartment. It's so cool. I like it when we stay over and watch all the people on the street and eat Japanese at Poks."

"Me too, Baby. Now let Paw Paw go clean it up.".

I have a cleaning lady who comes in once a week, but Little Margie doesn't need to know that. Let her think Paw Paw is just really neat.

"Okay, Paw Paw. I love you. Bye." Click.

That's my Little Margie. No fooling around. She makes up her mind, and that's that.

"I love you too, bye," I said, with no one to hear. But saying it aloud doesn't leave it echoing in my head for thirty minutes.

I was grateful Shannon and Roger had been able to keep the incident of two months ago from Little Margie and Maxoman. Since they don't attend public schools and don't watch much TV, Roger and Shannon told all adults not to mention it around the kids. I'd managed to keep my mug off the TV news reports and out of the newspapers through business influences and stealth. All of it together amounted to a lot of work, but was worth it. They think Paw Paw is 'so nice' and 'so cool,' and that's the way I want it, for as long as it lasts, along with being really neat.

Chapter 4

Thanks to the generosity of Samuel Bench I have an office/workshop/apartment above a Japanese Restaurant and Sushi Bar on 2nd Avenue. It's located in the newly renovated downtown district, one block off the riverfront.

The versatile space has it's own street level door that opens into a stairway that goes up the front of the building, over the sushi bar. There's a window under the stairway that allows a view into the restaurant.

At the top of the stairs, there's a left turn into a long hallway that goes back 43 feet, to the door of my office. Ten feet from the top of the stairs, there's a door on the right, the door to my apartment. Most people who came up the stairs didn't know this. The long hall is very mysterious. There's a ten foot ceiling perpendicular to dry wall that's painted a light Ralph Lauren gray. There are no pictures on the walls. My apartment door is an army green metal job that looks very janitorial, whereas the door to my office is stained red oak and inviting. On the office door at eye level is a gunmetal plaque with silver block letters making one word, 'TUCKER'. There's a video surveillance camera above the door that is capable of looking all the way down the hall. There are three monitors in my office and one in my apartment. Most people don't even notice the metal janitorial door. It's what I had in mind when I remodeled the place.

The oak door opens into a 22x12 foot room. Along the left wall is a light olive green fabric couch I picked up at Pier 1. The left wall is the one that goes back 22 ft. The back wall is the 12 footer and is the original old red brick. The other two walls are half-inch burnt pine tongue and groove panels I salvaged from an old house on the South Harpeth River.

On the brick wall are two lithograph prints, a Rance Hood named Crazy Dog Warrior and an Archer Black Owl called Cheyenne Burial. The Rance Hood is a number two of twenty artist's proof that I'd paid $275 dollars and a couple of years later found out it was worth a little over $6000. Cheyenne Burial was another blind luck acquisition.

Under the prints are two oak and glass barrister book cases that house my collection of flint and museum quality Mississippian pottery. They look prestigious and interesting in my office. Clients always commented on them, creating an effective ice breaker.

Besides, the security room in my house on Barren Fork Creek wasn't finished yet, so they were safer in town.

There's an antique cherry desk in front of the right-hand pine wall. Behind the desk is another door. This door is noticed by everyone. Think of a door that looks like it went to an old bank safe, with a big wheel on the front. That's exactly what it was. I found it at a salvage place that was run by a group of Mennonites down in Lobelville, Tennessee. It's actually a safe door from the early 1900's. It had been cut off during a robbery and was too interesting to toss. No one had ever used it for anything useful, like an anchor for a floating dock. Other than that, it had no use. It was just heavy and interesting, until I saw it. I bought it for next to nothing. If they were anything but Mennonites, I probably could have charmed them into paying me to haul it off. My charm only worked well enough to get them to sell it. I know it was my charm because one of them smiled, I think. I had the door sand-blasted, painted, and the combination mechanism rebuilt and renumbered by a locksmith friend who has taught me a few things about locks. We framed it in with metal I-beams and oak 2x12's.

The safe door opened into a gray carpeted room that is 22x10. At each end of the room to the left and right, were two gun safes. In the middle of the room stood an old pine dining table that could seat 10 people comfortably. The table was strewn with split, tanned, deer hides. They were great to put guns on when making a sale or when clients picked up guns I had smithed.

Above the safe door, facing the table, was another monitor. On the wall opposite from the safe door, another door opened into a smaller room, my work shop. My work bench sits in the middle of the room facing the door. A metal lathe, drill press, and other gun-smithing tools are arranged behind it. Above that door was another monitor facing my bench.

I get a good deal on surveillance equipment. People are always surprised to find how inexpensive black and white video cameras and monitors are. I can usually barter it out.

On the wall to my left, as I sat at my bench facing the door to the safe room, was a row of shelves housing tools, solvents, oil, etc. It looked like just what it was, a catch-alls shelf. However, it's really a secret door to my apartment. It was quite easy to build, you just have to know how. I have a friend who knew how. Now after paying for eighteen hours of labor, I knew how. I would most likely never apply this knowledge again, but I am very proud of it. Unfortunately, it was one of those enigmas, I couldn't show it off. It would defeat the purpose.

I pulled back the secret shelf, which opened into my bathroom between the toilet and shower. As it closed, I looked at myself in the full length mirror on the other side of the shelf and noticed I need a trim around the ears. That's about all I get cut, but for a few times a year when I get a couple of inches cut off my ponytail. My hair is naturally curly and when I grew it long during my Harley days, I found I could pull it back into a pony tail and that straightened it out. From the front I almost looked distinguished, along with a sculptured beard I trimmed myself (the only artistic outlet I have), I thought I look professorial. But for the remindful deep crescent scar starting just below my cheekbone and ending at the corner my mouth and depending on which profile your looking at, some said I look like a record producer, others said a pirate . . . same thing.

I walked through the galley style kitchen, past the Nordic Track and Bowflex machines into the living area, with windows overlooking 2nd Avenue.

I have two futon couches arranged at right angles. They can quickly be turned into beds. One has its back to the windows; the other is along the left wall when facing the windows.

I stood and looked down at the street through the mist of the December afternoon. It was a blur of red, white and blue; cowboy hats and scarves, boots with doggin' heels on people who didn't know what they were for: a country and western Picasso; a freeze frame of expectant glances hoping to see someone famous. Tourists dressed like Hee Haw characters (for some that's the only models they had), were not deterred by the inclement weather.

Once, this street had been mostly empty, with just a few businesses still open. The storefront for Randy Woods' Old Time Pickin'
Parlor, where I worked as a custom guitar builder and stringed
instrument repairman, would have been directly below me. In fact,
the window I was looking out of was once the spray booth window,
that used to contain a huge exhaust fan that blew the lacquer out
over the street where it would dry and dissipate into a fine powder
before doing any damage to the cars parked below.

There used to be a hardware store across the street and down
to the left the Shobud factory where they made their famous pedal
steel guitars. The other buildings were mostly abandoned two and
three story brick buildings, but for a few small businesses like the old
shoe shop where I bought dyes for my airbrush.

Now the street was bustling with street vendors and germs
(said with a hard g). The word was coined by a pissed off songwriter
or some such back in the late seventies. It was first said germs, like
the bacteria we all felt they were when they invaded Nashville two or
three times a year, clogging up streets and taking all the choice parking places. Then it was changed to the hard g sound so we could say
the word in their presence. Then when country music went ballistic
in the early 80's, the money became so outrageous, the word became
a term of endearment. Here come the germs, God Bless them.

Since the renovation of the downtown district, the real-estate
down here was untouchable. Now, there were wonderful restaurants.
The famous Wild Horse Saloon was across the street and down to
the left. There were street vendors selling everything from gold
chains to popcorn. I could sit here and see just about anything I can
think of. It was like a country music Bourbon Street, without the
visible alcohol.

I heard the creaking of a baggage car door.

Chapter 5

Brad Spain. It was hard to think about him without the years and circumstances melting away and feeling like yesterday. My second encounter with him was a month after the first. It was in January of 1983, after the Charlie Daniels Volunteer Jam. Brad had the occasion to stick his S&W .38 special service revolver in my ear and cock the hammer. There were many people that night on the 14th floor of the Hyatt Regency trying to get my attention, but that did it.

As I watched a couple come out of the Wild Horse all duded up for line dancing, the linear reflection of where life had taken me since I went to work at the Picken' Parlor in 1976, became lodged in my throat.

Now due to the generosity and gratitude (I'm not sure which came first) of Samuel Bench, I have this great space in the high rent district of downtown Nashville, with a 99 year lease, free of charge.

That night after Brad caught my attention at the Hyatt, he walked me to the elevator in handcuffs, walked me outside onto Commerce Street and around the corner, where he took the handcuffs off. He took me to a bar and sat me down. Of all the cops in Nashville, Brad was one of only two, who knew what I'd been through. He was there, and he was there for me that night. He saved my butt, in more ways than one. I've always been grateful to him.

I stayed in the music business for a couple of more years. Made a few more guitars, did lots of repair work, wrote a few songs, and then had to get out. When my friends in the Biz asked why I was getting out, I would just say 'It's not conducive to a healthy lifestyle'. That was true for me anyway. I was having too much fun not dealing with my grief. Fun in the way of Makers Mark, Grand Marnier, Marijuana and Cocaine. I was having so much fun I was incapable of taking care of my daughter and had to ship her off to her grandmother's in Louisiana where she went to high school for three years. Irreclaimable years.

Before Dec. 11th, the booze, due to my livelihood, was in my life only in moderation. The drugs, well, let's just say years before, were just business. I had handled grief and Post Traumatic Stress badly.

In 1984 I built my last two guitars for Amy Grant and her then husband, Gary Chapman. I used the money to buy a water sports business on the beach in Negril, Jamaica. After 3 years of traveling back and forth from there and three very close calls with the Rude Boys (the Jamaican Mafia called the Posse in the states) trying to get rid of me, I sold the business to an eager stupe from Long Island, who thought he was going to move to Magaritaville. Then I came back to Nashville and started shooting guns again. Something I grew up doing extensively and stopped when I started doing something else with my hands. Something legitimate.

That's when I started running into Spain again. I would see him at the gun range, and a friendship ensued.

It was time to make one of those decisions based on the information available in the present moment. You could never tell when one would be a pivotal decision. I decided I was hungry, that sounded safe enough. I checked my multipurpose blackjack, and saw there was just enough time to give the office the once-over before going downstairs to catch some Sashimi prior to the big shootout.

After straightening up a bit, I threaded my custom-made Bellioni holster on to my belt, reached under a pillow on the futon, pulled out my 1911 Colt .45, and slipped into the holster. I decided to keep my black cherry, chip toed Lucchese cowboy boots on and not change into running shoes. They put me up over six-one, which would tower me over Spain's five-seven, maybe intimidating some extra points for me during the impending shootout. I put on my Abercrombie and Fitch lamb skin brown leather jacket, donned one of my LSU caps, set the security code and went downstairs.

Chapter 6

When people asked where you're from, most usually reply by telling them the town they grew up in. Well, I grew up all over the world. I'm an Air Force Brat. My traveling dysfunctional family didn't move to the States for good until the summer between my sixth and seventh grade years. Before that, it was just visits that went along with either duck season, summer fishing, or when my sister, brother and I lived with my mother and abusive step-father, also an Air Force Officer.

When my father regained custody of my brother and I, leaving my sister with my mother and step-father, he was a Major. He was a firm believer in the aphorism 'children should be seen and not heard,' so I didn't have much opportunity to say the words 'Dad' or 'Father'. He was referred to as 'The Major'.

A year before the Major retired, we moved to Alexandria, Louisiana, his home-town. I did my junior high, high school and college in Louisiana. So, when people asked me where I am from, I said Louisiana. Most of the people who have known me for years associate me with Louisiana. The truth of the matter is, I've lived in Nashville and the surrounding area for over 20 years. That's longer than I have ever lived anywhere, but I *am* wearing an LSU hat.

Alexandria, known locally as just Alec: the land where the rednecks met the Cajuns met the Army boys from Fort Polk, met the Air Force boys from England Air Force Base, all of which bordered the beginnings of some of the most perilous swampland in Louisiana. One of which was one of my personal stomping grounds, a place called the Devils' Raceway. All in all, a very volatile and dangerous place. I had the scars to prove it.

I had a friend, Max Young, who ended up as a drill instructor at Fort Polk, sixty miles west of Alec. Every time a group of recruits would go out on their first leave, he would give the same speech. He told them that although they have been taught many ways to kill a man with their bare hands, not to think for one minute they were going to go into Leesville or Alexandria and whip up on any of the local boys. He informed his newly trained killers that the local boys grew up in a war zone, most carried guns and all carried knives, and 'they will kill you!'. They didn't always listen.

Chapter 7

As I reached street level, I paused in the shadow of my entrance alcove. It was good to check the street, get a feel for the pulse, the movement, or lack of it. I'm not paranoid, just cautious. Not everyone loves me. The octopus is still alive; he may be missing a few tentacles, but he's still alive.

I stepped onto the sidewalk, turned left, and walked the twenty feet to the doorway of Pok's. The tourist traffic wasn't too bad, so I was allowed to pause and check out my favorite hangout and eatery.

Directly in front of me was a display case containing Japanese art, sake services for sale and a nice selection of sake. The bottles were displayed around the varying services. It created a nice feng shui entrance to the establishment. You could see over the top of the display. You could turn to the left and go to the sushi bar or turn right and move into the radiant ambiance of the Red Dragon Restaurant. There were more than a few red dragons on display. Pok liked red dragons.

Nothing seemed out of the ordinary, so I turned to the left.

The sushi bar was a rectangle island with the far end being under the stairway to my place. It was almost full. There were couples and small groups scattered around leaving only a few unoccupied stools that faced the raw fish display cases. This didn't concern me, because down the far end on the right, against the wall facing the window to the street was my chair. It was unoccupied because of the 'reserved' sign sitting on the bar in front of it. The only reserved sign in the building as far as I knew.

This was also where Pok did his magic. There were never fewer than two sushi chefs working, and I'd seen as many as five in the center of the action. But, Pok worked just that portion of the island.

It may have had something to do with the fact that's where his platform was. Pok is very short. He may have had the platform built there because the stairway to my place made for less head room or maybe because that was the only place I would sit. Pok loved me.

I'd helped a drunken tourist out of his restaurant, and now he thinks I could do no wrong. Of course the tourist, being drunk and all, didn't want any help, didn't in fact, really want to leave.

I felt more comfortable with my back to the wall, with a view of the rest of the restaurant, and I could see out the window onto the street. Some call that the gunfighter's seat. I just call it the best seat in the house, any house.

As I walked around to the right and towards *my* seat, Pok spied me and gave me his million dollar smile (he's probably made that since opening this place two years before). He's a sweet guy.

."Hey, Mista Tucka."

"Hi Pok, how're you doing?"

"Mee? I'm goood. You want sake?" he asked, while making a rice ball for sushi. Pok was from Tokyo. He's about four and a half feet tall, muscular and perfectly formed. He looked like a little Arnold Schwarzenegger, only better looking.

"No thanks, Pok. Let me have some green tea and the small Sashimi plate," I said.

As I sat down in front of the reserved sign, some of the patrons sitting around gave me curious glances. I sometimes have that effect. It must be the scar.

After he wiped his hands on a towel, he stood like a western gunfighter, elbows out, palms towards his hips, and slowly swayed back and forth. He pretended to draw his imaginary six-shooters and said, "You working tonight?" Then blows the make-believe smoke from both index fingers. Pok watches a lot of TV, including the news.

Needless to say, this morphed many of the glances into stares.

Between the glancing and staring, I felt like a dart board. I tried not to make a face.

"No, I'm not working tonight Pok, just hanging out with some friends," I said.

He looked disappointed. I think he would have been ecstatic if I told him I was going out to whack somebody.

"I got yu favrit Sake, de one from Cororado."

"No thanks, Pok. Just green tea to start, but I'll have a Haake Beck with the sashimi."

Green tea was supposed to have the good kind of caffeine, whatever that meant. After such an exciting order, I must not have been so interesting, and the dart slingers retired.

Pok started shouting in Japanese, and a beautiful woman scurried out of the back.

It always amazed me, how oriental women could look graceful, even when hurrying. I loved oriental women. It must be my upbringing.

Her name was Lei. It's pronounced lay, but I'm not going there. It's been too long.

Lei came directly to me and seemed to ignore everything Pok was saying. He hadn't stopped jabbering since she appeared. Nevertheless she had eyes only for me. FANTASY! She was somewhere in her mid to late twenties and had been working here since the beginning.

She carried a tray with a hot rolled-up, white hand towel and a pair of plain wood chopsticks. There was a wooden bin behind the bar with over a hundred ornately lacquered chopsticks in their own numbered cases for regular customers. I preferred the wooden ones; the food doesn't slip out of them so easily. Pok and I sometimes got a conspiratory silent laugh out of the regulars dropping food because of their fancy slick sticks, but it was smart marketing on Pok's part.

She stopped next to me, stood with her feet together, slightly bowed her head and presented the tray.

"It is so good to see you, Mr. Tucker," she said, with just a hint of accent, that I found attractive.

"Lei, it is always a pleasure to see you," I said, as I took the towel and started to wipe my hands.

She set the chopsticks on a napkin on the bar, then slowly raised her head to make direct eye contact with me. It was so un-oriental of her.

I looked down, then looked up quickly and nodded to her. I wanted her to know how much I appreciated her lovely brown eyes.

She blushed and showed a modicum of even white teeth, "No, Mr. Tucker, it is my pleasure."

"Lei, if I was 20 years younger, I'd ask you to marry me. I would take you away from this horrible place," I said, with a wave of my hand to include the restaurant and Pok.

Pok was smiling like he was part of my joke.

Lei turned as red as the dragon on the kimono she was wearing, and as she short-stepped by me, whispered in my ear, "You no too old, you too scared," then disappeared behind the red door to the kitchen.

I almost dropped my towel. Pok started laughing very loudly, the way only oriental people could do and get away with it.

"She like you, Mista Tucka, " Pok whispered with a wink and a grin. "She think you soo handsome. Yes, she say this to me."

Stricken with a sudden case of aphasia, I did the smart thing. I looked around the room for buried treasure.

A few minutes later Lei returned with my tea. I deduced she wasn't ignoring Pok. My neck was getting hot, and I felt like I was walking in a field of land mines.

"Thank you, ma'am," I said, as I looked at the ceiling for more buried treasure. In my peripheral vision, I saw her look up at the ceiling, then I heard her giggle.

"I will bring your Haake Beck with your sashimi. Is that right?" she asks, not budging.

I realized I must show bravery. Pok was watching. I must not lose face. I would impress them with my witty repartee.

I turned my head, looked deep into her brown eyes and said, "Yes ma'am."

Pok was laughing loudly again. Lei looked at me with a smile that somehow let me off the hook, then they both got the giggles.

I liked this restaurant.

From the restaurant I detected movement aimed in my direction and saw a familiar face coming. It was Paul Macino with a very attractive woman in tow. He held his hand out for the shake and with a big smile on his round face said, "Tucker, it's great to see you."

"Paul, how've you been?" I asked, turning my stool to face them.

"Great, just great," he said, pumping my hand so hard water should be coming out of my ears any second now.

"I want you to meet my fiancé, Troy," he said, with his left hand on the small of her back.

As I stood, her hand came up to replace Paul's hand in mine.

"Good afternoon Troy, it's a pleasure to meet you," I said, looking into big emerald eyes, surrounded by short cropped blonde hair.

"Mr. Tucker. Please sit. We don't wish to disturb your meal. It's just that I've heard so much about you and what you have done for Paul and Ryan. I believe Paul brought me down here in hopes of running into you," she said.

Her accent sounded native Nashvillian and she reeked of old money, looked to be about 35, but was probably closer to 45. She wasn't a pumper. She was a holder.

"It's not Mr., it's just Tucker," I said, as I sat back down.

She knew how to wear makeup. I had to look hard to see it. It could've been misconstrued for staring.

"Is that your first name or your last?" she asked, with a mischievous glint in her eyes.

"Both," I said, giving Paul a glance. He looked constipated.

"I didn't put her up to that, I swear," he said.

Paul was in his early sixties but aging well. He owned a string of successful auto parts stores across Tennessee.

"That's true. He always refers to you as Tucker, and Ryan says Mr. Tucker. I asked him one day what your whole name was and he didn't know. I'm just naturally nosey," she said, as she tossed her head like her hair was longer and in her eyes. She was still holding my hand.

I felt my eyes squint with amusement. In the silence that followed, I could sense Paul becoming uneasy. My squinting escalated.

I could see that Troy was having a blast, her bright eyes were dancing as she moved the toe of her right shoe back and forth, pivoting on the spike of her high heel.

She didn't mind holding my hand. I didn't mind either. It was nice. She had a great manicure with pale pink polish, and the nails weren't so long as to be in the way.

"Well, *Tucker*," she said, with delight, "We expect to see you at our wedding in June."

I gave her hand a light squeeze and said, "It would be my pleasure to attend your nuptials, and may I say that Paul is indeed a fortunate man."

I liked her. There was an easy elegance about her.

"Paul said you were a nice man, although I had my doubts after you making the news. But I see Paul's perception of you is accurate."

Her expression altered, like a small embarrassing memory just came to mind.

"To be truthful," she whispered. "Paul wanted to invite you and I said not until I'd met you."

"So this is an inspection, and I passed?"

Now I understood Paul's uneasiness.

Paul groaned and started looking around for *my* buried treasure.

As I stood, she very naturally let go of my hand, allowing me to put my left arm around Paul's shoulder while I shook his hand. Paul's a standup guy and was exceedingly generous concerning the little matter I handled for him.

"Congratulations, Paul. It looks like you've got your hands full."

From the look on Troy's face, I couldn't have said anything more fitting.

Paul let out some air and in a relieved tone said, "You got that right."

Troy looked me dead in the eye and smiled.

"See you in June," she said, spun on her heel and left without a backward glance.

Paul, still shaking my hand, looked like he was going to apologize.

I said, "She's great, Paul. You're a lucky man, and I'm more than a little envious."

"Yeah, she *is* a bundle. Thanks, Tucker, for everything. Now I can send you an invitation."

"I'll look for it. Don't worry about the inspection. I don't blame her," I said.

He shook his head and seemed like he wanted to say something else, but Lei came back with my sashimi and Becks.

"See ya," he said, and hurried after the bustling Troy.

As I sat back down to eat, through the window I could see them walking on the sidewalk and thought back on how I'd met Paul.

Paul's son, Ryan was working at Davis Dodge, moving cars and trucks around the lots and being an all-around gofer. He'd landed the job at Davis Dodge on his own. Ryan was 18 and loved trucks and music, in that order. One day while moving a truck, he backed it out of a parking spot on the back lot, and ran over Ray.

Ray was a black gentleman, 62 years of age, who had worked at Davis Dodge for more than ten years. He was well liked and was affectionately known as Uncle Ray by all who worked there.

When I said Ryan hit Ray, that was an understatement. He not only backed into him, but ran completely over the old gentleman with the rear wheels of a double axle three-quarter ton Dodge Ram pickup. Uncle Ray didn't survive.

Ryan was arrested, taken downtown and charged with vehicular homicide, and subsequently, I got a call from a distraught Paul Macino.

Paul said he got my name from a patrolman who wanted to remain anonymous. Patrolman Anonymous had said that I may be able to help Paul because I had some friends down at the department. Paul also said he got the impression the patrolman didn't care much for the arresting officer.

I didn't know what I could do. Not being a private investigator, I was at a loss, and told Paul the same. He literally begged me to help him and had already arranged for me to see his son.

I heard the ache in Paul's voice and not knowing what else to do, I went to see Ryan.

When I arrived at the jail, it was obvious Ryan had been crying. I thought the cops had been grilling him. But after talking with him, I found he was frightened and completely devastated over having killed Uncle Ray. Ryan didn't seem at all concerned about what was going to happen to his self. He swore he looked in all the mirrors and looked behind him at least twice before backing out. He'd said, "There must be a blind spot or something in the truck."

As I left the interview room that had been set up for us, I ran into the arresting officer. A splotchy red-faced porcine man named Poteet.

Poteet wasn't happy to see me. Although I didn't know him, he seemed to know me and didn't like me. I asked him why an 18-year-old boy was charged with negligent vehicular homicide for accidentally backing into someone.

He informed me, "It wasn't any of my fuckin' business. But if I really wanted to know, the kid had a reputation for playing loud music in the vehicles he moved. And if he hadn't been playing the loud fuckin' music, he would have seen the old fart, and besides, he backs out too fast. He's just a spoiled rich punk who doesn't give a fuck about anything but himself."

I saw why cops were sometimes called pigs. Poteet was a real jewel. Yes, sir. A jewel shaped just like an asshole.

Through Spain, I got copies of the arrest report and pictures taken at the scene. I got the feeling Spain was Patrolman Anonymous. When I called him on it, he denied any connection, but did say Poteet was getting ready to retire and might be trying to go out with a bang.

As far as I knew, once a cop makes an arrest he doesn't try to prove the perp is innocent. Not all cops, but many consider it is their job to prove them guilty. It's the politics.

So, I found myself down at Davis Dodge asking questions just like I had a right to. It helped that Spain called the manager and asked them to cooperate with me.

Everyone was very cooperative. Everyone liked Uncle Ray. Everyone liked Ryan. It was a tragedy.

In the arrest report, Poteet said Ryan Macino showed no remorse for what had happened.

Co-workers of Ryan's and Uncle Ray's said that after it happened, Ryan didn't talk much, just stood there looking around. The cop would ask him questions, and Ryan would answer in a low monotone, then look around. When Poteet arrived at the scene, music could still be heard through the closed door of the truck and when he opened it, the music came blaring out.

One of the salesmen used to be a medic and said he thought Ryan was in shock. Sounded reasonable to me.

I was shown to the scene of the accident. As I looked around, I had the pictures taken at the scene, one of which was of poor Uncle Ray laying on his left side, facing away from the impact. What bothered me was he was lying perpendicular to the bed of the truck. It seemed to me if he was walking or standing behind the truck when it hit him, he would have been laying parallel to the bed. I looked at the pictures with a magnifying glass and saw small smudges on the palms of Uncle Ray's hands and the knees of his pants looked slightly soiled. It just didn't look right. There wasn't any blood. There were no eyewitnesses to the accident.

As I walked around the lot, I noticed small dusty paw prints on some of the vehicles. Kitty tracks, I know all about kitty tracks. My orange tabby, Miso, tracks up my truck with a vengeance. I also noticed some of the vehicles had been recently dusted. Not washed or cleaned, but dusted in places, places where a kitty might walk.

I got with the manager and asked him what Uncle Ray's duties were. He told me Uncle Ray was a custodian of sorts, kept the offices swept and vacuumed and sometimes waxed the floor at night after the dealership closed. I then asked him if Uncle Ray had a room or a place he kept all his things. He showed me to a small room between the offices and the garage. The room was about 8x10 and contained a cot.

The manager explained that Uncle Ray sometimes stayed over when waxing the larger areas or would come in late to work through the night. I snooped around and found a bag of cat food under the cot.

I showed it to the manager. He frowned and said, "I told Ray no pets allowed."

"Did you have a problem with Ray and pets?" I asked.

"Yeah, it was the kitty litter. You could smell it in the hall. Ray wasn't punctual about cleaning it out."

Anyway, it all came down to the fact that Uncle Ray had been looking for his cat, crawling around on his hands and knees looking under the cars and trucks. Uncle Ray didn't hear so well and hadn't heard the music or the running engine.

There was no way Ryan could have seen him.

Once these facts were pointed out to the Assistant District Attorney, the charges were dropped and Paul Macino got his son back. Ryan went into therapy to help him with the trauma of what had happened.

Poteet's jewel was exposed for everyone to see. He retired, reeking like something from his jewel.

I was just glad I could help, but felt badly about what had happened all the way around. I admired Ryan for going to work for someone other than his father, he was a good kid, and Uncle Ray was dead.

A week later, I found out that three years before, Paul had lost his wife to cancer. Like myself, he too, was a single father.

Chapter 8

Nashville, TN-December 11ᵗʰ Present Day

Nashville can be confusing for tourists and transplants. The roads on the west side of the Cumberland River aren't set in a square grid like most cities. The streets on the west side of Nashville are laid out more like a lopsided wagon wheel. The roads emanating from downtown moved out like spokes, with the rim of the wheel being Old Hickory Blvd. about 10 miles away, give or take a few miles, depending on how lopsided the wheel was at that point. The same street may also have up to four different names, again depending on how far out you go. For instance, Broadway, Nashville's main downtown drag changes to West End, then Harding Road, then Highway 100. That's how you get to my place in Hickman County about 40 miles out. The closer you are to downtown, the closer the spokes are. At one point in downtown Nashville, West End and 21ˢᵗ Avenue are only two blocks apart. By the time you get to Old Hickory Blvd., 21ˢᵗ has changed its name to Hillsboro Road, and is five miles away from West End, which has now called Harding Road. It's simple as long as you know. If you don't then you're lost.

I was in my blue Ford F150 Super Crew 4x4 Lariat going south on 4ᵗʰ Avenue, towards Lafayette Street, where I would turn left to go out to Gun World. By the time I get there, Lafayette will have changed to Murfreesboro Road.

Every year I find this day one of retrospective confrontations, so while driving toward one of the spokes, I thought of the Major. Maybe it was the orientalness of the restaurant.

Alexandria, Louisiana-1962

The Major was a highly decorated fighter pilot of two wars, World War II and the Korean War, a real live fire-breathing war hero.

I didn't know about that until one spring day when I was 12, not too long after he retired from the Air Force as a Lt. Colonel. But he was still the Major.

He ordered me to go out and clean up the storage shed next to our carport. Inside was his old service foot locker. Being naturally nosey, I started looking through it and found underneath a neatly folded uniform, a locked metal box about the size of a cigar box. I shook it and heard what sounded like money. Of course I pried it open with a screwdriver, one of the many tools hanging neatly on the wall.

When I raised the top expecting to find a horde of coins, much to my amazement and general state of pre-teen bewilderment, I found medals instead. There were medals with rotting ribbons attached, medals with no ribbons attached, medals from other countries, and a lone Zippo lighter. It was engraved. On one side it read:

> Tuck
> Squadron Leader
> The Fighting 395th

On the other side:

> We can beat any man
> From any land
> At any game
> That he can name
> For any amount
> That he can count

My feline curiosity won over any judgment I may have had at that age. The Major happened to be at home. I rushed in and laid the box in front of him like I had every right to break into his private locked up memories and demand to know what they were about.

The fact he didn't cuff me meant it must've really taken him by surprise, and from his ashen face, the contents of the box took him somewhere other than the kitchen table.

As he looked into the box, I felt time flutter. He reached in and took out the lighter. He turned it around a few times, clicking it opened and closed with his thumb, put it in his shirt pocket, gently closed the box and quietly said, "Take this back and put it where you found it."

I wasn't so dense I didn't know how much I had just screwed up and how lucky I was to get off without some sort of corporal punishment. It was a pivotal moment. I had learned a valuable lesson on privacy and respect without a hand being laid on me or the offense of a vituperative tirade.

I later decided it would be the way I would raise my children.

And unbeknownst to me at the time, I caught my first glimpse of the demons that tormented the Major to the abuse of alcohol that would unleash the anger and violence for which I would become the main recipient.

I took the box back where I'd burgled it with a reverence that wasn't there before, then sneaked next door to Steve Fleck's house and called Uncle Roy, the Major's oldest brother.

"Unca Roy, I jus founa buncha medals from te war in de Maja's ol foo locker an he jus tol me to pu em ba. I mean, like I bro' nto de box and he din't even git mad... really. Jus tol me t pu em back and I did, bu' I'm scared to ax him abou' 'em. Ya shoulda seen da loo on 'is face."

I had a habit of talking so fast most people couldn't understand a word I said the first time around. I think it was due to the fact that I had a Filipino mama-san from birth to 3, then a Japanese mama-san from 3 to 6. I spoke very little English until I was about six-and-a-half.

My Uncle Roy was a wonderful guy. He just laughed and said, "Slow down, boy, and run that by me again."

On more that one occasion I remember my grandfather, Paw Paw Tucker, asking the Major after I had been telling him something, 'Don, what language is that boy speakin' now?'

The Major's exasperated reply with a sigh was, 'That's English, Mr. Dee' (that's what the Major and my uncles called him). At which point Paw Paw would look sternly over his glasses and down his nose with a dubious glare.

After I was through turning gibberish into a somewhat comprehensible language, Uncle Roy said, "Look, buddy, your old man had a tough time in the war. He flew a lot of missions and lost a lot of friends. He's got more medals than any of us, more medals than anyone I know, but he's never been able to talk about it. He won't even talk to me. One time I made him watch an old movie with me, one of those where they show some real footage of aerial dogfights. When I looked over at Don, he was white as a sheet and was gripping the chair so hard his knuckles were white and we couldn't pry him loose. Hell, we had to call your stepmom, and after giving me a good cussin', she called the flight surgeon out at the base. By the time he got to my house, your dad was talking a little, but the flight surgeon had to talk to him alone before he'd let Don drive home. I gotta tell you, it was quite an ordeal. We never brought it up to him, and he never said a word about it."

"So that's why he'll never watch those kinda movies with me," I said in monkey jabber.

Uncle Roy must have understood some of what I said, because his answer, after a deciphering delay, was, "That's right. Now when you get a little older and can drive yourself over here, you come see me. I'll get your other uncles together and between us, we will tell you what we know. We all have stories about your Dad that we've heard from friends of his in the service. There still may be a few letters around explaining some of those medals."

That's just what I did.

Chapter 9

While navigating through the Nashville traffic on my way to Gun World, I thought about my grandmother, Gran Gran. Ten years ago, just before her death, she gave me some memorabilia she'd found in her attic. Among them was a newspaper clipping from the Alexandria Daily Towntalk. The Headlines read "Five Tucker Brothers Fighting On Four Different Fronts," with service pictures of them all. The Major was the only officer, only a Lieutenant at the time.

They were a bunch of tough bastards, because they all came back, alive.

When I arrived at Gun World there were no parking places in the front. There are only eight spaces, but they were full. I drove down a side street next to the building and found more cars parked on both sides. Some were Metro squad cars. This was very suspicious. Gun World closes at six. It's not uncommon for us to shoot after hours, but there shouldn't be this many cop cars here.

I parked about halfway between the Three Little Pigs and Gun World, opened the console, retrieved the extra magazine I kept there and slipped it in the left front pocket of my jacket.

I had to knock on the door to be let in as it was about 6:05. A young short-haired patrolman opened the door.

"Mr. Tucker, my name is Walker, Richard Walker," he said, with a nervous grin as he put out his hand.

"Patrolman Walker," I said shaking his hand.

Seemed like a lot of hand shaking going on today. I felt like a politician. That's not good.

Over his shoulder, I could see eight or ten men milling around the gun racks that filled the room between the front door and back counter. Most of them wore uniforms. They were all looking at me.

Leaning against the counter talking to Spark was Brad Spain. I'm always surprised when I see him. He's a very dapper guy.

Spain was wearing a gray light-weight wool pinstripe. The stripes were very thin lavender and pink with a cream randomly thrown in. Under the suit coat was a lavender shirt with a cream tie, with just a sliver of his tie-dyed suspenders showing. Black tasseled Damoni loafers grounded out his attire.

His black hair was shiny and parted down the middle, with braids lying across both shoulders, resting on his chest.

He grew them years ago while working undercover and upon returning to regular duty got to keep them because of religious practices. He's the Water Pourer for the Cherokee Sweat Lodge.

In a way, Spain looks like the actor Andy Garcia with long braids, the broken hawk-like Indian nose and his teeth being the only dissimilarity. Spain's teeth were a little bucky.

As I walked between gun racks containing a variety of long guns, the men moved to form an aisle.

"Am I busted?" I asked Spain, while more hand shaking was going on.

"Spark," I said, acknowledging him on the other side of the counter from Spain.

"Tucker," he nodded back.

"I guess somehow the word got out about you being here to shoot it out with me," Spain droned.

"Yeah, right," I said.

Then pointing my thumb over my shoulder at all the cops, I added, "You little Injun, I know you've been practicing for this or they wouldn't be here. I also know, you know I haven't been shooting much, what with the remodeling of my place downtown. It's not going to help you. Now I'll show you no mercy."

"The truth is, Tucker, since your Wyatt Earp act, you're quite the talk of the station house. These youngsters just want to get a look at you." Spain said, with an air of innocence you could shovel.

I looked over my shoulder, around the room, and found all eyes were on us. No one was even pretending to look at the displayed guns.

"Spark, give me a box of Winchester .45 hardball," I said, as I took out my Colt and released the magazine into my left hand, ejected the hollow point round in the chamber, setting it on the rubber mat on the counter.

"That's it," I heard someone whisper behind me.

I thumbed out all the hollow point rounds in the magazine, took out the spare magazine and thumbed those out, and started reloading the hardball rounds from the box Spark had laid in front of me. Both mags were eight-shot extended mags (original 1911 mags hold seven),and with one in the chamber gives me nine. Not as many as some of the new 9mm's that held 15 and 1, but I found it adequate.

There was a lot of murmuring going on behind me. Spark was looking like an amused catfish.

"That gun of yours is famous now," he said.

"It's just a gun," I said.

"Yeah, right," Spark said. "If you did as much work on a customer's .45 as you did on yours, it would be a two thousand dollar gun."

"Well, I don't know, Spark," I said, doing a fair imitation of him.

"Not to mention you iced two bad motherfuckers with it," Spark added.

I felt my mouth move while holstering the gun on my right hip.

"Did you just smile?" Spain asked.

"What's that mean?" Spark asked, looking worried.

"It means shut the fuck up, Spark," Spain said, about as fast as I've ever heard him speak.

"Let's get this show on the road, I'm hungry," I said, walking past Spain towards the door of the lounging area that contained a couple of couches along with some old and badly done taxidermy. You had to pass through this room to get to the basement where the range was housed.

"Hey Tucker!" Spark yelled from behind me. "The bullets are on the house!"

I wasn't far enough away to warrant the volume in his voice.

I turned to speak to him and ran into a wall of uniforms that had fallen in behind Spain and me. They parted allowing me to see Spark,

"It's okay, Spark. Just put them on my bill. I'll pick up the rest on the way out. Now, come on down here, I understand you're supposed to do the counting."

"Yeah. I'll be there in a minute, everything's all set up," he said, sounding relieved.

I bet, I thought. Something shady was definitely going on.

There were so many cops standing around, I could smell leather and after shave. When they moved, the creaking leather reminded me of riding horses. I could smell guns too, but I *was* in Gun World. I felt sure, even if I weren't, I would've smelled the same thing. Guns and leather, like kids playing cowboys.

I turned back to the lounge door and found Spain holding it open for me. He looked apologetic. As I stepped into the lounge, I saw why.

The lounge couches were full of cops. Some in uniform, some not, but I could tell they were all cops. Every non-uniform was wearing a jacket or a sport coat, concealing their weapons. As I walked in, I had to turn right to get to the basement door, and before I had made the turn, the couched cops were on their feet shuffling around. Some seemed a little nervous. Others were timidly curious. I recognized a few of the plainclothes. One was Larry Rizzo, a compact, thirty-ish yellow-haired, crewcutted detective with homicide.

"Tucker, how's it going?" he asked without extending his hand. He knew I wouldn't let anyone hold my right hand with this many armed strangers around.

"Rizzo," I nodded. "You know all these yahoos?"

He looked over my shoulder and eyeballed everyone that came in the room behind me.

"Yeah, everyone but him," he said, gesturing over his left shoulder with his head.

Sitting in an old battered armchair under a revolting stuffed elk head, reading a newspaper, was a man about my age. He looked up at the room in general without showing much interest in what was going on, then went back to his paper. Even from a sitting position, I could tell this short-cropped, salt and pepper haired man was very fit. He too, was wearing a leather jacket, almost as nice as mine.

I don't think even the dimmest of hit men would try anything here. He must be a customer of Spark's, here to pick something up and Spark hasn't had time with all the hullabaloo.

When I got to the doors that led to the basement containing the range, I would have to turn left, and that would put Mr. Mysterious behind me. That didn't worry me, because he'd have to shoot through a covey of cops.

"Tucker, we'll use the two lanes in the center," Spain said from behind me, as we walked down the narrow stairway.

I pictured him on his toes with a knife between his teeth. Ambush was imminent.

There were signs on the walls of the stairway reminding everyone to wear eye and ear protection. I knew both would already be laid out for Spain and me.

There were ten shooting lanes. At the bottom of the stairs, was lane three, which meant the remaining seven were to the right. That's the way I turned, putting the firing lanes to my left.

It was dungeon-like, but adequately lit, with more light down the 75-foot shooting distance to the inclined backdrop that absorbed and deflected the lead. Each lane had its own partitioned alcove, separating the view of the person shooting to either side. This was a safety precaution. It helped keep hot ejected brass from the person in the next lane, from going down your shirt or getting stuck in your collar. That was another reason I liked to wear a hat while shooting.

I worked on my own guns and could change the direction in which the brass was ejected with just a few minutes' work on the ejector. It's the other person's gun that worries me. I've been burned more than once.

I went to lane six and stepped in to look down at the targets that had been set up.

Normally we would shoot at the regular bad guy silhouette target, but I could see this was not the case today.

I heard men jockeying for position. The targets were paper plate sized, black bulls eye targets. The type when the bullet struck, a very bright florescent chartreuse spot would appear, leaving no doubt as to your aim.

The targets had been attached to pieces of cardboard, supported on a hanging metal frame that could be moved backward or forward by pushing a button on the right-hand wall of the shooting bay. Attached to the same wall was an empty gallon coffee can, with the word BRASS stenciled across a strip of masking tape.

I felt Spain step into my alcove, which was just big enough for us to stand side by side without touching.

"I thought you'd like these targets, what with your age and all, your eyes must be going," Spain said matter-of-factly.

I knew Spain had had trouble seeing at distances, so I said, "You must be worried to be pulling this sophomoric psych crap."

My eyesight problems were the common trombone playing kind, that was easily remedied with reading glasses from Walgreen's.

The vying for positions was coming to a standstill. It was time to get on with it.

"Okay, Spain," I said. "What's the surprise rule I don't know about?"

"What *do* you mean, paleface?" he said angelically.

"Let's just get it over with so you can buy me dinner."

Spain sighs, then brightens up, like he just got a great idea. I saw a cartoon light bulb over his head.

He said, "I know, let's make it interesting. What you say we put five in each gun and a spare mag, then do a speed load with the extra mag when we run out of the first. The first one through puts his gun back in his holster, then yells red ("red!" is what you yell to your partner when out of ammunition in a firefight). Any shots outside the black, we take a half second off the time."

I looked behind us where there were two uniforms standing with stop watches. Not only was Spain out to ambush me, he was planning a massacre, and if he said that many words in a row again, I was going to fall asleep. I wondered if that was part of his strategy.

"Just got that idea this moment, did you?" I asked dryly, hoping for a short response.

"What do you mean? You don't think I planned all this, do you? How dare you, for as long as you have known me, how could you think I'd do something that despicable? I can't..."

"Spain," I interrupted. "I don't believe there were any Cherokees at the Little Big Horn."

It took him a moment to get it, then he looked around. Yes, I was definitely outnumbered. He gave me his handsome bucktooth grin and said, "Yeah, well I can see you're intimidated."

"What're you shooting?" I asked.

He pulled aside his suit coat, allowing me to view a Colt .45 almost identical to mine. It had definitely been Tucker-ized. I had accurasized so many 1911's, there was no way to put a face to the gun.

"Whose is that?" I asked, knowing it wasn't Spain's.

"That's for me to know and you to find out," he said, straight faced.

"I suppose you've been shooting it for a while, getting ready for this."

"You're getting ready to find *that* out," he said, with a leer.

Spain is always psyching, but for the first time since the challenge earlier this afternoon, I saw myself buying dinner.

"Let's do it," I said.

Spain walked into his shooting station. I walked forward into mine and started loading my mags with the correct number of cartridges. I put five in the extra mag, pulled the mag out of the gun and ejected four into my hand, leaving four in the mag, one in the chamber. I always carry it chambered, cocked and locked; that way, all that had to be done after drawing the weapon, was to thumb down the safety and pull the trigger. The Colt has two safeties, one being a grip safety at the back of the grip that if wasn't depressed, the gun wouldn't fire. I remember the Major referring to it as, 'the lemon-squeezer'.

As I looked down the shooting lane at Spark putting something on the floor, I heard Spain in the next booth, doing the same to his mags.

"Spark, what's that?" I asked, as he fiddled with a contraption I couldn't see, because he was in the way.

"It's a new countdown light system I bought for just this type of activity," he said, moving out of the way, showing me a set of four lights stacked up on top of each other, about six inches apart. The whole thing was about four feet high and six inches wide. The lights were from top to bottom, two reds, one amber, and the bottom one was green.

"Reminds me of drag racing down in Opelousas," I said.

"Where?" about a half a dozen voices asked.

"Same principle," Spark said, as he lumbered back toward the booths. Spark moved like Spain talked.

Spark said, "I've got this set at one-second intervals, it starts at the top and goes down red-red-amber-green. You shoot on green."

"Duh," said a comedian from somewhere in the dark. It did get some laughs, but not from Spark, who was looking hard for the performer.

It looked like we were ready to commence. The cop who was going to time me was behind to my left, so he wouldn't be bombarded by my flying brass. I knew Spain's timer would be in the same position next door.

Spain peeked around the corner, and was now wearing a pink tennis visor, ear protection that looked like muffs, and shooting glasses with yellow lenses. He'd gotten rid of his suit coat, and his bright, tie-died suspenders were blinding.

"I'm going to order the full rack of ribs and drink two imported beers, cause you're buying," he said, grinning like a Cheshire cat.

"Spain, if you could see yourself right now, you wouldn't be smiling." I added, "Are you sure you like girls? What *does* Betsy do for sex?"

His grin was replaced by a baffled frown.

There was a lot of coughing going on in the dimmer parts of the cellar and a few small bursts of muffled laughter. As far as I knew, Spain was the highest ranking officer here. It definitely wasn't kosher to laugh at him.

"Okay, you two get ready!" Spark yelled, as he fingered his glasses back up on his nose.

"I'll count to three and turn on the lights. You two with the stop watches hit the buttons when the green light comes on."

"Duh," again followed by laughter.

Spain disappeared around the partition. I stepped forward, slipped the ear protection over my hat and put on the shooting glasses. They were so smudged with what I was sure were Spain prints, I had to take them off.

"Put your pieces on the bench and step back one step!" Spark yelled, sounding like a drill sergeant.

I drew my gun, set it on the table and stepped back. It was cocked and locked.

Someone, quietly cleared their throat, caused me to look his way. It was Patrolman Richard Walker, and he was shifting his eyes over towards Spain's booth.

I stepped back and looked into Spain's booth to find him in a two-handed shooting stance with his gun pointed at the target.

Ever since Spain and I've been shooting against each other, spanning over a decade, we'd been playing this game. I took all his shenanigans as a compliment.

"Spain, why don't you come over here and keep me honest," I said quietly.

His shoulders hunched, like a small boy caught in the cookie jar.

As he turned to look at me, I ducked back into my booth. When he came around, I could tell he didn't know if I had seen him or not.

"I trust you, Tucker," he said, with big innocent eyes.

"I'm sure you do, but I think we'd both have better scores if we could see each other. You know, make it a more interesting competition."

I looked around and said, "What about you guys? Wouldn't ya'll like to see us go at it, side by side?"

Almost everyone had crammed into the booths in order to see the targets, so they hadn't been privy to Spain's point shaving tactic.

There were nods and murmurings of agreement. There wasn't much Spain could do, but come over with me.

I scooted over, which put him to my left. I wasn't worried about his ejected brass hitting me. On all the guns I worked on, I made sure the brass went almost directly over the shooters right shoulder. That kept them out of the way of their partners in a firefight, and I had definitely worked on the gun Spain was going to shoot.

"Let's do this!" Spark yelled irritably. "I want to go home!"

I said, "Hold on, Spark, I've got to clean these glasses. There's something all over them."

I reached over, take hold of Spain's cream-colored silk tie and started cleaning the glasses.

"Thanks, buddy," I said. "This won't scratch the lenses."

He didn't say a word, just looked straight ahead like a guilty defendant receiving his sentence.

Spain set his extra magazine on the bench with the .45 next to it, and I did the same.

"You ready?" I asked.

"Yep."

I looked over at Spark and nodded, then looked at Patrolman Walker and caught his eye, took off my leather jacket and handed it to him. He gave me a sheepish smile and blushed. Walker was just a kid, couldn't be more than 22 or 23.

"One . . . two . . . three!" Spark yelled, and hit the button.

The lights started, red . . . red . . . . amber . . . . green.

By then I had tunnel vision, my heart rate had slowed, and *The Calm* had settled over me.

When the green light glowed, I stepped, picked up my gun, with slightly bent knees and a two-handed grip, both eyes open, I looked at the target and shot five times. BANG-BANG-BANG-BANG-BANG.

After each shot, as soon as the muzzle dropped back into the target, I fired again. The way I have my gun tuned, this happens about every three-tenths of a second.

After the fifth and last round, the slide locked back. With my thumb, I pressed the magazine release button and the empty mag fell on the bench. I shoved the extra magazine, that I don't remember picking up, into the gun, thumbed down the extended slide release as I aimed, pulled the trigger, starting the next five-round sequence, BANG-BANG-BANG-BANG-BANG.

The shots were so close together, it was hard to distinguish one from the other, it almost a continuous roar. Again, as the last round was spent, the slide locked back.

I yelled, "Red!"

I released the slide, thumbed up the safety, slipped the gun in my holster and stepped back.

"God damn, motherfucker, son-of-a-bitch," were just some of the less colorful expletives bouncing around the room. Cops have such broad vocabularies. I heard one say, "Fuck-me-running! Even a... "Shit the bed!"

I knew I'd shot faster than Spain; that was obvious. He was still shooting when I holstered my gun, and he didn't bother to say 'red'. But, had I outshot him? I don't see where my bullets strike when I'm shooting. I just shoot.

"Six point three seconds!" yelled the patrolman timing Spain.

I looked behind me, and the cop standing there looked like he was going to faint.

"I forgot to stop it," he said, looking at the stopwatch. He was in his late twenties with bright red hair and now, a face to match.

"Don't worry about it," Spain said with disgust, gesturing with his gun to the targets.

The black parts of the targets were about five inches in diameter. His had florescent chartreuse spots all over it and one black hole in the brown border.

My target just had one large bright area in the center about three inches in diameter, and in the center of that was a hole you could see through, indicating multiple hits in the same area.

Everyone but Spain and I started talking.

"Sumbitch, Tucker must have shot his in five seconds or less . . . naw, more like four seconds . . . no way six seconds . . . shit."

Spain looked at me, smiled with a shrug and said, "Looks like I buy again."

"I beat you with that comment about Betsy, didn't I?"

"No, you just beat me, again. I've been practicing with this thing (he looks at the gun in his hand) and this setup for a month. I bet I've got 20 hours, what with all the driving back and forth, and a thousand rounds invested in this shit."

"When I was a kid, I used to shoot a thousand rounds a weekend."

He looked at me like I had just grown a unicorn horn.

"You never told me that before," he said quietly, looking down to the targets.

"Thousand rounds a weekend," he mumbled.

Men were starting to mill around, and I felt someone pat me on the back. I'm not much on being touched from behind; I'm not much on being touched period. I spun around to find Richard Walker. He was stepping back, holding out my jacket with an alarmed look on his face.

"Ah . . . your jacket, Mr. Tucker."

I'd forgotten about my jacket.

"Thanks Richard, and drop the mister," I said.

From his face, you'd think I just told him he didn't have cancer. He did put himself out there by alerting me to Spain's game. He seemed like a good kid, not much older than my son.

"Why don't you come to dinner with us?" I asked.

"Why don't you *not* come to dinner with us," Spain said, looking firmly at Walker.

Maybe Spain *did* know it was Walker who alerted me.

"*Mr.* Tucker and I have some business to discuss, remember?" he said, raising his eyebrows at me.

"Maybe some other time, Walker," I said.

"Sure, Tucker . . . I mean Mr. Tucker," he said after getting another 'I'll scalp your ass' look from Spain.

After Walker left, I said to Spain, "A little tough on the kid, weren't you, or do you just want me to feel old?"

"Yeah, well, he may be a little too nice. It could get him killed someday. If he lives for the next couple of years, he'll make a good cop. He's a pretty good shot and getting better. He's been playing that game 'knuckles' you showed those recruits at the range last year. He's very fast. I think he's working up to challenge you. Then we'll see how old you really are."

I yawned. "Let's go eat. I'm driving out to the house after."

"You go on over. I've got a little business to attend to. It shouldn't take me more than five or ten minutes. We'll eat and talk about the interview and that other thing," he said, putting on his suit coat.

I nodded and turned to see the basement was almost empty, just a few men hanging around, probably the business Spain was referring to.

When I got back upstairs, Spark was behind the counter, waiting for the stragglers to leave. He also had my target. He held it up in front of his face and looked at me through the hole and said, "Well, I don't know, Tucker."

As I walked up to him he pushed the box of Winchester .45's I'd loaded my mags from and my pile of hollow points at me.

"Hand me a rag, will you?" I asked.

He reached behind him and pulled one off the shelves.

My gun was hard-chromed, making it the color of dull steel. This stopped it from rusting easily, but after shooting, you could see a powder blast smudge an inch or so behind the muzzle. I took the rag, wiped the gun clean, then started reloading my mags with the hollow points. I'd clean it properly when I got home. I handed the rag back.

"Spark, how did you get that name?" I asked, as I replaced a mag with eight hollow points, chambered a round, then dropped the magazine into the palm of my left hand, to top it off with a round before ramming it home, and holstering my gun.

"I played hockey in high school," he said. "The coach called me the 'Spark Plug' of the team because I had so much spirit and hustle, and it just stuck."

Spark just grew a unicorn horn.

Chapter 10

Upon entering the restaurant, I was reminded why Spain and I liked it, other than the good food. There were booths along the back wall, allowing us both to sit next to the wall with a view of the front door.

There were seven four top tables with red and white checkered plastic tablecloths, or would that be tableplastics? It wasn't crowded this Wednesday night, a few couples and a couple of singles having dinner, plus a guy who needed to go on Weight Watchers, hanging around the takeout counter.

Obeying the 'Please Seat Yourself' sign, I went straight back to a booth and took the left side. This would leave my right side toward the door.

A young lady came to take my order. I told her I was waiting for someone and just bring me a water with lemon. Thinking once I was home, I might pour myself a Makers Mark on the rocks. I seldom drank the hard stuff anymore, but when I did, I liked it strong. The Major liked it strong too, so did his four brothers, all alcoholics. That was another reason I seldom indulged.

What with the shooting tonight and thinking about the Major, I couldn't help but remember how I got started down this road. The Major taught my brother and me how to shoot his 1911 Colt just as soon as we were strong enough to hold it up. At one point he actually had two.

His P-51 Mustang took on a lot of lead during one of his missions. He was within a mile or so of the airfield and having trouble keeping *My Baby* (he named all his planes My Baby) in the air. He finally had to try to land, which turned into a small walk-away crash landing. He was still in Indian country and had to play hide and seek all the way back.

During his retreat, he found, much to his chagrin, he'd lost his .45. So upon his safe return, he put in a request for another one. In the meantime he borrowed an old Colt revolver from a buddy in the squadron. Days later he received his requisitioned pistol, but didn't open the box because he was getting used to the old revolver, said it was more accurate.

There was a lull in the fighting and some of the mechanics got together and went out to where his plane went down to salvage parts, and lo and behold, his pistol was found in the cockpit.

A couple of weeks later, his buddy wanted the revolver back, so the Major opened the box to clean and assemble the newly acquired .45. They came disassembled in a waxed box, all covered with cosmoline, which is a substance like Vaseline mixed with oil. You weren't supposed to have two pistols, but since the mechanics didn't report it, as far as the Army Air Corps was concerned, he only had one. The wild thing is they had consecutive serial numbers. The odds of that happening was like being delt a Royal Flush.

He managed to hang on to both of them and after the war had them ornately engraved in Italy. One he had nickel-plated and the other, black-blued. He carved out the inside of two Bibles, and sent them back to the states from different locations. He was an atheist, so for him this wasn't a problem. Only the black-blued one made it. That's the one he taught us with. It's such a beautiful piece, with the engraving magnificently done. During a recidivistic period, I carried it, and it saw me through more than one scrape. Now my brother has it.

These were the kind of stories I could finagle out of the Major in the years following the box of medals incident. Stories like this and him pissing himself because he was so scared while flying to a mission. Or how they'd have to pull him from his cockpit, lay him across a wing, then pull his pants down. He told me he would sometimes lay there for fifteen minutes before he could relax enough to urinate. Then he would go for five minutes. Never stories of why or how he had so many medals.

Those stories came from other sources.

Chapter 11

The Major and his four brothers taught my cousins and me to duck hunt on the famous Catahoula Lake at a very early age. Between the five brothers, there were two duck camps on the bluffs overlooking the lake. All but the Major were either builders, plumbers, electricians, or a combination of the three. There was my uncle Roy, the oldest, then Lloyd, Ed, A. D., down to the baby boy, Donald, my father.

I was 9 when I was first awakened in the middle of the night while sleeping in one of the many army surplus bunk beds, to the smell of coffee, wood smoke and frying bacon. Still snug in my sleeping bag, I watched the Major and my uncles move through the dim hazy light, smoking cigarettes with their coffee while breaking out the shotguns and putting shells in their hunting vests. The jocular mood of the night before being replaced by the quiet efficiency of few words, the faint smell of oil, with small clinks of gunmetal, resembling something I may have seen in a war movie.

I wasn't allowed to shoot a gun in the duck blind yet, but my brother Ben, three and a half years my senior, had gotten a new .410 Savage single shot for his birthday the past August and was going to hunt. I remember being so excited to be allowed to go, that I wasn't jealous.

I recall that morning, after a slow foggy boat trip in the 14-foot bateau pushed by an old Wizard outboard, how the duck-blind appeared through the fog like a stalking monster. It was brushed with pine boughs, still green and thick with the smell of turpentine.

The Tucker brothers had four sites on the lake for blinds. It wasn't uncommon in those days for disputes over blind sites to escalate into blind burnings, beatings and sometimes a shooting. Like when one pre-dawn morning, Taterbug Johnston was shot in the back with No. 6 shot, down at the boat landing. It didn't kill him, but did knock him down, causing weeks of considerable discomfort. No one ever messed with the Tucker sites.

As the Major got us settled in, nothing was said about the wet November cold, or if we were comfortable. We were there to hunt, and these issues were of no concern.

When the first light of dawn raked the horizon, I saw thousands of gnats and mosquitoes in front of my face. Every few seconds I would try and shoo them away with my hand.

The Major asked, "What're you doing boy?"

"Trying to get rid of all these bugs."

"What bugs?" he asked.

"All these mosquitoes and gnats," I said, again shooing them away by waving my hand in front of my face, while blowing with my mouth.

After a moment of silence, he put his arm around my shoulders and quietly said, "Those aren't bugs, they're ducks. We call it 'The Parade'."

I have never forgotten how, once he told me that, I just had to refocus my eyes to see he was telling the truth. There were literally thousands upon thousands of ducks, flying, darting, and falling like autumn leaves, through the blue and orange sunrise. As the ducks got closer, I could hear their calls and the air passing over their cupped gliding wings gave off a jet-like whistling sound.

We got to watch, and listen to "The Parade" for another ten minutes, until legal shooting time. Then the shooting started. It was busy, loud, and *very exciting* for this big-eyed boy. I spent many years thereafter watching "The Parade," and it never failed to make my chest feel too small for my heart and remind me of that first hunt. The hunt where I didn't have a gun of my own, a day when I felt my father loved me.

The brothers were all handsome, fun loving, hard fighting men. By then Uncle Roy and Uncle A. D. were in AA. The other three would only drink beer while in camp; otherwise, it could get a little dicey.

The Tucker boys got mean on hard liquor. They grew up fighting. Sometimes each other, but woe be to the man who harmed one of them. Through all their toughness, there was a gentleness and loyalty that felt a lot like love, though you could bet your last dollar not one of them would ever say that word to the other.

I remember them sitting around the old picnic table in the heart of the three-roomed camp; smoking, drinking beer, and telling stories on each other.

As I leaned in the open doorway, back-lit by the moonlight filtering through black silhouettes of tall Cyprus trees that skirted the lake, I could feel the cool November breeze move my hair along with the Spanish moss hanging from the live oaks that surrounded the camp. I could breath in the smell of water that hung in the air and listen to the ducks night calling on the lake. All the while I would listen to the brother's vibrant stories.

Wild stories of duck hunts, of pretty girlfriends they stole from each other, tales of knife fights and broken noses. Like the time Uncle Ed hit a man who was getting ready to shoot A. D. with a pistol. A dispute over a woman; I believe it was the man's wife. The man was standing at the bar when Uncle Ed hit him with his right fist; as he went down, his foot caught between the bar and the brass rail that ran along the bottom. The force of the blow broke his leg in three places, not to mention what it did to his face.

Nevertheless, as a small boy, I fell in love with all of them, at the duck camps, the deer camp, and the fishing camp on Spring Bayou where we fished for bull-nosed bream, bass, the sweet sacalait, and red-eared chinkapin too fat to wrap your hand around.

These men, all broad shouldered, barrel chested and narrow hipped, whose rugged tanned faces were creased with more than age lines—the scars of battles and laughter. They were larger than life to me. They were giants, men among men . . .and I wanted to be just like them.

We hunted rabbits, sometimes at night with a spotlight. This was called 'shining' and was against the law, making it all the more like outlaws on a midnight raid. It was more effective on a moonless night. We were always surrounded in the black night by the sounds of crickets and buzzing insects, the croaking of tree frogs and the shrill chirps of cicadas, along with an occasional growl of an alligator. We would aim the light into the darkness while walking along raised oyster shell roads through the marsh, looking for the shining red eyes of a big swamp rabbit. Once, while 'shining' the edges of a railroad track, I heard a woman scream in the distance, piercing the black wall of night sounds, like a leering dagger through a black cloth veil. A scream so loud and long, I just knew she was being murdered. Uncle Ed held my hand, as I leaned on him and began to shake.

"That's a panther," he said, then patted me gently on the shoulder. "A wild cat, and a big'n by the sound of her."

"Why's she screamin', Uncle Ed?" I asked.

"She's talkin' to her boyfriend."

"She sounds scared," I said.

For some reason he thought this funny and laughed out loud while holding my shoulders. "One of these days you're going to know all about that."

My heart was starting to slow down, but I still couldn't shake the image of a woman in a long white dress, blonde hair flowing wild with the wind in the yellow moonlight, her face twisted with fear, like something out of an old Vincent Price horror movie. Maybe he was lying about the cat to protect me, but to this day, I don't like horror movies.

The brothers, all having sons, leased 3,000 acres down in Avoyelles Parish south of Marksville, from a logging company and built a long-roomed deer camp with a kitchen room attached to the back and an outhouse, just a short walk into the trees.

The camps had no running water, so they built cisterns to catch the frequent rains. I've never forgotten the imagined fear of a little boy, afraid he was going to fall into the spider infested black hole cut into the seat of the outhouse, or the satisfying surprise of the fresh, slick, thirst-quenching taste of rainwater.

This is where my uncles started my cousins and me squirrel and rabbit hunting, and then we graduated to deer.

We called the big old swamp bucks, "mossy backs". The Tuckers weren't the type of men to hang stuffed animal heads in their homes. The racks of the big mossy backs were nailed outside the camp, from left to right under the roof, from one end to the other.

This is where I learned about the saying "You ain't ever been lost lest you've drunk water from a hoof print." In the swamp the only for sure good water is what the rain has left in a hoof print. I was once lost for 18 hours. I've never been lost again. It taught me to look behind me, as much as in front of me. The swamp all looks the same, but if you look behind yourself enough and study a little, when you need to go back, it looks familiar.

Like in life, it's good to remember where you came from. It may help keep you from losing your way.

During those years of my life when the very fiber of my being was seasoned with the hard deep darkness of abuse and braised with the searing white heat of violence, my only saving grace was the time spent with Margie or alone in a Louisiana swamp.

So, I, more so than my brother, was bitten by the swamp bug. I was either in a swamp slipping up on a mossy back or on the bayous, or the hidden sloked lagoons with names like Laccasiene, Locki-tyboo, or Coulinwaugh, fishing for bass, bream, and sacalait. Or, I could be found at sunrise, on Catahoula Lake, trying to feel my father's hand on my shoulder, while I watched . . . "The Parade."

Chapter 12

The waitress (is that politically correct or should it be server?) arrived with my water and lemon, and said she would return with the buttered hot water cornbread I'd forgotten they made here. The pieces of cornbread were almost as dangerous as Krispy Kreme Donuts. I made the sign of the cross with my fingers and shook my head, which rated a pretty smile as she left me to my reverie.

I thought of my first introduction to the art of pistoleroing.

Louisiana, 1963

When I was 13, I had the chance of seeing Mr. Bob Grayson from Cheneyville, Louisiana, put on a shooting exhibition at the National Guard Armory. Mr. Grayson was the man who taught many of the movie stars out in Hollywood how to do the western quick draw. I thought it was about the greatest thing I had ever seen. I knew I wanted to be like that. To be able to draw a six gun, and with a wax bullet, shoot off a playing card lying flat on someone's shoulder, and do it so fast you couldn't see my hand move.

One instant Grayson's hand was by his side, the next, the gun was in his hand roaring like it had a life of its own and he was just holding on. I hung around afterwards and met him. Later I started hitching rides with anyone I could down to Cheneyville, about 30 miles south of Alec, where he owned a store on the left side of the road to Baton Rouge that sold gas and homemade pecan pies his wife made.

I pestered him until one day he had me play a game he called knuckles. He put his right fist out, then told me to put my right fist against his, knuckles to knuckles. He then said he was going to raise his fist up and rap the back of my hand with his knuckles. All I had to do was move my fist out of the way. He explained that he could move his fist, twist it, and do anything but raise it or disconnect, to fake me out. This would make me all hurky jerky nervous, not knowing when he was going to strike like a rattler. I would jerk my hand back at the slightest movement, then return it to the knuckles to knuckles position. Once he rose to strike me, if he missed, it would be my turn.

He didn't miss for what seemed like a long time to a teenager. I would come home with the back of my right hand swollen blue green. At home, I would teach 'knuckles' to anyone willing to play. The back of my hand hurt so much, if anyone touched it, I felt like puking. So, I didn't let anyone touch it. I was unbeatable, unbeatable until Mr. Grayson got a hold of me again.

After the back of my hand healed, I would go back down to Cheneyville and try again. In retrospect, I believe he got a kick out of this. He had no mercy on me and gave me a good knuckle thrashing every time, every time but the last time we played, if you could call it playing.

It took a few months, what with the healing and having to beg rides with some of my older friends who had their driver's licenses. In those days, you only had to be 15 to drive. I walked into the store, where Mr. Grayson was sitting in a rocking chair holding a fine Colt .45 six-shooter, with rags and oil sitting on a small three-legged table that appeared to be homemade, next to his chair.

"So, Mr. Tucker, I see you again," he said grinning, showing me his tobacco- stained teeth. He always called me Mr. Tucker like the fine southern gentleman he was, when he wasn't beating the hell out of the back of my hand.

"Yes, sir. I'm back for the last time," I said resolutely.

"For the last time?" he asked, pushing back the old black sweat-stained cowboy hat he wore. "Sounds like you aim to beat me today."

I didn't tell him, but that wasn't what I meant. What I really meant was, if I didn't beat him, I'd never come back for him to beat me again. I was cock of the walk at knuckles back in Alexandria, and it was feeling too good.

So I just nodded my head and said, "Yes, sir."

He put the gun on the table, unwound his lanky frame from the old rocker, made a fist, stuck it out in front of him, and said, "Let's go."

I walked over to him, put my fisted knuckles next to his and looked him in the eyes. I never took my eyes off of his eyes. He twisted his fist a couple of times, and I never budged. Then he struck like a pit viper. It wasn't that he missed; my fist just wasn't there when his came down.

I don't know whose eyes showed more surprise.

"Well I'll be damned," he said with wonderment. "I've never been beat before."

I was too stunned to speak.

"Now it's your turn, sir," he said to a 13-year-old boy.

I went right after him, no twisting or faking him out. I was on a roll. Our eyes locked together, we went at it. In less than three minutes, the back of his hand was starting to swell, he laughed, stepped back and sat down in the rocker.

He picked up the old Colt and said, "Take a look at this."

I couldn't believe it. I knew something important happened, but wasn't quite sure what it was. I walked over as he handed me the gun.

"Check it, boy, to see if it is loaded. That's lesson number one," he said.

He then put on his belted holster and showed me the correct height to wear the gun. Not low down like the gunslingers on TV, but with the butt just below my elbow. This way the momentum of my hand coming up, pulls the gun out of the holster. Then he took out a piece of paper and drew a picture of a long cowboy boot with a spike coming out of the sole.

"Get your Paw to make you one of these out of heavy metal," he said, pointing to his drawing. "Make sure it comes up above the top of where your holster will be. Hammer it into the ground, so when you start practicing with live ammunition, you can walk up next to it and strap your holster on the outside of it. Tie your holster around it and to your leg. This way, when you discharge the gun too early, and you will, the bullet will just bounce off and go in the ground. It will keep you from shootin' yourself. When you get this made, get yourself a little Colt .22 six-shooter, then come back and see me."

That's just what I did.

Chapter 13

I heard the front door open and Spain came into the restaurant. It didn't take his eyes long to find me. He walked over and stood at the end of the table, looking down at me. I could tell he was enjoying being tall, although he's only a few inches taller than me when I'm sitting.

"How's the weather up there?" I asked.

He crossed his arms and looked down his nose at me with the warmth of a frozen lake, reminding me that he was considered one of the best interrogators on the Metro P. D. After an hour of listening to his voice and looking at his dark Sitting Bull imitation, the perp would feel as though he had been there for days and was willing to confess to anything, just to get away.

"Okay, I'm sufficiently frightened, now sit down," I said, gesturing with my glass of water to the bench across the table from me.

As he sat, the waitress/server came over and hovered.

"I'll have a Heineken with a glass, not a mug," he said, as he took a handkerchief from a back pocket, and started wiping down the table.

This didn't rate the smile I got from the waitress, as she curtly spins off.

"Let's get the important business over with first," he said. "Betsy wants to introduce you to a friend of hers, her personal trainer at the health club. She told me to tell you . . ."

"Stop," I said, holding up my hand. "What's going on? Did I ask to be fixed up?"

"Oh, are you seeing someone?"

"No."

"How long's it been, Tucker?"

"How long has what been?"

"Since you've been laid? Don't be dense."

I didn't have to think hard about that, but I had to think if it was any of his business or not.

His wife, Betsy, wasn't his wife the first time I met her. She was a patrolman, patrol-person, whatever. She was Spain's partner, and I met her at the same time I met Spain, on Dec. 11th, 1982. The events of that night so greatly affected her, she quit the force, unintentionally releasing Spain from his departmental restrictions on dating your partner. Now she's his wife and has her own real-estate business. She later told me that what she experienced that night bound them together, and was, in a sense, 'the glue' that held them through the hard times. Taking this into consideration, along with my long ongoing relationship with Spain...

"I've been alone and celibate for three years."

"Three years!" he yelled, his head forward, his neck veins bulging with his buck teeth sticking out of his mouth.

Amazing how this guy could look so much like a jackass. Some women considered him good looking.

"Damn, Spain, why don't you take an ad out in the Tennessean?" I asked, looking around the restaurant. "There could be some people in town that didn't hear you."

"That's about when you and Paula Stone stopped seeing each other, isn't it?" he asked.

"That's right."

The waitress brought Spain his beer and we ordered. Spain, had the full rack of ribs, and I ordered the smoked turkey breast plate with a Haake Becks.

After she was out of hearing range, Spain continued. "You never told me what happened between you two. I mean, damn, Tucker, she's like one of the most beautiful country singers in the business. She cut that song of yours, what was it called?"

"I'm Leavin You For Me."

"Yeah, the next thing I know, I read in Country Music Magazine how she says you two are still great friends, but nothing about the breakup. From the article, Betsy and I got the impression she was still in love with you."

I hadn't read that article, but I needed to do some bud nipping.

"It was me, Spain," I said.

"What ya mean...you?"

"Have you ever listened to the words to that song?" I asked

"I guess, but I can't remember them now," he said.

"I didn't write it about her, but it fits. Her life is so all-consuming, I couldn't find myself, and the bottom line is, I just wasn't in love with her."

"Jesus, Tucker, *I'm* in love with Paula Stone," he said disbelievingly.

"It was complicated. Besides, she's too young for me."

"How can a woman be too young? How long were you two together?" he asked.

"About six months, not counting the two weeks I was hired to watch over her because of that stalker thing. She was probably going to want kids, and I've been there, done that, got three t-shirts."

"Ya know, Tucker, I knew you were dating her, and from the way you were just, not around, I thought you were going to settle down."

I looked off, remembering another life when I was happy and complete, and some of what I went through when I lost it.

I'd had different therapists over the years to help me deal with the loss of my wife and due to the nature of that loss the PTSD that accompanied it.

Since her death I had trouble staying in relationships. I always seemed to compare the woman I was with, with my wife. It wasn't a conscious effort, but I was told I did it, never-the-less.

The therapists were all in accordance on a couple of my issues. One was that I would experience the affects of PTSD on different levels for the rest of my life. The trick was recognizing its' slippery serpent head, to which I believe I had shown a reasonable proficiency. The other concurrence was <u>*do not*</u> compare the new woman in my life to my wife, on this issue I was an astoundingly successful failure. I understood the concept, but for me, it was like trying to put a moonbeam in a pocket that was sewn shut.

The new woman was doomed from the outset. The loss of my wife had taken it's toll. I missed her, right now.

One of the upsides to Spain's slow speech pattern was he didn't seem to mind the long silent abysses I sometimes tumbled into.

"My wife's a hard act to follow."

Spain said, "I wish I could have known her."

"Yeah, me too," I said, thinking if he did, she'd still be alive.

The Weight Watcher candidate needed a dolly for his carry-out order. I wondered how many people could eat on what he was trying to carry out. Maybe it was for his family, a large one.

Spain and I locked eyes for just a moment, then he cleared his throat and asked, "How long's it been since you've talked to Paula Stone?"

"She called me awhile back and asked me to the CMA Awards, I declined."

"What did you say? How do you say no to something like that, and to someone like her?" he whispered, shaking his head.

I expected another bray, but he surprised me. I liked that.

"I told her it wasn't her, it was me. I had some issues I needed to work out before I could be with anyone again."

After ending it with Paula, I'd sat down and written out a description of the kind of woman I wanted to be with. Not just a physical description, but a list of qualities and traits. After reading it, I was struck with the certainty that this woman wouldn't have anything to do with a man like me. After weeks of thinking about it, I came to the conclusion that I must obtain these qualities if I were going to attract a woman with them. The smart-aleck remark, 'it takes one to know one', took on a new meaning for me. Now, three years later, I felt I was getting closer.

"Are you seeing a shrink again?" Spain asked.

"No."

"So, what you're saying is, you're not ready to see anyone at this time," he said in a way I could tell he was formulating what to say to Betsy.

"That's right."

"Don't you get lonely?" he asked.

"I'm learning to be alone without feeling lonely. There's a difference." *At least that's what I was told.*

While Spain was trying to figure out what I'd said, the waitress brought our food. Spain's rack looked delicious and totally artery clogging.

Spain looked up from his plate long enough to ask, "How many songs have you had cut over the years?"

"Just ten," I answered.

"You should be loaded, so you buy dinner," he said.

"Not loaded at all, just enough to keep the wolves from the doors. I paid cash for a lot of the work I contracted for the house in the country and the apartment. I've only had two in the top ten, none of which went to number one. I haven't written a song in years, and what with all the CD burning, the money's not what it used to be."

"Yeah, one of those was 'Unconditionally', the song about your wife. What was the other one?"

"Cowboys and Engines," I said.

"That's right," he said, "Great song, ah . . . I like the other one too."

"Thanks, but speaking of being loaded, Betsy's real-estate business seems to be doing well. I see 'Spain Real Estate' signs all over the place, and I know you can't afford that suit and those shoes on your pay."

"Okay . . . Okay. I'm buying," he said.

In between bites, he wiped his hands clean from the roll of paper towels the restaurant supplied for each table. The pile of used towels was mounting, so was something else. Spain appeared to become very serious.

"I found out something concerning those two shooters you took down. They were imported by Eddie Tuma."

Chapter 14

Eddie Tuma, 'the octopus' I'd been feeling at my back, was Nashville's turn of the century Al Capone wanna-be. I didn't know much about him, other than he's not one of the good guys.

Spain continued, "I've got it on good word that Bench borrowed a ton of money from Tuma to buy property on First and Second Avenues and was supposed to cut him in on the profits after reselling, and a percentage of the rental properties. Instead, he sent Tuma the money back with some interest. Kinda cut Tuma off at the knees. Not too bright of Bench."

"Uh-hunh," I said.

"I'll tell you what's worse," Spain said, looking straight at me.

I pushed my beans around on my plate. Bar-B-Q beans don't like me. I'd forgotten they came with the dinner.

"Your ex-client and apartment benefactor, Samuel Bench, has left the country with no need or intention of returning to the US, and Eddie Tuma has let it be known you're now his new hobby. He didn't take kindly to you spoiling his sweet revenge and his message to any other future business partners that 'you don't fuck with Eddie Tuma'."

"Uh-hunh," I said.

"You don't seem to be too shook up over it," he said.

"This isn't what you wanted to see me about. You said there was someone who wanted to meet me, some kind of interview."

The waitress came by and asked if we were through, and started clearing the table. She was all business, as if she could feel the vibe in the air.

"Do you know the name George Carr?" Spain asked.

It didn't take but a second for the name to register. It was on the news and in the Nashville papers.

I said, "He's the guy whose wife was killed in Houston, a car wreck, about three months ago, right?"

"Yeah. Anyway, about two months ago, he calls me. I know him through some real-estate shindigs Betsy's hauled me to."

The waitress brought the check and looked undecided as to which side to put it on.

"What's your name?" I asked her.

"Bonnie. What's yours?" she asked, with a dash of attitude. I think she was still miffed at Spain for wiping down what was for sure a 'Bonnie Cleaned' table.

"My name's Tucker," I said. Then pointed to Spain, "and the compulsive clean freak gets the check."

This brought back her pretty smile as she delighted in giving Spain the check.

Spain looked like he wanted to retaliate, but looked down to catch himself wiping his hands for the umpteenth time, stopped, dug out a credit card and handed it to her. She gave it a hard look before leaving with it.

"As I was saying," Spain continued, "he calls and asks if I know anyone who could check into his wife's death, someone I trusted. I gave him your name."

This came as a complete surprise.

"Why would you do that? I'm not a private investigator."

"I know that, but you did get to the bottom of the Macino boy's problem very quickly, and didn't you teach a class to the Houston Police Department, something about weak hand shooting?"

"As it relates to cover," I said, then added, "and I've done some gunsmithing for some of their Swat team and pistol team."

"Well, I figured you had some pull in the Houston P.D. and could maybe look into it. Oh yeah, speaking of classes, Debbie over at the Department of Commerce and Insurance called me and said the security companies are pressuring her to get you to teach some classes for the State Guard License."

"I don't do that anymore."

"Why'd you stop?" Spain asked.

"It's too dangerous, too many inexperienced people with loaded guns."

Spain laughed, "It's amazing what killing two men can do for business."

"What did you tell her?" I asked.

"That I would say something to you."

"Okay," I said. "You did."

Spain took a fingernail file from the inside pocket of his suit coat and started cleaning the sauce out from under his fingernails.

I wondered if he'd do that if a woman was present.

He looked up from his chore, raised one eyebrow and said, "George Carr called this morning and said he would like to meet you tomorrow."

This just didn't add up.

I said, "I read she was killed in a car accident and was burned beyond recognition."

"That's right. He had to have her dental records sent down."

I said, "One, why does he want it looked into? Two, why doesn't he hire a private eye from Houston? And three, why does he wait two months to meet me?"

"Remember, on the phone I said there was something strange going on? Well, I'd call this strange, wouldn't you?" he asked. "Tucker, this guy's got more money than Trump and Turner combined. He has his own bodyguards and security. I don't know why he waited so long to meet you, or why he just doesn't send some of his own men down there."

Spain took out a business card and handed it to me. It read, 'George Carr' along with a phone number.

As we walked through the door of the restaurant into the night mist, Spain edged past me to walk out first. We both paused and took in the street, checking parked cars for silhouettes of surveillance, or anything suspicious. Everything seemed normal, but, that's how it would look if the person or persons after me were any good.

We walked over to my truck, and I punched in the code to unlock my door.

"Tucker, I told Carr the particulars of the shooting."

"I didn't know there were particulars," I said, as the door clicked unlocked.

He took a deep breath, "There were 13 shots fired that night. Of the six you fired from your .45, there were two in each of the shooters' chests, just left of center. You could have covered them with a pack of cigarettes. There was one in each head, just under their left eyes. Smart, covering your ass in case they had body armor, just like you teach. Bench's personal body guards, Powell and Trent, fired their 9 millimeters twice each. They said the shooters were already dead on their feet by the time they got their guns out. Out of those four rounds, one hit the big guy in the leg, another round went through the gristle of the little guy's left ear. The remaining two were misses that hit the building across the street behind the shooters. Powell fired at the big guy, and Trent said he shot at the smaller one."

I noticed when Spain was speaking copese, he spoke at an almost normal speed.

There are three vital areas on a human, and an order of selection. One; center mass, the chest. Two; the pelvis, to break them down. Three and lastly; is the head. When shooting at paper silhouettes any hit above the brow or below the nose doesn't count for a hit. There have been too many recorded instances of bullets hitting a forehead then tracing the skull and exiting without much damage or ricocheting off a tooth.

With that in mind, I said, "I couldn't see their pelvis's"

I could feel Spain looking at me through the dim light.

"That little guy was very fast," I said, looking down the street at a man wearing a hooded coat crossing to the restaurant.

He said, "Tell me about it. All of the remaining three rounds came from that little fucker's .357 semi-automatic. Two of them went through your coat, just to the left of your heart and under your armpit, and hit the brick wall at Pete's. The other bullet is the one that hit a coffee cup the waitress in the same restaurant was holding."

I said, "I had that coat repaired. Little Vietnamese guy has a tailor shop out in Bellevue. I have his card at the office, if you ever need anything done, like a pair of pants taken up or something."

"Fuck you. What I'm saying is you made a lot of points with a lot of people that night. The big brass down at the station are starting to look at you a little differently now."

"Let me get this straight," I said. "This is the same brass that blackballed me from the range after finding out I worked on guns that belonged to some maybe unsavory characters from the northeast, and now because I killed a couple of guys from there, I get a slide."

"Yeah, that's about it."

"And this is a good thing?"

"You think it could've gotten worse than it was?" Spain said, as he picked something off of his coat sleeve.

"Cops are still talking about how you stepped in front of Bench and just stood there during the firefight. Trent said it was like you knew those two were going to try and hit Bench. He told me he couldn't tell who made the first move, you or them. Said when it started it was over." Spain snapped his fingers. "Just like that," he said.

"Trent's ex-secret service, isn't he?" I asked, not wanting to open my door and have the interior light come on, making an easy target of me.

Spain was looking down the street the other way, his suit coat was unbuttoned with his right thumb hooked behind his belt buckle. I wondered if he still had that .45 or his usual 9mm Beretta.

"Yeah. Trent said he didn't like it worth a shit when Bench hired you to help them. Said it pissed him off so much he wanted to kick your ass."

Spain chuckled, "I told him he had better bring his lunch when he decided to have a go at you. He gave me a weird look and told me he would probably be dead if you weren't there. Said they all would have been."

"How's Stretch doing?"

He looked at me like I was speaking calculus.

"What?"

"The waitress that got hit in the coffee cup."

"Oh, yeah, I forgot you know her. She's okay, told me it was too bad the cup was empty. It could've had hot coffee in it and would've burned the shit out of her, then she would have found somebody to sue, maybe you." He laughed at the thought.

Stretch was tougher than she looked, and she looked plenty tough. She always had some smart-assed remark; this meant everything was good with her.

"Just how well did you know Stretch?" Spain asked.

Standing beside my truck, I looked down at the backs of my hands, then turned them over to gaze into the palms, like there were answers in their shadows.

Over the years Margie and I knew her from different restaurants she worked where we'd go for dinner. We liked her. We could tell she liked us. She was attractive and funny. It was that kind of connection where everyone is attracted to each other, but no boundaries were being breeched.

I said, "Margie and I knew her from eating out. She was always the head of something, like bar manager or floor manager where she handled all the waiters and waitresses. Very tough broad. Looked a lot like Gina Davis, you know, the tall redheaded actress."

"Yeah, I can see that," he said, still searching the soggy streets.

"She took me home one night, back then, when I was really crazy, you know, afterwards."

Shaking his head slowly, he whistled and said, "Damn, I bet she was hot. She's not bad now, a little rough around the edges."

"Yeah, she's been doing that kind of work since I've known her. Those late nights will get to you. No one's immune. She likes her beer too."

I remembered that night. I had been trying to pickle my memories with Crown Royal and numb my pain with cocaine, and she took me home with her. My next recollection was of laying on her bed looking up at her face, which seemed about a mile away, so I asked, "How tall are you?"

She looked down at me and asked how tall I was, and I said "six foot even."

She smiled at me, she had a great smile with a little overbite, and said, "I'm five-twelve."

Sounded great at the time; at least I was taller.

That night, I found that tough broad exterior was just a wall. When she let it down, she was very soft and nurturing, a truly sweet woman. One of those surprises in life we live for.

"You know Spain, she's really a sweet nurturing person," I said.

"You're shittin' me, right?" he drawled. "No way that woman is nurturing. She said she would've sued your ass for being slow on the draw if that cup would've been full of hot coffee. I don't think she was kidding. She wasn't smiling when she said it."

When Spain says more than a couple of sentences in a row, it's like your grandmother telling you a bedtime story. I yawned and thought 'she still loves me.'

"Spain, why'd you take the time to help me, you know, back then, when I was crazy? You didn't really know me, but every time I got into trouble, it seemed like you showed up to keep me out of jail. Even when you were working undercover."

If he noticed it took me twenty years to ask that question, he didn't show it.

He pulled his braids from behind his back, laid them on his shoulders, and said, "I liked you because you always were kickn' the shit out of some cowboy."

I said, "About half the men in this town are cowboys or dress like one, including me."

He smiled and said, "Well, there you go."

We'd been standing beside my truck for too long, so I opened the door, the interior light came on like a stalag search light.

"If I were you I'd disconnect that light," he said.

I got in my truck, opened the console, pulled out a folded piece of paper and handed it to Spain standing in the open door.

He unfolded it and leaned into the truck to shed enough light to read it by.

"I found that under my wiper a few weeks ago," I said, scanning the street.

I knew what it said, in bold-faced type, 'YOU ARE A WALKING DEAD MAN. YOUR ASS IS MINE. SOON'. It was signed E. T.

"Shit, Tucker, what did you think when you got this?"

"I didn't think it was from a short little alien with a glowing finger."

"Why didn't you report this?" he asked.

Sometimes Spain has no sense of humor.

"And what would've happened if I did?"

Spain looked up from the note, folded it, put it in his pocket, and said, "Yeah, I see your point. He'd never come at you by himself, and there is no proof as to who wrote it."

"That's the way I figured it."

"You think he's going to make a run at you?"

"Yeah, I've felt being watched for a while now."

"Well, watch your back. After what you did to those last two, that's where it'll come from."

I closed my door, extinguishing the light, and started the truck. He rapped on the window.

After the window was down, he looked hard at me and said, "You doin' okay today?"

It was the first reference as to it being the twentieth anniversary of Margie's death. Somehow the term anniversary wasn't appropriate.

"It's been a bit reminiscent. Thanks for taking my mind off it for a while." I said, nodding toward Gun World.

"If you change your mind about meeting that personal trainer, give me a call."

I nodded and pulled away. Today was not the day to contemplate meeting a new woman.

Chapter 15

Brad Spain was looking at the taillights of Tucker's truck when he picked up his cell phone and dialed the number written on the paper on the seat beside him.

It was answered after only one ring.

"Hello, Brad," said the voice on the other end.

Spain thought 'I've got to block this number,' and said, "Yeah, well, I did what I could. I don't know if he'll call or not. Tucker doesn't think of himself as a detective, so I don't know."

"Thanks for setting that up tonight. It was very informative," the voice said.

"I told you he was good, didn't I?"

"Yes, you did."

"Well, what did you think?" Spain asked.

"You were right."

Spain looked at the rear window of Tucker's truck, but couldn't see an outline of the man through the tint.

"He's the man for the job, but you need to get him interested."

"Are you saying Tucker doesn't respond to money?"

"I've never known it to be a dominating factor in his life," Spain said. "I've seen him turn down high-paying gigs because the client was an asshole."

"All right then, thanks for your help, Brad."

"Thanks for the loan of your Colt for the past few weeks."

"It didn't do much good, did it?" the voice laughed.

"Not tonight," Spain said, just before breaking the connection.

He put on his left blinker, flashed his headlights at Tucker's taillights, then made his turn onto I-440 that would take him home to his wife.

He thought about Tucker and what an influence the man had had on his life, and how Tucker was completely oblivious to it.

In the months following December 11th, Tucker had, on occasion, revealed to Spain different periods of his past. Tucker being full of grief and guilt along with enough brandy and cocaine to amputate an appendage, would talk in a monotone drone with a thousand yard stare, while the anger crept out of his pores. Sometimes it would be after Tucker had lost it in some Nashville late night spot and had taken his anger out on some usually deserving bully. The police would be called in and Spain would intervene, leading Tucker away in handcuffs, not to jail but to someplace where he could talk him down. Tucker hated bullies, and when one showed his ugly side in his presence, the bully found out what ugly really meant. It seemed that Tucker felt guilty about beating the shit out of someone (once literally) who needed it, as if he knew beforehand it wouldn't be a fair fight. But, Spain thought it was Tucker's survival guilt. This guilt would sometimes cause Tucker to tell Spain about his shady past.

During one of these confessionals, the anger coming off of Tucker scared him, giving him second thoughts on his previous decision to remove the handcuffs. But, through it all, what he'd observed on the night of December 11th, through the following procedural investigation of Tucker's personal life, his own personal experience with Tucker, and perception of the man over time, led him to one general conclusion: he liked the man. In his line of work, that didn't happen often; in fact, it didn't often happen in his personal life.

He'd watched Tucker pull himself from a deep hole that he himself prayed he would never get a glimpse of. He had seen the man transform his life, personal and business; change himself into more than he was before his downward spiral into that fissure fate had bestowed upon him late one bloody night in December of 1982.

Tonight was the first time Tucker had confided anything of his new personal life. He was a virtual chatterbox compared to his usual self. Spain felt as though he and Tucker had crossed an invisible line that deepened their friendship. But, with this interview he'd set up for Tucker, he just hoped he hadn't initiated something that would get Tucker killed. He liked having him around.

Chapter 16

I drove back towards town with Spain following me in his unmarked Taurus Turbo. He lived in Brentwood and could have turned off twice to take shorter routes home, but didn't turn until we got to 440 on West End. He blinked his lights and was on his way to his devoted wife.

I was still in the Richland area when a car pulled out of a condo parking lot. This wouldn't have been suspicious but for the fact I'd seen the car a couple of blocks away, and it had plenty of time to pull out before I got to it. Also, its lights were off until I passed. It was a plain sedan, maybe a General Motors.

The GM was about four or five cars back. I decided to take a little detour to see if my imagination was running away. I turned on my left blinker. The car in question didn't, not that I expected it to. I made the left onto Wilson and kept my eye on the rear-view mirror. At about the right time a car turned in behind me, about four blocks back. As I approached Woodlawn, I slowed well ahead of the stop sign, to let it catch up. It didn't. I stopped at the sign, and turned the right blinker on. The car turned right a block behind me. Since I didn't really want to lose them, if they were following me, I turned right onto Woodlawn. There's a three way stop at Estes, and as I waited my turn, I kept an eye out behind me. Just as I started to move through the intersection, I saw a car turn right from a side street, and as it passed under a street light, it looked to be the same car.

I picked up my cell phone and punched in Spain's number.

After a couple of rings he answered, "Spain."

"It's Tucker. You got somebody following me, watching out for me?"

"No. Where are you?"

"I'm on Estes, taking a little detour to see if it sticks to me."

"You need me?" he asked.

"No, just checking. Wouldn't want to mistake a cop for some-one else."

He said, "Let me know if you need some help. I can have a squad car next to you, pronto."

"I'll let you know," I said and hung up.

Now, it seemed to me I was being followed. If he was any good, at some point he'd come up behind me, turn off again, then pick me up again. He knew my route home, or he wouldn't have been waiting for me where he was. My job was to pick the place where he could come up behind me, and hopefully, for my plan to work, there would be no cars behind him. I couldn't have this car behind me when I got out too far. It gets remote fast once you pass Belle Meade.

I stayed on Woodlawn until it butted into Kenner Street. I turned right on Kenner, then left on Harding, which was West End (one of the name changing spokes). That's where the tail picked me up again. I had just made what was an obvious tail-detecting maneuver and he must have known by now, that I knew he was following me.

As I was stalled at the red light at the intersection of White Bridge Road, the tail moved over into the right-hand turn lane and shot down White Bridge Road. If he was following me, he'd go down to Post Road and hang a left, which would put him parallel to Harding. From the speed of his car, I figured he would turn back onto Harding at either Hillwood or Davidson Road.

While waiting for the light to change, I removed my jacket. This did two things: it gave me better access to my .45, and it showed the Concealed Weapons Permit badge I have attached to my holster in front of the gun. The badge comes in handy if I inadvertently flash the gun under my coat while in the grocery store or such. I don't look much like a cop, and the badge has a way of relaxing people, if they should see the gun. It relaxes cops too; they may assume you're one of them. In any case, it lets them know you have the right to carry.

It was at Hillwood when he turned behind me about a hundred yards back. There was no one between us, and right now, no one behind. It was perfect. The next light was at Belle Meade Boulevard, just past the police department. Being one of the wealthiest commu-nities in the country, Belle Meade has its own police force.

I timed it for the light to turn red and I'd have to stop. The car had no choice but to pull in behind me. In my rearview mirror,

I could see there was more than one person in the car. If these were bad guys, they wouldn't try anything here. I could be wrong, but there's only one way to find out . . . right about now.

I opened my door, drew my gun as I got out and thumbed down the safety. In a two-handed walking shooter's crouch, I approached the car, keeping the truck bed between them and me. There were two men in the front seat and one in the back. As I approached my rear bumper, I moved the muzzle back and forth between the two in the front, first the head of the passenger, then the head of the driver, then back to the passenger. From their point of view, I was covering them all, and I had good cover behind my truck bed, and rear tire. I could only see the hands of the driver. The danger would come from one of the other two. If these were civilians, my badge would make them think I was a cop, and I'd be able to talk to them.

In the back seat, by the shoulder of the man sitting there, I saw what appeared to be the barrel of a shotgun, pointed at the roof. Okay, not civilians. I'd have to shoot him if it moved.

"Put down the gun! Show me your hands!" I yelled. It's good to give a verbal command. I used to teach this.

I was talking to the man in the back seat, but the two heads in the front now had big eyes. The driver rammed it in reverse and squealed the tires. He actually backed down Harding until he could back into the parking lot of St. George's Church, which is next to the police station. He did a K turn and was heading back the way he came, obeying the speed limit. It all took less than ten seconds.

Definitely bad guys, but the K turn was curious. It's something that's taught in law enforcement or the military.

That's no good, maybe now would be a good time to visit Houston. I got back into my truck and just made the green light. I dug out the card Spain gave me and dialed the number. It was answered on the second ring.

"Mr. Tucker, George Carr," the voice said.

Caller ID.

"Mr. Carr."

"I am very pleased you called tonight. I would like you to come to my house tomorrow. Would that be possible?" he asked.

"Yes. When and where?"

"One o'clock at 5302 Page Road, it's on the left about halfway between Belle Meade Boulevard and Chickering. This may take a while, so it would help if you could plan to stay for dinner. Will that fit into your schedule?"

This voice was one that was used to being obeyed, his politeness coming as a compliment.

"It fits," I said.

I knew the house. I'd watched it being built over a two year period, and it had only been completed about eighteen months ago. I thought it was going to be a hotel, but for the zoning. It was a stone monstrosity, maybe 20,000 square feet, on a ten acre lot where land sold for up to $500,000 per 2-acre lots.

"Good," he said, and hung up.

So much for the compliment.

Chapter 17

I watched my back all the way home. It would be obvious if I were being tailed. My house was at the end of a winding 800-foot downhill drive. To get to my driveway, you had to turn three times off Highway 100. Each turn took you down a smaller country road.

I like to describe my home as a Frank Lloyd Wright berm home. I wanted it to look like the hillside it came out of burped a stone house. It steps down quickly from the hillside, had a flat roof, and the side facing the creek was mostly atrium doors and windows.

There are two bedrooms, two baths, with a 600-square foot great room. The bedrooms are both about 260 square feet. The bathroom off my bedroom is 192 square feet with a 6-foot black Jacuzzi tub with a heater, a black toilet, a black urinal and two pedestal sinks. I have an 8-foot square open tiled shower with two heads. Some of the subs I contracted to help me build it said it looked like one hell of a bachelor pad. Since it was just my son, Emmett, and me living there, I suppose that's what it was. Emmett being 19, in love and away at college, was only there occasionally. I put a lot of custom amenities in it, like the warm floors heated by water that was pumped through thick-walled plastic pipes in the winter. But, I suppose I built it thinking one day a woman may come out.

My place was not easily approached without detection. I had a pretty good security system, a Catahoula hog dog named Razor. If Razor didn't know you, you didn't get on the property. Even if he did know you, you might not get on the property.

I also have two black labs. Buck, my 13-year old male who's blind in one eye, the result of surviving blastomycosis. The other eye had cataracts so bad the vet said he saw only dim shadows, and he's deaf as a post. I couldn't determine if his deafness was the product of having too many shotguns go off next to him over the years, or if it's selective hearing due to his age and general contrariness. Buck was retired from duck hunting and with his blindness, arthritis and deafness, his quality of life was kept high by eating, catching up on his sleep, and occasionally putting his big graying head in my lap for some petting.

My other Labrador is a 14-month-old female named Tuesday. She was born on Tuesday Sept. 11th, and I named her Tuesday as a reminder that a little joy came into the world on that day.

Labs don't make good security dogs, unless you have one with a poison tongue, that kills on contact. I'm training Tuesday for field and trial and hunting. I'm afraid she may be a little spoiled, but she's extremely bright and is a fast learner. She's an exceptionally beautiful dog, and her sweet disposition is truly a joy to be around. I've had three Black Labs since I was 19, and she's my first female. I'm afraid I am smitten.

After I fed the inside dogs and stopped Miso's meowing by putting fresh dry food in his bowl, I fed Razor on the flagstone patio, poured a Makers on the rocks and cleaned my Colt.

There's a certain satisfaction I received from cleaning a gun. I looked at the gun and realized it had never killed anyone, I had. The gun was just a tool.

I liked a gun that was functional and deadly in its simplicity. Like a good tool should be. I don't like all guns. I'm not one of those gun geeks you saw walking around gun shows in fatigues and jump boots. They gave me the willies.

Many guns had no place in my life. Guns were ultimately designed for one thing: killing.

Sure, you've got your target guns and your target shooters; nothing against them, it's a great sport. I was once quoted in a magazine as saying, 'Some guns are designed just for sport shooting. These sporting guns are so accurate, I can't imagine one missing just because it's aimed at a human'. I was told by the magazine's editor, it didn't go over all that well with the sport shooting community.

For me, when I practiced, it was to hone my killing ability with that particular gun. Even if the gun was designed for killing game, all guns would kill a man.

Some guns were designed to just kill humans. One of these and the most deadly in its simplicity is the Colt 1911 A-1 .45 caliber semi-automatic, designed by John Browning. It's strength and simplicity in itself suggested death. The semi-automatics expanded in moving parts from that design on. It was my experience that the more moving parts there were, the more room for error there was, which usually translated into a malfunction. In a gunfight, that malfunction most often translated into the one holding said malfunctioning gun, as dead. Other than design, metal quality was the next most important aspect, and the Colt 1911 was made of the finest Argentine steel, mined prior to the embargo.

When the time comes for me to need one, I'm most comfortable with this gun in my hand. I'm not actually holding it, it's a part of me.

Chapter 18

Tuesday was standing at the door, her demeanor saying 'haven't you forgotten something.' Buck stood beside her, his graying face swayed like Stevie Wonder at the piano. He knew if Tuesday was standing there, I'd come and let them both out. Buck didn't cotton up to Tuesday at first, but now he seemed to love her. She's his seeing eye dog. His nose was still in good shape, and if he couldn't see her, especially at night, he could sure smell her.

"Alright, guys," I said.

I wiped off what little oil I had left on my hands with a rag, and stood to walk over. This always got Tuesday spinning in circles with anticipation which made Buck back up, so he wouldn't be knocked over. He does this with a blowing sound humans make when exasperated over something a child does.

I opened the door, and Tuesday immediately attacked Razor, which he tolerated, then they took their gladiator practice off into the dark, with a stiff, limping Buck not far behind.

By the time I cleaned up after myself, took a shower, and got ready for bed, Buck and Tuesday were inside and getting ready for bed themselves. This usually consists of jockeying for possession of one of the two dog beds on the floor at the foot of my king-sized bed. One is for dogs with arthritis, very thick and plush. Tuesday usually steals it before jumping on the bed with me, surrendering possession to Buck.

By this time Razor is off patrolling the perimeter. I don't often see him sleep. I know he does; he's just sneaky about it.

I sat on the edge of my bed. Tuesday was laying on Buck's bed.

"Come here little girl," I said, patting the bed next to me. She looked up and shot me a 'Do not disturb me' look.

I was relentless, "Come're little girl. Come on, up."

She slowly unwound her lanky puppy frame and jumped onto the bed. I had to quickly slip under the covers to establish my territory. She always lies right next to my legs to the inside of the bed. If I don't hurry, I ended up with only a fraction of the edge.

I was quick enough to claim a comfortable tract before Tuesday finished making her bed next to me. She immediately started her groaning and grunting, sounding like a little pig. I called her Miss Piggy when she did this. If I moved during the night, she'd start her Miss Piggy talk.

I lay on my back with one hand under my head, the other one on Tuesday's head.

This was not my favorite time of the day. It was my lonely time, bedtime. The time I missed Margie most of all. After twenty years, you'd think I'd be over it. It's not always, not every night, that I miss the scent of her, the weight of her body next to mine, but when I do, there's a hole inside me where my heart should be that can't be filled. The depressing futility of that fact, was not lost in the energy it took not to cry and not to feel sorry for myself. As I looked up at the ceiling, I could acknowledge the romantic in me.

Not long ago, I rented the movie "Serendipity." A movie about love, destiny, and soul mates. Two people met and an unmistakable connection was made. They lost contact and the rest of the movie was about how years later they found each other and lived happily ever after.

Happily Ever After. One would tend to believe that after these movies were over, the couple lived together for the rest of their lives and both died in their sleep, at the same time, at the ripe old age of a 120. It's what I'd wanted to happen.

My time at 'Happily' had come and gone. I was happy. I was complete. I didn't want for love or a place to put my love. Then, in the space of a quick breath, it was taken away. The 'ever after' sucked. I'd like to believe *it* could happen again. But, after 20 years, the likelihood of that happening looked painfully slim.

I had tried a few times. Tried being the operative word. The trying was what was not right. If it was right, it would just be. If it was right, the trying would be the little arguments about whose turn it was to take the trash out, or where the remote control for the TV was. This would only come after years of being together, meaning we got along so well, that these were the only things we could find to argue about. That's how it was for us. I wanted that again.

With the women I had been involved with, involved enough to qualify as trying to be a couple, I was looking to find that same love, that same connection, and I indecorously compared them to her. Of course, they could never measure up. If they had, that would mean all that I had suffered wasn't vindicable. Talk about your catch-22.

Accepting where I'd gone afoul with my post relationships didn't lessen the ache of missing her, of being lonely, or the hopelessness of finding *it* again.

I turned off the bedside lamp, pulled a grunting Miss Piggy up close to my pillow, and wrapped my arm around her. She put her nose up under my chin, lovingly nuzzled my neck with her puppy softness, and licked my ear.

"I love you, little girl," I said, and closed my eyes.

Chapter 19

George Carr sat at his desk, alone in the private office of his home, the only room that was not designed by his wife, Jean. His heart ached for her. With all his money and power, he couldn't bring her back from the dead. For 30 years they had loved one another, and now she was gone.

She was killed in a car wreck in Houston, where they owned another home in River Oaks. Only, he didn't believe the wreck was an accident. His gut told him she was murdered. Carr's gut had never lied to him. He'd made a lot of enemies on his road to wealth and power, and couldn't shake the feeling his wife's death was aimed at him.

She had been burned beyond recognition, and at the funeral the urn containing her ashes was somewhat ironic. She'd always said she wanted to be cremated after she passed, ever since they first knew each other, over 30 years ago. He just never imagined he'd be the one to take care of it.

There was a light knocking on the door.

"Come in, Frank," he said.

The door opened and a tall lean man, with salt and pepper hair cropped close to his head, stepped into the office.

"Mr. Carr, Dennis is here. Would you like to see him now?" he asked, his clear blue eyes showing concern and care.

George Carr stared at his long-time body guard, head of security, and friend, Frank LeCompte.

"Mr. Carr. . . Dennis?"

Frank had worked for George Carr for almost 12 years, ever since he'd left SEAL Team Six at the age of 38. He was considered the old man of the Team. Instead of staying in the Navy and training new SEALS, he took the job offered by Carr. Carr was only a few years older than Frank. He was now like the big brother Frank had lost to the Vietnam War.

"Mr. Carr, should I have him come back later?" he asked, seeing the far away, grief-stricken look that could still take over his employer.

"No, bring him in. And Frank, stick around."

"You bet," Frank replied, as he turned to fetch Dennis James, one of the security team he headed up for Carr.

James and two others had been sent on a mission earlier in the night. A mission Frank thought was an unnecessary risk, but he couldn't talk George Carr out of it.

George stared at the door until it opened, and Frank entered followed by Dennis James. Dennis closed the door behind him. They walked over to his desk and stood, almost at attention, reminding Carr of how when he allowed Frank to do the hiring, he had hired almost exclusively ex-military personnel.

Frank LeCompte said, "Go ahead, Dennis, tell him what you told me. Just the way you told me."

Dennis James, considered small by those who didn't know him, cleared his throat as his face took on a pained expression, and said, "Mr. Carr, Frank was right about this not being a good idea. We pretty much let him know we were following him, ya know, like to scare him a little."

"What happened, Dennis? Get on with it," Carr said

"Well Mr. Carr, this Tucker fellow doesn't scare worth a damn. To tell you the truth, he scared the Bejusus out of us."

"How did he accomplish that, Dennis?" he asked, with a wryly curious tone.

"Before we got the chance to pull up next to him and scare him with the shotgun, you know. . . like the plan? Well, sir, we had to stop behind him at a red light, and, sir, he was out of his truck and had us covered with that Colt of his before we had a chance to do anything. He's very fast and, well, sir, it just seemed like the best idea for us to, ah . . . get out of there."

"Well, I'll be God damned!" Carr yelled, smacking his hand down on his desk. "I like this Tucker, I really do," he said with a small laugh. "You were right, Frank."

Dennis Jame's worried look was replaced by perplexity.

Carr looked at Dennis James and said, "He called. He's coming tomorrow."

"Really? He didn't look scared at all Mr. Carr," James said, then looked at Frank. "Not at all."

Frank walked Dennis to the door and, as he opened it, said, "Thanks, Dennis, you and the boys did alright. It went better than I'd expected. Take the rest of the night off and go drink a couple of beers." He patted James on the back on his way out.

As he closed the door, Carr heard James mutter, "More'n a couple."

Frank walked back to the desk and sat in the chair across from Carr.

Frank said, "That could have gone differently. Tucker is fast at killing. I would have hated to lose three good men tonight just to ensure something that was going to happen anyway."

"Do you really think he could've got all three?" Carr asked.

"I saw him shoot tonight. I have no doubt."

"So, he's that good?"

Frank LeCompte was very still when he said, "I've never seen better, anywhere."

"Coming from you, that's remarkable," Carr said.

Carr nodded at a stack of files and papers over a foot tall on his desk. "But I'm not surprised. After reading this investigative report on him, I would've been disappointed if he wasn't that good."

Frank shook his head. "I told you he's the same guy I heard about during my SEAL training. He was only 19 then."

Carr reached over and patted the stack of papers. "Tucker's had an interesting life, to say the least. I believe I may know more about him than he does about himself."

"I don't understand why you spent so much money having him investigated. Spain said he was the man for the job, and our preliminary investigation here showed Tucker's reputation was sound."

Carr reached over to a humidor on the right side of his desk and took out a Cohiba, clipped it, and with a lighter smoldered the end as he rolled it between his fingers.

"The last man we hired disappeared. He may have been bought off, and if he was, I just don't want to make the same mistake. Captain Spain said that, if Tucker took the job, he'd stick to it until the end and that he couldn't be bought. Hearing it is one thing, but I wanted to know more about the man, his background, his pattern of life."

Frank LeCompte didn't miss the 'we' in Carr's statement. LeCompte didn't miss much, period. It was like his employer to include him, even though he had no money invested, just his time. Just one of the reasons he loved the man.

Looking at the investigation stack, Frank grinned, "Well, you should be able to get a sense of the man now."

"Frank, you should really take the time to read *all* of this," Carr said, again patting the pile warmly. "It's amazing the man is still alive and was never arrested."

"Mr. Carr, when do I have time to read?" Frank smiled. "Besides, I feel like I know him. Don't forget, I compiled most of that file, and I heard all about him during my SEAL training. Every time we would be learning something or shooting at something, Levanda would say 'Tucker this . . . Tucker that.' Hell, to hear Levanda talk, the guy was a legend, one bad-assed fucker. And he was only 19."

Chapter 20

I was under a bridge, the water was rising, getting deeper by the second. It was now up to my knees.

I crawled up towards the safety and dryness of the road that crossed the bridge. I could hear the roar of the fast rising water, like the growl of a dog. I could hear the whine of wheels on the road, like the whimpering—of a—of a dog.

I opened my eyes. Tuesday was sitting next to my head, facing the window above me, whining. The little girl was afraid. I could hear Razor's low growl. He was just outside my bedroom.

Razor barked at deer, chased rabbits and raccoons, hid from skunks, and growled at people.

I rolled over onto my stomach, reached under my bed, and pulled the Mossberg 590 12-gauge assault shotgun from its slip-free fasteners attached to the frame. It held eight in the magazine and one in the chamber. It also had a side saddle attached to the non-working side of the receiver, that held another six shells.

Leaving my Colt under the unoccupied side pillow where it slept, I crawled across the carpet to the atrium door. As I started to open it, I felt Tuesday's cold nose on my bare butt. I jerked and bumped my head lightly into the door's glass.

"Tuesday, sit," I whispered. It was a moonless, cloudy night, and I could just make her out in the darkness. I could see a dark hole behind me, shaped just like a standing dog.

I sat down and pulled her close to me as I scanned the patio. I wasn't too concerned about anyone being on the patio. Razor wouldn't let anyone get that close without doing more than growl, which he was still doing.

I pulled up on Tuesday's collar, put my mouth close to her ear and said, "Sit," hopefully sounding forceful and loud.

She sat down and cocked her head, questionably.

"Good girl," I said. We're still training.

I opened the door and crawled out onto the patio with the shotgun in the crook of my elbows. It was cold. I was totally nude and shrinking fast. Razor was backing around towards me. I crawled over to the corner where there were no windows that might silhouette me against the night, and stood just as Razor came all the way around the corner. He never looked up at me, but kept his attention up the hill towards the gate, some 800 feet away. He stopped growling once his body touched my leg. The hair was raised on his back, his body leaning forward on high alert. His lips were pulled back and I could see his teeth.

I wished I'd taught him something like, "Sic' em!", so he'd charge up the hill and tear the crap out of whoever was up there. But, with me being the alpha dog in this equation, he was waiting for me to do something.

It was a still night, and through the sound of the mellifluous creek below, I thought I heard the faint sounds of footsteps barely rustling the gravel on the drive. By the sound of it, whoever it was, were still pretty high up, if they were there at all. Only one way to find out.

I ran barefoot up the stone steps that were laid through a tiered azalea and rhododendron garden. As I came to the lower level drive next to the house, I slowed and walked across the gravel as not to make any noise and because I have soft feet and the gravel hurt like hell. I stepped into the wooded island that was the center of my circular drive.

The ground in the woods was damp because of the wet weather we'd been having. Staying low, I moved quietly to the electrical transformer box that was about 30 feet up the hill. The box is a three foot cube and made of heavy metal and would make good cover, if I needed it. I sat down with my back against the box and waited for whoever was coming down the drive, if indeed someone was. As I sat there, I was struck with how cold it was, then thought, that's a good thing, there were no chiggers or ticks out.

I was starting to shiver, and the shotgun was getting colder by the second. Then I heard them talking. I'd lost track of Razor in the dark.

"Do you think he's got any dogs?" It was a loud whisper.

"It doesn't make a shit, I'll kill the fuckin' dogs, too."

I pushed the safety off and turned a little to my right. It sounded like they were coming down the right side of the island. I sneaked a peeked around the box to see if I could see them yet. I looked down at my legs and wished I had gotten a better tan last summer. I was very white and felt like a light bulb that was just turned off. All I could see was me. I didn't like that.

"Can you see the house yet?" said the same loud whisperer.

"Fuck, I can't see anything. It's fuckin' dark," said the one that was going to kill my dogs.

"We're gonna have to do this guy fast, just shoot him in his bed if we can, can't give him a chance. I don't want him shooting at me."

"Shut up, you fuckin' chickenshit," said the K-9 killer.

"Don't talk to me like that, Pauly. This guy's too good to let him shoot at us, I'm ....FUCK!"

Two shots rang out-Bang!-Bang!

"God damn it, Anthony! What the hell . . ."

Then another shot- "Bang!" Followed by the howl of a hurt dog.

"A fuckin' dog! It fuckin' bit me, fuck, fuck. I shot the fucker, fuck . . . fuck!"

They were no longer whispering.

Razor must have gone around the other side of the house and slipped up on them from behind. I turned all the way around, facing the sound of them, but kept the transformer box as a shield. I put the shotgun over the top of the box and aimed. I hoped it would be high enough not to hit Razor if he was still on his feet. I couldn't see them, but I knew where they were, about 25 yards away. There were a lot of trees between them and me, but I'd be shooting No. 4 birdshot and at that distance, the pattern would be about the size of two basketballs. I shot five times, fast as I could pump. Bang-Bang-Bang-Bang-Bang!

I ducked down behind the box as it was hit with what felt like a jackhammer, instantly trailed by the sound of automatic gunfire.

Down at the house, Tuesday was barking, and even old Buck was putting in his two cents, but only sounding like a farthing's worth.

I rolled over to my left and changed my position. Lying on my stomach, I felt sticks and leaves trying to invade my private parts, and was again relieved it wasn't summer. I eased the shotgun forward, and from down low on the ground, again peeked around the metal box.

Now that the echo's of the fired shots were fading, I could hear the sound of running feet on the gravel, going away. I knew I had two double-ought buckshot and two slugs in the magazine. I always load my shotgun like that. Out of nine rounds I load five birdshot and then two oo buckshot, then two slugs. The buckshot is like nine .38 caliber bullets being shot at once, there's nothing deadlier at close range or in the dark. A slug is a hunk of lead about half the size of my thumb.

I jumped up and moved up through the island about twenty yards, keeping the larger trees between me and them.

"That mother fucker's down there shooting at us! And that fuckin' dog bit me!"

"We gotta finish this thing. You go down to the right, and I'll go down to the left. We'll get him in a cross fire."

Sounded like a good plan to me. Too good. I didn't like it. I was naked and cold, with sticks and leaves trying to find their way up my ass, and I didn't like *any* of that, either.

I knew exactly where they were, up on the single drive, just before it splits to go around the island of woods I was on. I also figured they'd stick together and stay on the drive until they got to the split. There was a street light up at the top, where my driveway started, and it was casting just enough light I thought I might could see them, maybe. They were still 60 or 70 yards away, if what I saw was them.

I couldn't let them separate. What's more, I was so cold my manhood was in jeopardy. I ran straight for a large beech tree I knew to be about 50 yards from the split. As soon as I got to the tree I leaned against it and shot four times into the middle of the road a little ways up the hill from the split.

BANG!-BANG!-BANG!-BANG!

"Ahhhh Shit!"

I heard a body fall and hit the gravel.

I sat down with my back to the tree and started taking shells out of the side saddle to reload. All these were oo buckshot.

First, it came as horizontal lead rain. Hard slapping pops, ripping bark off trees, completely severing smaller saplings, then the sound of automatic gunfire, a wall of sound. Explosions and the horrific sound of wood being ripped apart and hammered. The ground around me exploded, showering me with leaves and dirt. I could feel the tree I was leaning against being hit with a rapid fire sledgehammer. I made myself as small as I could and closed my eyes to protect them from the debris that was flying around. I never stopped reloading.

I knew they couldn't know exactly where I was, but someone had seen my muzzle flashes and had homed in very close. All I could do was wait for them to run out of ammo and have to change magazines.

It didn't take long. The quiet was as startling as the noise was at first. I decided not to peek around the tree again. I knew one was down. I was pretty sure there was only two. That left one on his feet. I knew I'd never use algebra.

It made more sense to me to stay where I was and let him come to me. The closer he got, the better it was for me and my shotgun. Whereas he could sit up there and chop down the trees around me and maybe get lucky and chop me down. I wasn't cold anymore.

I heard some grunting and the sound of gravel being scraped. The sound was getting smaller. In a little over a minute, I heard a car door slam and tires spinning in the gravel up on Willow Branch Lane.

I sat there trying to hear out into the darkness over the sound of my breathing. I thought I might just sit here until daylight. I didn't know what time it was, so I didn't know how long that might be.

There could have been another man in the car waiting and that would make three altogether, meaning one could have been left behind to get me after I thought the coast was clear. That was more like algebra.

Deciding to stay put was a wise decision. I heard the soft rustling of wet leaves and a small twig break. Whoever it was, was good. He was very quiet. I could barely hear him as he moved down the hill and closer to me. This guy was smart, staying in the woods and off the gravel. I knew I'd have time for only one shot and I had to make it count.

It sounded like he was coming straight for my tree. I could barely hear him. I didn't want to take the chance of standing up. He was too close and would hear me for sure. As quietly as I could, I stood the shotgun on its stock in front of me. I didn't know on which side of the tree he would pass, and I had to be ready to shoot left-handed if he came around to my right.

He stopped moving. I could hear him breathing. He was on the other side of my tree. I could sense him searching for me in the dark. I cradled the shotgun with the palms of both hands next to the trigger guard, ready to lean the gun in either direction and shoot one-handed, almost over my shoulder, if need be.

He stopped breathing. I could hear my heart beating in my ears. I realized I'd been holding my breath ever since I'd heard him breathing on the other side of my tree.

Suddenly I felt a warm wet tongue on the side of my face. Razor had leaned around the tree and almost licked the leaves and sticks out of me.

"Damn, boy," I said, and realized I was whispering. I put my arm around his shoulders and pulled him close to me. They were gone. Razor said so.

I felt something warm and sticky on my chest. I stood and walked down to the house, feeling for the first time my complete nakedness. Before, it had been more environmental, how my feet hurt on the gravel, how the leaves and twigs were trying to invade my body, the whiteness of my body in the night, the fleeting coldness overrun by the rushing of battle blood being pumped by adrenaline. Small frames in a much larger film. A film of survival. Now that I had survived, I felt ridiculous and self-conscious. I may have to start wearing pajamas.

I'd left the door to my bedroom open. When I went in and turned on the light, Buck and Tuesday were on the bed. When all the shooting started, I guess they knew where the safest place was. I laid the shotgun next to them.

I pulled Razor in and checked him out. There was a lot of blood on the left side of his head. I wetted some paper towels with water and started cleaning him up. He had a perfect round hole through his left ear and a furrow of hair missing along his left jaw, leaving just a burn. The hair on the side of his face was singed and his left eye was a swollen and bloodshot. I checked his eyes with a flashlight, and his dilation seemed to be fine. I didn't know about his hearing though.

"Got a little close, didn't you, boy?" I said. "You want to stay in the house for the rest of the night?"

Razor looked over at the pansies laying on the bed, huffed and walked outside, back on patrol.

I looked at the clock. It was 4:44 a.m. I was starting to shiver. Some might think I was shaking, but it was just a shiver. I went to my walk-in closet and put on a heavy, giant hooded robe. On the way out of the bedroom, I reached over the bed and slipped my hand under the lonely passenger side pillow and pulled out my Colt. I went into the kitchen and made some tea, setting the gun down. . . close by.

Standing by my stainless steel stove top waiting for the kettle to whistle, it hit me. They knew where I lived. My son, Emmett, could have been home.

Emmett was the product of a relationship with a friend of Margie's and mine during a vulnerable period of my convalescence. Marriage was not an option for either of us. Emmett was legitimized through the courts and carried my name. Without the courts being involved, his mother and I shared equal time with our son. Since the age of two, when we started living in separate homes, Emmett stayed with each of us for two weeks of every month. Emmett was literally my salvation. He was my beacon and reason for living during a time of extreme nigrescence. He could have been home.

Later in the morning, I would have to call Spain and find out where E. T. hangs out. I'd have to have a chat with Eddie Tuma.

Chapter 21

I was cooking a mushroom, asparagus, and egg white omelet when I heard Razor's 'somebody's driving down the driveway' bark. Tuesday joined in, and Buck went into his Stevie Wonder impersonation. I looked at the clock on the double oven. It was 6:17 a.m., and not quite daylight.

I had changed into jeans and a sweat shirt. As I went to the single atrium door, I tucked the Colt into the small of my back and pulled the sweatshirt over it. Earlier, while drinking tea, I'd loaded the shotgun and sidesaddle back up to capacity, and it was leaning in the corner to the right of the door, barrel down so I could pick it up by the grip.

Before I opened the door, I saw a flash of colored lights and heard one small blast of a police siren.

I turned on the floodlights and waited. It only took about twenty seconds before Larry Deal, the constable of Lyles, was standing on the patio.

"Come on in, Larry," I said, turning and walking back toward the kitchen.

I heard the door close, and when I turned around Larry was standing there, his hat in his hand, displaying a bald shaved head sitting atop heavy shoulders. He had no neck, literally. He looked in the corner and saw the shotgun. It was black and ominous, looking just like what it was, a killing machine.

"Can I make you some coffee? I'm just finishing up this omelet and would be glad to share it with you."

"I gotta few calls earlier this morning, Tucker," he said.

"I bet you did," I said, slipping the omelet out of the non-stick pan onto a plate. "How about that coffee? I can make you a fresh cup."

"No thanks. What the hell was going on here earlier? Mildred Thomas called and said it sounded like a war over here."

Mildred Thomas is my closest neighbor, about a third of a mile away.

"Must've been someone shining deer up on Willow Branch," I said, sitting down at the dining table.

"With a machine gun?" he said. "That's what Mildred said it sounded like. And Wayne Baker called right after and said there was something going on over here, and it sounded bad, like a gunfight."

Wayne lives on the other side of the creek, way up the hill, about three quarters of a mile, as the crow flies.

"Yeah, that's what it sounded like to me, too. Scared me to death. I wasn't about to go up there and check to see what was going on. The only reason I didn't call you was, I figured someone else already had. Figured I'd see you sooner. It was over an hour ago I heard all the commotion."

"Ya know, Tucker, we read the papers out here, too. I know what you do for a living. Always kinda liked having you out here. I figured if you was still alive, you'd still be here, and if you weren't, well, there just wouldn't be any reason for me to hightail it over here so early."

Larry was a good ole country boy. He was born and raised here in Hickman County and got along with just about everyone. Constable was an elected office. He also wasn't going to get his head shot off if he had anything to say about it.

Larry Deal walked over to the corner and stuck his finger in the barrel of the shotgun, twisted it around, then pulled it out. It had a black smudge on it. He held it to his nose and sniffed.

"Smells like it's been fired recently," he said, then looked over at me. "What in the hell are you eatin'?"

"A mushroom and asparagus egg white omelet." I said, still chewing.

"Jesus, Tucker," he said, scrunching his face like he just got a whiff of something bad. Constable Deal was a sausage and egg man, the eggs cooked in the grease from the sausage.

"When's the last time you fired this here riot gun?" he said, holding up his smudged finger.

"Must have been a couple of months, at least," I said, with my mouth full. Dining etiquette would have been lost on him.

"Yeah, right," he said with a smirk. "And you always have it parked right here by the door."

"No. I guess I was nervous about those poachers up the hill, what with the automatic gunfire and all. I couldn't go back to sleep, so I got up and put that in easy reach just in case, you know."

"Yeah," he said with a grin. "Those *poachers* must have shot them a deer right up there by the split of your drive. My headlights picked up a shiny blood trail that started right about there and went up past your gate."

"Really?"

"Really," he said, twirling his hat around his finger like a cowboy twirling a gun. He was enjoying himself.

I said, "I never thought they were that close. You reckon they didn't know anyone was living down here?"

He walked back to the door and put his hand on the knob, put his hat on and said, "Well, I'm sure they do now. I'll go tell Mildred your poacher story, then go by and talk to Wayne. I like you, Tucker, but I hope you can keep your Nashville business in Nashville, know what I mean?"

I stopped eating and put my fork down. The anger was coming up. They had come to my home. My son could have been here, alone. I looked him in the eye and quietly said, "I know exactly what you mean, Larry, and I'm going to make sure those poachers get the message."

He suddenly looked like he needed to put on my heavy robe to chase away a chill. He nodded, then was gone.

After eating and cleaning up, I fed the dogs, then did some paperwork for about an hour. After changing into camo pants and rubber boots, I put Tuesday in the truck and drove the two miles to the Henry farm, where I had permission to use their pasture that contained a pond.

For the next hour Tuesday heeled, sat, and played baseball, a training exercise. Baseball is where she sat alone about 20 feet away. She's the pitcher's mound. I'm home plate. I throw dummies at the first, second and third base positions. I send her to each base where she retrieves the dummy and brings it to me, then goes back to the pitcher's mound for the next command. At least that's what happens when it's done properly. At the end of the hour I thought, maybe tomorrow it would be done properly. I was determined not to let anything get in the way of my daily routine. Everything will go on as normal.

It may have had something to do with the black shotgun laying in the grass next to me. Tuesday kept going over to it and smelling it, like it was somehow important. She knew it wasn't routine.

After returning to the house, I took a shower, shaved, tied my hair back, and got dressed. I pulled on a black t-shirt that I tucked into blue jeans held up with a custom-made, wide leather belt, sturdy enough to hold my Colt filled holster, and put on my Lucchese boots.

I sat down on the couch and called Spain.

"Brad, I need to know how to get to Eddie Tuma," I said after he answered.

There was a long pause then, "What do you mean by, 'get to'?

"They made a run at me last night. At my home. I can't have that."

"You okay?"

"Yeah, but one of his goons isn't."

"Did you kill him?"

"Only if I got lucky, shotgun in the dark, up the hillside from the house. I knocked him down. His partner hauled him off, left a pretty good blood trail."

Spain was quiet for a moment. I could hear the background noise of a police station.

I said, "Razor let me know they were there. I sort of got the drop on them when they were fumbling down the driveway in the dark."

"Sounds like fun."

"It was a blast."

He laughed and said, "Like I said, Tucker, what do you mean by 'get to'?"

"I just want to talk to him. Explain my side of it, you know, express my feelings. I wouldn't want anything bad to happen because of non-communication."

"Can I come and watch?" he snickered.

"That may put a damper on what I'd like to convey."

"Yeah, I bet."

"I want to talk to him where he feels safe, on his own turf."

"Can I have your gun if he offs you?".

"Sure. Where can I find him. . . tonight?"

He let out a long breath and said, "Fuck it. He owns a couple of titty bars, one on Nolensville Rd. and the other one is on Dickerson Rd. The one on Dickerson is called The Men's Room. He uses it as an office. He can usually be found there every night after 11 o'clock. His office is on the first floor. It's the door on the left in the back of the place. He'll have some muscle. Be careful."

Tuesday came up and put her head in my lap and I rubbed behind her ears. I took love where I found it.

I said, "Sounds like you have done a study on this guy."

"Fuckin' A, we'd love to nail this bastard on something. He's crazy, but he's smart and seems to be connected. Like I said, be careful, I don't want your gun that badly."

"Thanks, Brad."

"No sweat. I'm just worried that if you have to kill him, you'll leave the wrong witnesses."

"Well, there's that," I said. "But how ya gonna act?"

That had him laughing again, "Another Tuckerism?"

"Well, that's what life boils down to, isn't it?" I said. "No matter what happens, you'll be judged on one thing, so 'how ya gonna act.'"

"Tucker, what're you gonna do about Carr?" he said.

"I'm going over to his house this afternoon, at 1 o'clock. He wants me to stay for dinner, too. Sounds like a long interview. I hope I don't get sleepy."

"George Carr's anything but boring," he said.

I had the feeling he was leaving something out.

"What?" I said.

"Whatta you mean...what?"

"I just have a feeling you wanted to say something else."

"You're right," he said, and hung up.

Chapter 22

I pulled into the circular, tightly laid flagstone driveway of George Carr's mansion. It led me under two giant stone arches with cupolas at each end of a tall covered entrance before the front door. The door looked like something taken from a 17th Century church. It was all wood timbers and large metal hinges held together with nails, or more like spikes.

I rang the bell hoping I wouldn't hear someone yell 'come in'. I had my doubts about my ability to open the door.

The door opened and standing in the dim foyer light was a medium-sized woman whose gray and white uniform, and old face, didn't fit her beautiful hair or Gestapo gaze. From the lines on her face, she was somewhere in her mid hundreds, and by the ease with which she opened the door, I ascertained the door was either hung and balanced by an artist or this old biddy could clean my clock.

"Come in, Mr. Tucker, we have been expecting you." She smiled, and I was taken aback. She had a gorgeous smile, and her voice sounded like music. As I came in and closer, it became apparent the lines in her face I had taken for age, were scars. Hundreds of little scars. She'd had a very good plastic surgeon. I didn't know what had happened to her, but it had to have hurt, and she was younger than me.

"It's just Tucker, and to whom am I speaking?" I said, putting out my hand and looking her in the eyes, but not with the intensity of someone avoiding her face.

I must have turned on a little charm. She tilted her head just a little towards the floor, her shoulder length strawberry blonde hair falling around her face, then extended her hand that I gently held without shaking it.

"I'm Rachael, head of housekeeping," she said, her eyes darting to the scar on my face.

I found her attractive.

"This house looks like it would take some keeping," I said, looking around, still holding her hand.

She laughed warmly and slowly took her hand back.

Before she could close the door, I said, "Do you mind, I would love to close this door, if I can."

She laughed again and stepped aside.

As I closed the door, which took no more effort than any door, I thought, when my ship comes in I'm going to have a head of housekeeping, one just like her, with a laugh like that.

"That's amazing," I said. "I thought you were like Superwoman, when you opened that door.

"Then I shouldn't have let you, *like* . . . close the door." She smiled again, increasing the depth of the scars.

She turned and walked away from me into the foyer. She looked great walking away. She couldn't be any older than mid thirties, wonderful legs, and exceptionally fit.

The floor was granite with an array of Persian rugs with a few Kalim's strewn around. English Hunter tapestries hung down from 30 feet up. Pieces of art ranging from alabaster Buddha heads to an array of Edmondson sculptures stood atop pedestals surrounding the foyer. A chandelier hung in the middle that looked to be made of diamonds. The cut crystal shimmered like a sunrise after an ice storm.

"Rachael, could we just stand here for a moment? It's not every day I see something like this."

She turned around and walked back and stood by my side.

"I'm used to it, but you're right. To me, it's all become something to be cleaned, without being broken."

I took her hand and looped it through my arm and patted it. I leaned closer and whispered to her, "It must be a real pain...."

Looking straight ahead she said, "In the ass."

"Thanks, just the word I was looking for."

Turning her head, she looked at me and said, "You don't seem the type of man to lose many words."

I almost smiled.

"If it's not too personal, how long have you been working for Mr. Carr?"

"I've been with Mr. and. . . Mrs. Carr, for a little over nine years," she said, the sadness in her face making her look old again.

I hadn't met George Carr yet, but I was already liking him. Any man that could keep this woman employed for nine years must have something other than money going for him.

"Rachael, I'm sorry to hear about Mrs. Carr. I can see you liked her."

"We were very close," she said, looking through the foyer as if someone was coming, or maybe the absence of someone.

In a confidential tone she said, "It has been very hard on Mr. Carr. We are all close here in the Carr household, and not much goes on that I don't know about."

There was nothing to say to that, so I didn't.

"I hope you can help us, Tucker. Now it's time for you to meet Mr. Carr."

The way she said us, like a family, all I could do was nod.

She led me through opulent rooms to a hallway that had a different feel to it. It had been decorated by someone other than the one who decorated the rest of the house. At the end of the hallway was a plain solid oak door.

Rachael knocked softly, twice, on the door.

"Come in, Rachael," I heard from the other side.

Rachael opened the door, and I stepped into a large office, about 1,000 square feet of office. This was a man's office, and sitting behind a polished teak wood desk the size of a small dining room table was the man. He was sitting in a plush high- backed wine leather chair, the pleated tufts studded with brass. His hair was jet black, streaked with gray. It was thick and combed straight back, revealing a strong forehead. From 30 feet away, I could see the blue in his eyes. As he stood and walked around the desk, his movements were confident and graceful for a man his size.

"Mr. Tucker, I want to thank you for taking the time to see me today," he said, walking toward me with his right hand extended.

He had to be at least six-foot-six or seven. He reminded me of a retired pro basketball player, a fit one.

As I tried to get a comfortable grip in his bear paw, I said, "I am sorry for your loss, Mr. Carr."

His lean rugged face lost some of the confidence that I had first seen in it.

"Thank you, Mr. Tucker. I understand you are no stranger to loss, so your words are appreciated."

While still holding my hand, he put his left hand around my right arm and gently led me toward his desk. In front of the desk, facing each other, one to the left and one to the right of center, were two chairs identical to the one behind it.

On the hike to the chairs, I took in more of the office. The hardwood floors were randomly covered with rugs, some were Navajo, and looked old. There were bookshelves made of polished cherry, and a glass fronted gun case with a display of long guns and hand guns. Some were antiques, collector pieces. Two fish mounts, one a Grayling and the other a large German Brown, were placed on either side of a Pronghorn antelope high on the wall behind his desk. It smelled of lemon polish, wood and fine cigars. I liked his office.

"Please sit down, Mr. Tucker," he said, indicating the chair to the right.

As I sat down, I noticed a picture on one of the bookshelves behind his desk, he and a beautiful auburn-haired woman with a dazzling smile. He had his left arm around her shoulders, his right hand holding ski poles. The bright colors of their ski clothes burned through a light snow shower. I could see the fullness of their relationship embossed on their faces. They were in love and happy.

"That was my wife, Jean," he said, hoarsely.

I must have been staring at the picture. I continued to look at her. Her hair was like Margie's, auburn and thick, falling down around her shoulders. Her ski goggles propped up on top of her head, holding her hair off her face. The small laugh lines around her eyes and mouth were eye-catching, accenting her character as well as her beauty.

I slowly turned my head and looked at George Carr in the eyes. I didn't even notice that he'd taken the chair opposite me. We sat like that for a moment, looking into each other's eyes, each looking for ourselves in the other, I found 'the me' of years ago.

"It gets better with time," I said. "A lot of time. I know it's been three months and there are some people who think you should be getting better by now, that you should be getting on with your life. To hell with them. Three months is nothing. It's going to take years."

I could see him laboring.

"My name is George," he said.

"Tucker," I said.

He leaned over, put his elbows on his knees, looking at the floor. I could hear him breathing.

Through his teeth he said, "How did you get through it? Brad Spain told me about the car wreck that took your wife. I have never heard of anything so horrible."

He looked up at me, slowly straightened and sat back deep in the chair. "Brad said you probably wouldn't mind talking about your experience. He said you used to do it all the time when you did grief counseling. Would you mind talking to me? Or would it be too painful?"

This was one baggage car that was always open.

Over the years, between grief counseling, therapy and just plain venting, I came to identify grief as a sneaking, slithering monster that only attacked when I was least expecting it. It would never pounce when I was describing what had happened, even in a graphic way, but when I was alone, tired and vulnerable. I once watched a television commercial and saw a ballerina dancing in the morning mist and the tears just appeared. The naïve effort it took not to cry would break my jaws and the sob I wouldn't let out, burst in my heart. It took some difficult learning, to cry.

George Carr sat there, hands folded in his lap, waiting.

"Badly," I said.

He looked confused.

"You asked how I got through it," I said.

"Badly?" he asked.

"Oh yeah. I turned to booze and drugs. I couldn't eat. Every time I tried to eat, I'd cry. I cried in more than one restaurant."

"I know what you mean," he said, with a 'finally being understood' groan. "Why does that happen?"

"It takes a lot of energy not to fall apart," I said, nodding to his implicit sigh. "It also takes energy to digest food. Sometimes there's not enough to do both at the same time. But, then I found if I did a bump of cocaine and had a drink, I could stay on top of it."

He looked over at a closed cabinet and said, "Yeah, I've been drinking more than I used to."

"George," I said, "you do anything you have to do to make yourself feel better. Just know this, what you don't process now, you'll process later."

"What do you mean?" he asked.

"Grieving is a process and you *will* go through it. It helps to know what that process is, so when you experience it, you won't think you're crazy. I suggest if you haven't already started, get some grief counseling."

"Brad said you suffered from Post Traumatic Stress Disorder," he said uncertainly, like maybe he was overstepping a boundary.

"Suffered . . . that's an interesting word," I said. After thinking about it for a moment, I added, "Appropriate."

Riding the currents of a gentle breeze blown in from my past, I heard the faint sounds of a train clacking on the tracks.

I said, "I remember the first time I went grocery shopping by myself. It had to be about a month after her death. Grocery shopping was something we always did together. Pushing the cart was my job, and putting the groceries in it was hers. One moment I was pushing the cart, and then I was lost, not really knowing what to do. I needed her. The next moment I was in the car. I was trapped under her. I could taste and smell the blood. I was in the nightmare I couldn't wake up from. All the terror and fear was there, I was choking on her blood and spitting her brains out of my mouth. Then I could feel myself waking up, knowing she would be there by my side and everything would be okay. But when I woke up, I was on my back on the floor of Kroger, soaked in sweat with people standing over me. Then I had to deal with the fact it wasn't a dream, it was real. Then it started all over again, from ground zero. Any processing I'd done around grief was erased. That's Post Traumatic Stress. It took a few years for that to stop."

"Jesus," he muttered.

"Jesus?" I said. "At the time, I was certain he wasn't there."

Carr's perceptive stare said it all. "I've had my doubts about my faith in Jesus. . . and God too, since all this has happened. Jean was such a kind soul."

In his eyes, I could see the guilt boiling up like lava. His face had a pallid, beleaguered pallor.

"You said you've been drinking more lately." I said. "I think one now would be appropriate."

He stared at his watch. It was one so expensive, I didn't know what kind it was.

I said, "It's happy hour somewhere." I knew it was old and trite, but the timing felt right.

"Okay." he said. "Could I get you something?"

"Sure," I said. It was way too early for me to have alcohol, but when I looked into his eyes, I saw myself twenty years ago and knew what he needed now was a companion. Someone to share with, even if it was a drink at one o'clock in the afternoon.

Laughing, he said, "Fuckin' A."

Though he laughed, his demeanor changed. His lips thinned and his eyes took on a feral gleam. I saw a hard edge to this man. There was a steeliness that transcended the business type hardness I would expect from a self-made billionaire. Somewhere, at sometime, this man had rubbed against violence, up close and personal.

"I'm having a bourbon on the rocks. What can I get for you?" he asked.

"I'll have the same," I said.

He stood and walked over to the closed cabinet I had seen him eyeing earlier. After opening the cabinet and selecting a crystal decanter, he opened a silver ice bucket and tonged some ice cubes into two glasses next to the bucket.

"Just two fingers for me," I said.

"Before or after the rocks?" he asked.

"Before," I said. I found myself liking this man. I'm sure he could've had any one of many people come in and fix our drinks.

After bringing my glass, he sat down across from me and said, "Do you mind if we talk a little more . . . about . . . ," he looked at the ceiling searching for the words.

"What you're going through?" I said.

"Yeah . . . I suppose," he said, through another uneasy laugh.

This was a man unaccustomed to nervousness.

"What would you like to know?" I asked.

"Do you believe in God?"

I took a sip of my drink, it was Makers. "I don't believe in a white-haired holy man sitting on a throne up in heaven dishing out destiny and justice."

"What do you believe?"

"You may be asking the wrong person these questions," I said.

"No, I think I'm asking exactly the right person," he replied.

After thinking a moment I said, "I used to believe in God, before. But afterward, I figured He couldn't exist. Any God that would take a beautiful spirit like Margie and leave me here, wasn't any kind of God at all, so there must not be a God. Never-the-less I cursed Him. So, if he didn't exist, who was I cursing? In retrospect, I see that God loved me. He had to, because I have cursed Him so profoundly that if He didn't love me, I would surely be ashes in hell by now."

His gaze was intense. "So you *do* believe in God," he said.

"God is incomprehensible. So I believe God is the law of nature. Physics. That for every action, there is an equal and opposite, if you will, balancing reaction. The laws of the Universe. Space and time. God is nature and nature is God."

He took a sip of his drink and said, "Space and time? What's that about?"

"Time is so everything doesn't happen all at once, and space is so it all doesn't happen to me."

He smiled and said, "Sounds like you've read a lot."

"About eleven years after she was killed, I had a need to comprehend, spiritually, what had happened to me, to make some sense of it. George, you need to understand that this is happening to you, not to your wife. The anger you sometimes feel towards her is due to the fact that you have been left here to deal with this crap. She's in a better place. You're the one left behind to feel the pain and loneliness of grief and abandonment."

He said, "I've never told this to anyone. But, sometimes I do feel angry at her. I do feel abandoned. Then I feel like an asshole for thinking like that."

"You should feel abandoned, you were. What's good to work on, is fault. There is none. It just is. That includes yourself too. It's not your fault. It's just one of God's little Ism's."

"You seem to have come to terms with God."

"George, you don't come to terms with God. God, whatever you deem that to be, is a constant. It's us that fluctuates, you know, that free will thing."

I could see that he was physically hurting. I knew what that felt like.

"Listen, George, as I said, I've read a great deal, trying to understand what this is all about. I could give you a list of books to read, but I could also just tell you what I've gleaned from the studying I've done."

Leaning forward, he said, "Tell me."

I'm not a homiletic person, so I had to take a big breath and a likewise drink before saying, "Okay, here goes. There was once, only one. Just one, one entity, one intelligence. For millions of years *The One* contemplated his existence, and it came clear to Him what he must do. He divided himself into trillions upon trillions of pieces. These pieces became the universe and all it encompasses. All the planets, all the life forms, every atom . . .everything. The trick was, He could stay in contact with every atom on every level. As far as our level goes, the human level, we contracted to forget Him. Forget Him in order to find Him again. And the only way to find Him was through dysfunction."

"Dysfunction?" he asked, looking completely lost. "I don't understand."

"The best way I could explain it is, 'everything that has nothing to do with love and creation is dysfunctional'."

After thinking about it, he said, "If that's true, we all live dysfunctional lives."

"There you go," I said, raising my glass.

"How do we find God through dysfunction?" he asked.

"By living dysfunctional lives, we find out what doesn't work. Once we eliminate what doesn't work, what's left?" I asked.

"What does work," he said.

"And then we're closer to God," I said.

"How can we do that in one lifetime?" he asked.

"You can't."

"So now you're telling me you believe in reincarnation?"

"Yes."

"How can you believe in God and reincarnation at the same time?"

"If you think of God the way I do, it's the only way to believe."

"Do you believe in Jesus?" he asked.

"Yes, I do. I believe Jesus was a man, a remarkable man, who walked the earth and showed us how to be what we are capable of being."

"I think what I meant to say is, do you believe he was the son of God?"

"Yes, but so are you or I."

"How can you say that?"

"George, I'm not much on sermons. Like I said, this is information I've gleaned, information that for me was heartfelt, felt to be true. What one person feels to be true may not be the same for another. What's important to me and should be important to you, is what rings true for you."

He put his drink down and said, "I know this may not be what you thought you were coming here for, and you're right. But, I'm interested in how you came to terms with your experience. I'm having a hard time. I still can't believe she's gone. I've never been a very religious person. I tried the church scene a few times, and it just didn't fit for me."

"I had the same experience," I said, taking another micro sip of my drink. "Just remember this. I believe everything is in Divine Order. I don't have to understand it. Because I can't see the big picture, it's just too big. But somewhere down the road, some good will come from this."

He looked hard at me and said, "Are you saying that what happened to you and to me was Divine? That some good will come of it?"

"Yes," I said. "George, I like who I am today. I may not be as happy or feel as complete as I once did, but, I believe I'm a better person now than I was then. I feel I have more substance, more soul substance, if you will. I live a less dysfunctional life now. Don't get me wrong, I'm not telling you I'm some kind of enlightened being, and I've done all the growing this time around that I need to do."

I looked up through the ceiling and said, "You heard me up there, I hope I've had all my painful lessons, but if I haven't, give me the strength."

I raised my glass to the universe, took a vigorous swig, then rapped my knuckles three times on his desk.

George Carr finished his drink, walked over to the liquor cabinet and made himself another. He gestured questionably towards me and I shook my head, no.

As he walked back to his chair, the door to the office opened, and Rachael stuck her head in the door.

"Can I get you two something to eat?" she asked, as I stood.

It was as if she knew we were drinking in the early afternoon and may require food.

George looked a bit like a little boy caught drinking out of the milk carton.

"Not right now, Rachael, but thank you. I'll let you know."

"I'll check on you a little later," she said, ignoring his response.

As she closed the door, I stared at the space she had occupied.

"I like her," I said.

"It's hard not to. My wife found her and she's been with us ever since. She's very bright."

Almost blinding.

"I'd like to hear about it sometime," I said.

"Well, Rachael will be the one to tell you, not me," he said, knowing I meant her scars.

"I wouldn't want it any other way."

"Look . . . Tucker, you said you believe in reincarnation. Why?"

I turned around, faced him and leaning against the edge of the desk, stirred the whiskey and melted ice with my finger. I could feel the alcohol warming my blood, relaxing me and warning me at the same time.

"George, I'll tell you this one thing more. My spiritual philosophy is mine, a mish-mosh of Christianity, Judaism, Buddhism, Native American, and New Age beliefs. It's what works for me. It's what makes me accountable for my actions. You have to get your own. I am not, nor do I want to be a preacher, teacher, guru or any facsimile thereof. Nor do I want to be rude."

His face tightened, "I don't understand . . ."

"They're all roads leading to the same house."

He looked more contemplative than skeptical.

"Don't get me wrong, George, I have a long way to go. My road is my road, and I'll travel it quietly. After all, I've killed people."

He nodded with understanding.

'Tucker's Spiritual Philosophy 101', was over.

Chapter 23

He walked around behind his desk and sat down, facing me as I sat. The male bonding was over, and at last we were to talk business. He reached over, opened a large humidor, pulled out a cigar and said, "Would you like one? They're Cuban."

"No thanks, I'm doing my best not to take on any new vices, especially ones I can't afford."

"Do you mind if I have one?" he asked.

I knew if I said yes, he'd put it back. "No, I like the aroma of a good cigar. That's one reason I've avoided smoking them."

After the clipping and lighting ritual was over, he said, "Frank, would you please come in now?"

A few seconds later, the bookshelf behind and to the left of him opened and a man walked in. The shelf closed by itself, leaving the man standing to Carr's left.

"Mr. Mysterious," I said to myself.

I found myself standing, my right hand hooked into the edge of my coat, ready to pull it back and out of the way. I didn't really feel threatened, it was more of a reflex. I must have stood when the shelf started opening. Some surprises put me on auto-pilot.

"I told you he's good," said Mr. Mysterious.

"Sit down, Tucker, please," Carr said, with an amused expression.

I remained standing and said, "I've got one of those."

They exchanged queried glances.

"The secret bookshelf, only mine holds tools and stuff."

"This is Frank LeCompte, Tucker. Frank is my personal bodyguard and head of my small security force."

"Define small," I said.

Carr looked at Frank LeCompte and nodded.

"Six, not counting me," LeCompte said.

Standing there, LeCompte was even more menacing than when I'd seen him sitting, supposedly reading a paper, at Gun World. In a physical confrontation, I'd want this man on my side

"Oh, I believe I'd have to count you," I said. "Maybe twice."

"I saw you shoot it out with Spain last night," he said, with just a hint of Cajun.

"It was impressive," he added.

"What were you doing there, other than reading a newspaper?" I asked.

"Observing you for one thing," he replied.

I didn't remember seeing him once we had gone down into the basement. I wondered from what vantage point he observed.

Spain.

"And the other thing?" I asked.

"I had to get my gun back," he said, and pulled his coat back and exposed the Colt 1911 Spain had used last night.

I'd never seen this man before. I would have remembered him. But I had definitely worked on that gun.

As I was trying to figure it out, he smiled and said, "I've had this old Colt for a long time. It was hard to let it go for a month, while Spain practiced with it. Not that it did him much good."

"I don't remember you," I said.

"That's because we've never met," he said, with a smile that was fast morphing into a snicker.

"Okay. I give up," I said.

He laughed and said, "Jerry Melchior."

I nodded.

Jerry was a private gun dealer that periodically brought me 1911's to accurasize. He would either buy a few and have me work on them, then sell them for a profit, or take one in from someone that didn't know I existed and charge them approximately thirty percent more than I did to do the work. What I did wasn't cheap, so I knew that LeCompte was paid well for his services.

Frank LeCompte's features turned inquisitive when he said, "Tucker, what do you do to these guns? I used to carry a 9mm Sig Suaer. Then I shot one of Jerry's .45's that you'd worked on. Which, by the way, I didn't find out about 'til later. I couldn't believe it. I carried this Colt in the service and loved the caliber, but it used to kick like hell and was only accurate at short ranges. Now it's smooth as silk, fast as a cottonmouth, and as accurate as a little .22. I don't like carrying anything else."

His Cajun accent was more pronounced when he said, cottonmouth. Also, not many people even refer to that snake.

Jerry Melchior always got the works, the deluxe Tucker-ized version as it were.

I looked up at the Pronghorn antelope, took a breath and in my best gunsmithing vernacular, said, "I lowered the ejection port by 3/16 of an inch and radiased the port's back. What that does is allow you to shoot faster and also it doesn't ding up your brass, which will help stop jamming. Then I radiused the entire slide and barrel bushing, so you can get quick entry in and get it out of your holster without drag. I took a 25 degree radius off the back of the slide and also around the metal on the frame where the custom Pachmeyer Walnut Grips with finger groves go, to better fit your hand. I put on an extended grip safety, a combat hammer and an extended slide release. Took your trigger pull down to a plus or minus 31/2 lbs. I put on an extended magazine well to fit the new eight shot magazine. I added low profile front and adjustable rear sights, so when you're racking the slide back, you won't tear up your hand. I put in a brand new recoil system with a Smart Spring, along with a recoil buffer pad. I ramped and polished the injection port for a faster feed into the barrel. I buffed the rails on the frame, as well as the slide for a much smoother movement. And I added a beaver tail back-strap, with a speed well for faster magazine loading for combat situations. And I had it hard chromed, so you won't have to worry as much about rust."

He looked over at George Carr and blinked a few times. He looked back at me and said, "Sure you didn't forget something?"

"No. You're from Louisiana," I said.

"That's right. I thought I'd lost my coon ass accent," he said, smiling with white, even teeth.

"Almost. Most people probably wouldn't have picked it up," I said, still standing. He looked down at my right hand, then back up at my face.

"Levanda told me to say hi and 'Get Fucked'," he said, the smile turning into a grin.

That sat me down . . . hard. Bill Levanda, my best friend all the way through junior high and high school. Every year in high school the Navy would send some people, Navy SEALS, to try and recruit from the schools athletic department. They just wanted to talk to the football players and the track team. Later we found out why. It was because of the humidity. It was about the same as in Vietnam. They figured any kid who could play football or run track in that kind of heat would make a good SEAL. It was a very tempting presentation they put on. Every year one or two of the seniors that didn't get scholarships to college would go off after graduating and try and make the SEAL teams. Every once in a while, we'd hear someone made it. It always surprised me, they were never the best players or the toughest guys. That's why they didn't get scholarships.

Levanda was offered a football and a baseball scholarship to Louisiana Tech. He decided to take the baseball. After his first year, his girlfriend since junior high dumped him. He came home on summer break and over some beers told me he was going to SEAL Training Camp in a few days. That was the last time I saw him. That was a little over 30 years ago. I would hear rumors from some of the other guys that had made the teams about Levanda, but no one really knew what happened to him after the war. I knew he did three tours, but the last I'd heard, he hadn't come back from his last mission. Now, here was this man standing in front of me, I could see military written all over him, telling me my old best friend says hi and to 'Get Fucked'. Levanda was the only person I knew back then that would or could say that to me. I once told him not to be afraid of my temper. I promised him I'd never hurt him, he was my best friend. So any time I got out of line, he would tell me to Get Fucked.

"You were on the Teams," I said. "And Levanda's still alive?"

"Yes, and yes."

I felt myself getting angry. My best friend, that I thought was dead, was alive. And he was not there for me when I needed him. Bill, his girlfriend Brenda, Margie and me were inseparable. I still remember how Margie cried when we heard he didn't come back from his last mission. I'd always harbored the belief he'd survived and was still out there somewhere. I knew he would be an efficient killer. He was a math major and was going to be an accountant or CPA. He was always so calm, nothing ever got him riled, not even me. He once stuck a fork in my hand because I tried to take a roll off his lunch plate at the training table. It used to drive me crazy the way he would eat so damn slow and just one thing a time. He would eat all the roast beef, then all the potatoes and so on.

The last thing he always ate was his roll. One day I asked him if he was going to eat it, and he said, "Yes, I'm going to eat it, and if you try and take it off my plate, I'll stick this fork in your fuckin' hand."

Well, that surprised everybody at the table. Everyone knew there wasn't anyone, including most of the teachers at the school, who could take me. I didn't mind people thinking that either, it kept me out of a lot of fights. So, of course, I called his bluff. I reached for his roll slowly, to show how 'not afraid' I was. He stuck his fork in the back of my right hand. I mean stuck it, straight up, quivering like an arrow in a tree. Everyone at our end of the training table scrambled out of the way, and Coach Booth was down there in a flash to see what was going on. I'm sure it looked like a fight was about to break out. By the time the coach got to the scene, I'd already pulled the fork out and handed it back to Levanda, which he continued to eat with.

I never got mad. He told me he was going to do it. I never again, doubted his word.

I looked down to find myself rubbing the back of my right hand with a finger, across four barely visible, little white dots,.

"The fork?" LeCompte asked.

"He told you about that?"

LeCompte walked around and sat in the chair across from me that earlier had been occupied by Carr. Now we were both sitting down. I was starting to feel a surrealness to all of this.

He said, "I was standing next to Levanda the very first day of SEAL Training. This bad ass Master Chief instructor comes up, the first thing he said was, 'Any of you pussy assed numbnuts that thinks he can take me, step up here and let's dance'. I heard this guy next to me whisper under his breath, 'I wish Tucker was here.' It was Levanda, and it was just the first of many times he said that."

"He was my best friend. I don't know how to feel about him still being alive. I've missed him over the years."

"Well, he missed you too. I could tell by the way he talked about you. You were a big influence on his life."

"How and when did you talk to him?" I asked.

Frank LeCompte looked at his boss, who had been sitting quietly behind his desk, smoking and sipping at his drink. Carr nodded to him.

"When we started investigating you and I found out you were from Alexandria, I had to make sure you were the same Tucker he used to talk about. I mean, talk about your coincidences. I pulled some strings and called in some favors and found out where and who he's with these days."

Even through the surprised anger of finding out I'd been investigated, I was getting ready to ask him about my old friend.

He put his palm up toward me and said, "Don't ask, I can't tell you. He was one of the guys that couldn't or didn't want to come back."

"Come back? You mean he's still over in Southeast Asia?" I asked. He could at least tell me that. Southeast Asia is a big place.

"No, I don't mean that. I meant come back to a civilian or I should say a civilized life." His hand gesture encompassed the room and his eyes looked out the window, suggesting all that was out there.

I sat there, thinking about my best friend. He was the last one I ever had.

LeCompte said, "I talked to him on the phone, and it was scrambled so many times I didn't know where he was. He did tell me when he found out about your wife, it was hard on him. After everything Levanda has been through, for him to say that, he must have really liked her. He also told me to tell you, don't be surprised if one day he slips up behind you and slices your throat with a rubber knife, whatever the hell that means. He said you'd understand."

Now, that opened a baggage car.

Book Two

"BAGGAGE CARS"

Chapter 24

After being stabbed in the hand in a bar when I was fifteen, I went to see Mack. Mack worked as a car mechanic for a friend's father who owned Val Eskew's Garage and Towing Service.

Mack was a veteran of the Korean War and an infamous local bad-assed knife fighter and was covered with scars to prove it. I wanted to learn how to use a knife, so I wouldn't ever be caught like I was in the bar that night. He decided to teach me and had me go out and buy some toy rubber knives and some pool cue chalk.

We rubbed the chalk over the edges of the knives. We cut off the points and rubbed chalk on the small blunt ends as well. That way, after Mack and I fought with the rubber knives, we could tell every place we cut or stabbed each other. It would leave a green chalk line for every slice and a green chalk spot for every stab.

I remembered that first lesson. I had on a white t-shirt. Mack put one of the chalked up rubber knives in the back pocket of his grease stained blue coveralls and gave me the other one and said, 'Come and get me'.

I went after him. I was fast with my hands and knew it. I went in slashing and stabbing, never hitting anything. He grabbed me, and we wrestled around the garage. We had a small audience, my friend Val Jr., and some of the black guys that worked there. For a minute we danced around, while he held onto my knife hand just below the wrist. He pushed me away and said, "Stop, look at yourself."

I had little green stripes all over my white t-shirt, with five or six little green spots over my chest. I never saw Mack pull the knife.

Mack looked at me, "You're one dead fucker, Tucker." His poetry bringing on snickers and laughs from the audience.

"Now, the first thing to learn about knife fighting is you're going to get cut," he said, showing me his left forearm that was covered with scars. "But, if you can decide where and when, it might make the difference of walking away or being carried away."

His poetry sucked, but after two years of dancing with Mack, I finally turned the tables.

I used to practice on Levanda. I sometimes sneaked up on him from behind and cut his throat, leaving a green line on the left side of his neck. It used to piss him off that he could never hear me. Or, if I went at him head-on, that he couldn't get away from the rubber knife.

Chapter 25

Nashville, Carr's Mansion, 1:45 PM

"Yeah, I understand," I said, looking out the window behind LeCompte.

"I think I can guess," he said. "Levanda said you were something else with a knife. Even after SEAL Training, he said he would shoot you before going up against you with a knife."

"Well, if he said he'd shoot me, I'm sure he would."

"He also said you would have some kind of low profile knife in your right front pants pocket."

I reached down with my right hand and pulled out my Ken Onion designed Kershaw spring assist, flicked open the 4-1/2 inch blade, closed it and put it back. It only took a couple of seconds.

"I don't like knives," I said. "I prefer something that barks here and bites over there." I pointed across the room.

Frank LeCompte looked over at Carr. Neither had anything to say.

Carr reached down to the floor to the left of his chair and pulled up a stack of file folders and papers over a foot high, He set them down on the desk in front of him and said, "I had you investigated. I probably know more about you than you do."

I looked at Carr and said, "You had me investigated? What did you find out?" I asked. I didn't try to hide the irritation in my voice. Just when I was liking the guy and thought maybe I had a new friend. I didn't know whether to be pissed off or flattered.

As I sat there trying to decide, he said, "For one thing, I found out you were an outlaw."

"No," I said, "I have always been a Tucker. I had a third grade teacher named Outlaw. She was the meanest old bitch I've ever known. I still have nightmares about her."

Frank LeCompte laughed out loud and said, "I told you. Brad said he was a funny guy."

Carr was amused, but wouldn't waver, "You were a big marijuana dealer in the seventies. And you never got caught, even after the cops knew who you were and were gunning for you."

Having my secret past so accurately thrown in my face was surprising and unsettling, like suddenly having my cloths jerked off in public, and I'm a shy guy. I glanced at the stack of files in front of Carr, then over to LeCompte, then back to Carr. I have found it appropriate, when I find myself at a loss for words, not to go looking for them.

After a moment of silence, somehow giving my past an unwarranted respect, Carr said, "I have statements here. One being from a retired Shreveport Police Officer by the name of Gray. Gray states, in his words, 'you were one of his partners in one of the biggest and badist marijuana dealing crews in northern Louisiana."

One of my continuous torments has been to fugue particular felonious episodes during a time of my life when there are cherished memories of the same period that can rankle in my heart the love of my life that has been forever lost to the tactile textures.

My personal prevarication of those episodes was that I was caught up in the revolutionary Zeitgeist of the seventies.

"Robby always did think big," I said, feeling the first shimmerings of the locomotive that pulls the baggage of my past, coming full blast.

Clickity-clack . . . clickity-clack . . . clickity-clack . . .

clickity-clack!

Chapter 26

"I see by your application that you prefer to be called Tucker, and I can see why. What were your parents thinking?" asked Barry Woods.

"Trying to preserve a family name is what I was told," I said.

Barry Woods stood up behind his secretarial type desk that was totally misplaced in his wood-paneled office, adorned with various golfing and ping pong trophies.

"I usually hold two to three personal interviews with applicants. My business is very important to me," he said.

I could tell Barry Woods took himself very seriously. He was about five- eleven and weighed around 200 pounds. Take away the beer gut that hung below a yawning chest, take away the liquor lines that creased his face under blue eyes and a blond crew cut, there was an athlete. I took him to be about 35.

"Yes Sir," I said. Being an Air Force brat with an officer for a father, yes sir's came out involuntarily.

"I've checked your references and made a few personal calls to some cops I know in Alexandria."

"Yes Sir," I said. I needed this job, whatever it was. I'd filled out the application following a tip from a friend who had a friend that was a head hunter for an employment service. I had no idea what I'd applied for.

Sawbuck's Sporting Goods was the largest sporting goods store in Shreveport. It sold everything to everybody. From uniforms to the majority of the schools to every kind of ball, gun, shoe, racket, club, trophy, and the latest in sports fashions. The merchandise packed the entire three floors.

"You put down that you had experience with guns and listed some competitions you had won. I don't know much about guns, as you can see," he said, gesturing with a wave of his arm that encompassed the many trophies around the office.

He not only took himself seriously, he took himself as being someone important. He probably was, he owned the biggest sporting goods store in Shreveport.

"So, I made a few calls and talked to some friends of mine in the Alexandria Police Department," he reiterated. Not only was he important, he had connections.

"Yes sir."

"I was told you were very good with a handgun."

"Uh-huh," I said, thinking I would sound more intelligent if I varied my replies.

He looked at me. My responses might have confused him.

"I was looking for someone to help me in my golf department. I used to do it all, but my time is limited these days. What do you know about golf?"

What I knew about golf wouldn't fill a thimble.

There goes my chances for a job. But, I wasn't going to say I knew nothing.

"Looks to me to be about the same as pool. Just a bigger table and you hold the cue different."

He stared at me with no expression for about five seconds.

"Damn," he yelled, kicking the side of his desk. "I never thought of it like that. Okay, what do you know about pool, then?"

"Enough to know when to walk away with money in my pocket,"

"Now you're talkin'. I like a man who knows when to walk away with money in his pocket."

I didn't know it at the time, but I had just plucked the heart strings of a gambler.

"Well, Tucker, here's what I'm willing to do. I can move the manager of the gun department to the golf department, he's been overseeing both for the past few weeks anyway, and you can be my new manager of the gun department. How would you like that?"

I didn't know much, but I did know I wasn't applying for a manager's position. I was told what the wage was, and it definitely wasn't manager pay. I didn't say anything.

There was a stony quiet between us. But, since I was the one with the least information, it was easier to keep quiet.

"I'll pay you $300 a week, and you can charge whatever you want at cost and take as long as you like to pay it back. I'll never take it out of your check."

To me it sounded like, "I'll pay you a million dollars a day and you can have anything you want in the store."

I didn't want to appear over-eager, so I just sat there reading trophy engravings, while I thought about how to say yes without genuflecting. Managing the gun department, wow, Sawbuck's had a very large gun department.

"Okay, $350 a week and you start tomorrow," he said, blowing importantly between his lips, while rocking back and forth on his feet with his hands in his pockets.

Before I could answer, he said, "Your expertise and knowledge of guns has been called to my attention through my contacts, but I want you to know that's not the only reason I want you to work for me. I wouldn't normally hire a 21 year old to hold such a position, but, we work a lot with the Shreveport Police Department. We sell them everything from badges and night sticks, to guns and ammo. I've been told you know how cops think and what they want. I also saw you play in the 1969 Sugar Bowl. In fact, I won some money because they put you in."

Aha...Now we get to the meat of the matter.

I remembered how I got to dress out for the Sugar Bowl due to an illness that overcame the third string varsity linebacker. They pulled me up from the junior varsity to fill the bench. Due to freak injuries that overcame the fullbacks, I was the only one who had any idea of the plays. In fact, I knew so little, all they could do was give me the ball up the two, four, and six holes. It was just one of those fluke occurrences, it all just clicked, came together, jelled, all of that. I started popping the holes the line made for me, that built their confidence; the holes got bigger, and that built my confidence. I've had a while to think about that night.

"It was my first and last varsity appearance on the LSU gridiron," I said.

"You were just a freshman, right?"

"That's right."

"You were listed as a linebacker. Why'd they put you in at fullback?"

"I played both ways all the way through junior high and high school, fullback and linebacker. I didn't know you could just play half a game until I got to LSU. I got my scholarship to play linebacker."

"Why'd you quit playing after that year?" he said. "You were great. You came in from nowhere and they just kept feeding you the ball and you just kept on knocking off three to seven yards a carry, all the way down the field. You set up one touch-down and two field goals in the last quarter."

Wow! The glory days!

Margie and I were the first couple in the new married dorms with a child. She worked, I worked, and playing football and going to school at the same time didn't. I dropped out of school and we moved back to Alec. She got a job as an insurance underwriter, and then a year later she got a transfer with her company to Shreveport, along with a raise.

I said, "My wife's job brought us here."

It was hard for him. Evidently he wanted more.

After a few blinks, he shuffled some papers on his desk, picked up what appeared to be my application and after looking at it, said, "I see you worked for Southern Bell for a year, then you sold insurance for a while. With the same company your wife works for?"

"That's right."

"Why did you stop doing that?"

After thinking about it for a couple of seconds I said, "It seemed like a magic show to me. Selling something you can't see. You can't put your hands on it. Every time I made a sale, I felt like they just didn't know which shell the pea was under."

If he was asking me why I quit working for the telephone company, that answer wouldn't work.

"Be here at seven in the morning," he said.

Unbeknownst to me at the time, that was my introduction to a new career... crime.

Chapter 27

<hr>

About a week later

It was 2:30 in the afternoon when he swaggered in, in full uniform, night stick and all. Five-feet-seven inches of him, covered in leather and steel. That's how it looked. He couldn't have weighed over a 145 pounds. His revolver and all the police regalia took up most of the space he occupied.

He walked up to the counter as I was putting a freshly polished handgun into the display case.

He sauntered up to me like he was 10 foot tall and bullet-proof, stuck out his hand and said, "My name is Robby Gray. I saw you shoot at the Alexandria P. D. range a couple of years ago. You were shooting western quick draw. It was fuckin' unreal."

He had cold, clear slate-colored eyes, that didn't go with his youngster's grin. He looked about 13 and exuded something akin to Irish charm. Everything but his eyes wanted to make you laugh, so I didn't feel too bad about the smile on my face.

"I'm Tucker," I said. "Good to meet you."

"Shit, I know who you are. I saw you draw and shoot six rounds out of single action revolver faster than I could shoot six times with a semi-auto, fuck the drawing. We have a mutual friend who'd been telling me about this kid who could outshoot anyone on the force, so I had to go see for myself."

Two years ago I was 19 and had been married for two years, had a 2 year-old daughter, and had been shooting guns for more than half my life, and shooting very seriously for six years. I didn't feel like a *kid*.

But...his charm and enthusiasm was irresistible.

"I hope I didn't disappoint you," I said, closing the display case.

He turned away and started roaming around, looking at the guns and their new display. I had rearranged quite a bit in the week I had been manager.

"I've been coming here for years. I didn't know Sawbuck's had this many guns. Where did they all come from?" he asked.

"They've always been here. It's just a little trick I do with mirrors and crushed pecan shells," I said seriously.

He looked around carefully and said, "I don't see any mirrors."

"That's because of the pecan shells," I said, proudly.

He looked around and when his head was turned away, I saw by the small shrug of his shoulders, the sudden tilt of his head and a jerk that ended in stillness, he just got it.

He turned slowly around and looked me straight in the eye and said, "You're a funny fucker, aren't you?"

He wasn't smiling. I could see this little guy was dangerous.

In a blink he was once again, all smiles and charm. He laughed and said, "I like that. It's hard to get me. But, you got me."

"I have my moments," I said, crossing my arms over my chest. "They're far and few between, so I hope you won't mind if I savor this."

We both started laughing and were instant friends. Robby would come by three or four times a week while on duty. We started shooting down at the Shreveport P. D. range and within a couple of months, I'd met almost the whole department.

I started having special sales for just the Police Department. I did some exhibition shooting for the Department to help raise funds for charity. I took my beautiful wife to the Policemen's Ball and hung out with everyone from the top brass to the man walking a beat. Robby Gray and I double-dated with our wives, and everything was good.

Then one day Robby was in the store telling me how his partner had shined a light into a car and caught a couple of teenagers going at it. They weren't fighting. They were doing that other thing.

"Man, it was embarrassing," he said. "I mean the girl was buck naked, and the guy was about half way there. I had to shine the light around to make sure there wasn't a gun around, and she started crying and all. I told them to get dressed and get out of the car. We don't have to do that, ya know, we can just make them get out naked, but man I just couldn't do that, she was crying and all."

I wondered what 'and all' meant. I think it meant 'real hard'.

"Well, anyway," he continued, "we did a routine search, and we came up with a lid of grass." His face looked like Christmas. "You ever smoked any weed, Tucker?" His posture suggested confidentiality.

About a year before, I had tried grass for the first time. While my other friends had gone with the long hair and beads, smoking pot and hash, I had stayed with the blue jeans and cowboy boots. When one of my friends showed up back home during spring break and offered me a joint, I declined and started asking intelligent questions like, 'why are you smoking that shit? Why do you think they call it dope?'

His response was to use my own words the day I got him to drink his first beer, "Don't knock it unless you've tried it, Tucker."

I looked at Robby and said, "Yeah, I've smoked a little."

The truth was, from the first time I tried it, I liked it. My wife liked how it mellowed me out. Calmed my temper and 'those Tucker ways,' as she put it.

Pot left no hangover, and the only down side was the munchies. For the past year I had been getting my pot from Wayne, a high school friend who now lived in Baton Rouge.

During my senior year, Wayne had transferred from Los Angeles. In the *cool* department, he was a few years ahead of us hicks in Alexandria. He had long hair, he was a hippy and I don't like bullies. All of that translates into I came upon Wayne and Richard Pollard in the hall in front of the lockers. Wayne's locker was close to mine. Richard was just starting to push long-haired, skinny, hippy Wayne around when I arrived. Richard Pollard was a big tall strong mean, bully. For two years, we'd managed not to get into it. We didn't move in the same circles, and he seemed to usually stay clear of me.

I 'd already met Wayne. After all, he was from California and cool. I was a big athlete and tough and handsome and cool, so we had been introduced by someone who knew how to get the cool people together. He seemed like a nice guy, but we didn't have much in common; until that day. We had Richard Pollard in common. Wayne was being bullied and I didn't like bullies.

When I came up on them, I told Richard not to push Wayne again. He sneered at me and pushed Wayne again. I tore down his meat house, right there in the hallway of Bolton High School.

Within a few seconds he was on the floor leaking red fluid from three or four different locations on his face, and having a hard time breathing. After ascertaining he wasn't going to die, I turned to Wayne to make sure he was all right. His look was one of fear and wonder. We never really "hung out," but we became friends. No one ever pushed him again, at least no one who knew me.

Years later when I wanted to buy some pot for myself, I was told Wayne was a big dealer down in Baton Rouge. I got in touch with him by phone and let him know what I wanted. He was astonished, me being such a straight guy and all, but said he would take care of me. He used code words, like herb and rope. He asked for my number and said he would be in touch.

A few days later I got a call from a friend of Wayne's, Cutter. He sounded black. Cutter said he was in town and had something for me, from Wayne. I met him in the back parking lot of a Burger Chef. I thought I was going to maybe have to buy a whole lid or maybe two. I didn't know what to expect. So I took $50 with me just in case he had three or four lids. Lids were going for $10 in those days.

He gave me a brown paper bag that felt awfully heavy and disappeared. There was no talk of money. I opened the bag, and there was a package about twice the size of a cigar box wrapped in red paper and covered in plastic wrap. I took it home and opened it. It was a kilo of grass. I later found out it was called Columbian Gold. It was very good.

After telling Robby I smoked a little, he nodded his head knowingly and said, "I knew you were cool. You're just too mellow for someone who has a reputation as a bad ass."

"What're you talking about?" I asked.

"Look, Tucker, I've been checking you out since the day we met. I know all about your high school days and some of the shit you were into after school down in Baton Rouge. You've got a reputation of being very quick with your temper and your fists."

"I don't know what you're talking about."

After furtively looking to make sure there was no one around, he said, "Yeah, right. Well, look, what you say you and I blow a joint after work tonight?"

I gave him a hard look and said, "You're not a cop, are you? You have to tell me if you are, it's the law. If you lie, it's entrapment."

He looked back just as hard and sincerely said, "A cop? Not me. I hate cops."

"Okay, I'll see you after work."

He picked me up in his squad car. I couldn't believe it. We drove down an isolated road on the edge of the city. He called in a code that he was going to eat. We sat in his squad car and smoked pot and listened to the radio dispatch.

When he said after work, I thought he meant his, too. He was still on duty, and there we were, getting stoned. It was freaky to say the least. We ended up laughing our asses off. And unknowingly, I was being groomed to ride shotgun, literally, for future drug runs to Mexico that were financed by the Commissioner of Public Safety.

Chapter 28

I looked first at Carr, then over to LeCompte, and said, "I take it Robby Gray was in a loquacious frame of mind. That surprises me."

Carr looked at LeCompte and shrugged.

LeCompte said, "He wasn't at first. He seemed reluctant to talk about you at all. He wouldn't talk to the first man we sent down to interview him. So I went down to Shreveport. He's got a house out on Lake Bistineau. It's not a big house, but it's very well built and has the finest furnishings money can buy. No way he could afford that kind of place on a cop's retirement. I talked with him for awhile. When I told him about you snuffing those two hitters, he laughed and said something like 'those stupid fucks didn't know who they were fuckin' with.' He asked me why I wanted to know about you. I told him the truth. We were thinking about hiring you for a job and were just checking you out. He asked what kind of job, and I told him it was none of his business. He wanted to know who was hiring you and was surprised when I told him. He left the room and came back in about ten minutes. I figured he was checking out Mr. Carr. After that I didn't even have to offer him money, as I was instructed to do if need be. Before he started talking, he informed me that the statute of limitations was over and the Commissioner of Public Safety, a man named Darvoyce, had killed himself while awaiting trial. Gray told me he was retired, and nobody could touch his ass. He seemed quite proud of himself."

"Now, that sounds like Robby," I said. "Don't let his charm fool you, he's tough. And he's not afraid of anything."

LeCompte got up and walked over to George's desk and opened the humidor and got himself a cigar. It helped me define their relationship.

After lighting it and blowing a cloud of smoke towards the ceiling, he said, "Yeah, well, after talking to him, I realized his reluctance to talk at first, had nothing to do with him being afraid of the law. But, he was afraid of something, he was afraid of you. It was like he didn't want to tell me anything that might get you to come looking for him."

"I try my best not to think about him or those days," I said.

After another pull on his cigar he said, "He told me how he set you up as a small time dealer to make sure you were 'cool,' as he put it. And something about testing your mettle, by asking you to go with him while he had a chat with a guy."

As I thought of the implausible justified mendacities we adopted to cloud our lives, I heard a train coming down the tracks.

Chapter 29

Dealing pot in 1972 was like bootlegging whiskey during prohibition. At least that's what we used to tell ourselves. Our main angst was it would be legalized before we could make our big score.

Everybody smoked pot, I mean everybody, or so it seemed. It was as if the people who didn't smoke it, were the minority. Selling pot was cool, the money was good, and besides, I was a small-time dealer.

That's what I was that summer night when Margie and I were at the dining room table in an apartment we were renting in an upscale complex in south Shreveport. She was wearing jeans and a long-sleeved denim shirt with the tails tied in a half-hitch that showed her flat midriff. We were listening to John Denver singing 'Rocky Mountain High' and bagging up lids from a kilo of Columbian gold spread out over newspaper.

Suddenly, through the curtains appeared the flashing lights of a cop car, sending their red, white and blue illumination dancing across the walls of the dining room.

Margie looked up at me over a triple beam scale. Her blue eyes like large planets in a white sky. Her face was floured with fear. My heart leaped, and I jumped up with my .45 in my hand.

"Don't, Tuck, please," she said quietly. She always spoke quietly to me when it was important or when she really meant it. It always caught my attention.

I walked over to the couch, stuck the pistol under a cushion and said, "Don't panic, it may not be about us."

I looked at the dining room table that was in plain sight if someone came in the front door. There wasn't any sense in trying to clean it up. If the cops were coming for us we were busted, definitely.

Margie got up and went into the kitchen and came out with a large table-cloth, I could tell she was going to try to cover it up.

I smiled at her, what a trooper. It wouldn't do any good. The room reeked with the hash-like aroma of quality marijuana.

There was a heavy pounding on the door, followed by a deep voice, "Open up, Police!"

Well, so much for it not being for us. I went over to the peep hole and looked through. All I could see was the back of a cop's head, his patrol hat, and part of a shoulder.

My stomach turned and I wanted to puke; the blood was rushing in my ears. I thought, 'This had to be what it felt like just before you died'. My life was almost flashing before my eyes. I looked back at Margie and said, "Sorry, Babe, we're busted."

I opened the door.

Robby Gray was standing there with a leering grin on his face.

"You son-of-a-bitch . . . you son-of-a-bitch!" I yelled, jerking him into the room and slamming the door.

"I got you . . . I got you!" he said, laughing, pointing at me and dancing like a leprechaun, his police gear jangling and creaking.

"Damn, smells good in here," he said, looking over at Margie, who had her face in her hands, shaking her head.

I had gone over to the couch and pulled out my .45. Robby was looking at Margie, suddenly realizing what he had done.

He walked over to her, put his hands around her shoulders and said, "God, Margie, I'm sorry, I didn't know you would be here. Honest to God, I thought Tucker would be here by himself. I thought you were out with the girls tonight."

Robby knew my pot was coming in today, and I'd told him earlier that Margie was going shopping with some friends. It was Thursday, and all the stores stayed open until 8:30. Being the manager, I'd scheduled someone else to work, so I could bag up the pot. Margie, at the last moment offered to stay home to help.

Having tested the new shipment, we were both stoned. This just added to what would have freaked us out even if we were straight.

Robby was hugging her now and saying, "There, there, it'll be all right. I'm sorry, Margie, really."

When she started to shake, he turned around and looked at me. He saw me standing with the pistol in my hand, and his face started to turn white.

"Look, Tucker, put that thing down. Jesus, I was just fuckin' around. I didn't know you'd still be fuckin' with it."

I was thinking maybe I should walk over and hit him a few times, it would feel so good. Then I heard Margie, she was laughing.

She had this funny habit. When she was laughing hard, she wouldn't make any sound. She would just stand there with her mouth open, with tears coming out of her eyes, and smiling for all she was worth. You could tell she was about out of air, and when she finally caught her breath, her sweet laughter was so contagious, no one was immune.

It only took a couple of seconds, and we were all laughing. It was really good pot.

After we settled down, Robby pulled back the tablecloth and began picking up buds and smelling them.

"Damn," he said, "this smells better than that last shit you got. Tucker, that connection you have is great. I can't even get Columbian Gold."

He sat down and rolled a joint. He fired it up, took a couple of hits, and after all the coughing was done, sat back in a chair at the dining room table. Talk about ludicrous, a cop in full uniform sitting behind 2.2 pounds of pot, smoking a joint.

"How's Mickey Archer working out for you?" he asked.

A few months before, Robby had introduced me to Mickey Archer. Mickey lived in Oil City, about 15 miles north of Shreveport. He was a dealer of lids. The first night I fronted him 30 lids, stacked in a shoe box, at $10 each. In less than three hours he was back with $300 in the shoe box, wanting another 30 lids. I told him to come back in an hour. Margie and I worked fast to accommodate him. He returned the next morning wanting another 30. I was paying $75 a pound for my grass and could make 26 lids out of 16 ounces. Cha-ching!

"Marijuana Mick?" I said, "he's doing great. I front him and he's never ripped me off. He sells pot like he's killin' snakes."

"Of course he doesn't rip you off," Robby laughed. "After what I told him about you before you met and after your first meeting with him, he wouldn't dare. He thinks you're the baddest motherfucker in Shreveport."

The first time I met Archer, he brought his wife with him. He asked me beforehand if that would be all right. I said yes. It was perfect.

At the time, we lived in an old thirteen roomed house on Kirby Street. When they got there I was in the bathroom taking a bath in a claw foot tub. There was a wooden stool next to the tub with my father's hand engraved Colt 1911 .45 sitting on it.

As prearranged, Margie sent him back to the bathroom, telling him to just go in.

Archer walked in and there I was, naked in the tub with a gun only inches from my right hand. I wasn't smiling. I've been told that when I'm not smiling, I look like I'm pissed off, I have a turned down mouth.

"You Mickey?" I asked.

He was about five-nine, skinny with shaggy blond hair down to his shoulders, a scraggly blond goatee and very pale from lack of sun.

He said, "Yeah," looking down at me and . . . the gun.

"Gray said you could move some grass," I said.

"That's right," he said with shifty hesitant eyes.

"I'll front you the pot. If you ever rip me off, I'll find you and kill you, understand," I said, trying to sound like I meant it.

All he did was nod his head.

I stood up in the tub, my six-foot 225 pounds of muscle towering over him. He looked down at my left leg and saw the large round scar from a bullet.

I said, "Hand me that towel, will you?"

He found the towel hanging on a hook next to him and handed it to me with a shaky hand. I stepped out of the tub onto the bath mat and started drying myself off, still looking at him and never letting the Colt out of reach.

Something that didn't go unnoticed by Mickey Archer.

After I was about halfway dry, I pulled a pair of Levy's over my nakedness and said, "I want to hear you say it."

He swallowed and said, "I understand."

I didn't want this guy to think he could rip me off.

Then I took him into the living room, where there was a nice warm fire and two beautiful women.

His wife was a small, attractive, large breasted woman with long straight blond hair. She wore hip hugger jeans and a tight sweater that showed her belly button.

I never met a drug dealer with an ugly woman on his arm.

We smoked some grass and laughed a lot. I let him see the fun side of Tucker. He never ripped me off.

"Robby, what'd you tell Archer about me, before we met?" It just occurred to me, we had never talked about it.

"That you were the baddest motherfucker in Shreveport and if he ripped you off, you would kill him. I told him he wouldn't be the first either."

Well, that was a lie.

"What'd he say about the night we met?"

"Other than you had a big gun," he said laughing.

"Yeah, I let him see my .45."

"Tuck, sometimes you can be so dense," Margie huskily laughed.

"He said he would never, ever, think of ripping you off," he said, still laughing.

"So far so good," I said, wondering what was so funny.

Margie caught my eye and smiled a smile that said, I needed to get rid of Robby and fast.

God, she was sexy, but her timing was baffling.

Before I could think of a way to get rid of him, he said, "Tucker, come take a ride with me. I need your help with something."

I looked at Margie with a "get me out of this' expression.

"You two go on, I'll finish up here and clean this mess up," she said, giving me the same smile, knowing there was no need to tell me to hurry.

"Okay, just a second," I said and walked back to the couch to get the .45 and stick it between my jeans and the small of my back. An untucked t-shirt could conceal it in that position, and I had practiced getting it out.

After Robby and I were in his squad car, I said, "What's up?"

"You remember me telling you about that big redneck that kicked me in the balls to where I pissed blood for three days after?"

One night while off duty, Robby came out of a restaurant and walked right into a fight about to erupt. He went to break it up, not identifying himself as a cop, and the big guy didn't cotton up to it. He caught Robby off guard, and kicked the little guy and walked out.

"Yeah, about a month ago, wasn't it?" I asked. I noticed we were headed south on Highway 71. We would be out of the city limits in just a few miles if we kept this direction.

"Well, I know where he is, and I want to go have a chat with him. I found out he has a bad habit of drop-kicking little guys. I want you to watch my back."

"Where is he?"

"There's a bar about 10 miles south of here called Pop's. You know it?"

"I've seen it, never been in it," I said, thinking it wasn't my kind of place.

"It's a pretty rough place. A buddy in the Sheriff's Department called me about an hour ago and said the guy just pulled in. Maybe he's still there."

There didn't seem to be a graceful way for me to get out of this. I figured Robby would take my silence as a sign of compliance. I was in fact praying. I prayed this turned out all right, meaning I would walk away, and be able to be with Margie later.

We pulled into the gravel parking lot of Pop's, and Robby said, "That's his truck there, the red Ford with the dent in the door."

He took off his hat, badge, gun belt, everything that said 'cop'. "You're cocked and locked, right?" he asked.

It was a stupid question, so I didn't answer. Besides I wasn't finished praying.

"Okay, right, just watch my back," he said, reaching across me and opening the glove box. He pulled out an ominous black cylinder about eight inches long and a little thicker than a roll of quarters.

It was a kel-lite stick. Hand forged airplane aluminum and deadly in the hands of someone that knows how to use it.

He put the stick in his back pocket, rolled up the sleeves of his blue uniform shirt and slicked back his hair. It wasn't long enough to stay back, but it gets the sweat off your hands. I did the same thing, the hair thing that is.

I wore a t-shirt over a pair of Levi's and was wearing cowboy boots. Robby now looked like any blue collar worker going in to get a beer after work. And I looked like your typical short-haired, bearded, muscle-bound redneck. All I needed was a pack of cigarettes rolled up in the sleeve of my shirt.

We walked into the smoke-filled bar. No one turned to stare at us, the music didn't stop, a quiet hush didn't settle over the room like it does in the movies. We were just a couple of Bubba's out for a drink. Other than a couple of curious glances, we were invisible. Well, that was sure as shootin' getting ready to change.

We walked up to the bar, and Robby said to the skinniest bartender in the world, "Two beers please."

The bartender gave us the 'I've never seen you guys before' look and said, "What kinda beer ya want?"

I could feel Robby getting jazzed up. His adrenalin was starting to kick in. So, before he got into it with the bartender, I said, "Budweiser."

"Bottle or can?" the bartender asked.

"Can's fine."

"Yeah, I like mine in the can too," said the walking toothpick.

While he was getting the beers, Robby said, "That's him. Over there playing pool."

I looked over to the pool table where there were two guys playing. One looked about 40 and my size and build, the other guy was around thirty and about the size of . . . King Kong, or maybe Godzilla.

Oh shit.

"He's the guy about my size, right?"

"Wrong," said little Robby Gray

Shit...shit....shit.

When the bartender brought our beers, I said, "He's paying for it," pointing to Robby.

While Robby was pulling out his money, I surveyed the room. It was a typical southern bar. The décor was your typical beer signs on the walls, peanut shells on the floors, bar stools at the bar, and the clientele were your model . . . ex cons.

Shit...shit...shit.

There were enough jail house tattoos to cover a billboard.

"Robby, this might not be the place to do this," I whispered, trying to sound fearless.

"This is the perfect place to do this," he said evenly, staring a hole in Godzilla's back.

He picked up his beer and sucked it down in four long pulls. He softly set the empty can down on the bar, and the little man walked over to where the two biggest guys in the room were playing pool.

My back was to the bar, with my right elbow resting on it, my hand hanging just above my hip. There was no rush. There is plenty of time to do whatever needs doing. I didn't hear the music from the jukebox, I couldn't hear the chatter of barroom talk. I was as calm as a clear pond on a windless day. I wasn't praying. I was waiting.

Robby walked over and put a dollar down on the side of the pool table.

"I'll take the winner," he said, to no one in particular.

Then almost everyone was looking at the table. Not a good sign.

The smallest of the two big ones looked down at Robby and said, "This is our table."

"What the fuck you mean, your table? You own this place?" Robby said with a truckload of attitude.

He had positioned himself between the two. Godzilla was behind him. It didn't look good to me. I started easing my t-shirt up with the fingertips of my right hand.

Godzilla laid his pool cue down on the table, then reached over and put his humongous hand on Robby's right shoulder, grabbing him.

Shit.

It was fast, very fast. Robby whirled, his face was about even with Godzilla's chest. He threw an uppercut, getting the full force of his body into it. It landed right between Godzilla's legs. He followed it up with three more in rapid succession, each blow landing in the exact same spot as the first and ending with Robby on his toes.

Godzilla's mouth opened, but no sound came out.

Four or five guys stood up from their tables, and a small crowd looked to be forming.

No one moved toward them, yet. No one, including me, believed it was over.

Godzilla started to bend at the knees, slowly sinking. His face getting closer to Robby's. Robby bent his knees a little and gave him two more sharp uppercuts to the balls.

Now Godzilla's eyes were starting to bulge. When his chin was about even with the top of Robby's head, Robby calmly brought his left hand up and put it under Godzilla's chin, raised it and exposed what little neck was there. It was enough. Robby hit him in the Adam's apple with one fast overhand right and followed it up with four short, hard punches.

Godzilla went down hard. The guy had to weigh 300 pounds and when he hit the floor, dust rose.

Now there was a crowd, and it was starting to close in on the pool table.

The other big guy was just starting to realize what was happening. He turned his pool cue around and choked up on it, like he had done it before. Through the dust and smoke he started moving towards Robby's back.

There was a white chalk cone on the shelf under the pool cue rack. It looked like a new one, about ten inches high and still a good four inches in diameter at it's base. It was between the guy with the pool cue and Robby.

I shot it from the hip. I didn't remember pulling the gun. The .45 was very loud in the small confines of the bar, stopping all movement in the room. All but for Robby.

Through the white chalk dust cloud that was raining down over everybody within ten feet of the table, I saw Robby reach into his back pocket and pull out the kel-lite stick.

Over my right shoulder, I sensed the bartender making some kind of move. I quickly turned and having to reach only a little, slapped slim along-side his head with the barrel of the Colt.

He went down hard. When he fell, a sawed off shotgun dropped from his hands onto the floor.

Now everyone but Robby was looking at me. I motioned with the barrel of my gun for everyone to give Robby some room. I never really pointed it at any one individual. They somehow got the message.

The little big guy had dropped the pool cue and was now trying to blend in with the wall. It was hard to do. He was all white. His face looked like someone had thrown flour into it. Every time he blinked, he looked like a white owl, his eyes looking extra large through the chalk.

The back of Robby's blue shirt was speckled with chalk, and Godzilla had taken a blast of white chalk in his face.

I reached over with my left hand and picked up my can of Bud for the first time. I was thirsty. Everyone was looking at me. The only sound was the music coming out of the jukebox, Johnny Cash singing about some boy named Sue. I could relate.

That was the only sound. That is, until the first time Robby hit Godzilla in the mouth.

It made me wince. Me and everyone else.

Robby had the kel-lite stick in his fist like a roll of quarters. There was about an inch or so sticking out of each side of his closed fist. He had rolled Godzilla over onto his back and was sitting on his chest. He looked so small.

He would hit him once with his fist, then again with the part sticking out. He alternated this technique for about ten grueling seconds. Every punch after the first was a sound like someone beating a big wet graveled sponge. Ten seconds is a long time.

The blood looked brighter than it normally would. Contrasted against the white chalk it was reminiscent of Christmas. Blood was starting to pool on the floor around Godzilla's head.

Now, men were looking at me again. This time was like maybe I ought to do something, before Robby killed him.

I looked over behind the bar and saw Skinny was still napping. There was just a little blood around his head, or maybe it just looked like a little compared to what I had just been looking at.

I took another pull on the beer, then motioned with my gun again. Men started separating, making an aisle for me to walk through. It didn't look big enough. I motioned again. Now it was.

As I started walking, a man to my right sitting at a table I was going to have to walk by, with a black teardrop tattooed under his eye, made a small move. I knew he had a gun and was getting in position to pull it after I walked by.

Just before I got to the table, I moved and was beside and just a little behind him before he could pull it. I had the .45 stuck behind his ear. I put out my left hand, snapped my fingers and opened my palm. He didn't move, so I pushed the muzzle hard into his head, hard enough to bend him over. I repeated the hand gesture. He slowly took out a little .38 snub nose revolver and set it gently into my hand. Now I had two guns.

I walked over to where Robby was sitting on top of Godzilla. He had slowed down some. He was breathing rather hard now, and what had once been Godzilla's face was now bloody hamburger.

He was still alive, because I could see bubbles coming out of the hamburger every time he exhaled.

I looked over at the little big guy and motioned him further away. He moved. Still holding the .38, I leaned over and very gently put my left arm around Robby, hooking him under his armpits. I straightened up and set him on the floor beside me.

He was pretty tired by now, even though it had only been about thirty seconds since the first blow.

It was a busy half minute.

He looked up at me, then down at the bloody pulp on the floor. He looked like the American Flag. Red, white and blue. Mostly red.

He slowly unbuttoned his shirt, took it off and using the inside, started wiping the blood from his face, hair and arms. His wiry, muscular body was shining with sweat. He was as defined as any body builder I'd ever seen.

I could smell it, the blood. So could everyone else in close proximity. The jukebox had run out of quarters. You could hear the bubbling breathing of Godzilla, and from somewhere behind the bloody meat, what sounded like kittens mewing.

I heard a movement behind the bar, and found myself crouched, holding both pistols, aiming them at the bar.

Skinny's head became visible. After he focused on me, he slowly raised both his hands above his head and stood up.

I motioned with my gun for him to get out from behind the bar. He did. It was amazing how well these guys understood me.

Robby walked over to the little big guy and said, "When he recovers enough to understand what you say, you tell him I said, "When you kick a little guy in the balls, you better kill him. Also tell him if I see him in Shreveport again, I'll kill him."

"Who *are* you?" asked the little big guy.

"Just a little guy," Robby said and walked out the door, holding a bloody, blue and white shirt in his right hand.

"Who are you?" he asked me.

I motioned for him to go over to a table and to sit down. He did. I then motioned for everyone standing to sit down. They did. Some sat on the floor if there weren't enough chairs.

I backed out of the room toward the front door, raised my t-shirt and stuck the .45 in the front of my pants. I put my trigger finger to my lips and said, "Shush." I emptied the cylinder of the .38 onto the floor. The bullets made a racket in the hushed room. I wiped my fingerprints off with the bottom of my shirt, dropped the pistol, turned around and went through the door.

When I walked into the parking lot, Robby had pulled his patrol car around and the passenger door was open. I got in and we drove off. The door to Pop's didn't open, and I looked until it was out of sight.

"I don't think anyone saw your squad car," I said.

"You're really something, Tucker, yes sir, really something," he said, grinning at me.

"What the hell are you talking about?" I said. "I sure hope I never piss you off."

"Yeah, well, he had it coming. He'll never look in the mirror for the rest of his life without thinking of me."

"If he's got the balls to look in a mirror," I said. After we both realized what I'd said, we started laughing.

It was good to be alive.

Robby said, "You never said a word."

"What?"

"You never said a word. After I walked over there, you never said a word. You covered my back and controlled that whole bar without saying one word. You shot the shit out of that chalk cone," he said, laughing. "You are one cool fucker, Tucker," he said. "That's what I'll start calling you, Cool Fucker Tucker."

"No, you won't," I said. It didn't have the ring of Cool Hand Luke.

"If you ever call me that, I'll shoot you dead."

His laughter escalated.

What he had done to Godzilla was an ugly, ugly thing to behold. But, I had to give him credit. He took that guy on his home turf, and he didn't use his power as a cop to do it.

"What'd you do with the gun you took off that con?" he asked.

"You saw that?"

"Yeah, I looked over my shoulder once or twice, ya know, just to see what was going on. The asshole I was working on wasn't going anywhere."

I realized that if he was aware of all that, while doing what he was doing, he was the cool one.

"Yeah, well, I emptied it and dropped it on the floor. It was a cheap piece of crap."

"Damn, I could've used it. Oh, well, fuck it."

I didn't ask what he could have used it for. I didn't think I wanted to know.

He pulled over to the side of the road, got out, went around and opened the trunk and closed it. When he came back around, he was buttoning a black short-sleeved shirt.

He got back behind the wheel and peeled out.

"Did you see that teardrop tattoo on that con with the gun?" he asked.

"Yeah."

"Know what it means?"

"No," I said.

"It means that he killed someone in the joint."

"Swell." I said.

"Yeah, swell. How'd ya know he had it?" he asked.

"Body language, he telegraphed me."

We rode in silence for a few minutes. Then I noticed we had missed the turn to take me back home.

"Where we going?" I said.

"Just riding around for a minute. You in a hurry?"

I was thinking about Margie's smile. Our daughter Shannon had been spending most of her summer vacations with her grandmother down in Alexandria. It was a time we had come to cherish and take advantage of.

"I don't want to be out late. I have something to attend to."

He made a turn that would take us back to the apartment . . . and Margie.

"Speaking of business, how would you like to make 10,000 dollars in just a few days?"

I hadn't seen this coming.

"Doing what?"

"Same thing you're doing now, just on a larger scale."

"Larger scale, larger risk," I said.

"Tucker, what if I told you there would be no risk, no risk at all of being busted?"

"No risk of being busted? How's that work?"

"I'm a cop, remember."

"I don't know, Robby," I said, looking out the window, thinking what I could do with ten grand. Hell, if I didn't do it, someone else would. Anyway, pot was going to be legalized any day now.

"If there's no risk of being busted, why do you need me?"

"Protection."

This didn't sound good.

"From what?"

"We need to protect the money on the way down and the shipment on the way back."

"From what?" I asked again.

He pulled into my apartment complex and parked behind my car. He shut off the motor, turned to me and smiled. It was hard to believe this charming guy had been the same guy in that bar.

"Look," he said, "This is a foolproof deal, that is, concerning the cops. These days we're more worried about being hijacked."

"Hijacked?" I said, "By who?"

"This is a tight operation. I can't tell you about it until I know you're in. Why don't you think about it. Talk it over with your old lady and let me know in a couple of days."

I got out of the car and as I walked around to my apartment door, he rolled down the window of his squad car, and said, "Tucker, thanks for tonight, you're a cool fucker Tucker. I trust you, I know you can do this. It will be a walk in the park compared to tonight."

"I'll think about it," I said, shooting him with my finger gun before letting myself in.

Chapter 30

"Yeah, I went with him one night when he had a chat with a guy."

From their meaningful glances, I deduced Robby Gray had been extremely forthcoming in his explanation of 'chatting'.

Frank LeCompte reached over and put the ash from his cigar in the ashtray on the desk and said, "He did warm up to talking about the past, after a few drinks."

"You said Darvoyce killed himself?"

"That's right."

"That's strange," I said. "Darvoyce didn't seem to have the guts to do something like that. I remember hearing when they came to arrest him, he hid in the attic of his house and after they found him, refused to come down. Someone had to go up and get him. He didn't even have a gun. Just kept yelling he was the commissioner and everybody had to leave his house."

"Yeah, he told me about it," LeCompte said. "Said it happened just about like that."

"Does that sound like someone who would kill himself while waiting to go to trial?" I said.

Carr leaned back in his chair, smoke wafted out of his mouth, and said, "Maybe he didn't think he could handle jail. After all he was the commissioner of Public Safety. That's like the biggest cop there is."

"Or maybe someone else didn't think he could handle the trial," I said, etching the condensation on my glass with my finger.

LeCompte's head swiveled slowly, first looking at Carr, then at me, "You think Gray killed him?"

I said, "He could have done it, he's more than capable. It could have been him or one or two other men I know. But, of them all,

Gray would be the one. With Darvoyce gone, there would be no one to testify as to who actually went on those runs."

Carr leaned forward across his desk, his elbows supporting him, and said, "The same could be said about you."

I just looked at Carr.

After a moment of silence he said, "I know you didn't."

"How could you know that?" I said, enjoying the cigar aroma.

He patted the stack of files, smiled and said, "Call it instinct. And there's nothing in here that suggests you would murder someone."

I was beginning to get annoyed with those files.

"Seems like a lot," I said.

"What?" Carr asked.

"Of paper," I said, nodding towards the stack.

"You've done a lot of living, met a lot of people. They remembered you."

"Why go to all the trouble?"

"Let's just say, I was intrigued," he said, getting up to fix another drink. He didn't act like he'd had anything to drink at all.

"You don't get out much, do you?" I said, then immediately regretted it. I remembered some of the things I did to distract myself from dealing with grief.

Before I could decide if I needed to formulate a proper apology, LeCompte blew a large cloud of smoke between us and said, "Gray also told me an interesting story about your first run to Mexico. He said it got sticky and you unstuck it."

As Carr was starting to sort through and arrange some of the stack, he said, "Why don't you tell us about it?"

I had no intention of telling him anything. What I wanted to know was what he knew. And by the way he was organizing, searching, and thumbing through the papers, I figured he was looking for Robby's version.

"Why don't you read me what Robby said, and I'll tell you if it is accurate or not."

Carr stopped all movement for a moment. I watched his face change from a confused, 'I don't do that' expression to an acquiescent, 'this might be fun', grin.

He found what he was looking for. After separating a one-inch stack and setting it before him, he said, "Okay, here Gray starts by saying..."

As he began reading Robby's account, the doors to that particular baggage car opened, and without warning, my past galed over me.

Chapter 31

Shreveport, La. 1972

"$10,000!" Margie screamed. "$10,000!"

"That's right. He said I could make it in just a few days."

"Who do you have to kill," she said, jokingly.

When I didn't laugh, she froze. I figured if she thought I had to whack somebody, then found out it was just a drug run, she might go along easier.

I let her stew for a moment, then laughed and said, "Gotchya. It's just a drug run, don't worry."

I had waited until after we'd made love, and she was still in 'post coital glow,' before bringing it up.

She seemed to relax a little.

"I don't know, baby," she said. "For ten grand, it has to be dangerous or a big load or both."

That's what I thought, too.

"Naw, he said it was a sure thing. Robby's not going to take a chance on getting busted, he's a cop, for Christ's sake."

She got up off the bed and walked naked to the closet. Seeing her walk away always raised something in me.

"Why don't you come back here," I said.

She turned around and looked at me. I had the sheet pulled up to my chin.

"You look like a guy sticking his head out of a pup tent," she said, laughing.

I grinned at her.

"God, I love you," she said. "But, we need to talk about this, now."

"Come're," I said softly. It usually worked.

She reached into the closet, pulled out a robe and put it on.

"Get some clothes on sex fiend, and come into the kitchen. I'm going to open some wine."

As she walked out the door, she turned and found me standing next to the bed.

"Don't think this is easy for me," she, smiling passionately. "Cover that thing up before you come into the kitchen."

When she smiled like that, a mist seemed to cover her face, blurring it just a little. Like a photographer would do to a picture to make it sexier. It always made it hard . . . to breathe.

So, in the kitchen over a glass of wine, we decided that making $10,000 to do the same thing I was doing for a lot less, and doing it with a cop, was a reasonable risk. I had never been arrested for anything. The worst case scenario was that I got busted and got off easy, first offense and all. Besides, it was going to be legalized any day now.

I called Robby that same night and told him I was in.

The next day, he came by Sawbuck's. He walked in with another man. They were both in uniform. Robby in his cop attire, and the other guy was a fireman.

"Tucker, this is Phil, Phil Blackman," he said.

Phil Blackman was of medium build and looks. Medium length black hair, small black mustache, brown eyes. Very congenial type guy...right.

We shook hands, sizing each other up. It was almost intimate. He had a strong grip, not one of those guys that tried to break your hand, just a naturally strong guy. He was looking hard into my eyes, trying to see me.

"Good to meet you, Phil," I said.

"You too, Tucker," he said. "Robby told me about last night, sounded like a real rodeo. Sorry I missed it."

He was so soft-spoken, he almost whispered.

"Phil and I grew up together," Robby said.

Well, that said it all. I didn't have to worry about trusting Phil. Right?

He was almost the opposite of Robby. Where Robby looked and acted like a joker, this guy was all serious and unsmiling. But underneath, I could feel the same dangerous ripple that came off of Robby Gray.

"Can you get away so we can talk? I'm sure you have some questions," Robby said.

I looked at my watch and said, "Yeah, I'll take an early lunch."

We walked across the street to a popular meat and three called Sylvia's. Being too early for the lunch crowd to show up, it was almost empty. It was the only time you could eat there when it was quiet and they still had all the victuals on the specials.

We picked a booth well away from any ears. After ordering and the waitress left I said, "Okay, what's the deal?"

Robby looked over at Phil. Phil leaned back and crossed his arms over his chest. Robby was going to do the talking.

"Okay, Tucker, I'm going to tell you some of it. What I won't tell you now is who we're working for. Just know it's someone powerful enough that we don't have to worry about being busted."

"Okay," I said. " I believe you, we don't have to worry about getting popped. Last night you said something about hijackers, so I guess that's the problem."

"Right," Robby said, surveying the room.

"Listen, Tucker, like I said last night, this is a tight operation. There are as few people involved as possible. We try and keep a lid on the plans right down to the time we leave. Our problem, yours and ours," he said pointing to himself and Phil, "is leaks."

"Leaks?"

"Yeah. We're not worried about us, it's who's above us. We have no control over our boss and anyone he's dealing with. He's powerful, but sometimes I don't think he's dealing from a full deck."

"Sounds like a politician," I said.

Phil sat up a little straighter.

"I told you he was no dummy," Gray said.

Score one for the shot in the dark.

"Anyway, as I was saying, it's the hijackers. We used to have two teams to make these runs. We would take turns going down. On the last run the other team was hijacked on the way down, and they lost the money."

"How much money?" I asked.

"A whole piss pot full," Phil spoke for the first time.

"Maybe it was an inside job," I said. "Maybe they took the money and made up the part about the hijacking."

"Yeah, well, they didn't make up the part about being dead," Phil said.

A regular Mr. Sunshine.

"Well, that would tend to add credibility to their story," I said.

Robby laughed out loud, but Sunshine Phil didn't like it.

Robby quickly added, "That's why I got the okay to recruit you. I've been thinking about it for a couple of months, but needed to get to know you better before bringing it up."

"So, how long ago did this hijacking occur?" I asked, looking around, wondering if paranoia was contagious.

"Four months ago. There's usually a run every three months, but there's been a delay while we...ah, acquire the capital for another one."

Phil actually laughed. It wasn't nice.

"We plan on taking two cars down. One to carry the money and the other trailing behind. If the money car is hijacked, the trailer car comes in, and we got'em in a cross fire. You and I will be in the money car, Phil and another guy you'll meet later, will be in the trailer. They'll have a sniper rifle and an M-14."

"How about some hand grenades and a bazooka," I said.

Mr. Sunshine didn't like this. He leaned over the table and when his face was about halfway across he said, "Look, smart ass, those two who got killed were friends of mine, so, just shut the fuck up and do what you're told."

He was turning red.

I raised my eyebrows and looked at Robby. He just sat there smiling at me.

I leaned over until my face was about an inch from Phil's, smiled and said,

"I'm sorry about your friends, Phil, and I *am* somewhat of a smart ass. But, if you and I are going to work together, we're gonna have to learn to get along. Now, Robby said you two grew up together. That along with the fact he trusts you to go on these runs tells me a lot. I don't know what Robby's told you about me. But has he said anything, anything at all, that leads you to believe you can talk to me like that?"

"I ain't afraid of you, Tucker," he said between clinched teeth.

"Now, what reason would you have to be afraid of me, Phil?" I said, still smiling, while thinking about putting a thumb in one of his eyes. "We just met."

"Phil, don't push him," Robby said, putting a hand on Phil's shoulder and pulling him back against the rest.

"He's just a fuckin' kid," Phil said.

At 22, I was six or seven years younger than Phil.

"Now, I didn't make fun of you for being a big bad fireman, did I?" I said, sounding hurt.

While Phil was getting pissed off about that, Gray said, "Phil, make nice, can't you see Tucker's making nice with you? Even if you can't, I can...understand?"

Phil looked at Robby, then back at me. He decided to stay quiet.

"Don't worry Tucker, Phil will be all right. Besides, you two won't have to be together most of the trip."

Just as I leaned back, the waitress brought our food. We started talking about hunting and fishing. Phil's attitude changed within a few minutes, and he was almost congenial. He must get low blood sugar. I'd have to remember that.

Chapter 32

A few days later

After a hot weekend of Margie making sure I wouldn't miss her for a few days, I left the following Monday. She looked worried as I loaded my .45 and an old Winchester Model 12 pump shotgun I'd bought from an elderly black woman in Natchitoches. I packed two extra magazines ,a hundred rounds of .45's and a box of shotgun shells into a small Wilson gym bag that had a broken zipper.

"Tuck," she said, worry etched over her gorgeous face, "Do you think you're going to need any of that?"

"No, Baby, of course not. I just don't want to look unprepared."

Robby was outside honking the horn.

Margie came to the door where I had my gear and a small duffel piled up. It looked like I was going on a hunting trip, except there was nothing in season.

She hugged me and gave me a long wet kiss.

She said, "I love you for lying."

"I love you, too. Don't worry, I'll call you when we get there, and again on the way back. And, I wasn't lying to you."

"You think they'll let you?"

"They won't have any say on the matter. You're everything to me. I don't want you here worrying about nothing," I said, hoping the 'about nothing' part was true.

"I'll just stay inside while you go, okay?"

"Sure, Babe. Just think of it like a little hunting trip. I'll be back before you know it."

She held my face in her hands. Our eyes were locked, as she said, "I know *you* will. Take care of Robby."

I knew she meant, 'take care of yourself,' but saying that would have brought the danger too close. It was safer someplace else.

Earlier, Robby told me the money would be in the trunk of a white '68 Chevy Impala he'd pick me up in. A very nondescript car. I still didn't know how much money he was talking about.

He honked again.

After kissing Margie again, I went outside and threw my duffel and gym bag on the back seat, then laid the shotgun under a blanket that was on the floor behind the front seat. The broken gym bag was cracked open. Robby looked in and saw the ammo.

"You expecting a war?" he asked, from behind the wheel.

I sat down in the front seat, pulled the .45 out from behind my back and put it under a road atlas on the seat between us.

I said, "After hearing you talk about getting them in a crossfire, I didn't want to get caught needing and not having."

"That's cool," he said, his eyes tightening with thought.

"Where's Phil and the other guy?" I asked, looking out the back window.

"They'll be behind us."

"What kind of car?"

"See how long it takes you to spot them."

"Oh boy, a road game," I said clapping my hands and bouncing in my seat. I didn't look behind us again.

He laughed and back-handed me on the chest with his right hand.

I hadn't been told anything but what day we were leaving. I had only been told that on Saturday. Not the time of day, or where we were going, or how much grass we were buying. I was pretty much flying in the dark without instruments.

"When are you going to tell me where we're going?" I asked.

"We're going to Laredo, Texas," he said, firing up a joint.

"Don't you think we should curtail that until this is over?" I said.

"You can, but me, hell, I work the streets high most of the time. Gives me an edge when I need it," he said, then added sedately, "And calms me down when I need it, too."

I looked at him. I believed him.

He said, "On this run we're dealing with a new connection. One of the Mexicans from our last run, *my* last run that is, called and said he could get us a better deal through someone else."

"You trust him?"

"Sure, why not? I've dealt with him before."

"What's the time line?"

"We need to be at the Holiday Inn in Laredo by 5 p.m. Wednesday. We've got plenty of time. We don't speed, run stop signs, or do anything to call attention to ourselves."

"Makes sense to me," I said, thinking, *Master Of The Obvious.*

He reached under his seat and came out with a portable CB unit, the wires already attached up under the dash.

He keyed the mike and said, "Breaker . . . Breaker . . . good buddy . . . over," in an exaggerated country trucker accent.

"Come back . . . Teddy Bear . . . over," came out of the speaker.

He looked in the rear view mirror and said into the mike, "Just checkin' the connection, good buddy . . . over."

"Readin' you loud and clear, Teddy Bear, got you in sight . . . over."

"Check you later, good buddy . . . over."

I never got into the CB thing. But I knew enough to know they were on a closed channel. There wasn't any other chatter.

"Teddy Bear?" I said.

"Yeah, that's me. Don't I look all cuddly and shit."

"And shit? Yeah," I said, laughing. I must be getting a contact high.

"And who's 'good buddy'?" I asked.

"The guy you haven't met."

We only stopped for gas and food, making pit stops at the same time. It was at the third stop I noticed the same black Ford Bronco I'd seen at the second stop. I hadn't seen Sunshine Phil at any of the stops.

We were inside eating burgers and fries when I saw the Bronco parked on the edge of the parking lot. It was in approximately the same position when I'd first noticed it at stop number two, a truck stop north of Houston. We had been in touch with them over the CB. Robby would give them a mile marker number to let them know our location.

"So, Phil and Good Buddy are in a late model Bronco, black with a blue pinstripe." I said, then took a bite of my burger.

Robby's burger stopped on it's way to his mouth.

"That's pretty good, Tucker. Phil bet me a hundred you wouldn't spot them before Laredo."

"I was a Boy Scout," I said, with a mouth full of burger.

He stared at me and said, "Why doesn't that surprise me."

"When do they eat and make pit stops?"

"They have food in the Bronco and a gallon jug to pit in. They're not supposed to take their eyes off the car."

What he meant was the money.

"A jug might not accommodate a certain pit," I said, laughing. Sometimes I just crack myself up.

"Yeah, well, they've taken care of that when we've hung out in the parking lots after gassing up, stretching our legs or when I've looked at the map."

There were a few times we had pulled to the far edge of the parking lots at large truck stops after refueling, eating or pitting, and Robby would suggest we stretch ourselves by walking around the car or actually stretching in front of the car. They had been communicating a lot in police code, like 'What's your 10-20' and 'we want an 8-80'. I hadn't asked what they all meant because, one; I didn't care, and two; I think they were making it up as they went along just to mess with me. I also thought that 'Good Buddy,' was a cop.

"How'd you make them?" he asked, mopping up a glob of ketchup with his burger.

"Same vehicle in two different truck stops isn't that unusual, but the positioning was too coincidental. Both times they parked at the edge of the parking lot close to the road, when there were plenty of parking spots closer to the building. I guessed they got gas while we were stretching or when you're doing redundant map reading?"

I wondered why Robby needed to look at a map. He should know the route.

He looked over his shoulder at the Bronco, and said, "Yeah, they're not supposed to leave the Bronco at the same time, just in case the bad guys show up. You know, never lose site of us."

I said, "I guess now you've won your C-note, you guys can start speaking English over the CB, and you can stop looking at the map all the time. The stretching is good, though."

"Hey, we have to have some fun on these trips. Something to do besides drive and wait for a war to start."

"I guess they've never been more than a minute or so behind us, right?" I asked.

He shook his head, "More like thirty seconds. We try to keep about that close using the mile markers."

"Where were your buddies when they got hit?"

"About an hour out of Laredo, in the middle of nowhere."

"Did you know them well?"

After a moment of silence, he said, "Not as well as Phil. But I think they were stupid. I bet if it would've been you and me on that run, no one would have gotten the drop on us."

He was a cocky guy.

"I bet they were stoned," I said around a mouthful of fries.

"They weren't like you and me, Tucker."

"How's that?" I mumbled, chewing.

"Bad to the bone," he said, grinning with his mouth full, churned mustard visible around the edges. "That's why we're carrying the money."

That wasn't effective. Maybe too subtle.

I was just reinforced in my conviction that manners only counted with women and family. Even my manners went to hell in a hand basket around a bunch of guys. It was like using good manners around the guys might make you less of a man or too refined. But I knew real men talked with their mouths full of quiche.

The waitress brought the check.

"I take it you made reservations at the Holiday Inn before we left," I said, after I swallowed my food.

"Yeah, I made'm last week, adjoining rooms," he said, reading the check, then laying down some bills.

"Let's go outside and stretch," he said, getting up.

We moved the car to the far edge of the parking lot. As I got out, I heard Robby say into the CB, "Phil, you owe me a hundred bucks, he made you, game over . . . over."

I watched the Bronco move to the gas pumps. Two men got out. Phil started pumping gas, and the other one walked into the restaurant. He was on the other side of the Bronco and I couldn't get a good look, but there was something vaguely familiar about him. Phil shot us the finger.

By 12:30 a. m. Wednesday and we were an hour out of Laredo. For the past hour we had scarcely talked. Our senses were on heightened alert and had been for a couple of hours. There had been no joking CB chatter or idle talk.

I turned around in my seat, and on my knees, reached over and pulled the shotgun from under the blanket, turned back around and, racking it, chambered a round.

Robby didn't give me a second look. He was busy alternating his eyes from the road in front of him to the rear view mirror. I hadn't seen him put the pistol in his lap, the barrel pointing into the seat between his legs, the grip within easy reach of his right hand.

We had been on Highway 59 since Houston. We had gone through Victoria and a little place called Beeville. Probably a sweet town.

The two-lane road was lonesome and dark, with only a few headlights coming towards us. But often enough to keep us on edge.

Inside the Impala, the light from the dashboard gave the interior a greenish tint. The only sounds were the drone of the air conditioner and the whine of the tires interrupted by the little thumps the cracks in the road made as we ran them over. It was a desolate part of Texas and even the darkness couldn't hide the great expanse and flatness of the countryside.

I changed position, so I could look into the right side rear view mirror. I saw a light so far behind us, it looked like the head of a pin.

"Is that Phil and Good Buddy behind us?" I said, my voice sounding dry and small in the moving car.

Robby cleared his throat and said, "It better be. Any further back, they wouldn't do us much good if we needed them."

We could have called them on the CB, but, it would've seemed invasive to break the quiet that was giving us our razor's edge. Robby, Phil and Good Buddy must've had similar thoughts, the CB remained soundless.

Up until now, this trip was in some way nothing more than an adventure with a for-sure successful outcome. Now . . . well, it wasn't that I was having second thoughts. It was a little late for that. But, like many things in life, the idea of doing something is never the same as doing it. There were a few butterflies fluttering around in my stomach. But, I knew that like the butterflies I used to get before a football game, or before the ringing of the first round bell, these butterflies were my buddies. They would help keep me sharp, keep me quick, and, in this case, maybe keep me alive. Go ahead and flutter, my little gossamer-winged friends.

"Coming up behind us, watch it," Robby said evenly, looking in the rearview mirror. "They're coming fast."

His breath quickened.

"I'm getting in the back," I said, climbing over the seat. There was a roaring in my ears. I shoved the bags out of my way and started rolling the window down on the driver's side. When the window was almost halfway down, I had second thoughts about the bags and started piling them in front of my chest, between me and the window.

Just when I had everything situated and was ready to shoot, a Cadillac went flying by, honking as it passed.

There was no sound for a half a minute. I hadn't moved. I was still holding the shotgun, full of double ought buck against my shoulder, the blowing hot dry wind, itching as it rippled the sweat streaming down my face.

We both jumped, as the quiet was assaulted by the loud squelching of the CB, and Good Buddy's voice, "Bet that made your assholes pucker . . . over," followed by raucous laughter.

He added, "We followed them after they passed us long enough to see it was just a couple out on a late date . . . over."

Robby picked up the mike and said, "Naw, we thought it might be you guys coming up because we're getting close to Laredo, then the Caddy was by us before we knew it . . . over."

After a moment's silence, a disappointed, "Oh." There was no . . . 'over'.

Robby turned on the interior light and turned his head to look at me. I still hadn't moved from my 'ready to rumble' position.

"Motherfucker!," he yelled, laughing maniacally and pounding the dash. "What a fuckin' rush. What I'd tell ya. Look at you. No one's gonna get the drop on us. What a fuckin' trip."

After rolling up the window, I moved the bags from in front of me, realizing that the gym bag full of ammo was one of the bags I was hiding behind. I set the shotgun over on the front seat and climbed over.

"Man, that was so fine," Gray said. "You were like behind cover and everything. If those would have been hijackers, you would have blown the shit out of them. You were fast. Fast and smart. You're my man!"

He was bouncing up and down like a hyper-active kid waiting for ice cream. He really loved this.

"Yeah, right," I said, opting not to mention the bag of ammunition I was using for a bulletproof vest. I'd have to work on the smart part.

Fifteen minutes later we passed a sign that said Casa Blanca Lake, then a road to the north. I saw more light ahead, then a sign signifying the turn to the Laredo Airport. Almost directly across from the northbound turn to the airport, we turned south on Bartlett Avenue, went to the second red light and turned west on Guadalupe. It was one-way, and up ahead on the right was the sign for the motel.

We pulled into the parking lot of the Holiday Inn at 1:45 in the morning. We had a little over 13 hours to get rested before the deal was to go down.

Stopping under the overhang leading to the lobby, Robby said, "You stay here, I'll check us all in. Keep your eyes open, I don't see no fat lady."

While I was still looking for a fat lady, he came back and started the car.

He mikes the CB and says, "We're in rooms 156 and 158, in the very back, they're down and out...over."

"Roger that...over," came the reply.

We pulled around to the rooms. There were only a few cars in the lot and none around the rooms. Laredo was a real center of activity. It was perfect.

After parking the car, Robby said, "We've rented four rooms, we have 154 and 160, too. We'll leave them empty for a buffer while we rest and stuff."

I liked it, showed planning, I was starting to feel better about this.

"And stuff?" I said.

"I'll tell you later, after we're all together."

"So, I get to meet 'Good Buddy'?" I said.

"Ohh yeah," he exaggerated, then grinned an 'I've got a secret' grin.

He gave me the room keys and said, "Go open one. I'll get the money."

After putting my .45 behind my back, I got out and opened room 158. A minute later, he came in behind me. He closed the door, then threw a medium-size duffel bag on the first of the double beds. It was filled to a bulging rigidity.

"I won't even ask how much that is," I said.

"You know I trust you, Tucker. But this is your first trip and there are some rules we have to stick to."

"Don't worry about it. I'm not."

He smiled, opened the door and looked out for a few seconds then said, "I'll be right back, watch the bread."

He came back a minute later with our clothes, my shotgun wrapped in the blanket, a bottle of Jack Daniels tucked under his arm, and an unlit joint hanging out of his mouth.

"I don't know about you, but I need to wind down before I can go to sleep."

"Looks like you've got what it takes," I said, as he handed me the shotgun. I unwrapped it and laid it on the bed with the money.

I've never been much of a whiskey drinker. Being only 22 I hadn't had a chance to develop much of a taste for it. Also, the Tuckers had a history of becoming a little ornery while inebriated on whiskey, so I had mostly stuck to beer. But, tonight I might make an exception to the rule, the blood in my veins was amped with a few hundred volts.

Robby unscrewed the cap on the whiskey and took a long pull. He handed me the bottle. I didn't hesitate. I took a swallow, just one.

"I'd rather have a beer," I said, tears blurring my vision. I couldn't understand how anyone enjoyed the taste of whiskey. My face must have said what I was thinking. Robby laughed.

He lit the joint with a Zippo, took a hit, and passed it to me. I started to take it but in the mirror saw the reflection of the money bag and shotgun on the bed.

I handed it back and said, "I'll pass."

"Cool, more for me," he said, taking another toke.

I wanted to tell him to cool it, but, my instincts said not to. He was older and had done this before, and I had to trust he wouldn't get so stoned as to endanger me. My sole focus was to get out of this in one piece, without getting busted, and with 10,000 dollars.

"I need to call Margie," I said.

"No calls, until this is over," he said.

I quietly said, "I'm going over to that telephone and call my wife collect and tell her I'm here safe. If you don't like that, make a move."

It became very still in the motel room. The only movement was the marijuana smoke floating between us.

"I'm not going to let you make that call, Tucker."

I walked to within a foot of him. I looked down and said, "I've seen you in action, Robby...but..."

"But what,...boyo?" he interrupted.

"So far, you and I have been friends, but don't let your alligator mouth overload your mocking bird ass," I said, smiling.

We locked eyes. I could see him thinking, weighing the probabilities. I let him.

"You must really love her."

"You can't imagine."

"She is beautiful . . . and sexy," he said.

"You can't imagine."

"I'd be afraid to," he said, then ginned and took another toke.

"Just don't let me know when you do," I said. The tense moment had passed and now we were both smiling.

I picked the phone up to call.

"Don't mess with the collect thing," he said.

After going through the hotel long distance rigmarole, I heard her voice.

"Hello," she said sleepily.

I wanted to curl up next to her.

"Hey Baby," I said.

"I've been worried about you," she said, more awake now.

"No need to do that, everything's cool."

"I miss you. When are you coming home?" Her husky sleepy-voice always excited me.

"A couple of days, and when I get there, you're gonna need to find something to hold on to."

"Come're," she said, breathlessly. It's what we said to each other when we wanted to make love.

"Go back to sleep, Baby, I'll be next to you before you know it. And after I'm through with you, we'll go out and celebrate."

"When I get through with you, you're not going to be able to go anywhere," she whispered.

"I love you," I said. My heart was hurting.

"I love you more," she replied.

"Bye-bye, Baby."

"Bye, Tuck, be careful."

"See ya soon," I said and hung up.

I knew I wouldn't survive if anything ever happened to her. I've loved her since the moment I met her. I was 13 years old. But, we both knew that if anything was going to happen to one of us, it would be me.

"Cool," he said, looking at me with what looked like amazement mixed with envy.

"What?" I asked.

"Nothing, just cool," he said, taking another hit.

"Robby, when do we get paid?" I asked, sitting down on the bed next to the money.

"I was wondering when you were going to ask. Our money's in there," he said pointing to the bag. "Already separated. You'll have it in your hands by the time we leave Laredo."

That surprised me, but, before I could say anything, there was a knock on the door, to the rhythm of 'shave-and-a-hair-cut-two-bits'.

I grabbed the shotgun and held it in my right hand, out of sight below the edge of the bed. Robby saw this and grinned, put up his hand, signaling it was all right, walked over and opened the door.

Phil walked in and behind him was a familiar face, Allen Tucker, my first cousin. Allen's about five years older than me, the son of my father's oldest brother, Roy.

So, Allen was 'Good Buddy.' Allen is also a cop in Alexandria.

"Hey, Cuz," he said, grinning. "Close your mouth before something flies in it."

I surmised Allen was the mutual acquaintance Robby said we had on the Alexandria Police Department.

Allen was carrying a six-pack of Budweiser. He too, I knew, stayed away from the hard stuff.

"Allen's been on my team from the beginning," Robby said, through a cloud of reefer madness.

I stood up when they came in and was still holding the shotgun.

"I told you," he said, slapping Phil on the back. "You're not going to slip up on Tuck."

He knew better than to call me by my first name.

I threw the shotgun on the bed and walked over to shake his hand.

"I'm speechless," I said, while we were shaking. "A little shocked."

"Not as shocked as I was when Robby told me you were coming in on this. I'm glad to have you and your gun with us, Tuck. I had Robby come down to Alec to watch you shoot. Then you and Margie moved to Shreveport and look at us now."

Allen and I had hunted together as kids, but as adults we more often than not saw each other at the gun range. He and his wife, Lorna, lived in a nice house in the country outside Alec; too nice for a cop's salary. I always assumed Lorna came from money. Maybe not.

I was feeling much, much better about this deal. I had family here. I knew Allen would answer any questions I might have, and he wouldn't lie to me.

He saw the Jack Daniels on the dresser and made a disapproving face, looked me in the eyes and shrugged while winking. He threw me a beer, and a church key to open it with.

Allen was typical for a Tucker, good looking, muscular five-nine and about 185 pounds, brown hair with blue-green eyes.

I was taller, but I wouldn't want him mad at me.

He said, "Let's relax a bit and find out what's going on."

He looked questionably at Robby. That told me he didn't know much more than I did. The 'much, much better' was just reduced to 'much'.

I opened my beer and tossed the church key back, which he deftly caught.

He read my face and said, "Tuck, after what happened to the last team, things had to change, for security. We decided it best if Robby kept the plans of this trip to himself until we got here."

The seriousness of his demeanor just reduced it to, 'a little better'.

Phil hadn't said a word since arriving. He was standing by Robby, sharing the joint, watching the reunion. He didn't seem as antagonistic towards me. He was looking at me like he'd just met me, but this time, liked me.

"Tucker," he said, walking over with his hand outstretched, "I would like to apologize for being such an asshole. If we're going to be working together, we need to be friends. Allen's told me a lot about you on the way down, and I'm glad you're with us."

As I shook his hand, I said, "Thanks, Phil, but I'm probably still going to be a smart ass."

Everybody laughed, and Phil said, "Yeah, Allen told me that was your nature, but you could back it up."

"Yeah, my mouth has gotten me into trouble a few times."

Allen said, "I told them about the pennies."

"Great," I said dryly.

When I was 16, I was running with a rough crowd of older guys, between 18 and 20. I had a reputation for being tough, but, these guys were the real deal. We were sitting at a table in a bar called 'The Drive-thru', when in walked Richard Bardwell from Pineville. Richard was about 19 and also had a reputation. We almost got into it one night at a dance, but the cops showed up. I remember being relieved. Anyway, after he walked in and bellied up to the bar, I said, "For 2 cents, I'd get up and whip his ass." I suppose I was feeling like I needed to be tough.

The pennies hit the table bouncing and spinning, making a racket before settling. The guys I was sitting with had just called my bluff. They were not smiling. I remember instead of feeling tough, I felt stupid, and afraid. Richard Bardwell was a mean mother.

"Yeah, but he didn't tell me who won the fight," Phil said. "He just said it was a short, bloody one."

I said, "Nobody won that fight. I walked away, he didn't, but I'm sure it took me longer to recover. I really took a beating before landing a couple of lucky punches."

"From what I heard you didn't throw any punches, you never hit him with your fist. I heard you used everything but your fists." Allen said.

"Is that true?" Phil said to me.

"I just remember it was unpleasant. I try to forget unpleasant events."

Robby opened a beer and said, "Let's get down to business." He picked the money up off the bed and threw it on the floor with no more respect than a sack of potatoes.

I picked up the shotgun and propped it against the wall by the door, and we sat down on the beds with our beers, whiskey . . . and pistols.

After we were settled, Robby said, "Okay, this is the way it's going down. Teemo, that's our Mexican connection, you two remember Teemo, right?"

Allen and Phil nodded.

"Okay, Teemo's going to come by at 5:30 this afternoon and we're going to follow him down to Mexico and buy the pot, load it up and go home."

Allen and Phil looked at each other with equal confusion.

"What!" they said in unison.

"That's fucked," said Sunshine Phil.

"I don't like it," Allen said, looking at me.

"Don't look at me," I said. "I just got here. How does it usually go down?"

Allen said, "They usually bring it here, we load it in a U-haul trailer and go home."

I felt my jaw drop. This must be the *stuff* Robby referred to earlier.

"Excuse me," I said, "You're telling me you guys would load up a trailer with pot, right here in the parking lot of the Holiday Inn."

"Yeah," Robby said, chuckling. "It's great. The pot's in these boxes labeled tomatoes and we looked just like some vegetable entrepreneurs. Hiding in plain sight, you know."

I started laughing and said, "That's great. Why can't we do that this time? Why do we have to drive into Mexico?"

Robby looked at us one at a time and said, "After the last team got hijacked and whacked, Teemo called and said he had a new connection. A much better price and better quality grass, we just have to go and get it."

It was very quiet. The three of us who just got the news were weighing the risk. I didn't need to weigh as much as Allen and Phil, because it was all new to me. But their indecision was infectious.

Allen spoke first. "How do you see it happening, Robby?"

"In the morning, Phil goes and rents a U-haul trailer, one of those 8 or 10 footers should do it. After Teemo gets here, we follow him for a couple hours. That's how long he said the drive was. The route's all figured out, no problem. Allen, you stay here with the Impala. Phil, Tucker and I will pull the trailer with the Bronco. Teemo said we will need a four-wheel drive. We do the deal and call

Allen back here at the motel, after we know when we can meet up with him."

He made it sound easy. I could see some holes, but kept my mouth shut, for the time being. I also wondered just how much we were buying . . . an 8 or 10 footer?

We finished off the beers and Robby and Phil took a couple more swigs from the bottle, but no one got drunk. By 3 a. m., the memory of the road had stopped bouncing in my body, and I wanted to lie down. I was hungry, but wanted to sleep more than eat.

Robby yawned and said, "Let's get some sleep, and we'll talk again in the morning. If anybody comes up with any ideas that will help us get this done, we'll talk about'em over breakfast."

He gave Allen the key to the adjoining room, and we started getting ready for bed.

A minute later, the door to the adjoining room opened, and Phil said, "Sweet dreams, ladies."

He was holding a double-barreled sawed-off shotgun in his left hand. He left the door to their room open.

There was a lot of fire power in the two rooms. It would take some very stupid people to break into a motel room full of armed drug runners, I hoped.

I dreamed of making love with Margie and woke missing her. I felt like a little boy spending his first night out, wanting to go home where it was safe and sound. I could hear Robby's gentle snoring in the other bed. I lay there thinking about the holes in the plan I'd heard last night. I hope they wouldn't mind taking some advice from someone new. But, then again, this was new to them, too. After all, we wouldn't be loading boxes of tomatoes from a produce truck to a trailer. We were going to drive to Mexico and bring it back, at night. I felt sure they had the border figured out, but what about the dark? And who were these people Teemo was going to take us to? These questions would have to be discussed over breakfast. I was starving. I looked at my watch. It was 9:27 a. m. .

I got up and went into the bathroom. When I came out after my morning toilet, showering and shaving, Robby was up drinking coffee from a room service pot.

"Took you long enough. I had to use the john in the other room. Damn, your as bad as a woman," he said irritably. "Want some coffee?"

"Not if it makes me all warm and agreeable like you," I said.

"Fuck you," he said, with a smile.

While he was showering, I put on jeans, a black t-shirt, a pair of dingo boots and a long-sleeved denim cowboy shirt. I left the cowboy shirt opened and untucked, with the sleeves rolled up to mid forearm. I put on a cream colored hemp (I swear) cowboy hat that I had shaped myself over a steaming kettle. Pretty much my summer attire.

By 10:30, we were all in the restaurant, clean and awake, with an array of breakfast dishes laid out before us.

Robby had the money bag on the floor between he and Phil.

I had your regular bacon and eggs, with grits. They actually knew what grits were in Laredo. But the other three were definitely into the local cuisine. Juevos Rancheros and western omelets, even some kind of breakfast taco.

As the business at hand required, our table was away from other ears.

After we established an eating rhythm, Robby said, "Anybody have any ideas?"

For some reason everyone was looking at me.

After washing down some eggs and grits with milk and dabbing my mouth with a napkin, I said, "I have some questions and then, maybe some ideas."

I was proud of myself, watching my manners and all.

"Shoot," Robby said.

Allen laughed and said, "But not at me."

"What about the border?" I asked.

"Teemo said it's the dry season and there's a crossing about seventy-five miles south of here, around Zapata. The Bronco should make it easy. He said they drive it in pickups carrying wetbacks."

That sounded doable.

"Let me get this straight. We are going to leave here around 5:30 give or take a half hour, and follow this Teemo guy for a couple of hours into Mexico?"

"That's right," Robby said with his mouthful.

The swine.

"In Mexico, in the dark?"

They all stopped chewing

I looked at Robby, and asked, "Did it ever occur to anyone that the hijackers might have been Mexicans?"

Robby looked at Phil and Allen.

Allen said, "We always assumed it was someone from Louisiana, you know, a leak. One of the other team talked too much."

"Were they the talkative type?" I questioned.

They all three looked at each other, then shrugged.

"Maybe," Phil said. "Ronnie Leggit was pretty proud of himself and was getting cocky."

"Okay," I said. "Let's assume there was a leak. Why did the hijackers wait until they were almost to Laredo before ambushing them? Seems to me they could have done it a lot closer to home, save themselves a lot of driving."

Allen pushed his half-eaten breakfast away. He looked as if he'd lost his appetite.

In the silence that followed, the sounds of the restaurant became amplified.

Phil and Robby stared at each other, both looked constipated.

I said, "Robby, how'd you find out the other team had been hijacked?"

He rubbed his face with both hands, let out a long sigh and said, "Teemo called and told me the guys didn't show up with the money. He wanted to know if I had heard from them, and I told him no."

"What was his attitude?" I asked.

"He was pissed off, said this wasn't any way to do business and what was he going to do with all this product, wanted to know if we could get down here fast with some more money."

"What?" I said. "How long after the meet time did he call you?"

"I don't know. A couple hours, maybe three. Why?"

I looked at the three of them, one at time, and said, "Seems to me if the money was just a few hours late, it could have been because of car trouble or a wreck. There's quite a few reasons they could have been late. Why was he so pissed? Why would he ask for more money if there was a chance they could show up later, and wouldn't he know you couldn't get more money in the first place? Smells bad to me."

"I don't know, Tucker, Teemo has always played straight with us. I trust him," Robby said.

Phil nodded and said, "Me too."

I looked at Allen, "What about you?"

Allen grinned and said, "I don't trust anybody, but that's just my nature."

"Must be genetic," I said.

I leaned back in my chair, pushed my hat back and said, "To get back to my original question of how did you find out they had been hijacked and killed? You said Teemo called and said they were late, but when and how did you find out they were dead?"

"The next day, Teemo called, said they'd been found by the cops on some back road off highway 59. Said they were shot up pretty bad. It was on the news and shit down here."

"Did they have ID's with them?"

"Sure," Robby said.

"Then why would it be on the news down here before the police in Shreveport were notified of their deaths? Or were they?"

"Fuck," Robby said, as he leaned back and put his hands behind his head. Looking at the ceiling, he said, "The department didn't get notified until after I got the call from Teemo."

"You sure?" I asked.

"I'm sure, but that still doesn't mean Teemo was in on it."

"Were either one of the two a cop?"

"No, I'm the only Shreveport cop, that I know of, and Allen is the only other cop."

"That you know of," I said, drinking more of my milk while I digested what I'd just heard. "You're right, it doesn't prove anything, but I think it smells bad enough that we need to take some precautions and prepare for the worst case scenario."

"I'm with Tuck on that," my cousin said.

"Makes sense," Phil agreed.

"What do you have in mind?" asked Robby. "You do have something in mind, right?"

"Yeah, I've been thinking about it since last night, after I found out we'd be following them into Mexico . . . in the dark."

Allen chuckled, looking at Phil and said, "Told ya, didn't I?"

"Yeah, you did," Phil replied.

Robby and I looked like question marks.

"I told Phil on the way down that my cousin here," he said, pointing his thumb at me like a hitchhiker, "may be 22 but he acts 42, and out of all us cousins, is the smartest, toughest and quickest. I told Phil if he made a run at Tuck, Tuck would rip his arm off and beat him to death with it."

Robby was smiling at this and Phil looked a little uncomfortable.

Rip his arm off?

"The only reason I'd do that," I said seriously, "is because I have soft hands and they break easy."

Then I winked at Phil and smiled.

I *am* charming, and he couldn't resist.

"Fuck you," he said, laughing.

We were friends now.

The waitress came over and left the bill, which Robby picked up. So far, I hadn't dropped any cash on this fandango. There was some satisfaction in that alone, somehow giving credence to the professionalism of the operation.

We were back in the room, sitting around, when Robby asked, "Okay, Tucker, what's your idea?"

"I'll need the Impala for an hour or so, and some money to get some supplies."

Robby was shaking his head when he said, "One of the rules is, once we're here, we don't separate."

I thought back to the other rule, about no phone calls. Robby must have been thinking the same thing. He laughed and shrugged.

"How much money do you need?" he asked.

"Fifty will more than cover it. I'll bring back the change."

"I'll go with him," Allen said.

"Phil and I will get the trailer I reserved,' Robby said. "Then we'll come back and get some more rest."

Phil walked over, turned on the TV, and laid down on the bed with his hands behind his head.

I found it curious they didn't ask what I was going to buy.

"You better call and tell housekeeping to stay away," I said, looking at all the hardware laying around.

"Good idea." Phil said reaching for the phone.

"Where's the sniper rifle and M-14?" I asked.

Allen looked at me and Robby and said, "I told Phil with you around, I thought that might be a little overkill. Besides statistics show that most gunfights happen within 10 feet."

After a moment of sobering silence, Allen and I left to go get what I needed. It was good to be with family. We had a nice visit and caught up. We both felt sure marijuana was going to be legalized within the next year or two. They were lobbying for it in Washington, and some states, like Alaska, were going to legalize it for personal consumption. We were glad we were going to make some big money before it happened. He also told me he was only getting $7,500 for riding shotgun for the money and shipment. He knew I was getting ten grand, but it didn't bother him. He said I was earning it, taking a greater risk, hauling it home.

An hour and forty-five minutes later, Allen and I were back. We saw the Bronco parked with the trailer hooked up behind it. We walked up to room 158 carrying a number of bags and boxes. Allen knocked one time, softly, and Robby opened the door.

Robby and Phil looked on confused as we dumped our bags on the floor.

"We're going fishing?" Phil asked.

On the floor were over a hundred and fifty fishing corks, some fishing line, five cans of florescent orange spray paint, a roll of small diameter nylon cord, two newspapers, some masking tape, a 500,000 candlelight spotlight, a roll of clear plastic, and a light-weight mid-calf length cowboy duster.

"What's this shit for? I thought you were going to get some more ammo or something like that," Robby said, looking down at the mess with his hands on his hips. "Looks like we're going fish'n."

"This is going to give us the edge we need," I said.

"Listen to him," Allen said. "It's simple and makes sense. I like it."

I had explained my plan to Allen while buying the supplies.

"Okay," I said. "We're going to take everything but the duster, the light, and nylon cord into the two outside rooms. We'll split it up evenly. In the bathrooms, we'll tape the clear plastic to the walls around the bathtub and shower. We'll put the newspaper on the floors. We'll string the corks up on the fishing line, say 20 or 30 at a time, depending on how many it takes to reach the floor from the shower rods. After we get that set up, we are going to spray all these corks with the orange paint. We're using the outer two rooms so when Teemo gets here, it won't smell like paint."

Allen was enjoying the baffled faces on Robby and Phil. But, I had to hand it to them, they hadn't asked what the corks were for.

"What're the corks for?" they said in two-part harmony, Robby the high part, Phil the low.

Allen and I started laughing.

I said, "I don't know about you guys, but I'm not looking forward to be led into the Mexican desert or wherever they're taking us and not being able to find my way out, without their help."

I watched that sink in...it sank.

"We may not need this, but I'd rather have it and not need it than, need it and not have it."

They were all familiar with this saying.

I continued, "We're going to cut the fishing line about every fourth or fifth cork, and put them back in the bags, stacked so they don't get tangled. That will give us over 30 strings with 4 or 5 corks on each string. As soon as we get off the main road and think it's time, we'll toss a string out. We'll toss a string out at turns, crossroads, Y's, anywhere we think we'll need them. We'll only toss them out to the right side of the road, so we'll know which way to turn on the way back. But, so as not to get confused, we'll write down every turn on the way in. Like first turn, right, second turn, right, third turn left, and so on. We'll just reverse the turns on the way back. Our headlights, or the spotlight if need be, will pick up the orange, make them easy to see, and the strings will keep them from rolling out of sight when we throw them out. Like I said, we may not need this. Whatta ya think?"

Phil and Robby were both staring at the pile on the floor, nodding. The nodding became more active as their brains wrapped around it.

"Fuck yeah," said Phil, his grin grew with understanding.

Robby just dropped down on one knee and started separating the corks and newspaper into two piles.

He liked the strategy.

"Ah, what's the cord and big shirt for?" Phil asked.

"That's for you," I said, which brought on more confused looks.

"Go get that sawed-off double barrel you brought," I said.

While he went to get the gun, we finished splitting up the materials.

He returned with the gun, broke open the breech to show me it was unloaded, and handed it to me.

"Okay." I said. "I figure when Teemo gets here, if there is anything funny going on, he'll try and separate us from as much of our firepower as he can. Maybe all of it."

I could tell Robby and Phil hadn't thought about this.

"Have you done this before, Tucker?" Robby asked.

"Done what?" I said.

"This, a dope deal, in Mexico."

"No, why?"

"You seem to be thinking of a lot of stuff I never even thought of."

"Gray, you've just been a cop too long. I'm not thinking like a cop. On one hand, I'm thinking like a Mexican that's going to rip off some gringos, on the other hand, I'm thinking like that gringo that doesn't want to get ripped off and killed by that Mexican."

"I fuckin' told you, didn't I," Allen chirped.

"Speaking of dope deals in Mexico, who speaks Spanish?" I asked.

No one said a word.

"Teemo speaks English good," Robby said.

Probably weller than you, I thought.

I said, "That'll be fine, if he's the only one we're dealing with. But, if he brings others in on it and they start jabbering between them, we're screwed."

"How about you, you speak a little, don't you?" Allen asked.

I took three years of Spanish in high school.

"I know enough to ask someone's name, get something to eat and find the bathroom. I'm lost when they start talking fast."

The silence that followed was laced with trepidation.

"Okay." I said for the hundredth time today. Nothing was *okay*. "We'll just make sure to never let Teemo out of our sight, and if any one of us thinks he's messin' with us, we stick a gun behind his ear."

"Jesus, Tucker," Phil said. "We've never felt like we needed a gun around Teemo."

"Yeah, well, I'm sure the last two to come down here felt the same way."

Again, the silence was heavy.

"Getting back to the cord and duster," I said.

"Duster?" Phil the fireman said.

"The big shirt, asshole," Robby laughed.

The tension in the air started to subside, but I knew it wouldn't last.

I picked up the cord and made a makeshift sling for the shot gun.

"Come over here, Phil," I said.

He came over, and I put the sling over his right shoulder hanging between his body and arm, with the barrel aimed at the ground. It wasn't quite right, so I took it off and made an adjustment in the length.

"Okay, now, practice sliding the sling off your shoulder with you left hand and bringing the gun up ready to shoot."

While he was practicing, I said, "When Teemo gets here, we'll make sure my shotgun's on the bed. How many handguns do we have?"

Robby opened his overnight bag and pulled out two pistols. One was a .357 magnum revolver, and the other was a Llama 1911 .45 Colt copy. An adequate gun.

Allen went in the other room and came out with a couple of pistols. One was a Smith and Wesson .38 snub nose, and the other one was a Colt .45 like mine, without the fancy engraving.

"Do you cops have any holsters?"

"Yeah," they said, in concert.

"All right," I said. "Here's the plan. My shotgun will be on the bed. We'll all have our pistols showing, either in a holster or tucked into our belts in plain view. Put the pistol you're most comfortable with in the small of your back. Make sure your shirt covers it. When Teemo gets here, I'll be the bad guy."

"Whatta ya mean, the bad guy?" Robby asked.

"I'm the only new guy here. He doesn't know me. If any of you were to act out of the ordinary, it would alert him that something was wrong. So, I'll be the non-trusting asshole. I'll make sure he doesn't like me right off the bat. That way, we may be able to keep him off balance. If he is up to something, it may be easier to spot. You three know how he usually acts. If something's amiss, you'll know, and you can let me know."

"How?" Phil asked.

"As soon as one of you thinks something's not right . . . pick your nose."

They all three looked at each other.

"Just make sure you blow your noses prior to Teemo's arrival," I laughed.

I'd been watching Phil practice with the sling. He was getting better with it, for a fireman.

I picked up the duster and said, "Now put this on over the gun."

He did, and you couldn't tell he had a shotgun underneath.

"Now practice doing it wearing the duster."

He looked like he just understood for the first time the severity of the situation.

"Do you really think this is necessary?" he asked.

"Probably not, but why don't you do it anyway, just in case." He *was* a fireman, it might be wise to downplay it.

Robby and I made eye contact. Again I saw the hard, dangerous calm I saw the first time I met him. Then he nodded as if to say, 'Phil'll be fine."

While we were still looking at each other I said, "There's something I'm curious about."

"What's that?" he asked.

"Does Teemo know you've brought an extra car to run interference?

After a moment of thought, he said, "No, I just told him we would take precautions against another hijacking."

I looked around at everyone and said, "So, the extra two people could account for that."

Robby said, "Yeah, he's met both Allen and Phil at different times with me. When one couldn't get off work to come, the other did."

"Then we'd better move the Impala. Let him think we all came in the Bronco. It might end up being our 'ace in the hole,'" I said.

"Good idea," Allen said.

"I like it," Robby said, moving towards the door.

Phil was still practicing getting the shotgun up from under the duster.

I said, "That can wait. Lets talk about these guns some more."

Again, everyone was looking at me.

"My thinking is, if we have a lot of hardware visible when Teemo arrives and it makes him nervous, something's sour. I mean, why wouldn't we have guns, your partners were killed. He may try and separate us from the weapons. We let him, put him at ease."

"What?" Phil said, and stopped practicing.

"You're doing fine, Phil, keep it up," I said.

"As I was saying," I continued, "if he wants us to leave the hardware behind, for whatever reason he comes up with, we take the visible pistols and leave them here. Phil you take the shotgun and hide it out of sight in the Bronco before he gets here, lay the duster over the back seat. The three of us will have a gun stashed behind our backs when we leave. We have enough pistols to do that. I'll have my shotgun, that I'll have to leave behind. You two cops each have two pistols. Leaving one behind leaves each of you with one, and Phil will have the shotgun in the car. If this Teemo character wants to frisk us, Phil, you let him frisk you first, and I will take care of the rest. He won't want to frisk all of us, that would be too weird. When we get in the Bronco, make sure the doors are open long enough to give him a good look to satisfy him there are no guns in there. Just make sure the corks are well hidden in the back. We'll put them in some grocery bags and put some chips and stuff on top of them."

Robby looked at me speculatively, "Damn, Tucker, you really think they're going to make a run at us, don't you?"

"I hope not," I said. "Now, lets get these corks strung and painted so we can rest before we have to leave."

I noticed there was no talk of smoking pot, drinking beer or Jack Daniels. Their easygoing, for sure, money-making drug runs had changed. Suddenly the danger of being busted by the cops or being hijacked by other American dealers seemed small. I hoped on the way home I was accused of spoiling their trip.

Allen put his arm around my shoulder and said, "I'm glad you're here, Tuck."

I couldn't actually put my finger on the exact time I became the leader. I wasn't unfamiliar with the sensation. But, that didn't make it any less vexing.

At 5:47 there was a knock on the door. Our stage was set. Phil was sitting on the bed closest to the door with the money next to him. Allen was sitting in the chair by the closed curtained window overlooking the parking lot, and me, I was in the bathroom. I wasn't using it. It was part of the plan.

Robby went to the door and opened it.

"Hola, ey Rowbee, ow are jew doeen? Feel, you look good. Ilene ow are jew?"

"Hey, Teemo, good to see you . . . Teemo . . . Teemo," I heard from my throne position.

I heard the door close, then Robby said, "You by yourself, Teemo?"

"Sí, Rowbee, eets jus mee. We have pleenty time, you wan to smoke, you know to try the marywhanna? "

"You mean this is a sample of what we're buying, from this new source of yours?" Allen asked.

"Si, have a look at theese."

After a moment, I heard Phil say, "Man, this looks great. A lot of buds in this and not much seeds."

"I'll twist one up," Robby said.

"Eets a good night for theese deal, eese no moon, eet be very how you say . . . negro?"

"Dark," Phil said, sounding less enthused than Teemo.

"Jew goeeng to like deese shit, I promeese jew."

If I stayed in here much longer, I was going to have to use the bathroom. The power of suggestion was starting to take hold, and flushing the toilet before I made my grand entrance wasn't part of the plan.

I heard some coughing, then Phil said, "Shit . . . this is great. This is what we're buying, all of it?"

"Si, theese eez from thee sheepment. Wee jus have to go geet eet."

More coughing coming from Allen and Robby. I needed to get out there before they got too stoned to straighten up before we crossed the border.

I opened the door and walked out, quiet like.

Allen was still sitting in the chair by the window, Phil was standing next to the bed, Robby and Teemo were standing in the doorway to the adjoining room. Teemo was facing the doorway, his right side to me.

I stood there in plain sight for maybe five or six seconds before Teemo became aware of another presence in the room. He turned slowly and faced me.

I wasn't smiling. I was giving him my best hard ass look, which for me is easy, another genetic trait.

Teemo was about Robby's height, maybe a little shorter, but thicker with the start of a beer gut. He had an agreeable face, which had been smiling when he started turning. The smile faded and his pleasant brown eyes suddenly lost their amusing gleam.

"Who eese theese?" he slowly asked.

"That's our body guard," Allen said.

That was an ad lib. Then I realized that everything from here on out was going to be just that. We hadn't really gone over much dialog.

My shotgun was out of their sight, leaning against the wall to my left. I reached over and picked it up and held it in the crook of my right arm, in a relaxed, 'bird hunting' position.

"Bodyguard?" Teemo said.

It may have been my imagination, but his English seemed to be getting better.

"This is Tucker," Robby said. "I told you we had to make arrangements because of what happened.

"Tucker?" Teemo said.

I watched him as he tried to absorb this new development.

"Yeah, Tucker," Allen said. "You know, rhymes with bad mother-fucker?"

I was beginning to regret not having worked on dialog.

Teemo looked at each of them and said, "I no like theese, I do na know deese man, deese Tucker."

"I know him," Robby said.

"How jew know heem?"

I thought, 'this ought to be good'.

"I arrested him seven years ago, and put him in Angola. He's only been out a couple of weeks."

Oh, boy, it was all I could do not to look at Robby like he was loco. Angola, the worst prison in the U. S., where we all feared going. Feared enough that we'd rather shoot it out with the cops, than go.

Allen almost laughed.

"Angola?" said Teemo, looking at me with new respect. They'd heard of Angola, even down here.

"Wha jew do, Tucker?" he said to me.

It's about time, now I could get in on the ad-libbing.

"I killed two men that raped my sister."

Let's see what Robby does with that.

"Yeah, he was only 15 when he did that. The judge gave him time for manslaughter because he beat them to death," said Robby.

Damn, I *am* a bad mother-fucker.

"Yeah, and he killed two more men while in prison," said Allen.

And getting badder by the second. I'd better put a stop to this before I became a serial killer.

"Shut the fuck up," I said to no one in particular. "It's none of his fuckin' business who I am."

I hoped I sounded as tough as a guy who had killed four men before he was 22.

Teemo didn't like this at all. He backed towards the door.

"Theese no good," he said, looking at Robby. Then looking at each one of us, he said, "All deese gun, Rowbee, eets no good, you an me amigos. Deese man, he look... *peligroso*. I don wan heem."

So far, no one had to get rid of any buggers.

"Don't worry, Teemo, he's only here to protect us from hijackers. He does what I say. Isn't that right, Tucker?"

I looked at Teemo for a moment, then at Robby, and said, "If you're not worried about this guy, then I'm not. It's cool."

"No, Tucker, Teemo is my friend, understand. You're just coming along to help load the grass, get it...it's okay," Robby said, speaking very distinctly and slowly, crossing his hands with the palms turned down, like an umpire calling a slide safe.

Not only was I a bad ass. I was a dumb ass, too.

It was all I could do not to say 'duh,' so I just nodded and tried to look dumb and dangerous. Dumb I could do.

I must have pulled it off. The dumb part anyway. Teemo seemed to relax a little.

"Steel, Rowbee, all deese gun, eet no good," he said, waving his hands around, taking in the guns stuck in the front of pants and visible holsters.

"You don't expect us to go without a way to protect ourselves, do you?" Robby asked.

"Protect from wha?" Teemo asked. "You weet me, you mi amigo. You leave gun here, come back and geet after we do deal, hokay? Eets all feext up, evryting goeeng to be fine."

No one seemed to know what to do, so I said, as dumb as I could, "I don't need no gun to protect you from some fuckin' greasers."

I threw my shotgun on the bed, hoping I didn't overdo it.

"Thas righ, no gun, we all amigo...friends, si?" Teemo said with a big smile.

Robby looked at me and picked his nose, just for a second. It looked so natural I wondered if it was a signal.

Both Allen and Phil saw him do it and looked equally baffled. Maybe he had an itch and didn't realize he did it.

Before we had much time to think about it, Robby said, "Okay," and threw his pistol on the bed.

Allen and Phil did the same, and when Teemo looked at me for my turn, I pulled my cowboy shirt open to show I wasn't carrying a pistol. My Colt .45 tucked into the back of my pants was as warm and soothing as a hot water bottle. I imagined my fellow thespians feeling the same.

"Satisfied... *amigo?*" Robby said, smiling with deceiving boyish charm.

Teemo looked at us not quite sure, but other than frisking us, what choice did he have.

"Si, Rowbee, eez good, mucho mejor... how you say..."

"Better," I said. Some of my Spanish was still lingering around.

He glanced at me sharply. He didn't like that. And I didn't like, that he didn't like that I might speak the lingo.

What I did like was, he didn't know.

Now, Allen had a bugger, looked like it must be a big one. He must have picked up on the same thing.

"Allen, you stay here and watch the guns," Robby said, as he picked up the money.

Good touch, Robby.

Hearing this, Teemo relaxed, smiled and said, "Thas good, I bring dem back before soonnrice."

I didn't like this guy's accent. I'd bet he speaks English a lot better than he puts on. I couldn't put my finger on the reason why, but, it was there.

Robby opened the door, and we all walked outside. It was like walking into a dry sauna. It was close to 6 o'clock, and the sun was peeking at us through purple clouds to the west. It was going to be a beautiful sunset. I was looking forward to the cool nights that come to this part of the country.

In front of our room was a brand new Ford XLT pickup. A shiny black job that looked fully loaded. I felt the beginnings of a bugger. I couldn't help but think Teemo may have bought the truck with some of the hijacked money. But, if no one else had a bugger, why should I?

We walked past the XLT to the middle parking area where the Bronco was parked with the trailer.

As planned, we left the doors to the Bronco open while we loaded up, and Teemo did do a nonchalant inspection.

Before Robby could sit behind the driver's seat, Teemo said, "Robby, why don jew go weeth me, for . . . compañía."

We hadn't thought about this. Robby looked at me for a moment. I didn't know what to say, so I didn't.

Finally he shrugged and said, "Why the fuck not," then threw the duffel of money into the Bronco.

That didn't go unnoticed by Teemo.

After they walked over to the new truck, I said to Phil, "You want me to drive?"

"No, I'll drive. Better if your hands are free, just in case."

Sounded good . . . and, not so good.

We followed Robby and Teemo out onto Guadalupe. We drove west on Guadalupe until we came to Guerrero Ave. We turned south on Guerrero and were out of town within ten minutes.

It was a pretty drive. Often we were alongside the Rio Grande.

"That the Rio Grande?" Phil asked.

Again, I was reminded that the other three had never been anywhere around Laredo but the Holiday Inn. This was new to them, too. I didn't find any comfort in that.

"Yeah, I believe so," I said, remembering seeing it on the road atlas on the trip down.

"Doesn't look like we can drive across it."

"Not here anyway. It's supposed to get much wider somewhere south of here, and much shallower, you know, as it spreads out."

"Better get a lot fuckin' shallower."

"Yeah." What else was there to say about that.

Guerrero turned into Hwy 83. It was desolate country. Flat and brown with just a few scrub trees, mesquite bushes, and some kind of native junipers mixed in with cactus. We saw a few longhorn steers, and I marveled at their ability to survive in this outwardly barren country.

Highway 83 wasn't much of a highway, and Teemo was in no hurry. We never got over 50 mph. It was dark when we drove into what I supposed was the outskirts of Zapata. There were a few houses along the highway. I couldn't tell what tax bracket the owners were in, but the candlelight coming from some of the windows gave me a notion. It was hard to believe we were still in the U. S. of A.

Zapata wasn't anything to write home about. We were through it before I got much of a feel for it. From what I could tell, it was a ranching town. We crossed a body of water and the sign of the bridge said, "Rio Grande." It was about a quarter mile across.

"Now that's more like it," Phil said.

"I'm crawling over to get the corks," I said.

A minute later I had three brown grocery bags placed between my feet, the orange corks glowed from the dashboard lights.

"When're you going to start throwing them out?" Phil asked.

"Just as soon as I think we can't find our way back without throwing them out."

In one of the grocery bags was a pencil and a memo pad from the hotel. I put them in my lap. After a second thought, I pulled my .45 out from behind my back and put it between my legs.

Phil watched this in silence, nodding his head.

Chapter 33

<u>Almost to Mexico</u>

About 35 miles south of Zapata, we drove into a little dust bowl of a town called Lopeno. We passed a gas station that was open. In the washed out yellow light from the station, I saw a cowboy wearing dusty chaps, pumping gas into an old faded red pickup truck. Standing nonchalantly in the back of the pickup was a fully saddled buckskin quarter horse, with a lariat hanging from the saddle horn. His head was a full three feet above the cab of the truck, his ears standing straight up as he watched his partner gas up. There were no sides or anything to keep the horse from tumbling out sideways, only his steady balance.

I smiled as I thought, 'a real working team, those two'.

"Allen told me you used to Rodeo."

"Uh-huh."

"What'd ya do?"

"Calf roping and bull riding."

"No shit?"

"No shit."

"Were you any good?"

"Not at calf roping, had a great horse and bad ankles."

"When did you stop?"

"About a year ago."

"Why, get hurt?"

"No, a good friend did, got stepped on by a bull, in the chest, almost died."

He looked over at me and said, "Scare you?"

"Yeah, but not as much as my wife telling me she wouldn't give me anymore if I kept riding," I said.

With a small laugh, he said, "Yeah, I've seen your wife. That'd do it for me, too. No offense, Tucker, I meant it as a compliment."

I sat there, remembering Margie, standing in the candlelight wearing a shear negligee, holding a glass of champagne, when she gave me that ultimatum. I hadn't seen her in three weeks and had spent the last week of that sitting in a Fort Worth hospital with my rodeo partner, Jimmy Green. Waiting to see if he was going to live or not.

Her exact words were, 'Like what you see?'

I could only nod.

Then she said, 'If you ever get on another bull, you'll never get on this again.'

I never got on another bull. It wasn't that hard of a decision, because, something else was.

A few miles south of Lopeno, Teemo's right blinker came on. We turned west on a small dirt road.

"You gonna throw some out now?" Phil asked.

"Not yet."

"Whatcha waitin' for?"

"It's just the first turn off the highway, don't get nervous, we don't know how many turns we're going to make and how many of these we're going to have to use. I'd hate to run out somewhere in the real boonies."

"Yeah, you're right."

"But, I'll write this turn down, so we don't get confused as to when I started making notes," I said as I wrote down, '1- t-R'.

Phil said, "Good idea."

About half a mile later, the road started to veer back south, paralleling 83. A mile or so further, Teemo slowed and turned right again.

I rolled down my window and said, "Lag back a bit, let him get a little ahead before you turn. I'd hate for him to look in his mirror and see these flying out our window."

For some reason, this tickled Phil and he laughed. It sounded like nerves to me.

As we turned onto what was no more than a trail of tire tracks, I threw a string out, and I wrote '2- t-R', on the pad.

"Cool," Phil said, his teeth shining white by the console lights.

There was comfort in knowing that, if need be, we were going to be able to find our way back by ourselves. I hoped we wouldn't have to do that.

I laugh out loud.

"What's so funny?"

"I just got a picture of Teemo bringing us back out and him seeing all these orange glowing balls at every turn."

We both laughed . . . a little nervously. I noticed there were hardly any tracks on the ground.

Ten minutes later, Teemo stopped and in the light from his headlights, I could see water. His arm came out of his window and he motioned the go ahead for us to follow him, then slowly pulled into the water.

As preplanned, Phil and I jumped out to turn the front lugs, allowing Teemo to get the small lead we needed.

After getting back in, I rolled down the window, and Phil reached over and put it into four-wheel drive.

When I felt the time was right, I threw out two strings, then we followed them into the water.

It was easy going. The water never came up to the running boards. After what seemed like a mile, but, was probably closer to a couple hundred yards, we saw them come out onto dry land.

"Lag back..."

"I got it, I got it!" he said quickly.

"Sorry," I said. I could tell he was very nervous. "I guess I'm just a little nervous."

He looked over at me "Yeah, me too."

As soon as we got all fours on the ground, I dropped out two strings. I wanted to make sure we could spot these devices. The strings were so they wouldn't roll off.

In the headlights I saw some driftwood and brush piles that were piled up, like a current had made them.

"It's an island," I said.

"An island?"

"Yeah, see the driftwood and piles of brush."

He looked, then said, "I think you're right. I'll lag back a bit."

I dropped another string. There was no road, and we were leaving no tracks that I could see.

In less than a minute, Teemo entered the water again. I dropped out two more strings.

"Shit," Phil said.

This time the water was higher, it came up past the tops of the tires, making for slow going. Phil did a good job of not pushing the water up into the engine. We were going slow, the trailer was floating, but there was no current, so it stayed behind us. In just a few minutes, we saw Teemo's truck rise up on dry ground.

As we came out of the water, I dropped another string of corks. I could see scrub brush and cactus now.

"We're in Mexico," I said.

There was no road to speak of, and after a quarter of a mile of slowly following Teemo and Robby, I said, "Stop."

"What?"

"Stop!"

Phil slammed on the brakes, I leaned way out the window and laid a string on the ground, very carefully, parallel to the car.

"Go!" I yelled.

He took off, spinning the tires, raising a little dust behind us.

"What's that all about?"

"There's no road here. When we come back this way, we need to know in what direction to go. We didn't bring a compass, so the only way we can tell is the direction I lay the string."

His head quickly turned in my direction.

"Yeah," he said nodding. "Yeah."

"The next time I say stop, try not to raise any dust, okay?"

Looking straight ahead, he nodded, "I got it."

I only had to say 'stop' two more times before Teemo turned north onto a paved road.

The cloudless night sky was a dark blue crayon, the only light coming from the headlights and stars. There was no other traffic. I looked at the clock on the dash. It was 8:47.

We were following Teemo and Robby at a steady 65 mph. It felt like a 100 mph, jetting through the black night. The stars were bright in the moonless sky. The desert flatness giving the sparkling heavens above us, a bowl hanging over our heads effect. The inside of the bowl was covered with trillions of pin lights.

"What the fuck is that!" Phil screamed.

"What?" I said, jerking my eyes to the road.

"I saw something cross the road, it looked like a big leaf or something, but it looked alive.'"

I started watching the road for live leaves. A minute later, I saw three of them scurrying across the road in front of us, then a crunching sound when we ran over one.

"That, what the fuck's that!" Phil yelled.

My skin crawled, I shivered and felt sick to my stomach.

Then another one was moving from left to right, and there was a couple of brown greasy spots on the pavement where Teemo's truck had run over some.

"Jesus Christ, they look like..." Phil started.

"Tarantulas," I said. "They're fucking tarantulas...fuck...fuck."

I'd heard about this, but secretly prayed I would never see it.

I had a little arachnophobia problem. Okay. A big problem.

I was born in the Philippine Islands, the home of the largest spider in the world, the giant bird spider, at maturity reaching a diameter of 13 inches. The Filipino's called them potato spiders because they like to lay up in potato sacks and have their young. The potatoes taking the place of small rocks the spiders like to nest in.

When I was about three, my mother had rolled a G. I. bomb at one she'd seen coming across the utility room floor, where my parents kept the 50-pound sack of potatoes.

She was in the kitchen, and I, just coming in from the back yard, and being the toddler I was, simply stood at the door to the utility room and watched this giant bug walk across the floor.

A G. I. bomb, about the size of a can of shaving cream, was much like a hand grenade, in being that you pulled a pin and a few seconds later it would explode with about as much bang as a cherry bomb, expelling a cloud of DDT in a 20-some-odd foot circle.

This particular spider was a female and was carrying her young on her back. They were about the size of quarters.

Upon seeing this green cylindrical container rolling towards her, and her ugly babies, she, of course, pounced on it, trapping it easily. When the bomb exploded, I was covered with hundreds of them. They were all over me, on my face, crawling in my hair and in my mouth. These particular spiders have large fangs for holding on to the birds they jumped on in trees, but no venom. Needless to say, the babies had a nasty little bite. I was told the Filipino gardener almost drowned me with a water hose getting them off of me. But, not before they had done their psychological damage.

"Tarantulas!" screamed Phil, pounding on the steering wheel. "I hate fuckin' spiders, I hate them. I hate them!"

I was becoming very fond of Phil.

"They look like leaves blowing across the road," I said. "Let's just pretend that's what they are. They're leaves...they're leaves... they're leaves."

"They're leaves," he said, "they're leaves. Yeah, that's right, they're leaves."

It was our mantra.

An hour later, the leaves had become much less numerous, then stopped altogether. We didn't know why, and we didn't care, we were just happy not to see them.

Teemo slowed and turned on his left blinker. Phil was getting good at lagging. We made the turn, and I tossed out a couple of strings of corks. We found ourselves on a well-defined dirt road.

For another 20 minutes we followed Teemo down a straight road. We were definitely in the middle of nowhere. But, because of our strings of painted corks and turning notations, we didn't feel lost, maybe.

Teemo slowed again and made a left turn, that would put us heading south. I threw out another couple of strings, made another notation on the pad and said, "Ya know, if we hadn't been throwing these things out and making these notations, we'd be as fucked up as a snake in a lawn mower."

"That's for sure," Phil laughed.

The road we were traveling on was well defined, but suddenly, without putting on his blinker, Teemo made a sharp left turn off the road and onto the bumpy, cactus littered prairie. It was as if he'd almost missed his turn.

I managed to drop a string just as Phil made the sharp left.

"Sorry about that, Tucker."

"Couldn't be helped." I said.

We were definitely off road now. I couldn't ascertain what Teemo was using as a guide, as he wound his truck around scrub brush, cactus, through small washouts and dry creek beds. Then again, I was too busy to worry about it.

"This is bad," I said, as I rolled the window down all the way. As I got on my knees in the front seat, I kicked my .45 onto the floor. I pulled the bags of stringed corks close to the door, so I could get to them easily with my left hand.

"What're ya going to do?" Phil said quickly. He too was busy, fighting the wheel as he followed Teemo's erratic pattern.

I was hanging out the window so far my waist was resting on the edge of the door. I had a string of corks in my left hand, doing my best to keep them from becoming entangled. We had gone to great pains loading the bags, laying the strings in carefully and placing a piece of newspaper between each strand as we stacked them. I had been wadding up the paper to consolidate it, and every so often would drop a large ball of it out the window.

As Phil made a sharp turn, I leaned over as far as I could towards the ground, praying I wouldn't slap a cactus with my face, and laid a string down. Hopefully aimed in the direction we'd have to turn to find the next string.

I grabbed a bag with my left hand and put it on the seat behind me, as close to Phil as I could reach.

"When you get a chance, take some strings out and lay them across the seat next to me, I'm trying to lay them down with some kind of direction in mind," I yelled over my shoulder. "Tell me every time he turns and in what direction. I can't see him from down here."

"Gotcha," Phil said.

We dropped into a dry creek bed. I laid down a string, my hand only a foot off the ground. I hoped I'd laid it down at the edge of the drop so we could see it when we came back this way alone. I was starting to think we might have to, it sure seemed like Teemo was trying to lose us.

"Tucker, I think he's trying to lose us!"

"Yeah!" I yelled into the ground, laying down another string in the creek bed.

We drove down the creek bed for a snaky, bumpy five minutes, then Phil yelled, "He's turning left, going up the bank!"

I raised up from the ground long enough to pick a few strings off the back seat where Phil had neatly placed them, and was hanging again just above the earth when we went up the bank. I dropped two strands in a pile as soon as we came off the incline onto flat ground.

"He's turning left!"

My abs were starting to burn, and I felt bruised across my stomach. I didn't know how much more of this I could take. Plus, I was getting pissed off. I tried to keep the thought of leaves blowing across the ground out of my mind.

As we turned left, I laid down one more strand, and heard Phil say, "A fuckin road, we're on a fucking road. Not much of one, but a road."

I raised up to take a look and sure nuff, there were shallow tire depressions in the ground between Teemo's truck and ours. I was sweating, and my gut hurt. I picked up my pistol and sat it between my legs and rearranged what few strands of corks we had left.

"How many do we have?" Phil asked.

"I don't know. We'll either have enough or we won't, no use counting them," I said shortly.

At that moment, I wanted to be anywhere but where I was. Then I revised that, I wanted to be in my bed, lying next to Margie.

"Yeah, guess you're right," he said. "Looks like you may have been right about a lot of things," he added, unhappily.

"You know," I said, as I had the thought, "if I were bringing strangers to where I'd warehoused a load of grass, I might do the same thing. You know, make sure they couldn't find their way back to it."

"Hey, you're right, maybe we're just paranoid. I bet everything is cool," he said with some relief.

I wasn't quite there. There was a fine line between paranoia and careful. I always like to have a safety valve.

A couple of minutes later, Teemo's brake lights came on, and he slowed to a stop. In the light cast from his truck, I could see the rectangle front of an old adobe structure. It was about 20 feet across with a boarded up window on each side of a small wood door in the middle.

"I've got to take a piss," Phil said.

Now that he brought it up, I suddenly had to go like a race horse.

"Me too," I said, squirming, "but, let's not get out just yet."

I was cleaning up the cab of the truck, putting away any evidence of the corks and putting my pistol behind my back, when Teemo and Robby got out of the XLT and started relieving themselves.

Robby's back was to us, with his head profiled, and he was picking his nose like digging for gold.

"You ready yet?" Phil asked. "I've really got to go."

"Yeah."

I got out of the Bronco and started watering a cactus a few feet from the vehicle.

I heard Robby come up behind me and drop the money on the ground.

"We're fucked," he whispered.

"What's wrong?" I said calmly.

"What's wrong? We're fuckin' lost, aren't we? He's trying to get us lost so we can't get back."

I filled him in on my theory. How we'd probably do the same thing in Teemo's shoes. It seemed to calm him down, a little.

"Hey, amigos!" Teemo shouted jovially from the side of his truck.

"How did he seem to you on the drive?" I asked.

"Okay. He talked a lot, asked me a lot of questions about you. Made up a bunch of shit about what a bad ass you were. But you were my bad ass and would do whatever I told you."

"Uh-huh," I said.

"Did you see those fuckin' spiders on the road?" he asked.

"I don't want to talk about it."

"Man, you could hear them crunch under the tires. Teemo said they have these great big fangs . . ."

"Why don't you go in and check it out," I quickly interrupted. "We'll stay with the money until you come back and say it's okay."

That shut him up. My skin was crawling, like hundreds of spiders were on me. It took all my will power not to visibly shiver.

Phil had come around to stand with us, and we all looked over at Teemo. His teeth were gleaming in the headlights of the Bronco.

"Looks friendly enough to me," Phil said.

From where I was, I couldn't tell if he was smiling or leering.

"Okay," Robby said, "I'll go check it out, be back in a minute."

He walked over to Teemo and talked for a few seconds. Teemo looked over at us, then shrugged, and they both went through the old wood door.

I said, "Phil, go put your shotgun and duster on."

"Do you really think that's necessary?"

"Just go do it while you still have the chance, unless you want to walk in there unarmed."

"Yeah, okay. Up to now, you've been right about most things."

"Yeah, well, I hope I'm wrong about this. Stand in the dark when you put it on."

A couple of minutes later, Robby came out with a big smile on his face and waving us over, said, "Come on, it's cool. You guys are going to fuckin' love this."

He turned and went back inside, leaving the door open.

All right! It looked like everything was hunky-dory. I shouldered the bag of money, that I had yet to see a dollar of, and Phil and I walked over. The Bronco was still running and the headlights were on.

When we walked through the door, you could smell it, marijuana. The adobe structure was at least 50 feet deep. We were in a narrow hallway. The walls, all the way to the 8 foot ceiling, were made out of bricks, bricks of marijuana. About every 10 feet there was a cord hanging from the ceiling with a low wattage light bulb at its end, giving off a brown and yellow glow.

The hallway came to an end about 20 feet from the back wall. About five feet from the back wall was an old wooden table with another single bulb hanging above it.

Teemo was standing on the other side of the table with his back to the wall, next to a chair. Robby was standing on this side with his butt against the table, facing Phil and me, wearing a large smile.

Upon walking into the small clearing, I could see it was made by the removal of bricks. There were still a few stacks of bricks along each side wall to our right and left.

There had to be quite a few tons of pot here. I didn't feel like sharing Robby's smile. This was a *big* operation. You didn't leave this much laying around without men guarding it. Men with guns.

Behind the table to the left and to the right, were doors, I presumed leading to the outside.

"Give me the dinero, Tucker," Robby said.

He was relaxed and confident, so I handed it to him.

He set it on the table and to Teemo said, "$225,000, in small bills, just like we said."

My bowels turned to mud.

"How much are we buying?" I asked incredulously.

"3,000 pounds," Robby said grinning.

I wanted to slap the smile off the little bandy rooster's face.

Instead, I said, "We should have gotten a bigger trailer."

"It'll fit. We've done it before," Robby said, turning to face me.

Phil walked over to the right of Robby, and I was standing to his left. We were all about 5 feet apart. I saw Teemo look at Phil and take in the duster. I didn't like what I saw. I started trying to dig a Cadillac out of my nose.

Robby saw me and turned around to face Teemo, who was still standing on the other side of the table, with his back against the wall.

That's how we were positioned when both doors opened and in walked six Mexicans. Three on each side.

I didn't think they were here to help us load up the pot.

There seemed to be a lot of guns showing. No one, that I could see, had one in their hands. But, there were plenty of pistols sticking out the front of their pants.

The first one through the door on my side was a big mother and had a brown leather cord around his neck. The cord looked unusually tight to me. He also had some kind of big ass pistol sticking out of his pants I didn't recognize.

The next two both had smaller revolvers stuck in their jeans, but they may have just looked small compared to the big assed one.

Of the three, the one in the middle had a big gut, the one on the left had long greasy looking hair, and something that looked like a mustache trying to grow under his nose. Big mother was to my right.

I didn't pay much attention to the three on the right of Teemo. After all, there was just so much I could do.

Robby was backing up, moving a little to his right. Phil moved over to his left, getting closer to me.

"Keep spread out," I said quietly. This really wasn't happening. I was watching it, like a movie.

That stopped Phil about 5 feet to my right. Robby was a few feet on the other side of him.

Teemo's smile didn't look so friendly anymore. He put up his hands and said, "Rowbee, theys no need for jew and you amigo's to ge hur' jew know. Jew can jus leave de dinero and go. We no hur' you."

While I waited to hear what Robby had to say about that, I didn't take my eyes off the three on my side of Teemo.

I wondered if they spoke English, because they started spreading out a little and while doing it, were very interested in me. I felt my amigos may have overdone it, making *me* the bad ass body guard. The few extra butterflies that fluttered in my stomach said Teemo may have had a little talk with them when Robby came out to get us.

"Fuck you, you goddamned pepper belly, greaser motherfucker," Robby said, perfectly enunciating every word.

Great, a diplomat.

Everything slowed down. I thought about how I'd always told Margie that the last words I would speak before dying would be 'Margie, I love you'.

The three on my side went for their guns. They hadn't practiced as much as me. The big Mexican with the tight cord was reaching behind his back, and I figured he had a shotgun back there hanging from that leather cord.

"Phil!" I yelled, "Watch that big fucker...shotgun!"

My gun was in my hand and went off by itself.

"Bang!...Bang!" It doubled tapped.

The first two hit the one in the middle, high on his right shoulder. Of the three, he had his hand on his pistol first. He was up on his tiptoes for a moment, then slammed into the wall and started sliding down, leaving a bloody smear on the wall. He was no longer holding his gun.

"Bang!" That was from Robby's gun. I didn't have time to see if he'd hit anybody over there.

The long-haired Mexican was just bringing his gun out of his belt. His eyes were wide with surprise. He looked like he wanted to change his mind, but it was too late to stop his hand.

"Bang . . . Bang!" My .45 exploded in my hands, I was now crouched, in a frontal stance, holding the gun with both hands.

Longhair's right hand came apart as it slammed into his right hip, propelling his gun towards the middle of the room. He slammed against the wall, where he started listing slowly to the right.

I thought I may have heard Robby's gun go off again, but couldn't be sure, my ears were full from my .45.

I sensed Phil dancing beside me, fumbling with his duster.

The big mother with the cord did indeed have a shotgun, and was bringing it up to bear on Phil, who had danced between big mother and me.

I couldn't shoot over Phil. He was moving around too much, trying to get his shotgun out.

I quickly took one step forward, and with my left hand grabbed the back of Phil's duster and jerked him to my left. Over Phil's right shoulder, I shot once at the big Mexican, just as his shotgun went off, aimed at where Phil had been standing.

I felt a tug on the right side of my shirt, like a child had pulled on it to get my attention. Funny how that actual image came to me at that time.

The Mexican I had shot spun about halfway around to his left and sidestepped into Teemo, who quickly pushed him away. The shotgun was now hanging in his right hand, aimed at the floor, his arm looking useless.

When Teemo pushed him away, it helped to stand him upright, and I could see blood in the joint of his right shoulder.

"It's over!" I yelled, my voice sounding small in the echo of the gunfire.

"Fuck that!" Phil screamed from my left. I could hear the terror and adrenalin that laced his voice. Then, "Bang!" it was loud and I knew he had pulled both triggers.

It looked like the big Mexican had been hit hard with a giant feather pillow. His shirt depressed into his stomach. His stomach was pushed back into his spine. His mouth formed an operatic expression, like reaching for a high note. His hands came out in front of him as his feet came off the floor, like he was trying to touch his toes in mid-air. Then he gently kissed the wall with his butt and sat down on the floor. His head was now trying to touch his knees. There wasn't a lot of blood . . . at first.

No one moved. It was very still. The only movement was the light bulb hanging from the cord. It was gently swinging, moving the light it cast back and forth from the wall to the middle of the room, highlighting the smoke from the guns.

The smell of burnt cordite and dust was in my nose. But for the smell of marijuana and blood, I could have been at the gun range.

Teemo was still standing where he was when it all started, just a few seconds ago. To me, it seemed like at least five minutes.

Teemo was flat against the wall with his hands up around his shoulders. His eyes were mostly white, so was his face.

The three Mexicans on my side were down, one was dead for sure. Of the three on the other side of Teemo, two were standing with their hands high above their heads and one was lying on the floor. Because of the table, I couldn't tell what kind of shape he was in. The two who were standing, now that I had time to look at them, appeared to be twins. They were very dark complexioned, black haired, clean shaven, handsome men, in their mid thirties.

Robby started moving towards the table and the money, so did I. I heard Phil reloading his shotgun and turned toward him.

"You killed that guy," I said.

"No shit," he said matter of factly, followed by, "and, Tucker . . . thanks, you saved my ass back there. I guess I didn't practice enough."

"Yeah." Robby said, "And I'm going to kill this hijacking asshole." This wasn't good.

"Keep me covered, Tucker," Robby said, and walked around the table towards the now Caucasian Teemo.

With my left hand, I reached into my left back pocket, pulled out a full magazine, quickly dropped the magazine out of the .45 into the same hand, and slammed the fresh one home. I put the partially used one in the same back pocket. I was back to nine shots again.

The sound of the gun being reloaded was sobering and dangerous.

Robby had reached Teemo and was dragging him around to our side of the table. I kept my gun aimed in the general direction of the twins.

They didn't seem as afraid as Teemo, or as afraid as I'd like them to be. Although they did keep their eyes on me. Looking at them a little harder, I saw they were well dressed, nice shirts and slacks. They didn't appear to be any kind of muscle.

I leaned over the table and took a look at the downed Mexicans as Robby pushed Teemo against it.

The one on the left, long hair, was just rolling over onto his right side, leaning his back against the wall. His right hand was a gory mess, and there was blood on his right hip. It looked like I shot him in his hand and his hip, or through his hand into his hip.

That isn't uncommon at the gun range, when they spin a target around and the picture is holding a gun. You often instinctively shoot the first thing you see . . . the gun.

Long hair was starting to moan. Middle man was still sitting on his butt, leaning against the bloodied wall. He was looking at me in shock, literally, he was in shock. His body had just taken two rounds from a .45 in the shoulder, and I would be surprised if his shoulder wasn't shattered. His pistol was on the floor between his feet. It might as well have been a mile away.

I didn't look at the big Mexican.

"Before I kill you, tell me why you killed my friends," Robby said to Teemo.

I had no intentions of letting Robby kill Teemo, but at this time, I didn't have any good ideas on how to stop him. I also knew about that paved road to hell.

"I no keel you amigos, I no keel!" Teemo screamed.

Robby had his .45 up under Teemo's chin, pushing his head back with it. His finger was on the trigger; it was cocked with the safety off. In the rage he was in, he could easily accidentally shoot him.

Teemo was totally freaked.

"You're a fuckin' liar!" Robby screamed back. "Why'd you do it, you greedy bastard? Weren't you making enough money?"

I had to do something. I remembered Robby saying this was a new contact for Teemo, and how earlier, they said the pot was different. Was that tonight? It seemed like days ago.

"Hold it, Robby. Don't shoot him yet," I said, trying to sound matter of factly. Like he could shoot him later and I wouldn't care.

"What's up?" he said, still holding the pistol hard under Teemo's chin.

I couldn't see Phil, but knew he was behind me.

I was covering the twins with my .45. It still bothered me how unafraid they were. They were just *too* cool. Then the hair on the back of my neck stood straight up.

"Phil, cover the front door with that shotgun!" I yelled over my shoulder. Then pointing my gun at the twins, I said, "You tell whoever is out there not to come in. Do it now."

They looked at me like they didn't understand. I knew they did. For one thing; I had seen their eyes tighten when Robby said he was going to kill Teemo. For another; Teemo didn't try to translate what I had just said. I believed he was so afraid, he would have done anything to prolong his life.

The twins were standing so close together their shoulders were almost touching. I shot the wall between their heads, and the dried mud that exploded, showered them.

They both started yelling in Spanish. They said the same thing at the same time, sounding like a Mexican Doublemint commercial. They were definitely twins.

Robby, realizing there may still be some danger, backed off from Teemo, giving himself maneuverability space.

"I've got the front covered," Phil said behind me.

"Robby," I said, "keep 'em covered."

Putting my pistol down the front of my pants, I walked over to the closest pile of bricks and pulled one off the top. I went back to the table, set it down, took out my pocket knife, cut it open, broke out a fist full and dumped it on the table.

I stepped back and said, "Robby, check this out and tell me if it is about the same quality you've been getting."

While he was doing that, I kept my eyes on the twins . . . and Teemo.

Teemo was leaning against the table with his back to the twins. When Robby picked up the pot and looked at it and smelled it, Teemo slowly turned his head around to look at the twins. They barely shook their heads. If only one had done it I might not have noticed. I saw that being twins had its disadvantages as well as its advantages.

Robby said, "This is much better grass than we've been getting."

"Didn't you tell me Teemo said he had a new connection?"

"Yeah, so?"

"Well, it looks like he was telling the truth about that. Maybe he's telling the truth about not hijacking your buddies."

"Es verdad, Tucker," Teemo said, trembling.

"How you figure?" Robby said.

"I tell you how I figure," I said, turning and looking around at all the pot. I pulled my gun out and when I did, the twins looked like two Dobermans on alert.

I waved my gun at all the bricks and said, "This is a huge operation. Whoever owns all this," I looked at the twins, "doesn't need to hijack a couple of armed men and shoot them up to steal for money. That's a risky business. On the other hand, luring some stupid gringos down to Mexico, getting them lost, making them think everything is cool and just taking their money, well, that sounds much easier and much less risky. Gringos so stupid, they send down other gringos who are so stupid they get hijacked, killed and lose their money."

The twin on the right, couldn't suppress a slight smile. The one on the left was expressionless. He would be the boss.

"There's not much to respect...*respeto,* about that is there? No respect, no trust, not good business," I said for the twins' benefit.

"I don't know, Tucker," Robby said. "I don't know if I buy that."

"Let me ask you something," I said to Robby.

"What?"

"You want to walk outside first?"

That got his attention.

"We can take Teemo as a hostage," he said.

"I don't know about you, but I have no idea how many guns are out there waiting for us. I also don't know where they are, out there in the dark."

Robby aimed his gun at Teemo's head and said, "How many greasers out there? How many guns?"

Teemo's first reaction was to look over his shoulder at the twins. He stopped himself, but the intention was there.

"Robby." I said, "I think you're talking to the wrong man."

"Tucker!" Phil said loudly. "I think there's someone outside the front door."

"Shoot whoever comes through it, and I'll shoot . . ." I aimed my .45 at the twin on the left and said, "como se llamas?"

"Armando," he said in perfect English.

"And I'll shoot Armando here," I said.

Armando yelled something in rapid Spanish. I caught a few words... a lo sumo...something about the outside. The meaning was clear, stay outside.

Robby looked over at me and said, "What the fuck is going on?"

"I believe these handsome twins here, well, all this pot belongs to them, and Armando here, he's the jefe, the boss."

Armando looked at me and smiled, his teeth showing up white and even.

"Okay, so we use him as a hostage," Robby said, moving around the table towards the twins.

"I may have a better idea," I said.

Robby stopped and looked back at me, his eyebrows raised. We stood like that for a few seconds.

He said, "Let's hear it."

"First of all, let's all just relax a little, back off and take a breath."

In the silence that followed, long-hair began to moan.

Oh great.

I turned my head so I could see Phil. He was leaning easily against a wall of bricks, where he could see down the marijuana hallway to his left or into the makeshift room where we were.

For the first time, I saw a stool with a cowhide seat next to a short stack of bricks on my left. I put my gun in the back of my pants. I walked over, picked it up, brought it back to the table and sat it down across from the chair on the other side.

The light had stopped swinging, and the dust was starting to settle. The blood odor was stronger, like a dirty copper penny held close to my nose.

I remembered reading somewhere that Mexicans, most of all, admired and respected bravery, courage. So, I figured I had better get on with this façade before the shakes set in and I wet my pants.

I motioned to the chair and said, "Armando, would you like to sit?" I smiled and tried to sound polite, and unafraid. Then I motioned with my hand and said, "Of course, you can put your hands down. You and your brother, I'm sorry I don't know your name."

"Tom'as," said the other twin, speaking for the first time.

"Thank you, Senor Tucker, I believe?" Armando said.

"That's correct." I said. I've read enough to know how to sound proper.

After Armando sat down, I sat down on the stool.

Armando smiled handsomely and said, "I believe your shirt is no longer good, Mister Tucker." He nodded down to my right side.

I looked down and there was a hole about the size of a dime in the tail of my shirt, made by buckshot. I pulled the shirt out to get a better look and revealed two more identical holes. I remembered the odd picture of a child pulling on my shirt, trying to get my attention.

"You are very quick, Senor Tucker," he said, "and very lucky."

"Lucky?" I said. "Look at my shirt."

His laughter was genuine. Then he looked over his right shoulder at the three men laying on the floor, then back at me, and said,

"You are right, Mr. Tucker, I have no respect for someone who cannot protect themselves or their investment...or me."

Losing his smile, he said, "We have made a costly mistake. We underestimated you and your friends. We thought you would be, like you said, stupid. You are not."

"Where the fuck's this going, Tucker?" Robby said impatiently.

Without taking my eyes from Armando's, I said, "Give it a chance, Robby."

Armando smiled like a gambler with an ace up his sleeve.

"We're not lost," I said.

His 'ace in the hole' smile slowly faded. He looked over at Teemo, who shrugged.

"Don't blame him, he did his best. Don't misunderstand me, I'm not saying we could find our way back here, but we made sure we could find our way back to Texas."

He looked at me for a moment, his eyes searching my face. He nodded. He believed me.

"What do you propose to do now, Senor Tucker?"

I looked around the room and said, "You're in the marijuana business, right?"

He too looked around the room and said, "Yes, I am in the marijuana business."

"Well, we've got money and you've got marijuana."

"Your fuckin' with me, right?" Robby said.

I glanced over at Robby and said, "What do you want to do, Robby? Kill everybody and load up the trailer and go home? Then what? What about the next time your boss or whoever runs this operation wants you to make another run, what are you going to do then?"

He didn't have anything to say about that.

Across the room, Phil said, "Let him talk, Robby."

"What about the guys outside?" Robby asked. "What are we going to do about them?"

I stared at Armando and said, "I think the men on the floor were his best guns, and I'll bet the men outside would be perfect for loading the trailer."

Armando chuckled and said, "Balls."

Balls?

"I believe that's how you say it in English, no?" Armando laughed.

I looked over at Teemo.

He reached down between his legs and held his hands like he was holding two softballs, heavy softballs.

"The next time we do business, we would like for it to be like before, you bring it to the hotel and we load it up . . . like tomatoes."

Armando looked at Teemo. Teemo spat out some more rapid Spanish. When he was through, Armando looked back at me, then at Robby, nodded and said, "Si, muy grande balls."

I wasn't sure if he had agreed to what I'd asked, so I continued to stare at him.

"It will be as you say," he said.

"For the same price," I said.

He slapped the table with his right hand and laughed.

His quick movement almost got him shot. Robby was still holding his gun on them. He didn't seem to notice, but I didn't think he missed much.

"Next deal, same price, then we talk," he said.

I said, "We left the Bronco running. Please have your men bring it around and they can load the trailer."

Armando looked at Teemo and nodded.

Teemo started to move towards the back door on my right, stopped and looked at me.

I shook my head and pointed towards the front door.

"We'll just sit here and chat with Armando and Tom'as."

Teemo walked to the front door, said something, then walked outside.

Robby came over to stand close to me.

I looked over Armando's shoulder and said, "If you want to help your wounded...go ahead."

"They are no longer useful," he said.

"I think I like this guy," Robby said, with a wicked grin.

Armando looked at Robby, who was still holding his gun and said, "Senor Robby, the gun is no longer necessary. We all know each other...now."

After a small hesitation, Robby put his gun in his pants. It didn't go unnoticed that it was in easy reach.

There had only been two more Mexicans outside. They looked more like farmers than drug dealers. They loaded the trailer.

While they did, we learned that Armando and Tom'as' surname was Miranda and they were from Mexico City. They had no problem revealing themselves in this way. They either trusted us, or they were going to kill us before we left Mexico. It was hard for me to decide which. Thirty minutes later the trailer was loaded, and we were ready to go.

It was unsettling that the wounded men were still laying on the floor unattended. The one that Robby had shot was groaning loudly. He was gut shot. If he didn't get to a hospital soon, he would die. He might die anyway. No one seemed to care.

We were about ready to leave. Armando and I were standing alone, by the open back door on the left, the trailer just to the outside.

Armando was standing very close to me when he said in an intimate tone, "Teemo tells me you are a killer of men. You killed the men who dishonored your sister. The judge sends you to jail where you kill more men."

To say anything at all would just add to the lie. So, I didn't say anything.

"You are very quick with your pistol, a real pistolero, as we say in Mexico (it sounded like mayheeco). I find it odd you kill no one here today, Senor Tucker."

"I'm pretty quick, but I'm a terrible shot," I said.

He shook his head and said, "I think maybe you are a very good shot, and maybe you were not afraid for your life."

I'd have to think about that.

"Is there anything else you require?" he asked.

I had been thinking about the men I had to shoot tonight, the man who Phil killed, and I felt the early stages of deep anger welling up. I had not signed on for this. It was supposed to be easy, a sure thing, no sweat and all that. I was supposed to help guard against hijackers, and they may still be out there, waiting.

"Yeah," I said, "there is."

He stood there waiting.

"Have one of your men load up 50 more kilos."

He stiffened and said, "I beg your pardon."

"I said, have your men load up fifty kilo's."

"And why would I do that?" he asked, with a small amount of amusement, very small.

"Let's call it 'an underestimating and troublesome fee', and, it would make me feel better," I said, then pointed at the men and body laying on the floor. "About the extra work I had to do."

He never took his eyes off me.

"Chollo," he yelled out the door. Then he spoke so fast, I barely heard the one word I was looking for, 'cincuenta', but hear it I did.

One of the farmers came in and after two more trips, the extra 50 kilos were loaded.

We were ready to leave. I felt confident we could find our way back, well, maybe not totally confident.

"Mister Tucker," he said in flawless, accentless, English, "it is to my benefit that you get back to Texas (it sounded like Tehas) safely. I would not like you to be detained by the Mexican police, you know my name. I would also like to do more business with you. I believe you are a man of honor."

I knew he was going somewhere, I just didn't know the destination.

He looked at his watch and said, "I don't know in what way you assured yourselves that you could get back, but, I must assure you that time is of the essence."

I believed him.

"What are you suggesting, Mr. Miranda?"

This seemed to please him.

"I would like Teemo to go with you, to show you a faster way. You have my word that you have nothing to fear from me.

"I don't fear anything from you," I said. I needed to keep up the front of the bad ass.

He laughed and said, "Of course, but, please accept this gesture. It is to our mutual advantage."

Robby, Tom'as and Teemo had come up beside the door as we had been talking.

Robby said, "What was that last two loads all about? I thought we were through."

Armando Miranda and I looked at one another.

"A gift," I said, "to us, from Mr. Miranda."

Armando looked at the three newcomers and said, "A gift that Mr. Tucker negotiated for."

Then he put his arm around Teemo and said, "But I have offered a gift of my own. Teemo, I would like you to ride with the gringos. Show them the shortcut. Make sure they make it to the river on time, comprende'?"

Teemo's demeanor remained tranquil.

"Si, jefe," he said.

"That's not what we talked about, Tucker," Robby said.

"Yeah, well, nothing about this night has been what we talked about, has it?" I said to him.

"Do you trust him?" Robby asked, pointing at Armando Miranda with his chin.

"No, I don't trust him, but I believe him when he says we need to hurry. I think we can find our way back, but I think it will be slow going."

"Why do we need to hurry?" Robby asked.

Teemo was looking at Armando for acquiescence.

Armando nodded.

"The reever," Teemo said, "the reever is rising."

"What do you mean?" I asked, feeling a hollow spot in the pit of my stomach.

Armando sighed and said, "They close the dam, the Falcon Dam. Every night when the weather cools, they close the dam. In the late morning when it gets hot, they open it. For the turbines. The air conditioners in the gringos' homes uses much electricity."

I believed him. They didn't expect to have to go back tonight. And they probably figured we would go back through the regular border check, since we wouldn't be carrying any marijuana back, so they thought.

I hadn't the time nor the energy to get angry over this new-found knowledge.

"Let's go!" I said, and turned to leave.

"Mister Tucker," Armando said.

I turned back around and said, "Yes?"

"I would like to shake your hand."

I put out my hand, and we shook. Then I turned and put out my hand to his quiet brother, Tom'as.

After all the respectful goodbyes were over, we left.

As we pulled away, I looked back and saw Chollo and the other Mexican farmer pulling a body out of the building. There was no sign of the Mirandas.

Phil drove and I sat shotgun. The old term for sitting next to the front seat window was fast taking on new meaning, or should I say, the old meaning. Robby sat behind Phil and Teemo behind me, a little to the center so he could lean over the back of the front seat and give directions.

We went only a few hundred yards when we came upon the first orange string of corks. They were very bright and easy to see.

"Wha's that een the road?" Teemo said.

"That's our way home," Phil said with a delighted chuckle.

It gave me a feeling of well-being, to know we really weren't lost. It was only a hundred yards or so when we came on the next string off to the right, our signpost to turn right and off the road. This would take us into the washout, I could see it all in my mind. We didn't really need Teemo.

"You see it?" I said to Phil.

"Got it," he said, slowing to turn.

"No, no, keeps going, no turn," Teemo said quickly. "Eez mucho slow tha way. We have no time."

Phil kept slowing, looking over to me.

"Do as he says," I said. "Think about it, if we get busted by the Mexican police, so does he."

In less than a minute, we had turned right onto a larger road and passed the strings of corks that we had dropped when we turned off the main road onto the desert. We had already made up ten minutes.

Teemo pointed to the corks and laughed.

"You some smart gringos," he said, pounding me on the back. He sounded friendly and relieved.

We were pitched forward as Phil slammed on the brakes and said, "I've got to get out, I'm going to puke."

The Bronco was barely stopped when he opened the door, holding on to the steering wheel with his right hand, he leaned over the road and threw up.

He may have just realized he killed someone tonight. As I thought about this, I wondered why I didn't feel sick. I had never shot anyone before. Maybe because I had trained to do just that for most of my life. All those hours of practicing, I was practicing to shoot someone. Now that I had done it, it didn't feel much different than shooting the pictured targets of bad guys pointing picture guns at me, so far.

When we came to the river crossing, the pile of corks I had dropped were hung on a bush, floating.

We stopped at the edge of the water and watched the current. There hadn't been any when we came across earlier.

"What'a ya think, Teemo?" I said.

"I don know," he said, leaning over my shoulder, his head stretched out towards the windshield.

There was that fluctuating accent again.

"Robby, look behind you and see if you can find that spot light," I said, trying to make it sound like a suggestion.

I heard him rummaging, then he handed it over the seat. I plugged the 20 foot cord into the cigarette lighter hole and pushed the button to see if it worked.

"God damn," Phil said, as we were almost blinded by the light that filled the cab. It was a very, very, bright light.

"Teemo," I said, "come with me."

I got out and went around to the front of the Bronco and stood on the front bumper, getting the light as high as I could by raising it over my head. Teemo stood next to me, and I shined it out towards Texas. We could see the island, it wasn't completely submerged yet and I could see the string of corks still laying down in the middle, on dry ground.

"Si . . . Si!" Teemo yelled. "We go, rápido, rápido!" Then he jumped down, and ran around waving for me to hurry. He was a funny little guy. It made what we had just been through even more bizarre.

It was close. The water was dangerously close to drowning out the engine. We had to keep our forward motion so as not to allow water to go up the tail pipe.

We all had suggestions for Phil as he forded the first crossing. Robby and I were yelling instructions at him, and he was cussing and telling us all to shut up, the entire time Teemo was yelling in Spanish. At one point, the almost airtight trailer, full of what the river considered wood, started floating and wanted to jackknife into the rear bumper of the Bronco. It was a comical circus, and we were all laughing by the time we touched Texas. But, touch Texas we did, and Texas was in the United States.

There was an all around sense of relief, even Teemo was laughing and pounding Robby and me. You wouldn't know that less than an hour ago, Robby fully intended to blow Teemo's brains all over an adobe wall.

Surviving a gun battle and going from feeling betrayed, to the understanding of good business, does strange things to a human being.

Now, the fact that all we had to worry about was getting three thousand, one hundred and ten pounds of high-grade grass back to Shreveport without getting busted or hijacked, seemed a small matter.

After passing the gas station where I had seen the horse in the pickup, I looked at Teemo and said, "Where do you want us to drop you off?"

"Eet no matter, where er' jew wan, I jus make call an dey come for me." Then after thinking for a second or two, he said, "Soamplace wit food and cerveza."

The perfect answer, it pleased everyone. It looked like Teemo was going to live, at least for tonight.

While driving through Zapata, Robby had me reach under the driver's seat and pull out a portable CB unit, and no sooner did he turn it on than we heard Allen's voice.

"Come in, Teddy Bear, Come in, Teddy Bear . . . over." He sounded as if he had been saying that for a long time.

"Teddy Bear here . . . Good Buddy . . . over," Robby replied.

There was a stunned silence, then, "Everything cool, Teddy Bear?"

Robby looked at me. In the dim light of the cab I could see him grin. "Everything is cool, start back the way we came and I'll contact you within the hour...over."

"Ten-four . . . over."

Why doesn't he just say 'I'm a cop'.

Just north of Zapata, we passed an all night truck stop with a beer sign in the window.

"Phil," Robby said, tapping him on the shoulder, "turn around and go back to that truck stop."

A minute later, we pulled into the truck stop to let Teemo out. As he prepared to leave, he stared almost bashfully at Robby and said, "I jus do wha dey say to do, Rowbee. Dey say no going to keel jew, jus take dinero, dey say eet weel be eesy." Then Teemo laughed and slapped his leg and pointed to me and said, "He naw so eesy, eh, Rowbee, no?"

Robby and I locked eyes in the light of the truck stop. I wasn't sure how he was going to take that, but he smiled and said, "No, you're right Teemo, there's nothing easy about Tucker. He just seems that way."

I looked at the sign in the window and said, "I don't know about you guys, but I sure could use a cold one and maybe some Cheetos or something."

That turned out to be a popular idea. Robby, Teemo and I went in and bought some beer and a bag of snacks. We were back in the parking lot in a few minutes, the three of us standing by Phil, with his window rolled down.

Teemo smiled at all three of us and said as hopefully as a child asking for a bicycle for Christmas, "Eez how jew say, no har feelingz?"

Robby looked at me, I looked at Phil, Phil looked at Robby, and we all started laughing. After all...how ya gonna act?

Robby had contacted Allen on the CB, and it was easy to rendezvous with him. Three hours later, all four of us were in Freer, Texas eating breakfast in a little restaurant on Highway 59. The sun was just coming up, and I'd have to say it was one of the most beautiful sunrises I had ever seen.

As usual, we were as far removed from any other patrons as we could get, and we had a window booth so we could see the Bronco and trailer.

I didn't feel like talking. I was tired, and I missed Margie. But, Phil and Robby had nothing holding them back. They filled Allen in on the night's activities, and like most retelling of anything exciting, certain liberties were taken with the facts. By the time they got to the part about the extra load of bricks being made at the end, I had almost forgotten about it.

It was easy to do, since I had just learned we had taken on about 20 of the 'baddest motherfuckers in Mexico' and killed them all, but Teemo and the 'jefe'.

Robby looked at me over a cup of caffeine and said, "What was all that gift shit about Tucker?"

"Before I answer that," I said, "when do we get paid? We gave all the money to Armando."

Allen grinned and said, "I've got yours. We took it out of the duffel when you were in the bathroom, back at the motel. It's in a paper bag, all ten grand of it. When we leave, I'll give it to you. I've got paper bags for all of us. You and Robby take the load in the Bronco. Phil and I will follow you in the Impala, just like on the way down. We're home-free, man, home-free."

I looked at each of them and said, "Well, we've come out a little better than you think. I've got us an extra 50 kilos to split between us, it's ours. It has nothing to do with the shipment we came to get."

It took a few seconds for that to sink in.

I could see Phil trying to do the math.

"That's twenty-seven and a half pounds apiece." I said. At 200 a pound, which should be easy to get, that's . . ."

"Fifty-five hundred fuckin' dollars!" yelled Phil, the mathematician.

Allen looked perplexed.

"I'm not a drug dealer," he said. "How am I going to get rid of it?"

I could see Phil and Robby thinking the same thing.

"What!" I said. "What did we come down here for. What's in that trailer out there?"

I couldn't believe my ears.

"We don't sell it," Robby said. "We just get paid to come and get it. Our boss takes care of the distribution. It works that way, we don't know who sells it, and whoever sells it doesn't know who goes down and gets it."

"Kind of like one hand doesn't know what the other is doing?" I said.

"Yeah, kind of," Robby said.

I thought back on how many times Marijuana Mick had asked me if I could get pounds. He said he had guys all over north Louisiana begging for pounds.

"Okay," I said, "I'll get rid of it for you, at say . . . $125 a pound. It may take me a few weeks, but I'll move it."

Phil was almost counting on his fingers.

"That's a little over three grand," I said.

Within five seconds, they were all grinning and nodding their heads at me.

I had just moved up from dealing lids to dealing pounds.

Robby and I took turns driving and sleeping. The CB was quiet. We decided not to use it unless there was danger of a bust or a hijacking. We were tired and strung as tight as a banjo. The silence was as welcome as a warm breeze in the middle of a hard winter.

I was driving, still on Highway 59, going through Livingston, Texas, when Robby started to stir and rub the sleep from his eyes.

"Where are we?" he asked sleepily.

"About 60 miles north of Houston."

"I need some coffee," he said, as he stretched as much as he could in the restrictions of the Bronco. As small as he was, it was a lot.

"It's time for a pit stop anyway," I said, eyeing the gas gauge and squirming to relieve bladder pressure.

After gassing up and getting some Hostess Cupcakes to go with our coffee, Robby pulled to the edge of the parking lot where we waited for Phil and Allen to finish their end of the now much practiced routine, and, like routines go, it was beginning to get boring.

To compound the boredom I was tired. Maybe that was one reason I couldn't stop thinking about Margie. I had fallen in love with the girl across the street, literally.

There was a bond between us, a bond that had been forged out of surviving hardships together. There was the hardship of being in love at an age when all the adults in our life were telling us 'we didn't know what love was'. We had lost our first child, not to death, but to the authorities, who had taken her away from us. Our parents, thinking they knew what was best for us, made Margie go to an unwed mothers' home, where the nuns made her take care of her newborn baby girl for a week, then took her away. They said it would be a good lesson for her. She was only 15 at the time. It broke her heart.

After the first couple of months in the home, one of the nicer nuns took pity on Margie and allowed her to contact a friend of ours, who contacted me. Until then, I didn't know where she was. I was sick with worry and anger. A strong anger. I still remember the joy when I found out where she was, my first love, my sweetheart, my baby. After getting the phone number, we found ways to talk to each other throughout her pregnancy and our daughter's birth. When she called and told me the baby was gone, we cried, together. But when she told me what the nuns had done and how they treated her, like some sort of slut, well, that was when I started hating nuns, and I wasn't even Catholic.

A little over a year after she returned, my father informed me we were moving to Florida. He had talked to the coach at Florida and finagled a scholarship for me. We wouldn't let them separate us again, so we got pregnant again, knowing there was no way they could not let us get married. We did get married, in August, the summer before our senior year in high school. We were very much in love, and that love had always kept us together through the hell our parents put us through. They were very creative in the hell they dealt under the guise of wisdom and love. We dreamed of getting married and then finding our daughter, Patricia Elaine, that's what we'd named her, and surely they would give her back to us.

When that dreamed was shattered, our love for each other and our second daughter, Shannon, kept us together. I lived with her family for a year, then we got our first apartment. So, when I say we had a bond, it was made of steel. We had never lied to each other. We had no secrets. I was having a hard time thinking this may be a time to hold something back. It may not be wise to tell her everything that had transpired.

"George Darvoyce."

"What?" I said.

"Our boss is George Darvoyce, the Commissioner of Public Safety. He's the one who pays us."

It was like hearing the Pope was the devil, it just didn't compute at first. I had seen him on TV, speaking out against drugs and how he was personally going to stamp it out. I had seen him setting fire to piles of marijuana. He would do it at an abandoned airport and always with a lot of publicity. Television crews from all the local stations would be there along with the major newspapers. He was quite the public figure.

I knew Robby was serious. It all made sense now. Why he wasn't worried about getting busted by the cops, and how he got the time off.

"Does he know about me?" I asked. I had never met him.

"Yeah, he knows about you. I had to clear it with him. He knows I've been grooming you. I told him what you could do with a pistol, and he's heard about you from other cops."

I was confused. There was a protected warmth flowing through my body, and a cold drowning sensation in my head.

While I was deciphering my emotions, he continued.

"I've known him most of my life. He was a friend of my father's, when my father was coming up in the force. Darvoyce was an assistant D.A. at the time. Anyway, he caught me smoking a joint behind my father's carport at a Bar-B-Q a few years ago. I thought my ass was grass," we both laughed. "But, he told me not to worry about it, it would be our little secret. A few months later he took me to dinner, and we talked about the futility of the marijuana war and how it would probably be legalized soon. One thing led to another, and we started taking the pot we seized on busts and putting it back on the streets."

"You mean, those burnings on TV were faked?"

He continued to drive for a minute before answering. "Not exactly. That was one of my first jobs for him. I would replace the bales and bricks, with hay and alfalfa, wrapped up to look like marijuana, leaving only about 10 percent of what we actually burned marijuana. I just made sure it was left on top."

"What happens to the rest of it?"

"It goes back on the street. I don't know who's involved with that part of the operation, just like they don't know about us. I assume there are more cops involved, but I don't know. That's where the money for this run came from. Darvoyce really put the pressure on to make more busts the past few months."

"Yeah," I said, "I've noticed more publicity about it lately."

He laughed, and said, "It's really weird to see it on T V and knowing all the while, he's just scrambling to raise more money so we can make another run."

The more I thought about it, the more sense it made, that is, me doing this. It was a tight operation and only a few people knew about me and they all had more to lose than me.

"And, Tucker, thanks to you, from now on our runs will be a breeze. If you don't think what happened down there will get around to the other dealers and possible hijackers, you're crazy, and I'm going to make sure Darvoyce knows about it."

I didn't remember thinking anything like that, but Robby often talked that way, transferring his thoughts to others.

"I suppose so," I nodded, looking out the window as east Texas rolled by, a little too fast. This conversation was lulling me into

believing even the Texas cops were in on it, so just to make sure
it didn't do the same to Robby, I said, "Better watch your speed,
wouldn't want to get stopped this close to home."

His head jerked around, and I could see the lights come on
behind his eyes. He looked quickly down at the speedometer and let
off a little on the accelerator.

"Yeah," he whispered, more to himself than me.

We stopped at a storage place, where I rented a unit, and we
unloaded the 50 kilos. We did it just like we knew what we were
doing, hiding in plain sight. Robby said he would take care of the
rest. We pulled into my apartment complex at five in the afternoon.

So, when Margie opened the door after we honked, I looked
like I was returning from a hunting trip. She was wearing a black
halter top, white short shorts and was barefoot. My mouth mistook
her for an ice cream cone and salivated accordingly. She jumped on
me, wrapped her legs around me, and showered me with kisses.

"I love you . . . I love you . . . I love you," she repeated over and
over. The worry she had been experiencing since my departure, was
running down her exquisite cheeks.

Robby was standing beside the Bronco smiling, I heard the
door slam, and as he drove off, he yelled, "Miranda was right, you're
a lucky bastard!"

After throwing my duffels on the floor and unloading my shotgun and putting it away, she stood in the bedroom with her hands
on her hips. Her dancer's body looking totally feline, her face covered with the realization that I had not unloaded my weapons until
that moment. If I had come home from hunting, they would have
been empty before entering the house. I would have to watch that
next time.

"Tuck," she said huskily to me. Her voice dripped sex, like a
pheromone from an insect.

But, I knew there was something besides making love on her
mind.

"What is it, Baby?" I said, turning around from the closet with
the brown grocery bag full of money.

"I don't know if I could take another one of those trips."

I walked over to the bed and poured $10,000 onto it. It was
mostly in 20's with a few 100's and 50's mixed in. It was a lot of
money, and it looked like more than it was.

She stood at the side of the bed and looked down at it for a full minute. She slowly turned her blue eyes to me, moving her shoulder length hair out of her face so she was framed in a thick auburn mane with gold highlights. She said, "What are we going to do with it?"

"Well, I've been thinking about that all the way home. I was thinking that I would quit my job."

"Quit your job?" she said apprehensively.

With the storage unit in my mind, I said, "Yeah, you see, I have more, just about that much again, and it's all ours. And, in a few months I'll go down to Texas again, and, well, it looks like I don't need that job anymore, and I thought I would go back to school."

As she absorbed that information, her face transformed from nervous fear to the joy of possibilities.

"Me too? Can I quit my job and go back to school, too?" she said, barely whispering as if afraid, if the words were too loud, they would shatter and fall, before making the journey to my ears.

Now, Margie made a lot more money than I did. She was an insurance underwriter, and had her own office with the company she worked for. She had seniority and benefits. But, the look on her face was like a little girl asking for the best birthday present imaginable.

"You bet," I said, the tears forming as I was able to grant her wish. "We'll both quit and go back to school. But, before we use the money to do that, what you say, after I take a shower . . ."

As she pulled me down on top of her and the money, she said, "The shower can wait."

I eventually took that shower, then we nourished ourselves, with food. After making love through the night, lying in the comfort of her arms, a place of total honesty, I told her everything. Leaving nothing out and with no embellishments. When I was through, she proceeded to beat the stuffing out of me. She had a pair of strong dancer's legs, and she could spin around on her round bottom and crash down on me with her heels. She learned long ago that was the only effective way of exerting her smaller stature over me.

Chapter 34

"What are you smiling about?" LeCompte said. "From what Gray told me, there wasn't much to smile about on that trip you made into Mexico."

Smiled. I wasn't aware I'd smiled.

I wasn't smiling about the trip.

I looked at Carr and a sadness swept over me. I said, "I was thinking about when I got back."

Carr tore his eyes from mine and looked down at his cigar and knowingly nodded.

Evidently my smile had interrupted Carr's reading of Robby's account. I was aware of his voice droning behind my thoughts, but hadn't been listening. I decided to shorten this interview.

I said, "Just what did Robby say about that first trip?"

"Frank taped the interview with Gray," Carr said, as he was again sorting through the files and folders on his desk.

"I'll bet he didn't know about that," I said.

"Of course not," LeCompte said.

Carr held up a stack with at least a hundred pages in it and said, "I instructed Frank to have all interviews taped, and then I had them transcribed. This is Robby Gray's interview. If even half of what he says happened is accurate, it's fascinating reading."

"Just the condensed version, if you don't mind," I said, wondering who had done the transcribing.

Carr's eyes shifted over to Frank LeCompte's and with almost an imperceptible nod, turned the telling over to him.

"For one, he said if it hadn't been for you, they would have lost the money and the connection. Said when the shooting started, you shot three Mexicans before he could get a shot off. And shot each one of them twice."

"Seemed like the thing to do at the time. I knew *he* was going to shoot somebody."

LeCompte smiled at me through a blue cloud of smoke and said, "He said the same thing about you."

"What?" This didn't sound like the same gunfight to me.

"Yeah, he said when he heard you say, 'Margie, I love you,' he knew you were going to draw. Said it sounded like you were saying goodbye to her."

Now, this was a surprise.

"I didn't know I said it aloud."

"Was that what you were doing?" Carr asked. "Saying goodbye to her?"

I took a drink and said, "More or less."

LeCompte said, "He said you didn't shoot to kill, you just wounded them, but in the right places."

"I had never killed a man. I've always been lucky concerning violence and I was naive enough to think I was good enough to just wound someone, to incapacitate them. And, I think maybe I just had difficulty with killing a man."

"You don't seem to have that problem anymore," Carr said, unsmiling, from the other side of his desk.

"Like I said. I was naïve." Then added, "And things change."

After a moment of silence, and to no one in particular, I said, "I've done a lot of that since then."

LeCompte said, "How'd you feel after killing those two hit men?"

His question wasn't out of idle curiosity. This was a man who wanted to compare notes.

After the shooting I'd had ample opportunity to examine my feelings, or lack of them, concerning the death of those men.

I've felt more grief over killing a deer. A beautiful, majestic, gentle animal, truly one of God's innocent creatures. One moment they would be eating acorns off the ground, and the next moment they'd be dead. The deer never did anything to me or to anyone else, and they sure didn't have a gun, but, I still killed them. I tried to honor them, by killing them quick and as painless as possible, and by not wasting any part of them. I still have the hides of every deer I've killed. I don't deer hunt anymore.

I said, "I can live with it."

LeCompte and I looked at each other.

I said, "There are human animals running around that like to kill human beings, not have to, like to. There needs to be someone between the animals and the human beings."

"Which are you, Tucker?" LeCompte asked. "One of the animals or one of the human beings?"

Again, LeCompte and I looked at each other.

"Would you like another drink, Tucker?" Carr asked, taking LeCompte's eyes from mine.

"I better not. I have some business to attend to later." I said, thinking about my impending chat with Eddie Tuma.

"I've got some Haake Beck," he said.

"That would be fine," I said, wondering if he always had it on hand or if he had done *that* much research on me.

Instead of pushing an intercom button or using some hi-tech method of communicating with Rachael, he got up and walked over to the bar. After fixing himself another drink, he opened what looked like a lower cabinet and pulled a Haake Beck out of a small built-in refrigerator.

After opening it, he reached back into the refrigerator and brought out a tall heavy pilsner glass. He poured it without leaning the glass over, making the perfect head and letting off the ideal amount of carbonation to best experience the taste.

I felt LeCompte observing me as I watched Carr prepare my Beck's exactly as I like it.

After Carr brought the glass over to me, I looked up at him and said affably, "If you would have told me where it was, I would have gotten it myself."

His smile was only in his eyes as he looked down and said, "Well, now you know."

Yeah, I also knew where I was. In the middle of something I didn't understand.

He walked back around to his chair, set his fresh drink down on the desk and stood behind the chair, resting his hands on the back of it.

I said, "Mr. Carr, just what is it you would like me to do?"

He looked a little hurt that I had used 'Mr.,' just a little.

"You have obviously gone to a great deal of trouble and expense to check into my past, a past that I am neither proud of, nor wish to remember. A past that wouldn't enhance my current profession if it were to become public knowledge."

George Carr held up both his hands as if to ward off impending blows, and said, "Tucker, let me assure you, you have my word, this information goes no further than this room and the people in it. Believe me when I say that the record we have compiled about you is, to me, an asset for what I would like you to do."

Before I could say what was on my mind, he read it, and said, "Don't worry, it has nothing to do with dealing drugs or anything against the law."

I still didn't get it. I didn't know if I was just dense or he was being obtuse.

"From what we have learned about you through a compilation of written and verbal interviews, you have a reputation of being tough, honest, and honorable. You are well liked and respected. You also seem to be lucky. Put all this together, and you are a person I would want on my side."

"On your side to do what?" I said, trying again.

He was on a roll, it was as if he'd rehearsed his words, and wasn't going to be quelled at this point.

"Who taught you about honor? We were told by more than one person that 'if Tucker says he is going to do something, it's as good as done.' Even as an outlaw, you had a good reputation, and you were a young man. Where did you learn about honesty and honor? In the business you were in, those traits aren't common occurrences."

He was genuinely interested. I didn't think he was going to like my answer.

"Louis L'Amour," I said.

I was right, his eyes darkened and his frown grew into a silent snarl. This was a man that was in the habit of being taken seriously at all times.

With as much sincerity I could muster, I said, "I'm serious. I started reading Louis L'Amour books when I was about ten or eleven and read everything he wrote. I didn't stop until he died."

As my words soaked in, his face relaxed, once again revealing the man I liked.

"You didn't learn it from your father?"

The 'it' he was referring to was really more than one thing. After a moment's thought, I said, "I didn't have a very good relationship with my father. We didn't get along. But, from him I did learn one of the things you spoke of. He taught me that if I said I was going to do something, I better do it."

I'm sure my tone said this wasn't one of the lessons I enjoyed. But, learn it I did. It was a good thing to learn, even if the learning of it was painful.

His smile was slow in coming, and it was mixed with knowing compassion. He said, "It may have been an epidemic of our generation, not getting along with our fathers."

I nodded to him and said, "I learned a lot from my uncles, about what it meant to be a 'Tucker.' They all liked me. But, for the most part, I learned what kind of man I would like to be by reading L'Amour's books."

"Like what?" he said.

I said, knowing that L'Amour may never have said the exact words, "Like 'there are times you have to be tough, but you never have to be mean,' and taught you the difference through his characters. The difference between a bad man and a mean man, a bad man wasn't necessarily mean, but a mean man was always bad."

Carr and LeCompte exchanged looks.

"Well, you asked," I said, as I recalled the basic outline of the relationship with my father, after hours of therapy.

It started when my parents got divorced. I was maybe five or six at the time. My father didn't think I was old enough to understand what was going on, and he turned all his attention to my older brother, Ben. He explained to him how it wasn't his fault, Ben's, that is, that they were getting divorced. He told Ben how much he loved him, how he would always love him and would always be there for him, he pretty much ignored me and my little sister, Kathi, I guess he thought we were too young to know what was going on.

Because my alcoholic mother and equally alcoholic and physically abusive stepfather were such unfit parents, my maternal grandmother was going to testify against her own daughter. Four years after the divorce and without a court battle, my father regained custody of my brother and me. It was years later that I found out my father wanted only my brother, but Ben said he wouldn't go without me. I also learned that my brother's sometimes malice towards me was his way of dealing with his own set of problems. The time we spent with my mother and stepfather we were so neglected that my brother literally raised us. He would make sure we ate and stayed clean. I can still see him at the kitchen counter making us peanut butter sandwiches or heating up Campbells tomato soup. He protected us as well as he could. It was a big responsibility for such a young boy. I literally did everything he said...like he was my dad. It must have been very hard for him to let go of that responsibility after my father gained custody of us. It caused quite a bit of conflict between my father and me as well as my brother and me. But, we did the best we could. I trusted my brother more than my father. Ben was the only constant in my life. My father would give me chores to do and then my brother would want me to do something else. I usually did what Ben wanted...it gave a whole new meaning to "the middle child."

It wasn't until I was in my mid-forties that I found that the reason my father didn't want Kathi was because she wasn't his daughter. Kathi was conceived while my father was out of the country, on TDY. My half-sister, to this day, doesn't know. When my brother told me and found out I didn't know, he was amazed. I remember being angry and thinking, 'how would I know, no one ever tells me anything'.

Needless to say, I wasn't my father's favorite son. He used to introduce me to his friends at the American Legion bar as his number two son, his number one shitass.

My uncles once told me they'd told my father I was the best son he had, and the reason he didn't get along with me was because I was just like him.

Being so much like my father was an enigma, at least for him. My father had a hard time dealing with himself, I don't think he liked himself very much. He was well thought of and respected by his peers, by everyone...by me. He had a reputation of never taking any shit from anyone. I was the same way.

My father didn't want to take a close look at himself. He was a womanizer and an adulterer. He drank too much and was a mean drunk, mostly to me. I'm sure a lot of it was due to the war. But, in those days, Post Traumatic Stress had not yet been coined.

Since I was so much like him and he didn't like himself, well, you see how that goes. He didn't like me because I was so much like him and just couldn't see it. And I liked him because of the same reason. He was so much like me, I recognized that and it felt right. The more I loved him, the more he rejected my love.

I was told (by a professional) that was one of the reasons I used to do so many dangerous things. Death was nothing compared to the rejection of my father's love. I loved him, I "saw" him. I knew him. He and I were the same. But, if we were the same, why didn't he *love* me, why didn't he *see* me? Louis L'Amour saw me.

Can you say, *'baggage'*?

Carr thankfully interrupted my reverie, "I've never read any Louis L'Amour, but I've seen a couple of movies made from his books," Carr said.

LeCompte was grinning at me when he said, "I've read a lot of his books. I can see it." He looked at Carr and said, "Yeah, I can see it. Tucker's just an old cowboy, a real rootin' tootin,' damsel saving, gunfighter." His statement held no sarcasm.

Now, that appealed to me. I felt my eyes crinkle and held up my boot to show it off.

"My damsel's beyond saving," Carr said, erasing LeCompte's grin and bringing us back to why I was there.

Chapter 35

"If you would tell me what you would like me to do. I will tell you if I will do it."

I couldn't say it any more clearly.

Carr stood up and turned his back on me, "I don't think my wife's death was an accident," he said, looking at the picture of him and his wife on the bookshelf.

When he turned around to face me, he'd aged a hundred years. "I believe she was killed to get to me."

"Why?"

"I'm worth over a billion dollars," he said, with no pride what-so-ever. It was a flat statement with an underlying poignant tone that said, 'I would give it all up for a minute with my wife.'

I've never thought about money and that many zero's at the same time before.

"The process of making that much money sometimes means other people lose money, or don't get to make it when I did," he continued. "I've been threatened over the years, and I believe my wife was killed as a means of revenge."

That would explain LeCompte's presence.

"Why would you think that? Did someone contact you?"

"No."

"When was the last threat made?"

"A little over fifteen years ago," he said, with the weight of forethought.

Now, that seemed like a long time to me.

"Was that threat to you or your wife?" I said, looking up at him, wishing he would sit down before I had to go to the Chiropractor.

"It was to me," he said as he sat down.

Why is it always the little wishes that are granted?

I was beginning to feel like I was sitting in a rocket science class.

Trying not to sound exasperated, I said, "Okay, so, you think your wife was killed to get back at you, because . . . ?"

I was now convinced he was being obtuse.

"Because the private investigator I hired disappeared a few weeks after I hired him."

Now, this was pithy information.

"Would you care to elaborate?" I asked, looking at both of them.

Carr held up his glass between himself and the window, looked through the melting ice cubes, and said, "I hired a retired Houston PD Detective, turned Private, named Manske. He came highly recommended, and after a few weeks of getting nowhere, he called and reported he had a promising lead. That was the last we heard from him. Frank has called someone he knows in Houston. His house was staked out for a few days, and he was a no show."

Noticing his glass was sans whiskey, I asked, "What was this lead?"

LeCompte said, "He didn't say. Said he wanted to be sure about it before he said anything. He did say it was heavy."

Heavy?

"What did the Houston PD have to say?"

They both just stared at me, their vacant faces saying it.

"You didn't report it, did you?" I sighed, remembering how they said it might get messy. My *house* gets messy.

As Carr got up and headed back towards the bar, he said, "We talked it over and thought it best if we didn't call any attention to the investigation."

"Why?" I asked, trying to keep my head above the waterline.

"A couple of reasons," LeCompte said. "One, we figured if there had been any foul play, we'd let it cool off. Whoever was involved may think we've given up. So if we sent someone else, they might be able to pick the trail back up. Two, I got the impression that someone in the Houston PD might be involved."

"You got that impression, did you?" I said, thinking, did he really say *foul play?* He had definitely been in civilian life too long. I also didn't think he was telling me everything. But, what do I know.

"Yes, I did," LeCompte said. "I talked to him last. When he said this lead was getting heavy, well, that's the impression I got."

I hadn't been around this man for long, but long enough to get a sense of his sense.

"Sounds reasonable," I said. "So, when you said foul play, you believe this Manske may be dead. Is that right?"

LeCompte's face turned sour and he looked between Carr and me, said, "Foul play? I didn't say foul play, did I?"

Our combined silence was palpable in the large office.

LeCompte said, "Yeah, we think he's dead or bought off, probably dead."

I couldn't help thinking, *messy, messy, messy.* But I was beginning to connect the dots.

Carr was just sitting back down with a topped off glass. I hadn't been counting, but I still didn't detect any of the telltale signs of him being drunk.

I glanced at Carr and said, "George, did you think your wife was murdered from the beginning, or only after Manske got foul played?"

I was looking at LeCompte when I finished the question. There was no humor in my voice. I didn't think anything about this was amusing. I'd been asked over here for a job interview. So far, I've had my iniquitous past stacked on a desk then thrown in my face, been flattered, had words like dead and bloody replaced by foul play and messy. The only reason I didn't walk out was, I liked George Carr and Frank LeCompte; I liked the skiing picture of him and his wife; I liked Rachael and the way she looked for the ghost of a woman to walk into the foyer; I liked the room I was sitting in; I liked the flattery; I needed something to do; I was starting to feel the stirrings of intrigue; and I was getting hungry.

That's the only reason I didn't get up and walk out.

Carr, hands flat on his desk, leaned toward me and said in a voice barely devoid of tears, "After Manske disappeared following his last report, I became convinced she was murdered. I need someone I can trust to go to Houston and nose around, see if there is any lead that can help me find out what happened to Jean. I believe Manske was onto something and it got him killed. If he was bought off, he most likely wouldn't have disappeared. Why would he? Tucker, I loved my wife. I owe it to her, and what we had, to do everything in my power to find out what happened to her."

I started thinking, *if there were bad cops involved, I wouldn't be a bad choice to ferret them out. It's not like I don't have experience in that arena. And, me not being a cop or never having been a cop might be an asset. I do have some cop connections in Houston. Another thing, this Manske's disappearance may have nothing to do with the investigation into Carr's wife's death, it could be related to another case, or something from his cop days. But I knew Carr didn't want to hear that.*

Carr inhaled through his nose and said, "Tucker, I would imagine you might feel violated by all of the, ah, research we've done on you. Please understand and believe me when I say, it started out as a routine background check, something I would do before hiring anyone. I may have gotten a little carried away, but, the more I learned about you, the more I wanted to know. The more I learned, the more certain I became that you are the man for this job."

I looked at my past stacked on his desk and said, "A little carried away?"

He stood and looked down at me and quietly said, "Look, goddamnit, I'm not sorry, okay? I know you are the man I need. You want the job or not?"

I'd bet that was as close to begging that Carr had ever come.

"If I take the job, can I have a copy of my life?" I said, pointing at him with my finger and thumb, like a gun.

He stared at my finger gun for a moment, looked confusingly at the stack on the desk, then back at me, and said, "Of course."

I was curious as to how my life was perceived by others. I believed we never see ourselves as others do. Maybe I wouldn't read it.

"What happens if I find that someone did murder your wife? What happens then?"

LeCompte answered, "If you find out who did it, your job is done. I'll take care of the rest."

I pulled myself out of the chair, walked over to the gun cabinet and stood in front of it. I wasn't looking at the guns. I could see my reflection in the glass; I was thinking about Margie. I was thinking if someone murdered her to get to me, would I want to know that. Probably, the guilt would be bad, but not as bad as knowing her killer was walking around with a fuckin' smile on his face.

"What're you thinking, Tucker?" Carr asked.

"That if I find out she was murdered, I'd better make damn sure who did it before I tell LeCompte."

"Then you're going to help me, you're going to do it?"

I turned from the guns and walked over to the desk and with my legs against it, leaned over and held out my hand.

Carr held out his and as we looked into each other's eyes, we shook on it.

LeCompte walked behind the desk and stood to the left of Carr and softy said, "Hooya."

That's how we were when Rachael opened the door and walked into the office.

Chapter 36

"Excuse me, gentlemen," she said. Then her eyes gleamed with understanding, and she said, "I'm glad you are going to help us, Mr. Tucker."

Again, I heard the 'us', as in, family.

As Carr and I disengaged, she walked towards us. She had changed into a black long-sleeved shirt with the sleeves rolled half-way up her forearms, tucked into faded blue jeans. On her feet were soft brown leather boots, obviously custom made. The attire accented her broad shoulders, the strength of her arms, and the length of her legs.

Before I could reply, she said, "Dinner will be ready in 30 minutes."

"Splendid," Carr said. "I'm sure I heard Tucker's stomach growling a few minutes ago."

She walked over and stood next to me and looked sternly at George. She smelled faintly of roses and expensive soap. From the side, I saw that her face was only scarred on the front half. From the corner of her eye back, her complexion was flawless. I could see her pulse in the contours of her neck. I liked her neck.

"And from the looks of you, you need to eat," she said, still boring holes into Carr.

Carr looked down at his whiskey glass, embarrassment red was starting to creep up his jaw line. He meekly said, "I've only had a couple, Rachael, ask Frank."

She quickly looked at me and caught me checking her pulse. "I think I will ask Mr. Tucker how many you've had."

I was looking into her blue eyes and just getting a grasp on the fact, she had taken over some of Mrs. Carr's duties. Like watching out for Mr. Carr's health. I didn't get the impression there was any sexual tension between the two. It was more of a motherly, or sisterly energy. Then, I realized why I thought of sexual energy. She was standing very close to me, and she expected me to respond to the question.

"I would really like to call you Rachael," I said. "So, if you don't drop the Mr., I will have to call you Miss . . . what is your last name anyway?"

"Wallace," she said, maintaining eye contact.

"So what's it going to be, Rachael or Miss Wallace? It is Miss, isn't it.?"

I was enjoying her proximity and was surprised by my unpremeditated flirting. It took her a moment to realize it. She blushed, turning some of the more pronounced scars pink. She immediately dropped her head and looked at the floor. I was sorely cognizant that she was aware that blushing highlighted her disfigurement.

I felt like an ass. I didn't quite know what to do.

In almost a whisper, she said, "Miss . . . it's Miss."

I gently put my right index finger under her chin, raised her face up until we were once again looking at each other, and said, "So, what's it going to be?"

"What?" she said.

"Rachael or Miss Wallace?" I said.

"Rachael, of course," she said, with a small tinkling laugh, not quite a giggle.

"Okay, then, I'm Tucker, or Tuck, whichever you prefer."

She turned her head towards Carr, taking her chin from my fingertip in the process, and said, "Twenty-eight minutes." A note to her diamond edge exactness and household power.

She looked at LeCompte, curtly nodded, turned and walked towards the door. Halfway there, she spun around, and caught me noticing what else the jeans accented, and said, "I believe I will call you Tuck."

Before I could antically respond, she said, "And, Tuck, don't think I didn't notice you never answered my question."

"I never heard a question. Did you hear her ask me a question George?"

"Not me," Carr said, "You, Frank?"

"Not me."

She stared at Frank a moment longer, then looked at me and said, "I cooked Crawfish Etouffe'e', I hope you'll like it."

Then to George, she said, "I let the kitchen staff go home early." She left without another word.

I looked at Frank and said, "What's with you and her?"

"I don't know how she does it, but she can tell when George has had more than a couple of drinks. She asked me to make sure he doesn't drink during the day."

"I'll drink when I'm damn good and ready," George said. "And I'm damn good and ready now."

He started over towards the liquor cabinet, and Frank said, "How 'bout I open some wine, something to go with the Etouffe'e."

Carr stopped in mid-stride and said, "Did she say *she* cooked?"

"I was wondering if you caught that," Frank said.

I looked from one to the other and said, "I guess it's not a common occurrence when your head of housekeeping cooks."

They both were obviously taken aback.

"Who's head of housekeeping?" George said.

Frank started laughing, and I said, "She told me she was head of housekeeping."

Now they were both laughing. George Carr's laughter was loud and full of release. The hilarity of a man who hadn't done much laughing. I was reminded of the forgetting of grief, and how freeing it was, momentarily.

"What?" I asked.

After his laughter subsided enough for him to speak, George said, "Rachael *is* head of housekeeping, and head of everything else, including my investments. The woman graduated Suma Cum Laude, with an MBA, from Harvard. She literally keeps my house and my money together."

I looked back at the closed door she had just walked through.

Frank said, "And, the fact that she is cooking means she likes you. She is one hell of a cook. She got the recipe for Crawfish Etouffe'e from my mother and prepares it like a true Cajun."

Carr put his glass down without refilling it, walked back to his desk, sat down behind it, and said, "Rachael doesn't like many people. Her experience with other's reaction to her face has left her a bit cynical concerning the human race. She prefers animals, mostly horses and dogs."

I sat back down in my chair as Frank opened another book-shelf, revealing a hidden wine rack.

"I *don't* have one of those," I said. "I am glad she likes me, but I don't know why she would. I've just met her."

Frank's hand stopped in mid-air as he was reaching for a bottle of wine.

George Carr cleared his throat and said, "Ah, well . . . Tucker, Rachael sort of transcribed and arranged your file."

Now I really didn't know why she'd like me.

"Is there anyone else who knows more about me than, as you said, I do?"

Carr stood, walked over to the wine rack, pulled out a bottle of wine and while looking at the label, nonchalantly said, "I did have a psychiatrist I know read it, and give me an overall review of what kind of man I might expect to be dealing with."

My appetite was fading. I had already taken the job. There wasn't much point in getting mad about it. I had been around enough therapists not to be intimidated by them or their opinions. At times like this, it all comes down to one thing, 'how ya gonna act'. That's what life's about. A series of actions we make in relationship to information and situations.

So, I said, "I like red wine."

"Me too," Carr said.

"Me too," LeCompte said.

Chapter 37

I walked back to the gun cabinet as Carr and LeCompte selected and opened a bottle of wine. I looked at my watch and saw that it was almost 6:30. I had been in Carr's office for almost five and a half hours. It felt like days. My brain had been wrenched by memories, long put away.

Thinking back on my dealing days wasn't the hardest part. It was how Margie and I were at that time. It was edge living and it kept us close. Not closer, we couldn't have been any closer. It kept us in a constant state of intimacy and trust for the few years we were in the business.

Looking at the guns in the cabinet reminded me how she'd always trusted me not to get killed. How she liked to watch me shoot my guns and do some of the quick draw tricks with my western six-gun rig. I knew it made her feel secure. Like there was no way I could be shot in a gunfight. I didn't share that feeling, but could never let her know that. And, by the frequency and the intensity when we made love, I wasn't all that certain about her exact sentiments on the subject of my prolonged existence. It was fast times.

"It's open," Carr said. "Look at whatever you like."

I opened the framed glass door and plucked an old Colt Peacemaker from where it was hanging on a wooden peg by the trigger guard. I thumbed back the hammer until it released the cylinder, opened the bale and slowly spun the cylinder to check for rounds. It was empty. Then I did something so natural to me, I didn't even think about it. I gave it a half forward spin, then a full back spin until it settled in my palm, thumbed the hammer back and pulled the trigger. It was something I did to check the balance of a gun, how it fit in my hand and the sensitivity of the trigger.

LeCompte whistled softly and said, "Now, *that* was pretty."

Like I said, I did it without thinking and when I turned my head towards LeCompte, he saw my confusion.

"What you just did, I've seen it done before, but not with such a natural . . . acquaintance."

As George poured wine into generous crystal goblets, he said, "If you look in the bottom drawer of the cabinet, you'll find a holster that goes with it. I wouldn't mind if you tried them out, you know . . . quick draw."

I heard it as 'queeks draw', like in Queeks Draw McGraw, from the old cartoon. I always did.

"Maybe some other time," I said, returning the old Colt to its resting place.

"Come on Tucker," LeCompte urged, "don't go all shy on us."

"You know what Confucius said?"

They both shook their heads.

I pretended to draw two guns from imaginary holsters hanging on my hips and pointed both finger guns at them, squinted my eyes and said in my best English/Oriental accent, "Showoff's always shown up in showdown."

Carr looked surprised.

"So, you read Confucius," he said. "Again...you surprise me."

"No, fortune cookies," I said.

I could see them weighing this. I took advantage of the silence, walked over and picked up the glass Carr had set down on the desk, across from the chair I had occupied. I held it under my nose, smelled the wine, then swirled it in the glass, just like I had seen on TV, and took a sip. I didn't aerate it like they did on TV. It makes an unseemly noise.

"This is great stuff," I said, eloquently.

They both smiled.

"It's a '97 Cakebread, a Cab," George said. "One of our favorites."

No sooner had the 'our' come out of his mouth when the smile disappeared and again, we were reminded why we were there.

My eyeballs were rapidly starting to float around in their sockets.

I was still standing holding my wine glass when I said, "I need to find a bathroom." It wasn't as urgent as I made it sound, but I wanted to get out of the room for a few minutes.

"Right through that door," George said, pointing to the wall to the right of the secret bookshelf, behind his desk.

I had to look hard to discern the knob.

"Do you have one a little further away? I'd like to walk around a little."

"There's at least a dozen in this place," George said, unpretentiously. "After leaving the hallway to the office, turn right. As you head towards the windows in the back, there's one on your right, just before the entrance to the kitchen."

Ahh, the kitchen, my second objective. I took my wine with me.

Chapter 38

Carr watched the door to his office close after Tucker, then turned towards Frank LeCompte.

"I *know* those Canadian mother-fuckers are behind her death, Frank, I just know it. I can feel it here," he said, holding his hand over his stomach.

LeCompte set his hardly touched glass of wine down on the desk, looked at his employer, and said, "That feeling has served you well in business over the years."

George Carr stared back without comment.

What LeCompte saw were two black holes, where a moment before there had been clear blue eyes. Throughout his employment/ friendship with Carr, he had never seen that look. Never that is, until recently.

He *had* seen that look before. On stone-cold killers or on men who had been *in country* too long. Until recently, he thought he knew everything about this man, but, now he knew he didn't know everything. This didn't set well with his training.

Frank broke the glare, walked around Carr and over to the gun cabinet. He stood there for a moment, looking at the reflection of his boss in the glass, until he saw Carr turn towards him.

"Mr. Carr, is there something you're not telling me?" he asked as he turned, hoping to use some of that training to distinguish any one of many telltale signs of lying.

The Mister standing out, and not missed by Carr. When they were alone the Mr. was dropped.

"About what?" Carr said, his eyes once again blue and clear.

"About anything."

"Hell yes," George Carr said. "What kind of question is that?"

Before Frank could reply, Carr followed it up with, "You want to be a little more explicit?"

'So much for catching him in a lie,' Frank thought as he smiled to himself. Once again he was reminded why he was the employee and not the employer.

"About anything pertaining to this mission you are sending Tucker on?" he said, after choosing his words carefully.

Carr walked over to the window and looked out for a moment, thinking. The word *mission* reminding him he had hired the best fighting man he could find and that man was trained by the military. The very best. Over the years of their relationship, LeCompte had seemed to have become more civilized, for lack of a better word. Now he grasped, that was surface clutter. LeCompte was confused as to why he couldn't go to Houston and take care of it.

Carr turned slowly to face Frank and said emphatically, "No."

"I still think you should let me go."

"I don't doubt you, my friend."

"Then why . . . ?

"You don't have his connections to the cops. Hell, he has connections he doesn't even think about. And if there are bad cops in the loop, he's much more equipped to deal with them than you are. Look at yourself, Frank, take a good look. You look just like what you are. A ramrod straight, tight-assed, squared away soldier. Who is going to talk to you? Manske didn't even look like a retired cop, all sloppy and out of shape like he was."

"He came highly recommended, and personally, I thought he was smart and tough," Frank said, with just a trace of defensiveness.

"Frank, stop it. I don't blame you about Manske. It was supposed to be a simple preliminary investigation that you would have taken over if anything turned up. It just so happened that what turned up was Manske's disappearance. Let's just let Tucker take it from here. If he turns anything up, you'll be the man who takes care of it. If that's what you want."

"She was my friend," LeCompte said quietly.

For the first time since his wife's death, Carr heard the loss in his friend's voice.

"I know, Frank, and that's another reason I don't want you to go."

"That doesn't make sense, George."

"Sure it does, you were her friend, too, Frank. She loved you as such, and if I let anything happen to you because of her, she would come back and haunt me."

LeCompte's smile was slow in coming.

"She would, too," he softly said.

"Besides, Tucker's expendable and you're not," Carr continued.

"Well, thanks," LeCompte said, astonished. "But, I thought you liked him."

"I do. But it would take me forever to find someone to take your place. You know how much I hate breaking in new employees."

After a small chuckle, LeCompte said, "For a second, I half-thought you were paying me a compliment, a personal one."

"That's what you get for half-thinking," Carr said, taking a sip of his wine, through a trace of a smile.

Chapter 39

After christening the stellar facilities, I walked into the doorway of the kitchen. If that's what you call a 600 square foot room, full of granite, Sub-Zero, and Vulcan stainless steel.

Across the vastness was a figure made small, not just by distance, but also by standing in front of the giant restaurant grade Vulcan stove. Her right elbow mimicking the circular motion I knew the utensil in her hand was making in the skillet. If she was making Crawfish Etouffe'e' properly, it would be in an old cast iron skillet, preferably a Griswold.

She hadn't yet detected my presence. I was standing on an oriental runner, holding my glass of wine. My next step would have my cowboy boots echoing on a stone floor.

"Helloooow," I said softly, through my unoccupied cupped hand, making my voice sound like it was a yell, coming from across a mountain.

I must have said it too softly.

"Helloooow," I kicked it up a notch.

Her hand stopped moving, but she didn't turn around. Her posture was one of listening. It was a big house, *house*, wrong word. Structure, yeah, it was a big structure. I'd bet she heard lots of distant sounds, and often had to stop and listen. The far-off holler skit was losing its spontaneity, and just as I was about to step onto the stone floor, she turned and saw me.

I raised my empty hand over my eyes, like a man shielding the rays of the sun in order to see something in the distance.

Her laugh came from her belly and was almost contagious. I was vaguely aware of a drifting thought. *Why did I want to make her laugh?*

"You get used to it," she said.

Wow, she gets me.

From this distance, I couldn't see the scars.

"How did you get away from those two?" she asked.

Not wanting to give her TMI, I said, "I just needed to stretch my legs, you know, take a hike. Once I was out and about, I just followed my nose."

She laughed again.

I walked over towards her, around an island of granite that contained a stainless steel sink. When I was within a few feet, I said, "Now, that smells like you better not put that food on your head."

After a moment of thought, she asked quizzically, "What's that mean?"

In my best Cajun accent, I said, " 'Cause yo tongue gonna slap yo brains out tryin' to get to it."

She turned her head before laughing. I figured so I wouldn't see her scars turn into what she'd considered hideous laugh lines.

Again, her laughter was almost communicable.

After a moment, she turned, looked up at me, and said, "You don't smile much, do you?"

"I thought I was."

After a few small breaths, she looked down at the floor and whispered, "No, I'm not sure what you are doing."

Her soft words fell heavily to the floor.

"Well, you don't seem used to smiling and your laughter sounds a little foreign," I said, then wishing I would have bitten my tongue off instead.

She turned back towards the stove and continued whisking the Etouffe'e', a little too briskly.

Finally, she said, "I have my reasons. What are yours?"

I took a small sip of wine and said, "We all have scars, Rachael."

She stiffened and said, "I don't like where this conversation is going."

I walked to within a foot of her back. With my left hand, I reached around her and set the wine glass down on the edge of the stove. I never touched her, but, I could smell her. From the back, she looked just like any normal, extremely fit, statuesque, beautiful woman. I was suddenly overcome . . . with the fact that I didn't know what I was doing, either.

I stepped back and said, "I apologize."

I was leaning with my butt against the granite island, with my palms resting on the counter on either side of me. I was looking down at my boots, trying to determine my strange feelings towards this woman. It didn't feel like pity. It felt more like attraction, but it had been so long, how would I know?

Rachael picked up my wine glass, turned, took a couple of steps closer to me, gave me a close-up look at the scars, and said, "Accepted."

Instead of staring into her eyes, I looked at her face, all of it. Without the scars, she would be an incredibly beautiful woman. With them, I found her very attractive.

She said, "Earlier your eyes were green, now they are blue."

"They do that," I said.

"Mine too," she said.

"I know," I said.

She slowly raised my wine glass to her lips, and just before taking a sip, I saw there were no scars on her lips.

After what was more of a nervous gulp than a sip, she said, "This has to be Cakebread. I'm surprised."

"Why's that?"

"It was her favorite and I think this is the first bottle he's opened since the accident."

"So, you think it was an accident?"

"Yes."

"So, you think this investigation is a waste of money."

"Not necessarily."

We were back to eye contact, and she evidently saw my confusion.

"George Carr is a very wealthy, powerful man, used to being in control. When his wife was killed, he wasn't. I believe his guilt is now controlling him. Hiring you gets him back in control of something."

"Of me?" I asked, maybe just a little too incredulously.

Still holding the glass close to her mouth, she looked over the rim at me and said, "I would think George knows better than that. No, just in control. Doing something about what he believes."

Her voice came from the glass, in a sharp, high-end crystalline tone.

As she drank from the glass again, this time much more daintily, I said, "What about the disappearance of Manske?"

As she handed the wine glass back to me, she said, "I'm sure an ex-cop turned private-eye would have some enemies. And I believe he drank to excess. Who knows what happened, maybe he just took the advance and ran off someplace for a few months."

Must've been a hell of an advance.

I held the wine glass to my mouth, and just before taking a masculine sip, said, "So, you think it's just a coincidence, the detective disappearing during an investigation?"

She shrugged her athletic shoulders, and said, "Who knows?"

I handed the glass back to her.

As she took it, I countered with, "I read somewhere that there are no coincidences."

She raised her eyebrows and said, "In any case, George Carr has so much money, hiring you to make sure he had no part in her death is going to make about as much difference as taking a molecule of water out of the swimming pool in the back, and it's a big pool."

"I don't think you can do that," I said.

"What do you mean?" she asked, just before her flawless lips touched the rim of the glass.

"A molecule of water?"

"You *are* a wiseacre, aren't you?"

Wiseacre, wow, I would have to watch my language around this one.

"You could take out a drop of water, now, you could do that," I said, nodding all knowingly.

She took another sip of wine, and I swear it looked like she was holding it in her mouth, with thoughts of spitting it on me. Then her eyes twinkled and I knew I was safe, for the moment.

She finally swallowed and said, "I'm sure you get the picture. So, thank you again, from me, for taking the job."

'The job,' oh boy, I was employed again. I didn't know how much I was going to be making yet. That made me feel somewhat detached from myself. Like I had been swept up into something that was going to be one of those pivotal thingies. It wasn't an altogether pleasing sensation.

In fact, I was close to losing my appetite, again.

She tried to hand the now half-full wine glass back to me, which I refused with a shake of my head, and said, "I've had enough for today. I would really like some coffee. I'll make it myself, if you'll just show me the stuff."

'The stuff,' so articulate of me. Why did she do this to me?

"You don't like the wine?" she asked.

"No, I mean yes, I like the wine, it's just that I have to talk to someone later tonight, and I, ah, don't want to be dull for it."

"Dull?" she said with a smile. "I'll tell you what, if you'll cook the rice, I'll make you some French pressed."

"Cook the rice?" I said, "Is this a test?"

"Of course," she laughed. "I'll find out if you're still a Louisiana boy, or if you've been in Tennessee too long."

She opened a cabinet next to the stove, pulled out a boiler, then pulled a canister across the countertop that contained rice.

"Now, what else do you need?" she asked.

"Just some salt and a measuring cup," I replied, hitching up my pants, like I was getting ready to chop wood.

As she was getting what I'd asked for, I said, "Do you mind if I taste your Etouffe'e? I need to see how much salt to put in the rice."

"Of course, help yourself," she said, handing me the tasting spoon from the stovetop.

After tasting it, I said, "Definitely."

"Definitely what?" she asked.

"Don't put it on your head."

Again, her face was at a scar-hiding angle.

Chapter 40

After Carr and LeCompte entered the kitchen carrying another opened bottle of wine, the meal was served buffet style, that is, help yourself at the stove.

Rachael had pulled a large salad bowl, chock full, from the Sub-Zero and set it on the counter next to the stove, along with a four stack of fine white china plates.

As the guest, I was gestured to serve myself first. When Rachael observed my small self portioning, she gave me an almost hurt expression.

"I still have that business to attend to tonight. If I eat too much in the evening, I get kind of groggy, especially on carbs," I said, sincerely enough to get a reluctant nod of understanding.

It wasn't the time to think about what I was going to do about Eddie Tuma.

We were seated for dinner in a hidden nook off the kitchen that was surrounded on three sides by windows overlooking well-kept gardens. The nook was hidden by some more of those 'can't see' doors, I had seen in George's office.

From the outside, it must have looked like a small plant-less greenhouse sticking out into the garden.

The table was shaped like a roughed out picnic table, but was made from a solid piece of walnut that appeared to have been hand-rubbed with tung oil. Instead of benches, there were eight individual cushioned stools that swiveled on their affixed pedestals like bar stools, allowing easy access. It all had a George Carr office appearance to it. There was no 'head of the table' position.

George noticed I was drinking coffee, so didn't offer me any of the second bottle of wine. They seemed to be waiting for something. I hoped they weren't going to ask me to say grace, one of my secret waking nightmares.

"Go on, taste it," LeCompte said. "Tell me what *you* think."

Of course. The guest gets first bite. Whew, that was close.

I took a bite, chewed slowly, then after swallowing, said to LeCompte, "Don't wear it as a hat."

He laughed aloud and said, "I told you she could cook it."

Before Carr could ask the query in his eyes, I said, "And, the rice is beyond perfect."

Someone kicked my leg under the table. Wearing the boots was a good idea.

This familiarity between Rachael and me was perplexing, to say the least.

After the meal was consumed and the dishes stacked into the dishwasher the four of us were back in Carr's office. This time, more to the front of the room, closer to the door. We were seated around a coffee table sized slab of stone, on legs of twisted iron. Rachael and I sat on a couch that looked and felt like worn saddle leather. Carr and LeCompte were seated across from us and the table, in individual chairs that matched the couch.

On the table was a large, thick manila envelop.

Carr started this little meeting with, "Tucker, before we talk any more business, there is something I would like to ask you about."

"What's that?" I asked, thinking that whatever was coming would probably be a curve or a knuckle ball.

"In the interview with Robbie Gray, he mentioned something that was curious to me. He said to ask you how you got the cop to pay the money he owed you. Listening to the tape, it sounded as if he didn't know, and wanted to. Now, I want to know."

My stomach did a full barrel roll, endangering my Etouffe'e. This was a baggage car I had sealed and welded shut.

Shreveport, La., 1973

In the process of getting rid of the extra pounds of pot I'd persuaded the Miranda brothers to give us as compensation for their miscalculation of our ability to protect ourselves, I developed my own network of dealers. They wanted quantity and quality.

Around three months after the first run, I made one more for Darvoyce. It was the same crew, Robby Gray, Phil, Allen, and myself, making the same trip with different vehicles, but of the same type.

It was a breeze. We stayed at the same Holiday Inn. This time arriving in the early afternoon. From the time we pulled into the parking lot, until the load was in the trailer, was less than two hours.

We had just finished loading the *tomatoes* into the U-haul, when a shiny black Cadillac sedan pulled up next to us. The electric window on the passenger side disappeared into the door, and I was looking into the white smile of Armando Miranda.

"Buenas tardes, Señor Tucker, I hope everything is satisfactory."

I was hoping to see him.

"Everything is fine, Armando," I said, lowering my head to see who was driving.

"Hello, Tom'as."

"Hola, Tucker," he replied, with his agreeable smile.

Teemo and Robby had just gone into the room before the Mirandas pulled up, and were now walking across the parking lot towards the car. Teemo was carrying the gym bag containing the money. I noticed a small movement by Tom'as, and the trunk popped open. I didn't know enough about Cadillacs to discern if that was an option on that model, or something the Mirandas had customized.

Teemo walked past the driver's side and around to the rear, threw the bag in and slammed the trunk closed. Robby was standing next to Tom'as, looking over the roof at me.

On the trip down, I told Robby I would not be making another trip with the crew and I was going to talk to the Mirandas about going on my own, but on a much smaller scale. He wasn't at first agreeable, but after explaining my home situation with Margie (she didn't like me going off on these runs) and school, he came around. He wasn't happy about it, but he understood. Besides, what could he do about it, really?

Before they pulled away, I said, "Armando, there is something I would like to discuss with you, if you have the time?"

Politeness goes a long way with Mexicans. I had injected just enough respect into my question to get his attention and to imply it was business.

"Of course," he said, like he expected it.

He looked over at his brother, and said, "Tom'as, please."

The back door next to me opened by itself. I knew that wasn't stock. I looked over the roof at Robby, and said, "I won't be too long, I know we've got to roll. Explain to Phil and Allen. Okay?"

I said this more for the Miranda's than Robby, I didn't have time for them to take me to dinner and ply me with Mexican hospitality.

I got into the back, and just before closing the door, saw Phil and Allen looking a skosh alarmed over by the trailer. After closing the door, it occurred to me, not only could the door be automatically opened from the front seat, but it might also be locked from there as well.

As we pulled away and the windows were going up, Armando shifted in the front seat so he could see me and said, "It is a shame you must be in such a hurry. There is a wonderful Cantina on the other side of the border I would love for you to experience."

It swiftly came to me, this was the first time I had been with the twins without a gun in my hand. It was nestled behind my back, bringing me no more comfort than it would if I were riding along with any of my friends.

"I would enjoy that, Armando. I would like to know you and Tom'as better. I hope to have that opportunity in the future."

I've been told that I have the knack of picking up on the way people talk. If I'm around Cajuns, I'll start talking with a small Cajun accent. If I'm around hard-talking farmers, I swiftly turned into one. Now, I was around two educated Mexicans that spoke proper English. I wondered if I could take this back with me and hold on to it. Maybe, probably not...no way.

My reference to the future held an implicit connotation. Tom'as was driving with no apparent destination and Armando was looking expressionlessly at me. They were both silent, waiting, reminding me, they were big-time drug dealers and, without a doubt, very dangerous men.

I said, "This will be my last trip to Laredo with Robby."

"And, you would like to do business with us by yourself," Armando said, smiling and nodding with understanding.

No wonder he's the jefe. He was very quick to grasp my intention.

"Si," I said.

Without commenting on my bilingual agility, he tapped Tom'as on the shoulder, and pointed out the windshield to something. Tom'as turned left into the parking lot of a dry cleaners, put the car in park, and turned to where he, too, could see me.

"What is it you have in mind, Senor Tucker?" Armando Miranda asked.

They were both watching me with interest. I was rapidly losing my confidence that they would go for my proposal. Why would they? They just sold a ton of marijuana to us. Why would they sell less to me, much less?

"Armando, Tom'as, I am married to a beautiful woman who I love very much. I have a beautiful daughter who I also love very much. I am not really a, how you say, a bandito. The things Teemo told you about me were made up, to make me one. I have never been arrested for anything. I am using the money I make with your marijuana to pay for my wife's and my education. My wife does not like me going on these trips, with these men. She is afraid that I will, one day, not return."

"There is always that risk in this business." Tom'as said seriously.

"I understand that risk and accept it," I said. "But, is it fair for me to ask my loved ones to sit and wait for me to maybe not return?"

Tom'as started to say something but Armando slowly raised his hand to thwart any response from his twin.

"What is it you want?" he asked.

I made a quick decision to just throw it up and see where it landed.

"I would like to be able to contact you directly. Come down with my wife, like a little vacation trip, pick up anywhere between 25 to 50 pounds and drive back. Enjoy the trip and sightsee along the way."

The shock was plain to see, but I misread it.

"Your wife would come with you, she has agreed to this?" Armando asked, his eyes widening.

"It was her idea," I said. "She wants to come. She wants to be with me. She doesn't like being left out of any part of my life."

They both started laughing, and began speaking Spanish faster than I could grasp, even if I was capable of grasping. After a minute of their laughing, talking and observing my silence, Armando asked, "Do you have a picture of your wife?"

Now, that was a fast-breaking curve ball. I reached in my back pocket and pulled out my wallet. In it was a picture of Margie, sitting on a table at the fishing camp on Spring Bayou. She had her hands flat on the table next to her legs and was leaning forward, laughing at something I'd said just before taking the picture. She was wearing hip hugger pants and a halter top, her full-bodied auburn hair spilling around her face onto her bare shoulders. It was one of my favorite pictures of her. It showed her fine athletic figure, her beautiful hair, her sexy smile, and the sun had somehow managed to light up her blue eyes. I pulled out the picture and handed it to Armando.

He stared at it for a full ten seconds, then handed it to Tom'as. Tom'as looked at it for a few seconds, then whistled softly through his teeth.

"She is very beautiful, Tucker," Tom'as said.

"She must also be very strong, in here," Armando said, tapping his chest over his heart. "She must be, to want to come and help you with this business."

"She is very strong," I said, "and, very tough. She has helped me before. I trust her to do what needs to be done, when it needs to be done. She is my best friend."

Armando took the picture from Tom'as's hand and eyes, then said, "I would like to meet this woman of yours. What is her name?"

"Her name is Margie."

Armando looked at Tom'as. Tom'as nodded, then they looked at me. Armando reached in his inside coat pocket, pulled out a business card, and handed it to me. The card was a plain cream-colored card that read, Miranda Enterprises, with a phone number on the bottom edge.

"That is our home number. We live together. We have not, as yet, met the kind of woman your Margie seems to be. You say you are not a bandito, Tucker. You may not be, but you are in a business that is full of banditos. I have seen you in that business, and how you deal with banditos, and I would have to say you are very... professional. If you say your wife is strong, I believe you. Call us when you are ready for your little vacation."

To this day, I don't know if the banditos they were speaking of were themselves, or... if they would have done business with me if I hadn't had that picture of Margie.

A couple of months later, Margie and I did drive down to Laredo. The Mirandas invited us to their home. A beautiful ranch about two hours' drive from Laredo, into Mexico. They were perfect gentlemen and Margie liked them both. Over the months, we met with them and were introduced to many different gorgeous women who were trying to snare the Miranda twins. Apparently, no one knew what kind of business they were in, no one but Margie and me.

About a year after Margie and I first went down to Mexico, Tom'as married a lady from Austin, Texas. Her name was Lori, and she looked a lot like Margie. Our trips became a little shorter, as Tom'as could provide what little I needed right there in Austin.

The Miranda's had become good friends, but, after Tom'as got married and moved to Austin, we didn't see much of Armando. He decided to move back to Mexico City, saying he could conduct business from there, now that Tom'as was living like a gringo, in Tehas.

Looking back, them doing such a small business with me was only because of our friendship. Friendship and trust. I never felt like I was almost fifteen years younger than them, and they never treated me that way.

So, while developing my own network of small dealers, one was a cop from Alexandria. Barry Johnson, with whom I'd played junior high and high school football. Allen had told me about Barry, assuring me he wasn't going to bust me by telling how they had done some business before, illegal business. So, I really had nothing to be worried about.

Well, he was right about one thing, I didn't have to be worried about being busted. I needed to be concerned about being paid.

Most of the dealing in those days was done on a front basis. Meaning no money exchanged hands until the end. This did two things. One; if you were dealing with someone you had just met, or didn't entirely trust, you could give them the pot without any money exchanging hands. No money exchanged–no dealing crime–no bust. Two; it allowed people like myself to help someone under them develop a network without an initial investment by the underling. This was important, as most small-time dealers, that is, people dealing in lids, quarter pounds and such, usually didn't have enough cash on hand to buy 3 or 4 pounds of high-grade grass. I would front it to them and they would pay me as they sold it, hopefully before buying themselves new sound systems for their cars or color TV's, etc. Eventually their cash flow would increase and they could pay cash for part or all of their shipment. It wasn't unusual, for someone I was fronting, to get a little behind, owing me for one or two pounds, out of five I'd fronted. They usually caught up within a couple of deals.

Now, we get to the subordinate that develops his own pound business. In other words, his lid business would get so big as to be dangerous. If one person starts selling too many lids to too many people, his chances of being busted increased with the size of his business. That's when it's time to turn his lid customers into small pound customers and let them take the chances.

I could sell a pound for $175, that I paid $65 to $85 for, and the ancillary could turn around and sell it for around $250, give or take $10, making himself a fast $75 per pound.

If he could do this with 10 pounds, to one or more people, he just made $750. If he had his ducks in a row, he could do this easily in a few hours of one day.

The excuses for being short on payments, ranged from, 'my dog ate it', to, 'my guy got busted before he could pay me.'

I had this one guy who swore his dog pulled his trash bag full of pot out of his garage. Said his tore it up and spread it all over his back yard and there was just no way he could recover it all. It wasn't that I didn't believe him, but I told him I would be right over and help pick it up.

When I got there, he said he'd picked up most of it. As I walked around his back yard, I did pick up a few buds and stems. I never knew if his dog did it, or if he had to put some pot in his back yard for me to find.

Now, getting back to Barry the cop.

Barry had built up quite a large pound business. Being a cop, he had access to all sorts of would-be dealers who were always looking for a little help.

I started by fronting him 10 pounds, for $200 each. I always charged more for a front; it was good incentive for them to pay cash.

Business between Barry and me went well for almost a year.

He had been gradually building his network, so, he needed more and more quantity. It wasn't unusual for him to come to me needing more, before all of his cash from the last transaction was in. So, he always had a running balance with me. Before I knew it, he had a balance of 12 grand.

After, not hearing from 'Barry-the-cop' for a couple of weeks, my concern over the money started hurting my stomach, literally. This was not a good sign. I believe not enough people listen to their stomachs, in more ways than one.

I called my cousin, Allen, explained the situation, and asked what he thought I should do. After all, Barry was a cop.

Allen said he would look into it and get back to me.

The next day I was sitting on the screened-in back porch, when the phone rang. Margie answered it, and said it was Allen.

After Margie handed me the phone, he just said, "Tuck."

I didn't like the sound of it.

"Yeah," I said, as I watched her walk back into kitchen. I loved watching her walk away.

"I think you're fucked," I heard through the handset.

"Why is that?" I asked. I stood and walked over to the screen, to view the horses grazing in the green pasture across the gravel road behind my house.

"Barry says one of his guys ripped him off and has some incriminating evidence on him, so he can't get the money."

"Ever?" I asked.

"Doesn't sound like it."

"Do you believe him?"

After a five-second pause, he said, "No."

Now that sucked.

If he had said yes, I might have been able to let it go. I had already paid the Mirandas and that 12 grand was all mine. But, he said, no.

"Why don't you believe him?"

"Because it's the first I've heard about it. Seems to me if it was true, he would have said something to me before I had to ask him about it. And, it's his attitude."

"What about his attitude?" I asked, as the strawberry roan kicked the bay.

"When I told him you weren't going to be okay with it, he said, 'What's he going to do, kill me? I'm an old friend and a cop'."

As the bay ran across the pasture to get away from the roan, I said, "He has a point."

"Tuck, you're not going to let him get away with it. I know you better than that."

As the bay turned to fight the roan, I said, "Tell you what, you tell Barry, my old friend, that I'll be in touch."

I gave Barry Johnson a couple of days to stew. Then after checking with Allen to make sure Barry was home, I went to a pay phone and gave him a call. I didn't have to worry about *his* phone being tapped. After all, he's a cop.

"Barry, it's Tucker," I said, after he answered.

After a few seconds of silence, he said, "Yeah, I figured you'd be calling. I've been trying to get some money together, but those guys that ripped me have disappeared."

Sure was a lot of information without a question.

"What happened?" I said. I was curious as to what kind of story he came up with.

"Ah, these two guys I was working with, they're brothers and one of them lives here in Alec and the other one lives in Lafayette."

"Uh-huh."

"Well, they've been good guys and have always been on time."

"Uh-huh."

"Yeah, I guess they've been working me for a while, ya know, taking more and more, paying up, and then hauled ass to points unknown when they got enough fronted to them. That's all I can come up with," he said, with practiced conviction.

"I'm sure you've used all your resources on the street to find these guys, right?" I said, all cop-like.

"Hell, yes, I've been on it for over a week. I knew you'd be calling after Allen asked me about it. I don't know what to do, Tucker. I can't find these assholes, I don't have the money, I don't want you all pissed at me . . .

"Just a minute, let me think," I said, already thinking how his tone had changed. It had just the right amount of whine to it and showed enough respect for me, that I may be able to make him believe I believed him.

After a planned pause, I said, "Barry, can you get me anything, anything at all? If you can, I might be able to get us out of this hole."

For what I had in mind, I didn't want to seem too easy, and his answer would tell me what I wanted to know. If he had spent all the money, was he sitting on it, or was he setting something up for himself. I also hoped the 'we' would add some depth to the problem.

"Whataya mean?" he asked, sounding surprised.

I had him.

"If you can come up with a couple of grand, I'll use it to get us some real good stuff, something new. Something you can get top dollar for, and I'll front it to you at my cost. The way I've got it figured, three or four ventures like this will not only get you out of hock with me, but you'll make some on the back end."

I could hear the wheels spinning through the phone.

Then I closed on him.

"Even if you had to borrow it from somewhere, you'd still come out. You and I would be square. I could pay my guys, and if you ever get the money back from the guys who ripped you off, we'll talk about that."

"I might be able to put something together in a couple of days, ya know, talk to a couple of buddies," he said, a little too quickly.

"Great, Barry!" I said, with a feigned sigh of relief. "This'll work out. You've just got to watch your clientele from now on. Okay?"

"Yeah, no shit. Look, Tucker, I'm real sorry about all this, but I'll make it right. I promise."

"I know you will. Shit happens in this business. We'll fix it and move on."

"I'll give you a call in a couple of days, when I get it together," he said.

"Okay, when you do, I'll get the rope (code for marijuana). You can drive up here, we'll have us a visit and get this thing fixed up. Wait till you see this stuff, you won't believe it."

"Cool, call you in a couple of days," he said, then hung the phone up.

Now, what did I learn from our conversation. One; he was waiting to see how I would react to his not paying me. Two; he had most or all of *my* money. I knew this when he said 'Whataya mean, instead of, 'I don't know, or no', or something along those lines. Three; he's thinking not only will he get to keep my twelve grand, but make some more money and stay in business with me. And, four; he's dumber than I thought, so I really don't want to do business with him.

I looked down at Boone, my black lab, patted him on his beautiful broad head and said, "You're a good boy, Boone, a gooood boy."

My bowels felt like water and bile was in danger of rising at the thought of what I had planned to do, to get my money.

Four days after our phone conversation I was sitting on the front porch of the house I'd rented in the country, waiting for Barry.

A nice, semi-remote place on Dixie Garden Drive. It was just outside the city limits where the city police had no jurisdiction, and where the sheriff's department didn't know about me, I hoped.

I was sitting in one of twin rocking chairs that overlooked an acre of front yard that was studded by five 50 foot pecan trees, that dripped a sticky residue on any cars that were parked beneath them. Some people said it was aphids doing it, but I always thought pecan trees just dripped.

Boone was lying on the porch to my right, between the chairs, with my hand on his head, when Barry pulled into the drive.

Boone was seven years old and extremely friendly. So I put my fingers around his collar so he wouldn't try to get up when Barry got out of his car and started up the porch.

Barry wasn't a big man, about five-nine and a trim 150 pounds. At 24, his brown hair was already thinning, and his parents evidently hadn't believed in, or couldn't afford an orthodontist. Margie thought he was kind of handsome until he smiled, which he was doing now.

We'd played football on the same team for six years and against each other on baseball teams all the way from Rebel League through Pelican League. We never really hung out, so when I suggested to Margie that she may want to go out for a while, until Barry and I did our business, she didn't find that suspicious.

Besides, she needed to get out of the house to take her mind off of something that was bothering her, and given that 8-year-old Shannon was down in Alexandria visiting her Grandmother, I would be left alone.

She knew he owed us, but didn't know what I had been planning. It was one of the few times I didn't confide in her. Under the circumstances, I thought it best. She would find out soon enough, then I would have to deal with her reaction.

At the top of the steps, Barry said, "Hey, Tucker, nice day, huh?"

I chose not to reply, and I didn't get up when Barry offered me his hand. I let go of Boone's collar, and after shaking Barry's hand, he bent over and ruffled Boone's ears.

"How ya doin', Boone, old boy," he said.

I looked down at Boone, and thought, 'he didn't look old, he was only seven, and he was beautiful.'

Barry sat down in the chair to my right. Boone was between us, looking back and forth with his intelligent brown eyes.

"How was the drive up?" I asked, knowing full well how the drive from Alexandria was, two hours of flat boredom.

"I made it in an hour and forty-five minutes," he said proudly.

"You must have been hauling it."

"Yeah, well, it helps to be a *cop*," he replied.

"Not all the time," I said, gently rubbing behind Boone's ears.

I started to hear little rushing noises in mine, like water shooting through a pipe.

My reply was hanging in the air, and when I looked at Barry, I saw the first signs of alarm register.

Looking at the pecan trees, he said, "You doin' okay, man?"

"Hunky-fucking dory," I said, smiling thinly at the same trees.

"Where's Margie, she around? I'd love to see her."

Yeah, I bet you would.

She had been a cheerleader for two different football teams for five years, until we got pregnant with Shannon, in the 11ᵗʰ grade.

It was no secret all the players had lascivious thoughts of the cheer-leaders.

"She went shopping and to run some errands."

Barry had married a girl named Rochelle. We called her Roach, but she had a great personality.

One of my father's pearls was "never sleep with a girl you wouldn't marry."

I didn't believe Barry's father gave him the same pearl. If he did, Barry didn't listen. There were a lot of teenage pregnancies in the sixties.

"That's cool," he said.

"Yeah?"

"Sure," he squeaked, the alarm now in his throat.

Barry cleared his throat and continued, "We can get our business done and I can get on back to Alec, get the ball rollin', ya know."

"How much could you put together?" I asked, methodically rubbing Boone's ears. I'd just about put him to sleep.

"I got $2500," he said, after what I thought was too long of a pause.

Well, he either just added or subtracted $500. I was betting on added.

My hands were sweating and the rubbing of Boone was keeping my right hand dry and that was a good thing.

It's funny how things worked out sometimes.

I felt the itchy sweat as it rolled from my armpits and down my sides.

"Did you get that good shit you were talkin' about?"

"You bet," I said.

Between the rushing in my ears and the sweat dripping down my sides, I started to feel like I *was* 'humidity'.

He made a show of reaching into his right-hand pocket of his Levis and taking out a wad of hundreds.

When I took on a new recruit, I usually gave my, 'always keep your money in your left-hand pocket and my money in your right-hand pocket', speech.

It had always worked for me.

Actually, he pulled out two wads. One had twenty hundreds in it, the other had five.

There was no need for paranoia. There wasn't much traffic on Dixie Garden and, after all, he was a cop, right?

He handed me the money, and after counting it, I put it in the left front pocket of my Levis. This didn't go unnoticed by him. After all, he's a cop, right?

He made no comment on the fact that I'd counted it.

I was starting to get angry at what he was forcing me to do. I detest being angry, it tends to make me angrier, another catch-22.

"How much can you front me on this first run?" he asked, actually rubbing his hands together.

"I'll be right back," I said, standing. "Make sure Boone stays on the porch, I don't want him running out into the street. It would be my luck that the only car that came down the road today would hit him."

"I'll take care of him," he said, already starting to pet Boone's head.

I wanted to hit him with a 36-inch bat.

I went through the house to our bedroom. Under the bed was a walnut box I'd put there right after Margie left that morning.

I pulled it out and set it on the bed.

Could I really do this? I need to go to the bathroom, and I suddenly had to take a huge breath. I hadn't been breathing.

I opened the box and looked at the contents.

A Smith&Wesson .22 cal. semi-automatic, on a Colt 1911 frame. It had two barrels and slides. One was a .22 magnum and the other was a .22 long rifle, with a silencer attached.

I'd purchased the gun in the back room of a bookie's bar for $75 when I was 18. The bookie was an Italian. The gun supposedly came from the northeast and was used for a hit in New Orleans, and I believe, was supposed to be Red River bound. You never know about these things. So, I had never showed the gun to anyone.

The gun, extra slide and barrel with the silencer, were inlaid into purple felt. It only took a moment. While I listened for the sound of the front door to open, I assemble the gun with the silenced barrel, rammed a full .22 long rifle magazine up the grip, and racked a round in the chamber.

I thought I did a damn quick job, considering my hands were wet and shaking.

I had to get it together. I was angry, really pissed off. I was also afraid of what I had to do and what it may do to me, and Margie.

I wanted to cry.

I walked back to the front door, stood there, looking at the back of Barry's head, and thought how easy it would be, to just shoot him from here.

I took another big breath, let it out, took another one and slowly let it out.

I could see the wind riffling the leaves of the pecan trees, a woodpecker knocking away at a limb, but all I could hear was the rushing of water. No... it was blood.

After making sure it was on safety, but ready to fire, I tucked the pistol between my left hip and my jeans and pulled the t-shirt over it. It's not where I usually a gun, but it was perfect for what I had in mind.

After another big breath, I wiped my palms on the front of my jeans, opened the door and stepped out onto the front porch.

As soon as I walked out, Barry turned his head and looked at my empty hands. He couldn't see the bulge of the pistol because it was on my left and he was on my right.

"What's up Tucker, where's the shit?" he asked, half-rising from the chair.

I casually motioned him to sit with my right hand and walked over to the steps. I looked up and down the street to make sure there were no cars coming, which seemed to relax him back into the chair. He thought I was checking before I brought out the pot.

I knew he was carrying. After all, he's a cop.

I walked slowly down the steps until I was halfway down and about 10 feet in front of him. As I did, I crossed my arms over my stomach.

Again I looked up and down the street, careful to keep my left side unexposed.

"Looks clear to me," he said, from behind and to my right.

"Yeah," I said, turning to my right to face him, and uncrossing my arms.

By the time I was fully facing him, the gun was in front of my stomach, in my hand. I knew to him, it looked like it just appeared.

He didn't move . . . at all. He sat there staring at the end of the silencer.

The gun was hidden from anyone but him and me, if there had been anyone else around, which there wasn't.

Then he heard the click of the safety, as I took it off.

His face was pale and the fingers of his right hand were twitching.

I said, "I know you're carrying under your shirt. You wanna try for it? It might make this a little easier for both of us."

"I'm no match for you, and you know it," he croaked, like his throat was stuck.

"You want me to give you a better chance?" I asked.

He didn't answer. He just sat there looking at the silencer and all it implied.

I waited. I didn't trust myself to talk again. My throat was so tight, you couldn't have pulled a hair through it without slitting it.

I don't know how long we stood like that. It could've been ten seconds or ten minutes.

Finally he said, "You can't do this." It was almost a whine.

"Oh, and why is that?"

"I'm a cop, for Christ sake, and a friend," he said, his voice one testicle heavier than before.

"You think I want to do this," I said, with the anger I felt.

"Go for it," I said, with the first signs of tears in my eyes.

"No." He said. "I'm not going to make this easy for you."

It was going to be hard to see through the tears if I didn't do this soon.

"Easy!...Easy! You think this is going to be easy for me?"

I was really pissed now, and he could see it. Ray Charles could have seen it.

"The people I get my dope from want their money!" I lied. "I tried to explain the situation to them. They told me to get the money from you, or show them a picture of your body!"

The tears in my eyes was what did it. He knew he was about to die.

"I'll get it! I'll get it!" he screamed.

For the first time, Boone started to get up.

"Stay, Boone!" I said loudly.

The silencer had never left the straight line to his nose.

"Please," he pleaded, "just give me a chance."

"I gave you one, and you lied to me. No one ripped you off. The question is, just how much of my money have you spent?"

"I've still got most of it, I swear, I swear. You'll have the rest of it tomorrow. Please, Tucker, don't do this. You can't do this!"

"I don't have a choice, you'll just go back to Alec and never come up here again. Then, I'll have to go down there and have to do this all over again, only it'll be harder for me, you're a cop."

"I promise. I promise. I didn't know what kind of people you're dealing with. Allen said you were real tight with the Mexicans."

Thanks a lot, Allen.

"I'm sorry Barry. I'm sorry," I said softly, as the tears flowed freely down my face and into my beard.

It was time, the dreaded moment I knew was coming, what I had planned was at hand. It was time.

"You son-of-a-bitch," I said hoarsely, as I moved the silencer from his nose to his forehead.

"Noooooooooo!" Barry screamed, leaning so far back, the rocking chair was on the back tips of its runners. His hands came up in front of his face as if to ward off the bullets.

At the last split second, I turned the silencer to Boone's beautiful head, and pulled the trigger twice.

Phhitt-Phhitt

The little .22 bullets hitting Boone made a thwapping sound. The movement of the slide and the brass hitting the concrete steps was louder than anything else on the porch.

Through the rushing blood in my head, all noise was muted and distant.

Boone's head slumped down, as if he had quickly fallen asleep. His legs twitched a little, then I took my eyes off of him and back on Barry.

It took less than a second.

"Jesus . . Jesus . . . Jesus . . . . . Jesus," he whimpered.

"He ain't here, you piece of shit!" I screamed.

"Look what you made me do. You know how much I loved that dog. You know. Tell me you know!"

"I know, I know . . . I'm sorry . . . please . . . please," he was begging.

I hadn't realized it, but the gun was again pointed at his nose. We were both crying.

Uh-oh. I'd better get myself under control before I really fucked up.

"I'm going to lower my gun," I said softly. "If you move, I'll shoot you. If you say anything, anything at all, I'll shoot you. If I hear you breathing, I'll shoot you. Right now, I *really* want to shoot you."

I didn't like that the last thing I'd said wasn't far from the truth.

"Get off my porch. Get in your car and get the fuck out of here. Tomorrow before the end of the day you'll give Allen $9500 in cash. If he doesn't call me before 10 o'clock tomorrow night, I'll come down there and finish this, and you won't know when."

I'd been lowering the gun, and when it was almost next to my right leg, he started to say something. I whipped the muzzle up and again it found his nose. His mouth slammed shut. He sat there like a small child waiting for someone to tell him to come out of the corner.

"Now go. I have to bury my dog. I can't believe I did that. I'd rather have shot you. Go. Go," I said, the sound of the truth terrifying him, and me.

I turned on the step, giving him room to walk by me, and as he did, he was looking down, not wanting to meet my eyes, the front of his pants were wet.

As he walked by, I said under my breath, but loud enough for him to hear, "At least I don't have to worry about getting rid of your body and car now."

His knees almost buckled, but I couldn't hear him breathing. He made it down the steps and to his car.

I walked slowly back into the house. I never looked back as he backed out of the drive and drove off.

Once inside, I ran to the bathroom and threw up in the sink. I couldn't make it to the toilet.

Four years ago Boone had fallen off my 1960 Ford flatbed truck while I was going about 50 mph. In my rearview mirror, I saw him literally tumble head over heals. It looked like he broke his neck, but when I went back for him, he seemed fine. I never took him to the vet because there didn't seem to be any reason to.

Two months ago, Boone went down and couldn't get up, so I took him to the vet. By the time we got there, he was back up and seemed fine, but my vet wanted to take some x-rays. When the pictures came back, they showed a curved spur on one of his vertebrae and it looked like it was touching his spine.

The vet said the spur was most probably due to the fall years before.

He said the next time he went down, he wouldn't get up again. We'd have to put him to sleep, forever. The vet said it would just be a matter of weeks, if that.

Two days ago, it happened. Boone went down while playing in the back with Margie. We had been pampering him and loving him since.

I had been struggling with taking him to the vet, or putting him down myself. That's what had been bothering Margie. She thought we should have the vet do it, but I was having a hard time with that, I believe Boone would have known what was going on if we took him to the vet. He would have sensed it. I didn't want that for him.

After talking to Barry on the phone four days ago, a plan had intruded my brain. It wasn't a pleasant thought, what I was thinking. But, when, two days later Boone went down, it seemed like an omen.

My plan was sketchy, and I really didn't have any dialog worked out as to what I was going to say to Barry.

As it worked out, he thought my tears and anger were because I didn't want to kill him.

The scary truth was, I would have rather shot him. I didn't love him. And Boone was my little boy.

I felt bad about using Boone that way, and Barry . . . well, 'how ya gonna act'.

I never told Margie the circumstances around Boone's death. I just told her I didn't want to do it when she was at home. She thanked me for it.

I never told her the truth.

The next morning we drove Boone out to Catahoula Lake and buried him behind Uncle Roy's duck camp. A place he loved.

After a small ceremony, we drove back to Alexandria and picked up Shannon, our little girl. I wanted my family around me.

I picked up my money from Allen, at 3:00 in the afternoon. Barry Johnson and I never spoke again. I saw him once, but he avoided me.

Chapter 41

George Carr's Mansion, Present Day

From a far off place, I heard a voice.

I was slowly coming back.

"Excuse me?" I said, not quite back in the room yet.

"Your were going to tell us how you got the cop to pay you," George Carr said.

I looked at Rachael and saw the interest in her face.

I never told Margie.

Looking first at LeCompte, then George, I said, "No I wasn't."

I never told her . . . and now I couldn't.

All three were quietly assessing me. George was the one to break the silence.

"Okay, then," he said, as he reached over and picked up the manila envelope.

He opened it and dumped the contents onto the table; A cell phone, a credit card and some cash, two business cards and one printed page.

"This cell phone is already programmed with my private numbers, here and in Houston. I want you to stay at our home in River Oaks."

Our.

"I have a cell phone."

"I would like you to use this one. It never goes out of range. It works off special satellites, I think you'll like it."

"Okay."

He picked up the credit card.

"I thought it would be easier for you to use this for your expenses," he said, sliding it across the stone table towards me.

I picked it up, saw it had my name on it, one word, Tucker. I turned it over and saw the place for my signature was empty.

"You're pretty sure of yourself," I said.

George just nodded and picked up the money.

"Here's two thousand cash in advance of your fee and for any expenses you can't put on the card."

He slid the money across the table for me to pick up.

I left it laying and said, "We haven't discussed my fee."

"What's your fee for body guarding?"

"Four hundred a day plus expenses, or a hundred and fifty an hour. But I won't be body guarding anyone. I'm not sure how to charge for something like this. I'm not a private investigator."

"I'll pay you the same by the day, and will give you a bonus if you find proof she was murdered, and another bonus if and when you give me the name or names of the killers."

With no more thought about how much to charge for what I was about to do, I said, "Starting when?"

"The moment you leave for Houston. I can fly you down on my private jet, just say when."

I don't fly well. Not after an Air Jamaica plane lost an engine, turned upside down, and dropped almost 20,000 feet before the pilot could get the nose down so he could restart the jet.

"I'll be taking my truck."

"I'd planned on flying you down. You can use any one of three vehicles still at the Houston residence."

"I'll be taking my truck."

Carr frowned at LeCompte, then at Rachael, who was smiling at him.

"George," I said, "control is an illusion."

"What?" he said, again looking back and forth from Rachael to LeCompte.

"I get the feeling you're trying to take the reins before the horse is saddled."

After a moment of silence, Rachael said, "It's what he does."

"I'll keep that in mind."

"Whatever," George said, with a dismissive wave of one hand, as he picked up one of the business cards with the other.

"This is one of the last known people to talk to my wife."

I took the card. It read, Ernie Miles, and under the name, *Certified Advanced Rolfer,* then a phone number and an e-mail address. There was an address written in a feminine hand along the border.

"What's a Rolfer?" I asked.

"I don't know," Carr said, somewhat annoyed. "Some kind of body work, like massage or something." Then remembering, said softly, "She was always going to get it done, said it helped her posture, which was perfect."

Must have helped.

"Okay. What's the other card?"

He reached across the table and handed me the card. It read Harold Manske, Private Investigations, under that, a phone number and an e-mail address.

I put both cards in the right pocket of my sport jacket.

He reached over and picked up the typewritten page and handed it to me.

It was a list of the times Manske checked in with Carr and what he had to say. Not much, until the last entry which referred to the maybe bad cops.

Right. 'Just had a feeling'.

I knew LeCompte wasn't telling me everything.

I handed it back, and said, "I don't think I'll be needing this."

"I thought it might be useful, considering this bad cop angle. You might want to show it to one of your cop friends there."

"I won't be pursuing that angle."

"What do you mean you won't be pursuing that angle?" he said loudly. It was the first time I noticed his alcohol intake.

"Yeah, whataya mean?" LeCompte echoed, obviously perturbed.

Only Rachael remained quiet and watching.

"I haven't had much time to think this out, how to approach this investigation. But, it doesn't take much to figure out that going to my buddies in the Houston Police Department, and telling them I think there's a bad cop or two involved in a murder, is the wrong way to go about it."

These were smart people, and it only took a second for what I'd said to sink in.

"Then how are you going to get information about it then, just out of curiosity?" Carr said, fully interested.

"Just off the top of my head?"

"Yes," they said in unison.

It was obvious, to me.

"I think I'll go down there and investigate the disappearance of one of Houston's retired finest, gone private."

George Carr said, "What about my wife's death? I'm not paying you to find out what happened to Manske. I don't give a shit what happened to him."

"Then send someone else," I interrupted. I took the two business cards out of my pocket and dropped them on the table next to the phone, money, and credit card.

That shut him up.

I said, "I see you've thought this out and have an agenda. Maybe you should go down there and do it yourself, or find someone that's going to follow your plan."

Carr looked like a fast-ripening tomato.

I had to give him credit. Even when the color in his face looked like he was about ready to pick, he held his tongue. Probably between his teeth.

Before he burst and lost his seeds, Rachael said, "Tell us why you want to find out about Manske."

Looking at Carr, I said, "One is that I'm sure to get more help from the police using that approach, and two, if his disappearance *is* linked to your wife's death, I need to know that. So it doesn't happen to me."

Carr's color was returning to a normal.

"He's right," LeCompte said.

"Very much so," Rachael whispered.

I could see Carr wrestling with himself, beating himself up for not seeing such an obvious tack.

"George, you and your people are too close to this to be objective."

"I should have thought all that out, at least one of us should have," he said, staring at LeCompte.

With their eyes following, I got up and walked over to the desk.

I put my hand on the stack of papers that was my secret past, and said, "I think you've been preoccupied." I said this with as little sarcasm as I could. I didn't do very well.

All three saw the truth of my words. That stack of papers was a multitude of investigative research.

Carr responded with, "Okay you're right. But, like I said before, I thought it best to know as much as I could about you, before hiring you."

"Yeah, or you might just be nosey."

That got a laugh out of the other two.

Before Carr could retort, I said, "Then, there's the distraction factor."

"Distraction?" Carr asked.

I walked back over to the stone table. Standing next to him, I put my hand on his shoulder and said, "It's not uncommon for a person that's going through grief to be easily distracted from doing that very thing. Grief is a long, painful, arduous process. Sometimes the tools we use to distract ourselves become obsessions . . . or addictions. I was the master of distraction."

As my words hit home, his shoulders slumped and he lowered his head, as if to cry.

I knew what he was going through. He couldn't articulate it yet. His body was feeling the momentary release of the distraction, and that left only one thing, grief.

Looking out the window, a poem by Aeschylus came to mind.

I said, "In our sleep, pain which cannot forget, falls drop by drop upon the heart until, in our own despair, against our will, comes wisdom through the awful grace of God."

I walked back around and sat down on the couch next to Rachael.

Carr was visibly shaken, his face was ravaged, his eyes full of pain and unbearably tired.

Rachael's and LeCompte's compassion and individual pain were palatable.

I didn't know if Carr had heard me, then he said, "What's it mean?"

"It means you need to sleep." I said.

I leaned toward the coffee table and picked up the cell phone and put it in my left coat pocket so it wouldn't bang on my .45, and put the cards and money in the right pocket.

I stood and looked at my watch. It was 8:36. It was time to think about Eddie Tuma, and how I was going to deal with him.

"I've got a couple of things to do before I leave for Houston. I should be able to leave in a couple of days. I'll call you."

"Okay." LeCompte said, "When you do, I'll give you the address of the River Oaks mansion and anything else you need.

Rachael stood and said, "I'll walk you to the door."

Carr made an attempt to look at me, but I don't think he saw me. I remember wearing that face and what it felt like. A wooden mask you couldn't see through.

LeCompte stood, shook my hand and just nodded. His attention was focused on George.

As Rachael and I were leaving the room, I heard Frank LeCompte say, "Come on, George, let's go upstairs."

At the front door, which I was allowed to open, Rachael said, "I know what yesterday was for you. I don't know if you know it, but I transcribed the investigation George did on you. There was a detailed police report that Brad Spain made available to me. I was surprised to see it was actually done by him, twenty years ago."

I stepped out into the night's cool breeze and was surprised I wasn't angry with Brad Spain. Through the flood lights that surrounded the entrance, I could see the riffling winter browned leaves of a red oak, but couldn't hear their rustle.

She was behind me and without turning, I said, "He was there."

She moved around in front of me. I was trying to see if there were any stars out, but the trees were too thick and the light too bright.

"It must have been a horrible, horrible experience for you," she said, looking up at my face.

I was still looking up at something that wasn't there.

I looked down into her eyes and said, "It was an experience."

She blushed and looked down at the flagstoned space between us.

She said, "I'm sorry. I apologize. I didn't mean to hurt you."

"You didn't."

Still looking down, she moved even closer and said, "You must have loved her very much. It's been twenty years, I can feel your love for her, as if she were still alive."

I was looking at the top of her head, feeling the full weight of her words.

"Damn it," she said, "I'm not usually like this. It's just that I feel like I know you so well. But, I realize you don't know me at all. How could you?"

"I'll always love her. But, it's more than that," I said.

That brought her face back up. Her eyes asking me to continue.

"She saved my life. Twice."

"Really," she said. "How?"

I looked over the top of her head and saw nothing, as I said, "I was a very angry boy when we met. Broken home, alcoholic parents, verbal and physical abuse from both sets of parents. The usual scenario that can turn out a bad boy. I was headed for jail. I would have eventually killed someone, probably by accidentally beating them to death. We met when we were twelve. My family moved across the street from hers. She actually went into her house and told her mother she had just met the boy she was going to marry. We started dating when we were thirteen and, well, I'm sure you know all that. Anyway, over the years, she literally tried to love the hate and anger from me. She was always trying to turn the bad boy into a good man."

"That's very romantic," she said.

I said, "Yes, I suppose it is. She always thought so. She was still working on it when she was killed."

"She reprogrammed you."

"Yeah. She had some great software," I said, quietly.

Rachael looked shocked.

"What's wrong?" I asked, feeling I had said something inappropriate.

"You just smiled. You're beautiful."

Margie used to say that.

"I'm not beautiful. Men can't be beautiful," I said before I had a chance to think. It's what I always said to Margie.

Rachael was quiet for a moment, her eyes still on me, then said, "And the second time she saved your life?"

I looked down into her scarred face and said, "That was the night she died."

Her eyes seemed to enlarge to twice their size, making them all the more beautiful.

"I don't understand," she said, timidly.

"There's no reason you should."

I was starting to feel that protective numbness that sometimes permeates my body when I recall that night.

Still looking up at me, she said, "I'm sorry, Tucker, it's none of my business. I don't know what's come over me. I just . . ."

"We grew up driving in the days when there were no seat belts in cars. I used to think about what I would do if we were ever in a wreck while I was driving. I don't know why I did things like that. Worked out scenario's ahead of time, just in case. I still do that. I started driving when I was 15. So, I had years of driving and knowing what I would do if we were in a head on collision, if I had the time. My plan was to throw my body in front of hers, so she wouldn't hit the windshield. We weren't wearing our seat belts. Growing up without them, it just didn't seem important. An under-aged drunk driver hit us and knocked the car off the road. I saw all these trees in front of us. After being hit I couldn't control the car. I didn't even think about it, it was a reflex. I threw myself in front of her, my back to the windshield, my head just under her chin. My side of the car was crushed down through the steering wheel by a telephone pole. The anchor wire that was attached to the pole cut off the top of the car on the passenger side. It actually skipped across the top of my head, hitting her at the base of her nose. There was a space about the size of a laundry basket in the front of the car that a human could survive in. I was in it. Part of the molding from the diver's side was stuck in my mouth, through my cheek. I could feel it between my teeth, it didn't even break one. I thought she was still alive, at first. The doors were welded shut by the force of the wreck. I was stuck there, under her, until the adrenalin kicked in and I tore the door off. So, you see, if she wouldn't have been in the car, I would have been killed."

I heard the echo of the monotone litany in my head.

She grasped my hands, and softly jerked down, bringing me out of my head and said, "You were trying to save her life, and in doing that you were spared. You both would have been dead if you hadn't done what you did."

"That's what my daughters said."

"You should listen to them."

"Yeah, they said that too," I said, with a tone that suggested something on a larger scale.

Rachael shook her head and said, "You're amazing, you go from where you just were, to flippant. How do you do that?"

"You're reading too much into it. I'm a simple man."

Still holding both my hands, she said, "I find you many things. Simple is not one of them."

I opened my hands, thinking she would let go of them. She didn't. I looked at my truck and wanted to be behind the wheel, driving somewhere.

She let go of my hands and said, "Right, you're a simple man that reads and recites Greek poetry. I think you're a very interesting man, Tucker."

"Naw, I read it in a paperback novel once and it kind of stuck, was apropos at the time."

She laughed aloud, which made her face look like a cute old lady, and said, "I don't know whether to believe you or not."

"Maybe that's what you find interesting," I said.

Then I walked to my truck.

As I got behind the wheel, I thought I heard her say, "Tucker, you are a good man."

Book Three

"THE CHAT"

Chapter 42

For most of the day I'd had to put any thoughts of Eddie Tuma and his attack on my home on a back shelf. Until now. They knew where I lived. My son could have been home alone.

The fervent anger I felt earlier had slowly festered into a resonate bestial rage that was fast surfacing. I knew I had to show some restraint. A lot of restraint.

I didn't really have a plan and had learned long ago that plans had a way of blowing up in my face.

If you want to make God laugh, make plans.

I was better off to just have a general idea of what I was going to do and let it unfold from there. My general idea was to have a chat with Mr. Tuma, a serious one. With a lot of restraint.

I picked up my cell phone and hit the speed dial for Spain.

He picked up on the second ring and said, "I was hoping to hear from you before you went to see Eddie."

No hello, just straight to the point. For some, caller ID has eliminated phone etiquette.

"Yeah. That's why I'm calling."

"Whataya need?"

"For starters, what's he look like?"

After he finished laughing, he said, "You've never seen the man who's trying to off you?"

I took it as a rhetorical question.

"How'd the interview go?" he asked.

"Very strange," I said.

I felt dressed for the first time since early afternoon.

"Other than being long, how so?"

"I'll tell you later. What's Tuma look like?"

"God damn it, Tucker. Did you take the job or not?"

"Yeah, I took it."

Why did I have the feeling he already knew that.

"When do you leave?"

He must be a friend, I hadn't hung up on him.

"Never, if I don't get this thing with Tuma straightened out."

"How do you plan to do that?" he asked, with a worried edge.

"First, by finding out what he looks like."

"Oh, yeah. Well he looks pretty much like any thirty-five old, guinea, whop, goombah. About five-nine, 180 to 190 pounds, no neck, no fat, with thick black grease ball hair.

"My, my, that's pretty racial coming from a redskin pig."

"I just talk that way about bad Italian Americans."

"Right."

"What time are you thinking about having this little talk with him?"

"That's one of the things I was calling you about," I said, as I turned right onto Harding. I was headed back downtown towards my office.

Spain said, "If it was me, I'd surprise him around midnight. He'll be in his office by then. I did some checking while you were at Carr's. About midnight he checks the receipts from the first show."

"Show?"

"Yeah. His girls aren't just your regular titty bar babes. He's supposed to have a couple of real class acts."

Somewhere in that statement I heard an oxymoron. But what do I know?

"Tucker?"

"Yeah."

"You're just going to talk, right?"

"That's the plan."

"But, you're going to be carrying, right?"

"Right."

He said, "Listen. From what I hear, Eddie Tuma's a nut case. He's volatile and been known to blow up and clean up his mess later."

"That's what you hear?"

"That's the word on the street."

"He's evidently good at it," I said.

"At what?"

"Cleaning. He hasn't been busted, right?"

"Right."

"Spain."

"Yeah."

"Thanks for the information."

"Yeah . . . yeah. Call me when you're through with him, if you can."

"It'll be late."

"Call my cell. I'll be up."

Chapter 43

I went to my office to pick up something I might need. My kel-lite stick, a gift from Robbie Gray. Eight inches of hand forged airplane aluminum, the diameter a little larger than a roll of quarters.

As I sat by the window overlooking Second Avenue drinking Starbucks and thinking how Emmett could have been home by himself when Tuma's men showed up, my blood began to boil.

I knew I had to calm down.

Watching the people on Second Avenue gave me cause to ponder. Every individual was in his own life's process. The people on the street looked so happy and carefree. Did violence touch their lives? How many had lost a loved one? How many had killed someone? How many of them even thought about such things? Even if any of them did, maybe they weren't now. They were on vacation.

Maybe I could use a vacation.

I drank three cups of high test coffee, and by 11:45 was quivering in my truck, in the parking lot of The Men's Room.

I was wired for 220 volts and pissed off.

Five minutes before midnight, I left the car and walked up the front door ramp. I thought of two things: I remembered midnight was the witching hour; and I was surprised to see this place was wheel chair accessible.

For some reason, things were already slowing down.

Before getting out of the truck I'd slipped the kel-lite stick vertically down the front of my pants, directly behind my belt buckle. It would stay there and be reasonably comfortable, unless I had to sit down, which I wasn't planning to do. I was wearing my leather jacket. It made getting my .45 out just a little quicker than a sport jacket. And it was a little too big for me, making it easier to move faster.

I opened the door and was greeted by a security guard. He asked if I had any liquor or bottles of any kind and after saying no, gestured me to the cashier's window.

The cashier was typical security type. A big and muscular dull-witted jock.

In a broken nose whine, he said, "That'll be twenty bucks."

"There's a cover?" I asked. I'd never been in a place like this.

"Hey, man, you don't think you're going in there for free, do you?"

After giving him a twenty from my clip, he asked, "How many ones do you want?"

"Ones?" I asked.

With a 'I'm talking to a moron' sigh, he said, "Yeah, ones. Ya know for da girls. There's change machines inside, but it's easier to get it here."

I'd been careful not to make eye contact with anyone. As I peeled off another twenty, I was hard put not to give him one of my famous 'soil your pants' looks.

I didn't want anyone to be able to recognize me in a lineup. You never know.

After getting my twenty ones, I went through the only other door in the foyer.

I was assaulted by rock music, smoke, flesh, and a disc-jockey type voice talking about the girls and up-to-the-minute specials. "Table dances only $5 for the next five minutes".

The place was packed. There was one of those spinning mirror globes hanging above the dance bar. There were several laser lights hitting it, giving the whole room, top to bottom, an eerie, ethereal ambiance.

Satan hides in heaven.

There were topless women passing out drinks and dancing at tables occupied by both men and women.

In the middle of the first floor was a square bar, but not for selling drinks. Upon closer scrutiny, I saw that it was a raised rectangle dance floor with chairs all the way around it. None were empty.

The dance floor was about 30 feet x 50 feet, and there were two completely naked women dancing, one at each end. One of the dancers was almost straddling a women's face. Oh well. They were very pretty, all over. Then again what did I know. I hadn't seen a naked woman for a spell.

To the right of the center stage, the room tiered up three levels. Each level one step above the other. Each tier containing four top tables.

There was a stairway at the opposite end of the room from the entrance, where women were leading men up and down.

At the top of the stairs was an open room that contained big overstuffed chairs and love seats. I couldn't tell what they were doing up there, but by the sex eating grins on the men coming down, it didn't take much imagination to figure it out.

I thought for a man that had been celibate for three years, this might not be the best place for me to do this. Talk about your distractions.

I felt someone looking at me. It only took a few seconds to home in on his radar.

Sitting in a dark corner, in the back right-hand side of the top tier, was a man surrounded by four scantly clad women. I could barely make out his face, but had no problem seeing his left leg wrapped in bandages. It was propped up on a chair and the pants leg was slit to accommodate the bandage. He was very still and had moved the women out of the way so he could get a better look at me.

I had no doubt he had been out to my place poaching deer.

I had to move fast if I was going to get this done.

In the back left-hand corner of the ground floor was a door and standing off to one side, a man guarding it.

This guy didn't look like the jocks at the front. He was older, about 35, very fit, and was definitely of the Italian, shark skin suit persuasion. He was around my height with boots on, six- two, a full head of black hair, swept back, giving me a clear view of the scar tissue around his dark eyes.

I walked over to him, which was no small feat unto itself. By the time I had waded through the legs and breasts that were offering me everything from a lap dance to a drink, he had a definite fix on me.

As I approached the door, he stood in front of it, and with a thick Jersey accent said, "Beat it slick. This ain't the john."

By the bulge under his right arm, I knew he was a southpaw and was carrying a shoulder holster. Typical. A lot of gangsters or wanna be gangsters carried their guns in shoulder holsters. It's so cool. Good for me, bad for them.

There's a lot of distance between the hand by your side and the butt of the gun. And, once drawn, the gun could only come to bear on the target in a horizontal motion. The average man's body is less than 2 feet wide.

Drawing the gun from the hip, where it belongs, gives you the entire length of a mans body to connect with something.

He was giving his best stare, trying to make me poop my pants. I didn't even have to pee.

"I wanna see Eddie Tuma."

"Fuck off, pisshead."

Pisshead? What happened to slick?

"Tell him Tucker's out here."

Now, that got his attention.

His stare seemed to invert. His face looked a little strained, like he had to think.

He cleared his throat and said, "Wait here."

He started to turn and open the door, then at the last second pointed to a spot about 5 feet off to the side and said, "Stand over there."

After I had moved to my designated position, he opened the door and went inside, closing it behind him.

So far so good, I was still alive.

I glanced over to the other side of the room where bandaged leg was still looking at me. I was hoping he couldn't get up.

Carrying a tray full of drinks a fully clothed cocktail waitress hustled by and I said, "Excuse me ma'am. I think that's an old friend of mine over there, the one with the bandage on his leg. What's his name?"

She looked at bandaged leg, who was now talking on a cell phone, then back at me and frowned.

I moved over closer to the office door, leaned against the wall and said, "I'm just waiting for Eddie to get through so we can go out."

Then I did something I hadn't done in years, I winked.

She smiled and said, "Oh, that's Tony."

Gee, Tony, I wonder what that's short for.

"Yeah, I thought that was Anthony. What happened to his leg?"

She said, a little breathlessly, "I think it was some kind of hunting accident."

My charm was making her faint. It couldn't be she was getting tired standing there holding up that heavy tray.

"I notice you're not dressed like the other girls."

"I haven't yet graduated to their level," she said, with a laugh that almost made me forget why I was here.

It was obvious she never intended to *graduate*.

"I'm Tucker," I said.

"Sheila," she said, taking in my scar. It dawned on me that it might not be a good idea for her to be seen being friendly with me.

"Sheila, I lied to you. I'm not a friend of Eddie's. In fact, I'm sure he doesn't like me, even a little. So if anybody asks what we were talking about, just tell them I was hitting on you. Okay?"

She gave me a big smile and said, "I like you even more than I did before."

As she hustled away, over the loud music, I could barely discern her singing, 'That's my story and I'm sticking to it.'

It's the scar, makes me look sexy.

I felt good, almost happy . . . almost. If I had time to give it much thought, I'd worry about myself. Considering where I was and what I was here to do.

Just as I finished adjusting the kel-lite stick for comfort and concealment, the door to the office opened and Sharkskin said, "Alright," as he backed into the office.

He was careful to keep his body between me and a man sitting at a desk 20 feet away. Had to be Eddie Tuma.

"Close the fuckin' door, shithead," Sharkskin said, reaching up under his coat.

Shithead? What happened to pisshead? I think I like pisshead better.

I could have killed him five times.

I stepped into the office, onto a plush carpet, and closed the door. I heard it lock. How clever. I loved it.

By now his gun was out and pointed at me, a 9mm Beretta.

Six times.

I had expected this.

Sharkskin said, "Pull back your coat, let's see what you got."

I pulled back both sides of my jacket and turned all the way around, so he could see that all I had was the one gun.

"Take it out with two fingers, real slow, and hand it to me."

As my thumb and forefinger touched the grip, I thought . . . seven times.

I held it out for him at arm's length.

He took it, gave it a good look, whistled between his teeth, and said, "Niiice. I might have to keep this."

He stuck it in his pants, a little to the left of the belt buckle.

"Raise your pants' legs, dickbreath."

Yeah, pisshead was better, definitely.

I pulled my jeans up to the tops of my boots.

"Now turn your coat pockets inside out."

"They don't really turn inside out," I said, as I turned the pockets so he could see they were empty.

I was beginning to think I'd heard that voice before, in the dark.

"Okay, boss, he's clean."

He must be homophobic, any rookie cop would have found the kel-lite stick. He hadn't even touched me. I'd gambled and won, the first hand anyway.

He stepped aside, allowing me to see Eddie Tuma.

He was pretty much just as Spain had described. He was wearing a blue blazer with brass buttons and a white Polo shirt. I could just make out the horse. The first two buttons were open, so I could admire his chest hair. On his left wrist was a gold and diamond Rolex, and he had a diamond pinky ring... really.

This was going to be okay. Just the three of us in the room. No other doors, even hidden ones, that I could see, and I was looking.

Eddie Tuma must have assumed I was looking at all the large framed pictures on the wall behind him and the walls on each side of us.

They were obviously strippers who worked there, or had worked there. They were big pictures, about 3 feet by 2 feet.

In a thick Jersey accent, he proudly said, "I've fucked every one of those bitches."

No howya doin', no, it's good to finally meet you. I didn't feel properly greeted. But, I could tell he was a real classy guy.

"Well, I'm sure they say the same about you."

He started to smile and nod his head, then, his brow plowed with thought.

Not only class, but smart.

I was still 15 feet away from him, too far.

I walked past Sharkskin towards the desk. Sharkskin fell in behind me and poked me with the muzzle.

Eight times.

This might be easier than I thought.

When I was 2 feet from the desk, I stopped. I could see the room behind me in the reflections of all the...bitches.

I was pretending to look at the women, and as I whistled admiringly, I moved a half step to my right, allowing me to see the left side of Sharkskin, reflected over a gorgeous blond.

"I gotta hand it to you, Tucker, you got balls."

"Yeah?"

"To come in here like this."

"I didn't know your phone number or I would've called first."

He chuckled, drumming his fingers on his desk.

Sharkskin was only a couple of feet behind me.

"I got your little note on my windshield," I said.

"Yeah?"

Well, at least he didn't deny it.

He started moving things around on his desk top, very cool. First he picked up a pencil and stuck it in a pencil cup that had 'Stud' painted in freehand on it. He wanted me to see it. Then he moved an old flip type rolodex from the right-hand side to the left.

I could see he liked to print instead of cursive. Me, too, maybe we could be buds.

It was time to switch gears. I held my hands out in front of me, palms up.

In my finest apprehensive voice, I said, "Ya know, Mr. Tuma, I think there's been a terrible misunderstanding between us."

"How's that?" he asked, looking over my shoulder at Sharkskin with a 'this guy's about to piss his pants' grin.

I started moving my weight nervously from one foot to the other.

"I didn't know Mr. Bench and you had any trouble. I was just hired that very morning. I swear if I had known you and he had a beef I wouldn't have taken the job, I swear," I whined.

I wondered if I could tear up a little. Maybe not.

I heard Sharkskin snicker behind me, then, "Ain't so fuckin' bad without your gun, are you turdface?"

316 R. O. Barton

Turdface?

Then it happened.

Looking at the blonde, I saw Sharkskin slide his Beretta back into his shoulder holster.

Still shuffling nervously, I put my left hand in my jacket pocket, like I was cold, and hooked my right thumb inside my pants, right behind the buckle of my belt.

I said, "Gee Mr. Tuma, I don't want any trouble with you . . ."

I made sure not to make eye contact, opting to look at the pictures, but more importantly, their reflections.

I used the nervous movement of my body, along with my left hand in my pocket, to cover up my right hand.

Sharkskin was now going "heh, heh, heh."

I think it was a laugh.

I snapped his left knee with a side kick of my left boot, at the same time I pulled out the stick. The knee sounded like an old dried out cane pole breaking from the weight of too large a fish.

Sharkskin screamed. Literally. Like a woman, high pitched and long.

As he started to pitch forward, I came up with an uppercut and hit him in the mouth with the blunt end of the kelite stick. As his teeth shattered, it sounded like I'd hit a gravel road with a hammer.

When Sharkskin's head came up from the force of the blow, I reached over with my left hand and pulled my pistol from his belt, and in one motion, pointed it at Eddie. The move shielded my right hand, as I slipped the kel-lite stick in my back right pocket of my jeans. It was never seen.

It took less than three seconds.

Eddie Tuma looked like he'd just given blood, all of it.

Sharkskin was down, moaning loudly and bleeding profusely on the fine plush carpet.

"Stand up, Eddie, and put your back against the wall."

He didn't move.

"The last thing you'll ever hear will be this safety going off."

I made a show of picking my thumb up and slowly lowering it to the safety. I always carried my Colt at full cock with safety on, ready to shoot.

He got up and put his back against the wall. His hands had never left the desk top and now with his back against the wall, I wouldn't have to worry about him unlocking the door. I loved it.

"You're dead," he said, his color returning.

"Yeah? How do I look?"

Sharkskin's moaning was aggravating.

I backed up a couple of steps until I was next to his prone body. He was laying on his back, his head lolling back and forth, groaning, making little red bubbles. Now there was blood in two spots on the carpet, large spots.

I took a quick gander at Eddie, then jumped up and came down with both boots and my 200 pounds, right over Sharkskin's heart, rebounded off his chest and back onto the floor.

That shut him up.

I felt nimble.

"Jesus . . ." Eddie's voice cracked.

With one eye, I was watching Sharkskin's chest for movement. Glancing at Eddie, I said, "If he doesn't start breathing pretty soon, you're going to be the one to give him mouth to mouth."

The muzzle of my .45 never left his chest.

It took a few seconds but Sharkskin started gurgling. With my boot, I moved his head to one side so he wouldn't drown on his blood and vomit. Then I bent over and took out his Beretta and tossed it away.

"Looks like you're off the hook," I said, after straightening up.

"Now what?" he asked.

"What's his name?"

"What?"

I snapped the fingers of my left hand and said, "Come on, Eddie, you need to get with the program here."

I head gestured to Sharkskin and said very slowly, like I was talking to a child, "What is his name?"

"Pauly."

"Yeah? Tell me, Eddie, how come everyone around you sounds like they came from the set of 'The Godfather' but you?"

"Whataya mean?"

I snapped my fingers again and said, "Come on, out there on the floor, you got Tony with a shot-up leg and down here you got Pauly with..."

I gave the floor a quick once-over and said, "You know, I think he swallowed most of his teeth."

"You better kill me, mother fucker." He *did* sound tough, really.

"Now, Eddie, I was hoping we could come to some sort of agreement, you know, so I won't have to do that."

"You think you can just come in here and get away with this shit and live. You're fucking crazy, man."

"You think you can send this asshole and Tony out there, to my house! My house! I've got a son!" I was raising my voice. I hate to raise my voice, it makes me violent. It stems from my childhood. Yelling always ended in violence.

I slowly raised my thumb over the safety.

"Okay. Okay. Look, Tucker, you can't do this. You don't know who you're fuckin' with, man . . . I'm connected."

How dumb could I be? Jersey accents. Italian names. It was coming to me, slowly, but it was coming.

A couple of years ago, I had Tuckerized a couple of 1911 .45's for one Sonny Medica, from New Jersey. Sonny sent the guns to me, but when I finished, said he would prefer to come down and get them. Shoot them to see if they needed any fine-tuning, a custom fit, as it were.

Sonny and I hit it off nicely. He was more than a decent shot and pretty quick. I took him to the police firing range (I was still in their good graces) and he seemed to get a big kick out of that, the fact we were shooting right next to a bunch of cops.

While having dinner after shooting, I asked him what he did in Jersey. He told me he was a body guard for some big shot up there, a man named Tumanello. I couldn't remember the first name.

Sonny hung out for a couple of days. We did some more shooting,. I made a few adjustments on the trigger pull, and buffed the rails again. We got friendlier, and he told me the big shot was a distant relative. I figured he worked for the mob up there and probably did more than bodyguard.

He liked my off hand shooting, with either hand, and asked me if I would give him a few tips. I did, and before he left, he said if I was ever in Jersey, to look him up and we'd have some fun, eat some good Italian food. He also said if I was up there and ever got in a fix, to drop his name, it might help.

"Eddie, you know Sonny Medica?"

"......No."

It took him too long.

I walked over to the desk and grabbed the rolodex. I looked under the M's and there it was, 'Sonny'. The number looked familiar. I pulled it out and set it on the desk.

I looked under the T's and the first entry read, 'Frankie,' that's it, no last name.

That's the first name I couldn't remember, Frankie, Frankie Tumanello.

I set it next to Sonny's number.

"Whataya doin?" Eddie asked nervously.

"Take it easy, Eddie."

There was a cordless phone laying on the desk. I picked it up and saw that it had one of those caller ID buttons. Just for grins, I pushed it. When the last number that called showed, I punched the talk button.

The phone rang three times before it was answered, a voice said, "Yeah, boss?"

Outside the office door, I could barely hear the music, but now it was in stereo.

"Tony, you got your phone on vibrate or what?" I said with a raised voice and my best Jersey accent.

"Yeah, boss, everything okay in there?"

I took it Eddie liked his help to call him boss.

"Good, stay put," I said, and hung up.

I was confident he couldn't tell the difference between my voice and Eddie's over the music.

Eddie was still against the wall, but was looking at the two cards on the desk.

I punched in Sonny's number.

"Ahh, man, don't do that," Eddie said, not so toughly.

It rang twice before it was answered. There was a short pause before I heard Sonny's voice, "This better be good, Eddie, it's fuckin' late."

Caller ID again.

"How ya doin', Sonny?"

Another pause, then, "Who the fuck is this?"

"Tucker."

". . . Shit. Just tell me, is he still alive?"

"Yeah, for now."

"What did he do?"

"How ya doin', Sonny?" I asked again.

This got a little laugh as he said, "I'll be doin' a lot better after you tell me what the fuck is goin' on."

"What's goin' on is, I'm in Eddie's office at The Men's Room. He's against the wall, alive, and Pauly's on the floor in dire need of an oral surgeon and maybe an Internist."

"Okay. Okay. That's a start. Now, why are you there?"

"Eddie sent Pauly and Tony out to my house in the middle of the night to kill me. They didn't."

"Fuck! I told him not to fuck with you."

"He didn't listen."

"Fuck!"

"Yeah, that's kinda how I feel. My son could have been home, Sonny. I need to do something to make sure this never happens again. Got any suggestions?"

"Just a minute, let me think."

I gave him a couple of seconds.

"Tucker?"

"Yeah?"

"How'd you put it together...you know, Eddie and me."

"I was just about to cap him when he tells me he's connected (*a little white lie couldn't hurt*). I'm a little slow on the uptake sometimes, but it wasn't a long way from Tuma to Tumanello, not with all the Jersey accents around here."

"Yeah. I get it," Sonny said.

"Sonny, I've got Frankie Tumanello's phone number, but I thought I'd call you first."

"For God's sake, Tucker, don't call Frankie."

"You'd better come up with something, Sonny."

"Listen, Tucker, when all that shit came down, I told Frankie about you. He understood it was just business, even though you took out two of his best shooters."

"He still has you."

"Yeah, well, I don't do that kind of work anymore, I made my bones years ago."

"Why would Frankie send them down here to begin with?"

"It was for Eddie, he lost a lot of face over that real estate deal with Bench. They were kind of on loan."

"Pretty high interest," I said.

That got a small laugh.

"You got that right," he said.

The whole time I never took my eyes off of Eddie. He wasn't a happy camper.

"Ya know, Tucker, I couldn't believe any one man could have taken those two, not 'til I heard your name connected with it."

"It was close."

"Really? I wonder if that had anything to do with the fact I showed them your style of shooting? I even got them to wear their pieces on their hips, where you say they belong."

"Do me a favor, Sonny."

"What's that?"

"Stop doing that."

"Whatta you care, you're still walking around. I just helped make your life more interesting."

"What're we goin' to do here, Sonny? I'm getting kind of tired holding this gun up, and Pauly needs to go to the hospital, oh yeah, what's Eddie to Frankie Tumanello?"

"Nephew, not his favorite either, 'cause Eddie really wants to be a wise guy, and we're trying to get away from that image."

"Has anyone told Eddie that?"

Another chuckle, "Yeah, not that it's done any good."

"It's late and I'm getting tired, Sonny."

"Okay, give the phone to Eddie."

I slid the phone over the desk top and motioned for Eddie to pick it up.

Eddie looked at it like I would look at a spider.

He finally picked it up and said, "Yeah."

It was amazing how one word could sound so wise guyee.

After a full minute of him listening to what sounded to me like a chipmunk barking through the phone, he said, "I was just trying to take care of business, Sonny. I just wanted to make Uncle Frankie proud."

After another full minute of barking, Eddie said, "I gotta do something Sonny, I gotta do something."

More barking, then he pushed the phone back across the table.

I picked it up and said, "Yeah?"

"He ain't gettin' it, Tucker. I know him, and he just ain't gettin' it. Stay where you are for a few minutes, I'm going to have to call Frankie. I hope like hell he isn't asleep. I'll call you back in five."

"Okay."

After putting the phone down, I looked around, then said, "Eddie, go sit in the corner."

"Whataya mean, go sit in the corner?" he asked disbelievingly.

With the muzzle, I pointed to the right-hand corner of the room behind the desk, about eight feet away from the desk chair.

"Go sit in the corner. I'm not going to tell you again."

About that time, Pauly gurgled.

Eddie went and sat in the corner.

I walked around behind the desk and sat in the chair.

After a full minute of silence, I said, "Eddie, ya know, the name 'The Men's Room', it sounds like the smell of urine. You should consider renaming it. It's really quite nice out there, doesn't smell like piss at all."

"Fuck you."

"No, that's no good. That sounds more like an advertisement. You need something more subtle."

He didn't want to talk anymore. While he sat there thinking of a new name, I opened the top drawer of his desk.

Among the regular things one might find in a desk was a little .22 cal. derringer. I picked it up with my thumb and forefinger, like it was road kill.

I scrunched my face like I'd just smelled a skunk and said, "Damn, Eddie, you really *are* a bad ass. Evidently you're not afraid to just piss somebody off."

Unless you put a round directly in a man's eye, you couldn't be sure to stop someone with one of these. And you had to be close... very close.

He still didn't want to converse with me. I'd get over it.

The phone rang. I answered it.

"Yeah," I said.

"Tucker?"

"It's me."

"Go ahead and call Frankie, he's waiting."

"Okay."

"And Tucker?"

"Yeah."

"Frankie Tumanello comes from the old school."

"Yeah?"

"Respect goes a long way. Think you could fake it? It might help."

"I'll give it a shot."

"Bad choice of words."

I remembered why I liked Sonny.

"I'll give him a call."

"Right," he said.

I hung up the phone and looked at Eddie.

"Who ya gonna call?" he asked, looking scared for the first time.

"Ghostbusters."

I punched in the number, and it was answered on the first ring.

"Mr. Tucker?" The voice was smoker deep and resonated from his chest.

"Mr. Tumanello?"

"Yes."

"Oh shit," Eddie whispered from the corner.

I waited.

"Mr. Tucker, Sonny has spoken highly of you."

"As he has of you, Mr. Tumanello." *Won't hurt to schmooze.*

"As I understand it, you have my nephew at gunpoint; is that correct?"

"That's correct."

"In his own office?"

"Correct again."

"And just what is it you want?"

"Not to have to worry about your nephew sending someone to my house, again, to kill me or my son if he happens to be home, because I did the job I was hired to do."

"You're putting me in an awkward position, Mr. Tucker. It is not good that you are holding a gun on my nephew while we negotiate."

I put the gun on the desk.

"I'm not doing that now."

"Thank you, Mr. Tucker. Now, what can I do for you? Oh, by the way, that was an impressive piece of business you attended to in Nashville. Now, again what can I do for you?"

I deduced he was referring to me killing two of his men. His voice sounded genuinely impressed and not at all angry.

I said, "It's not just what you can do for me. But what you can do for us, all three of us."

"How so?"

"Mr. Tumanello, no disrespect to you sir, but, your nephew is confused."

"Confused?"

"Yes, sir. His issue is with Mr. Bench, not me. It seems Mr. Bench is too hard for your nephew to find, so I believe he is taking his frustrations out on me. I was just doing my job. In fact, if I didn't do my job, I wouldn't be here talking to you."

"I see," he said.

I believed him.

"I have a family, sir, I love my family. Eddie sent people to my home to do me harm. He had people try to kill me in my car."

"What?" Eddie said quickly from the corner. "I didn't do that."

Ignoring him for the moment, I continued, "I don't know what interest you have here in Nashville and it is of no concern of mine, but with all respect, Mr. Tumanello, I cannot and will not live my life in fear that Eddie will hurt my family."

I was trying to make sure it didn't sound like a threat.

"I can understand that, Mr. Tucker."

I must have done good.

I said, "Thank you, sir. Do you have any suggestions?"

"Sonny has told me you are a man of honor, Mr. Tucker."

"I try."

"Yes, as do I," he replied with a sigh.

It must be harder for him.

"Mr. Tucker, if I give you my word of honor that my nephew will make no further attempts to harm you or yours, would that suffice?"

"Of course, Mr. Tumanello," I replied without hesitation. Thinking about it wouldn't earn me any Brownie points.

"Please, call me Frankie."

Oh goodie, I have a new friend.

"Of course, Frankie, and I'm just Tucker," I said, grinning at Eddie, who looked back with disbelief.

"I believe you are more than *just* anything," he said.

"Thank you, sir, you are too kind." *Schmooze, schmooze.*

"Tucker, would you be so kind as to hand the phone to Eddie?"

"My pleasure, sir."

I covered the mouthpiece, held the phone out to Eddie and said, "Frankie wants to talk to you."

Eddie got up and walked over to me, looking like he was going to tear up.

He took the phone, "It's me, Uncle Frankie."

For the next minute, he listened without uttering a word. I couldn't hear Frankie Tumanello's voice at all, so I assumed he wasn't raising his voice.

After talking to him, I'd bet the softer he spoke, the more dangerous he was. I also had the impression he was a well-educated man, kind of reminded me of Armando Miranda. I wondered what had become of the Miranda brothers.

Finally Eddie spoke, "But, Uncle Frankie, Pauly's laying on the floor and he's really fucked up, needs to go to the hospital, his teeth . . . yes sir, sorry . . . yes sir. Yes sir.

This went on for another minute or so, plenty of yes sir's, and I'm sorry's.

While Eddie was studying his shoes, I put my .45 back in it's holster.

He finally looked up, handed the phone to me and said, "He wants to talk to you again."

I took the phone and said, "Yes?"

"Mr. Tucker, Sonny didn't apprise me of Pauly's condition. Did he know?"

Uh-oh, back to *Mr.* again.

"I told him."

"I see. Mr. Tucker, Pauly is also a relative *(that must be why they call it 'The Family'),* and he was just doing what he was told. I hope you won't take it as personal."

"I don't. That's why he's still alive."

"Yes, of course."

I could hear him breathing.

Just when I thought I had angered him and he was going to hang up on me without another word, he says, "Tucker, how would you like to go to work for me?"

Uh-oh, a change-up.

"Excuse me?" I couldn't keep the surprise out of my voice.

He made a sound I was sure was a laugh.

"Eddie is my little brother's boy. My brother was killed when Eddie was only 5. It was his wish that I keep Eddie out of the business. I have done my best. We changed his name, moved him down to Nashville and set him up in a legitimate business. It seems he is reluctant to be legitimate. I'm not talking about that Bench business. Mr. Bench not only had an agreement with my nephew, but me as well. Rest assured, Mr. Bench will hear from me sooner or later. Do you have a problem with that?"

"Not as long as I'm not working for him at the time," I said, feeling all rested and assured.

"Yes, of course. Now, getting back to business. I would like to hire you to keep an eye on Eddie for me."

For Eddie's benefit, I said, "You want me to keep an eye on Eddie?"

Eddie rolled his eyes, shook his head and groaned.

Frankie Tumanello said, "Yes. Just to make sure he doesn't get into any trouble. Keep me apprised of his standing in the community."

"I have a client at this time, Mr. Tumanello." I was getting the hang of this *Mr.* thing, to use it when talking business. "You couldn't have more than one client?"

"This is going to take me out of town for an undetermined time."

"Yes, of course. I see."

"But, when I come back, it would be my pleasure to drop in on Eddie from time to time to see how he is doing. As a favor to you," I said, showing Eddie my teeth.

Frankie Tumanello's laugh seized the irony of the situation.

"Tucker, I don't get much humor in my life these days. Thank you. I may take you up on that. And, if you ever come to the northeast, it would be my honor and pleasure to entertain you."

"I would be delighted," I said. I wondered if he had some kind of talent, like telling jokes, or playing the guitar. I doubted it.

A loud groaning gurgle came from Pauly.

Frankie Tumanello asked, "What's that?"

"Pauly," I said.

"How bad is he?"

"He's going to need an oral surgeon, an orthopedic surgeon, and maybe a plastic surgeon, and maybe a chest surgeon," I answered truthfully.

"Pauly is a very capable man, Mr. Tucker. Just what did you do to him?"

" I never learned to play fair."

"Of course. May I please speak to my nephew again, so he can get Pauly to the hospital? He's my cousin Sylvia's boy."

"Yes, sir. Goodbye."

"Goodbye, Mr. Tucker, and please call me when you return from your business. I think having you look in on Eddie might be a good idea."

So did I.

"Here's Eddie, Mr. Tumanello."

"Frankie," he said.

"Frankie," I said.

Just when I thought I was getting the hang of the *Mr.* thing.

I held out the phone to Eddie.

"Yes sir," started and continued for another minute. Eddie ended the conversation with something different, "Yes, sir, Uncle Frankie."

He put the phone down on the desk, looked at me and said, "I'm supposed to apologize to you and say it won't happen again. Give you my word and all that."

I crossed my arms and waited.

He walked over to Pauly, who was starting to make a lot more noise, looked down at him and said, "God damn it! We've got to get him to the hospital. Give me the phone, I'll call an ambulance."

I picked the phone up and held it as I crossed my arms again, waiting.

He stared at me for a full ten seconds, then said, "Okay, okay, I apologize. It won't happen again."

"You don't sound sincere," I said.

"Well, that's all you're getting."

"What about your word?"

He looked down at Pauly. His throat bobbed as he swallowed. He said, "You've got my word."

Now, that sounded sincere.

I tossed him the phone.

While he was punching in 911, there was a knock on the door, along with, "Hey, boss, open up, it's me, Tony."

Just who I wanted to talk to next.

"Where's the button for the door, Eddie?"

"You can open it from the inside with the knob. What are you going to do?" he asked, looking down at Pauly.

"Talk to Anthony. Don't worry, I'll play fair."

While he was giving 911 the address, I walked over and opened the door.

The music blasted by me and Tony stood there with his mouth open, leaning on one crutch.

Tony was about five-ten, 185 pounds, short thinning sandy hair, no facial scars, and looked to be in his late twenties. He was what women might consider cute. But his dark eyes were too close together for me.

I stayed close to him, so he couldn't see past me, and I backed up as he hobbled through the door.

"Close the door, Tony," I said, after he was in the room.

He closed the door, muting the music, and when he turned around, I'd stepped aside, giving him a good view of the room.

Pauly, in all his gore, was completely visible.

"What happened to Pauly?" Tony asked, to no one in general.

I had to give him credit, he was calm. Maybe it was shock.

"He slipped and busted his lip," I said.

Now Tony was looking at Boss, calmly waiting for an answer. Okay, not shock. He was just mean.

"Tucker did it. I've called an ambulance. Go get some of the boys, so we can get him out of here when the ambulance gets here."

"No," I said.

"Whataya mean, no?"

What a dumbass.

"You'd better not move him until the EMT's get here, his chest may not be in one piece. And, I want to have a little chat with gimpy here."

Tony turned to face me and said, "You're going to pay for this, motherfucker."

I walked over to him and did something I've always wanted to do. I kicked his crutch out from under him and said, "No, I'm not."

He was tittering, but standing. For the first time, I noticed his sport jacket was thicker around his left forearm, probably a bandage. Must be Razor's handy work.

I got in his face and spoke softly, "Take a good look at Pauly over there. See his face? That happened because he had a potty mouth. My name is Tucker, you can call me Mr. Tucker. If I ever see you within 5 miles of my home, I'll kill you and figure it out later. Understand?"

He started to turn his head to look at Eddie, who was still standing by Pauly. I quickly reached out and gave his bandaged arm an unkindly squeeze.

"Tony, don't look at Eddie, look at me."

It hurt, but he didn't make a sound as he looked back at me.

"Did you understand what I said?"

Through clenched teeth he said, "I understand."

I let go of his arm and said, "Good. By the way, my dog's in better shape than you."

After gently patting his bandage, I eased the toe of my boot under his crutch and kicked it up so he could grab it.

"Now, go take a good look at Pauly," I said, after he had the crutch under him.

He gimped over and looked down at Pauly who was now wheezing pink bubbles. He probably had a punctured lung.

"Jesus, Mother Mary, and Joseph," he said, as he crossed himself like a good Catholic.

By now Pauly's mouth was hard to discern. It looked more like a big red hole with loose white corn floating around.

"Tony, in a few days, when Pauly can understand you, you can tell him my name. It's Mr. Tucker. He was having a hard time with that tonight."

Looking at Eddie, I said, "Earlier you said you didn't have anyone try and kill me in my car. Is that the truth? Don't lie to me. It will not make me as congenial as I have been tonight."

Without hesitation, he said, "I don't know what you're talkin' about. I swear, I don't."

I believed him and I didn't want to. I hate algebra, all those x's and unknown factors.

I looked back at Anthony and saw the bewilderment in his face. This whole situation was flying over his head like a missed shot at a mallard.

"Anthony, stop thinking, you're going to hurt yourself. Your boss will tell you all about it."

I looked hard at Eddie, at least I was trying to, and said, "Eddie, make sure the next time I see you, it's because *I* want to."

I turned my back on them, opened the door and walked out into Satan's heavenly hideaway.

As I walked through the hordes of sexually frustrated men and women, I felt good, light, I was walking on a cloud. I felt alive. In tune with the universe. I could see everything occurring around me. The connectiveness of the human race to nature. I walked in a straight line to the door, and people parted like Moses parting the waters. I held no judgment of the people in this place, they were right where they're supposed to be, just like I was. Everything's In Divine Order . . . EIDO.

I walked out of the Men's Room into a light snow. It snowed that night, after Margie was killed. I used to like snow...before.

Chapter 44

By the time I was seated in my truck, letting it warm up, my spiritual high was waning.

I read somewhere God wants us to live in the present. To live every moment like we were children. Like seeing everything for the first time, full of joy, being overwhelmed by the wonders of life.

For me, it's much easier to live in the present when my life is in danger. Where any thought other than what is happening at this very moment, could end my life.

But, it wasn't always so. I used to be able to make love to *her*.

Now, the wonders of life are so much easier for me to see when I have just survived a close call. The closer to death, the longer the awe lasts.

By the time the truck started blowing warm air, I was back on the ground again, the night not quite as sharp, the snowflakes not as white, the resolution of life's picture dulling. The missing of her a black bulge in my chest that held tears that wouldn't come.

My phone chirped at me. I picked it up and said, "Yeah," not looking at the number because I knew I wouldn't be able to see it through the wooden mask I had unexpectantly adorned.

"I see you're still in one piece," Spain drawled.

"Yeah."

"I heard there's an ambulance on the way to The Men's Room."

"Yeah."

"You okay?" He asked.

"Yeah."

"You've been sitting there for a few minutes. I was beginning to worry about you."

I looked around. Double parked out on Dickerson Road, was Spain's unmarked.

"How long you been there?" I asked.

"Since midnight."

I looked at the clock on the dash, it was only 12:27 a.m.

I hadn't given it much thought, but I would have figured it for later.

"You worried about me?"

"Not since I saw you walk out unassisted."

"Thanks for the backup."

"Who's the meat wagon for?"

"Guy named Pauly."

"Pauly Manfredy?"

"We weren't properly introduced. He seemed to be Eddie's right-hand man."

"What did you do, Tucker?"

"I hurt him," I said, as I pulled my truck out onto Dickerson Road and drove past Spain's car.

We looked at each other as I passed him.

"How bad?"

"It would be good for the ambulance to get here soon," I said.

"Was it necessary?"

"He was one of the guys that paid me a visit this morning, I mean yesterday morning." I wasn't used to these night owl hours.

"Sounds necessary."

"Spain, do me a favor."

"What's that?"

"If Pauly dies, don't come get me until after 9:00 or 10:00 in the morning. It's been a long day, and I'm going to the office to crash and burn."

"Pauly's a tough bastard, he'll probably live, unfortunately. What about Eddie Tuma, you resolve anything?"

"Yeah, he won't be bothering me anymore."

"You sure?"

"I'll tell you about it later. Thanks again, and goodbye."

I slapped my phone shut and set it on the console.

The caffeine had evidently worn off. I was having a hard time keeping my eyes open.

I didn't have to worry about my dogs. Before I left the house that morning, I'd made arrangements for my closest neighbor's son to ride his four-wheeler over to my place and feed them. I often paid him to check on them when I was going to be in Nashville overnight or out of town. I was missing Tuesday. Maybe I'd take her to Houston with me.

The phone rang again. In a reflex I picked it up. It was Sonny Medica.

"Tucker? What the hell did you and Frankie talk about? He called and said you were going to work for us when you get back from some business trip."

"That's not going to happen, Sonny. No offense, but I don't knowingly work for wise guys. I can't afford it, personally or professionally."

"No offense taken, Tucker. But why'd you tell him you would look in on Eddie? You did say that, right?"

"Yeah, Sonny. I told him I'd do it as a favor. You know, keep your enemies closer."

Sonny's sense of humor was warped and after he stopped laughing, he said, "For some reason the old man likes you. Says to me to make sure you come up and have a meet with him."

"Go figure," I said, too tired for wit.

"Yeah, go figure."

"Sonny, it's been a long day and I'm beat. Thanks for the help tonight. Without you it could've turned out differently."

"Hey Tucker!" he said loudly.

"Yeah."

"*Fuggedabowtit.*"

The phone went dead and I turned mine off.

I just wanted to get in the bed and curl up. I missed . . . Tuesday.

Chapter 45

I was at the edge of a precipice, again. Waiting to take that step into the dark unknown. Not knowing how deep it was or what it contained. I did however, know what it didn't contain. A safety net. Just like I liked it.

The phone was ringing, but I couldn't find it. It was dark, I was groping around on all fours. Just as I started sliding around in something slick, the sun instantly blared.

I found myself in a pool of blood and brain matter. Somewhere on the edge a pig was grunting, snorting as he ate from the blood pool.

I couldn't find the phone. It wouldn't stop ringing. I had to get off my hands and knees. Get out of the blood and brains. A distant memory told me I had been here before. I *had* to stand up. I stood. I woke up to the sun shining through the windows, onto the futon I'd been sleeping on.

I was in my office. The phone was still ringing, the machine must be off.

"Tucker," I said, after finding the portable phone on the floor.

"It's Spain."

"What's up?" I said, opening and closing my eyes. Letting the dream bleed from behind my eyes, so I wouldn't see red.

"Pauly's dead."

That opened my eyes.

"That's bad timing. I was going to leave town in a couple of days. What do I need to do? You want me down at Metro?"

"Naaw, I'm just fuckin' with you, you hardass. He's alive, barely. His chest is crushed, left lung was punctured from a broken rib, he's going to need a new mouth and a new knee. What the fuck you hit him with?"

"Me," I answered, thinking I could leave after all.

"Yeah, okay. Anyway, you can leave, no charges are being pressed. They say he fell down some stairs."

"Could of happened like that," I yawned.

"Right."

"What time is it?"

"7:30."

"Damn it, Spain, I told you not to call me before 9:00."

"Just thought you'd want to know."

Remembering the dream he woke me from, I said, "Thanks, Spain."

"You want to get some breakfast?"

"Thanks, but I've got a lot to do before I leave. I'd better get on it."

"You mean you're going to make me eat doughnuts."

"You don't have to."

"They're Krispy Kremes."

"Okay. So you have to. Eat one for me."

"Tucker."

"Uh-huh."

"Come back."

"Christ, Spain, I'm just going to check on a wreck."

"Yeah, well, deep shit has a way of getting under your boots."

"Spain."

"What?"

"Go eat a doughnut."

Chapter 46

I brewed some Hazelnut Cream Decaf and called Emmett. It was early enough that I was hoping to catch him in his dorm.

"Hello," he said after the first ring.

"Hey, buddy, howya doin'"

"Hey, Dad," he sounded happy to hear from me. "I'm good. You okay?

"Yeah, fine, how are your classes going?"

"Great! I really like my English Lit. professor. He's very cool, doesn't seem stuck on fundamentals."

That's right up Emmett's alley.

"I know you like that."

"Yeah."

"How's the job at the library?"

"I really like it. It's quiet and no one bothers me. I got putting the books back on the shelves down," he said laughing.

"Do you need anything? How're you doin' for money?"

"I'm okay," he said, "but if you want to give me some, that's cool."

"I'm leaving town tomorrow or the next day. I'll put some in your account before I go."

"Where you going?'

"I have to go to Houston."

"For how long?"

"I don't know. But if you do come down, I think it would be a good idea to stay at your mom's."

Emmett liked to stay at my place when I was out of town. He liked to bring his girl over and hang. So the silence I was experiencing on the phone was understandable.

"What's going on, Dad?"

The shooting had shaken Emmett up. He's a laid-back kind of guy, a real sweetheart, a gentle soul. But, I taught him to shoot anyway. He took to it like I did at his age. He really loved shooting the pistols at the range. He was a very good shot, and underneath that gentle exterior, was a Tucker. I could see it in his eyes as he observed people.

After it happened he was very quiet about the incident and didn't seem to want to talk about it. I didn't know how he took it, or what he thought about me, and I cared.

It was a couple weeks after it happened when he opened up. He told me it was okay, what I had done. He was glad it was them and not me, said they got what they deserved. Said he was proud of me. Go figure.

"What's going on, Dad?" he asked again, a little louder.

"Had a prowler in the middle of the night, up on the upper end, by the columns."

"What happened? You okay?"

"Oh, sure, I'm fine. Razor ran them off, but I think he got a piece of them."

"Them?"

I never could lie worth a damn. There's always too much to remember.

"Yeah, well, there may have been more than one. Anyway, they took a couple of shots at Razor and ran away."

"Razor okay?"

"He's got a nice round hole in one of his ears, and he'll have a nice scar on his head."

"Sounds a little random, Dad."

This wasn't going like I had planned. There I go again, making God laugh.

"Probably some poachers."

"Yeah. Right."

"Anyway if you come to town while I'm gone, you should think about staying at your mom's."

"I'll think about it."

Emmett and his mother were struggling with the proverbial apron strings. I didn't want to think about Emmett being home alone. I would have to do something about that.

"Do what you want. But if you stay at the house, keep Razor close. I'll be taking Tuesday with me."

Emmett had his own shotgun under his bed, so I didn't have to mention that. I didn't want to mention that.

"I understand," he said.

"All right then. I'll call you from Houston when I know more about how long I'll be gone."

"Be careful, Dad."

"I'll be fine, Buddy, I'm just going to look into something for a friend." I didn't feel like I was lying, I liked George Carr.

"Okay. Gotta go Dad, I'll be late for class. I love you."

"I love you too."

The connection was broken.

Emmett's biscuits were done. I didn't feel there was much more I could teach him. He was off on his own for the first time and loved it. He was making his own decisions and learning from their outcomes.

I worked out for an hour on the Bowflex. Donned some gloves, and hit the heavy bag for twenty minutes. When I worked out on the bag, there're a lot of forearms, elbows, feet and knees working. The only reason I hit it with the gloves is for aerobics and timing. I aim for the throat a lot.

It took the rest of the morning for me to shower, eat breakfast, finish up the pistols I had been working on, ship them off, set the timers for the lights, and lock down the office.

I went downstairs and informed Pok I'd be gone for a few days and to watch the place for me. My place didn't need watching, but it made Pok feel good.

Chapter 47

It was one o'clock and I was headed out to my place in the country.

I called George Carr.

"George, it's Tucker," I said.

"When are you leaving for Houston?" he asked curtly.

He may have been feeling his overindulgence of the night before, or it could just be his natural demeanor, or a product of grief. But, how would I know?

"I'm trying to get out of here by early in the morning, but I need some things from you."

With a little more enthusiasm, he said, "All right, what do you need?"

"Fax me the address of your place in River Oaks, Harold Manske's address, and a letter of introduction."

"A letter of introduction?"

"It may help to set people at ease when I start asking questions about your wife's accident."

"It wasn't an accident, Tucker."

"That's what you're paying me to find out. Until I find out differently, that's the way I'm going to approach it."

While he was mulling that, I added, "I would also like a list of her friends in Houston, anyone that may have talked to her in the week before it happened."

"I'll get Rachael on that right away. What's your fax number?"

I gave him my fax number at home.

"Oh, and, Tucker there will be someone at the house when you arrive. I still keep a small staff on hand. And I've made arrangements for you to eat at the club and use their workout facilities whenever you'd like. They'll have a card for you at the gate."

"The club?"

"The River Oaks Country Club. The house is only a few blocks away."

Wow, *'The Club.' I'm moving up in the world.*

"Thanks, George, I'll call you when I get there. Oh, yeah, just one more thing."

"What's that?"

"I'll need Robby Gray's address and phone number."

After a considerable pause, he sarcastically asked, "You going to have a little reunion with your old partner in crime?"

I didn't answer him.

After a few seconds he said, "That was uncalled for. Tucker, I apologize."

"Accepted. I'll get in touch when I get there and keep you informed of any promising leads."

I hung up. I hoped I sounded like a 'Private Eye.'

Chapter 48

I stopped by my closest neighbor's house, Aaron and Sandie McFeely, and negotiated a price for their son Brandon to come over and feed Razor. I'd decided to take Buck to my daughter's, where he would be pampered by Max and Little Margie. I know one day soon, I'll have to make a decision, but not today. As for Miso, like any good cat, he takes care of himself.

It took the better part of two hours to collect Buck, his food, medicine and bed, take him to Shannon's and get back. Then I called my weekly cleaning lady, Sue. I told her I was leaving town and would call her when I got back.

I spent the rest of the afternoon thoroughly cleaning my house, so it would be that way when I returned. It didn't really need it. Sue had just been there a few days before, but it gave me something to do while I thought about what to pack in the way of clothes, as well as hardware. Also it's the best time for me to clean. It makes me feel like I'd accomplished something, it's so clean when I'm done.

The faxes must have come through while I was vacuuming. I like vacuuming. There's something very Zen about it.

I set the faxed pages on the coffee table, intending to look at them later, then decided to mop the great room.

With Buck at Shannon's and Tuesday with me, there wouldn't be any dogs tracking in and out of the house. Razor doesn't like to come into the house, that's for sissies.

It was after 5 o'clock when the house was pristine and since I'd decided to leave around 4:00 a.m., I fed Razor and Tuesday, then set about feeding me.

I've had this great hand-hammered wok for so long, it's seasoned perfectly. I made ginger shrimp with asparagus, green onions, yellow bell pepper, and a few artichoke quarters. I use the best peanut oil. It smells like roasting peanuts when hot in the wok. When it was ready, I dumped it into a big bowl, grabbed some chop sticks and a bottle of water, sat on the brown leather couch, put my feet up, and ate looking into a cold fireplace.

After cleaning the kitchen, I sat back down and looked at the faxed pages. The ones I was most interested in were Mrs. Carr's friends and Robby's address.

There were eight names, all women, along with phone numbers for each. A notation read, 'These would most likely be women she would have contact with.' It was signed, 'Rachael.'

She had a beautiful round cursive style, like someone else I knew. It's strange how one woman's handwriting can look so much like another's. Men's never do.

Robby Gray's address was 4589 Cypress Cove, Lake Bistineau, no zip, but then I wasn't going to send him anything. His phone number was also there.

Knowing Houston's weather is about the same as New Orleans in the winter, and the fact that I may be talking to some River Oak belles, helped me decide my wardrobe.

On the bed, I laid out a raw silk, cream sport coat, a black sport coat, leather jacket, two pair of brown slacks, two pair of Diamond Gusset jeans, a rain parka, a couple of sweatshirts, one blue dress shirt, seven black and dark blue t-shirts, seven pairs of jockey shorts, seven pairs of black cotton socks, one pair of running shoes, my boots, a pair of leather Merrill clogs, and a pair of Trask buffalo hide, brown lace-up shoes.

After studying the layout on the bed, I didn't see anything I could leave behind. I packed everything but what I was going to wear traveling, jeans, black coat, t-shirts, the Merrill's, and of course socks and undies.

As soon as I started putting clothes on the bed, Tuesday remained close in sight, or should I say I remained in her sight. She was perched on the bed, attentive to my every move.

"Don't worry little girl. You're going for a ride," the last three words causing her ears to perk and her tail to beat a para-diddle. I'm sure she smiled.

After packing my clothes in a soft duffel, I packed my dop kit, put it in the bathroom, then took the duffel to the truck.

Tuesday followed a half step behind. After putting the bag in the back seat and closing the door, she stood there with her 'aren't you forgetting something' face.

"Not now, little girl. Come back inside," I said, with what felt like a smile.

I wasn't sleepy, so I poured a couple of fingers of Maker's Mark over ice, sat down to watch the ten o'clock news, and think about hardware.

Tuesday was good about leaving me alone when I'm sitting on the couch eating, but drinking and watching TV was altogether another matter. She was curled up next to me with her head resting on my thigh, sound asleep. There was no way I could get up and leave without waking her. Life was good for her.

The news was typical Nashville news. A couple of shootings, a robbery at a convenience store where the video camera got some good pictures of the brilliant thief, sans mask. An ongoing investigation of a wife who'd disappeared over three years ago. The family of the wife were sure the husband had something to do with it. The husband was now living in Mexico with his two kids, where he couldn't be harassed by the media. The family wanted him back here to answer questions concerning new evidence they've uncovered. 'The police at this time have no comment.' Sounds like Spain.

Now, hardware. There weren't many situations I could think of where I would need more than my Colt and a few extra magazines, and those I could think of didn't seem applicable for what I was going to do in Houston. Whatever *that* was. So, even though I knew better than to try and foresee what was going to happen in Houston, I felt comfortable traveling light.

By the time the news was over, so was the Maker's and I was feeling relaxed enough to hit the hay. I don't normally drink right before going to bed, it left me edgy in the morning. But since I would be on the road, that edge would keep me awake until the coffee I planned to pick up at a truck stop on I-40, kicked in.

I got up from the couch, alerting Tuesday, walked into the kitchen area, put the glass in the dishwasher and turned it on for the night wash.

Tuesday went to the door like she wanted to go out, but I knew better. She just didn't want to be left behind.

"It's time to go to bed now, little girl," I said, in dog talk, Emmett says it's baby talk.

She immediately wagged into the bedroom, where I heard her jump onto the bed. I'd bet she was on my side.

I took a walk around the house to make sure it was ready for me to leave, turned off the lights and went into the bedroom. I would've won that bet.

After loudly brushing my teeth, this sometimes works in getting Tuesday to move before I come to bed, I walked back into the bedroom. She was conked out on my side, with her head on my pillow.

Before sitting down on the bed, I had to complete our bedtime ritual. I pulled back the comforter and tossed it over her, covering her completely.

She immediately started moaning with her Miss Piggy talk.

After stripping and tossing my clothes over onto the valet, I slipped under the covers, hipping Tuesday over with small repeated nudges.

After much Pig talk, we were both satisfyingly situated.

The only time I miss the days when I drank too much, was at bedtime. I used to fall asleep on the couch or climb into bed and be asleep so fast, that upon wakening, I wouldn't even remember getting in bed.

These days I was subject to any number of mental ambushes as I waited for sleep. The most common waylay was dream fretting. I always dreamed, but what about was the issue.

Tonight was different. Laying in bed with Tuesday's love by my side, I deliberated. When did I become the person that in my youth, I'd pretended to be out of fear?

Chapter 49

During my recidivistic dealing days, it was useful for people to perceive me as a bad-ass. It wasn't a conscious effort, but a sequela of survival. I used to wonder how long it would take before I was exposed. I lived in fear of being seen for what I was. A coward.

Somehow I faked my way through it. My mantra was, 'fake it 'til you make it'.

As I survived highjackings, shootouts, undercover cops trying to bust me, knife attacks, and just plain ass whippings, my reputation grew.

No one was more astonished than me when I came out on top. I believe the fear adrenalized me, altered time, gave me strength and speed, and I survived. My peers mistook my calmness after these altercations as bravery. In actuality it was the elation of being alive, the wonders of living. Everything was always brighter, sharper, colors were deepened, and as I observed these wonders, others saw calmness.

So, when did I become so hardened, allowing me to do the things I did last night and over the past few months.

I had to go back quite a few years.

I got out of the drug business intact. For the next seven years I was an artist (Margie liked to call me that). After her death, I got into cocaine, a drug that carries a lot of bad karma. To do as much as I was doing you either have to be rich or deal. I wasn't rich. But since my customers were my friends in the music business, there was no reason for guns. It was a passive affair.

For me, drugs and alcohol were just a slow suicide. I once tried the faster approach, but was stopped by the amnesiac effect of Halcyon and alcohol. I woke up in the morning with a cocked 38 Special snub nose in my mouth.

Then Emmett was born and I decided to live. I left the drugs behind and never had the urge to do them again. Emmett assuredly saved my life in that regard.

Even after I started Tucker Security, nothing truly dangerous ever came up. Was that perception also a derivative of my hardening?

Then a couple of months ago, I was in a shootout. I killed two men. I stood in front of Bench and was almost killed myself. Was I being brave? Or was it, that I just didn't care?

I can't fool myself. I'm still pretending. I'm still a coward. A coward of the worst ilk. I'm not afraid of being hurt or killed, because I really don't give a shit about that. It's pride. I'm afraid to lose, at anything. My loss of pride would slowly consume me.

I've always known that killing myself wouldn't work. If I did, the powers that be wouldn't let me see her. But if I died protecting someone, then for sure we would be together up there, over there, wherever there is.

I'm really not needed by my family anymore. I have enough insurance that Emmett would be okay, and like I said before, his biscuits are done. I know they'd grieve my passing. But if that happened, then that's their life's process, they'd get over it. It's not like losing your best friend, lover and wife.

Was I being selfish?

I remembered how after the wreck, I could cry over a Hallmark commercial. My empathy and sympathy would meld with compassion and often left me a wretch.

After years of reading and therapy, I came to view the tragedies of human life as each person's Divine process. Everything is as it's supposed to be. I had to come to this conclusion. It was the only way I could deal the hands I've been delt.

With every murder, rape or tragic accident, a debt is being paid and hopefully a lesson learned, not to be repeated.

The events of 9/11 affected me more than I would have thought. My brain was telling me one thing, my heart another.

My rationale was, that the grief all the survivors of the victims were going through, was strong in the collective consciousness. It bled out onto those who could feel it. I wasn't alone.

In short time, I came to view the survivor's grief process in the same way as I viewed the deaths of their loved ones . . . EIDO. Everything Is In Divine Order.

Hopefully, anyone surviving me would one day come to that same conclusion.

I never saw it coming. This twenty year commemoration of Margie's death has been the most retrospective and arduous of all. I literally had memories hurled at me at light speed. Memories of violence, shame, guilt, and pain. And memories of love. Some I've tried my best to let go of. Some I may never be able to let go of. And others I shouldn't let go of. I've never felt this lost. Even in the swamp.

All my post relationships had failed. Was I afraid to love like that again? Afraid it would be taken away and I would have to go through it all over again? Did I really want to know the answers?

As I laid with my hand on Tuesday, I thought, where does that leave me? I'm middle-aged, alone, and not at all sure the process of life has much appeal for me.

Then I remembered how much I liked to travel. I like the weightlessness of a road trip. And...money's good.

Tomorrow I'm driving to Houston, and hopefully I will be able to help a man get on with his process of grieving, so he can heal. I hope he's better at it than I was.

What if I did find out his wife was murdered and who murdered her? What would I do? What am I doing? I knew better than to make plans. I try not to be the constant source of God's amusement.

But I couldn't help feeling like a warrior about to take his first step on a spiritual journey.

Me, a spiritual warrior, I found that somewhat humorous and somehow . . . appealing.

EIDO.

Lyrics

Unconditionally

1) I remember working hard
   Staying out late at night
   You always greeted with a smile
   In the dawns early light

2) You knew I was always true to you
   No matter how it seemed
   And you were always true to me
   While I was chasing my dream

(Chorus)
Oh how you loved me
So unconditionally
Oh how you loved me
Unconditionally

3) Now that I'm all alone
   Taking good care of myself
   I know I owe it all to you
   Couldn't have done it by myself

4) You showed me I was a good man
   And how you believed in me
   You helped make me strong
   And you taught me how to see

(Chorus)

(Bridge)
   Everyday I thank the Lord
   Even though he took you away
   For the gift of knowing you
   And how you never gave up on me

   And how you loved me
   So unconditionally
   Oh how you loved me
   So unconditionally

Cowboys and Engines

1) I played cowboys and engines
   When I was a kid
   But not the same way
   As ole Gene and Roy did

2) Now I'm ridn' my horses
   And it feels so good
   Two in the trailer
   300 more under the hood

(Chorus)
   So it's
   Cowboys and engines
   On the open highway
   Cowboys and engines
   All American made

3) Them ole boys out west
   Are drivin' their herds
   And riding their fences
   In whirlybirds

4) They got a chuck wagon
   With fuel injection
   Big monster tires
   And positive traction

(Chorus)

(Bridge}
On motorcycles and four-wheel drives
All those cowboys keepin' this country alive

Guitar ride

5) The king had his Harley's in Memphis
   And he loved to ride
   Now singers in Nashville
   Ride with him by their side

6) Now I'm a motorcycle country boy
   And I love to roam
   Ridin' high in the saddle
   On thunder and chrome

Chorus repeat

I'm Leaving You For Me

1) Someone's treated you bad baby
   That's just old news
   Why you making' me pay
   Someone else's dues

2) Mama always said take care of number one
   But I look in the mirror
   And I see my face
   Between a rock and a hard place

{1st Chorus}

    I've been trying to tell you
    I've been trying all night
    And just about now
    Is just about right

    I'm leaving you for me
    I'm not leaving you
    For just anybody
    I'm leaving you for me

{Bridge}

    I've bent over backwards
    I've tried all I can try
    And I'm telling' you baby
    I've just said my last goodbye

{2nd Chorus}
    I'm leaving you for me
    And I want you to see
    I'm not leaving for just anybody
    I'm leaving you for me

3) I have no choice
   I would be a lie
   To say I don't care
   But my hearts already said goodbye

Repeat 1st chorus

Acknowledgements

To Carol Crosslin who had the misfortune to read my first draft. Thank you Carol for your guidance and taking the time to make me a better writer.

To Debbie Starrett for believing in Tucker and me, and for being the remarkable woman you are.

To Emmett Barton...son, editor, designer, writer, adventurer... just to name a few.

To Carter and Nan Andrews, Steve Prati, David "Doc" Zinsser, Dr. Leah Marcus, [Professor of English Literature, Vanderbilt University], Sidney Lohan, Betsy Miles, Nancy Belser, Trish Warren, Cathy Nakos and Melissa Messer, for their efforts and being fans of Tucker.

To Brad Spain for his permission to use his name and likeness.

To Aaron, Sandie, and Brandon McFeely for allowing me to use their names.

To John Rivers Bicknell for writing beautiful music for my words.

To Tim and Mary Schoetlle for the rekindling.

To Tony Bellioni, gunsmith extraordinaire, who built Tucker's .45.

To my brother Ken... for being there when it counted.

To Roger, Shannon, Max and Little Margie for being the best.

If there is anyone I missed, be sure to let me know and I will catch you on the flip side.

About the Author

R.O. Barton lives in Middle Tennessee with his beagle Angel and his hawk-headed parrot Hank, a force to be reckoned with.

CPSIA information can be obtained at www.ICGtesting.com
Printed in the USA
LVOW07s1359211015

459173LV00018BA/549/P